HELL
house

DAKOTA WILDE

D1519488

To the readers who could never choose just one book boyfriend.

Content Warnings:

This book is intended for an 18+ audience. It is a dark romance, with graphic and explicit content. Significant profanity is present. This is a why choose, enemies to lover's romance. MFMM scene is present. Praise kink. Breath play. Anal. Underage drinking and drug use. Death of a parent. Stalking. Murder. Foreign object play.

This book was made to be inclusive. I believe books should look like the world around us, therefore, there are LGBTQ+ characters, a non-binary character named Javelynn whose pronouns are they/them, and people of color as characters. This book touches briefly on racism and homophobia as the characters encounter the topics.

Want to listen to the Hell House Playlist? Be sure to check out Dakota's Spotify.

HELL house

DAKOTA WILDE

Hell is empty and all the devils are here.

-William Shakespeare

The Boys of Hell House:

1.   Pierce "Pride" Ledger

2.   Garrison "Greed" Hayes

3.   Walker "Wrath" Hart

4.   Emmett "Envy" St. James

5.   Lukas "Lust" Ledger

6.   Graham "Gluttony" Monroe

7.   Sloan "Sloth" Hendrix

The girls:

1.   Salem Knox

2.   Skye Dannon

DAKOTA WILDE

PROLOGUE
Pierce
TWO YEARS AGO

The woods are alive with sin tonight. My face is covered by a black bag, my vision is obliterated by the dark material, feet stumbling over errant twigs and divots that cover the ground. There are seven of us who are being initiated into Tartarus House, or more commonly known on campus as Hell House. My foot twists and I slam down hard on my knees, a rock jabbing through my jeans. Strong hands hoist me up and I feel a surge of wetness slide down my shin. Ah, fuck. I was bleeding. The guys and I'd pregamed a few shots so it didn't hurt as bad as it should have. Bet I'd feel that in the morning though. The sound of waves hits my ears, and the murmuring from the guys dies down. We must be close, though I can't see shit. The terrain changes beneath my feet from the hard mossy ground of the woods we'd just tracked through to sand, my shoes sinking with each step forward. Someone still has their hand wrapped around my arm, leading me to the secret initiation site.

Kildale Academy is located on an island off the Pacific Northwest Coast. It takes either a ferry or helicopter to get here, which meant you had to have a shit ton of money to even be accepted. Most of our parents were CEO's or heirs to a multimillion-dollar fortune. There was only the occasional scholarship offered, and to even be considered to join the only fraternity on campus, money and connections were imperative for your selection. My twin brother Lukas and I had been easy shoo-ins, being legacies with both our father and grandfather having been in the fraternity during their college years. It was expected that we'd follow in their footsteps. No questions asked, we had to uphold the Ledger legacy.

The guy's voices start back up sounding like a chant. Their voices echoing off of something. I feel my pulse increase, the vein in my neck throbbing. I was ready to take this fucking bag off my face and get this over with. I take one more step before I'm shoved down onto my knees, the bag ripped off my face. I blink fast, my eyes trying to adjust. We're in some cavern, close enough to the ocean that I can hear the waves slapping against rocks nearby. The air smells dank, the stench of fish wafting in the sea breeze air. My knees burn, and my head swims with alcohol. The cave is dark, the only light is coming from the moon and a few phone flashlights. I notice I'm kneeling next to Lukas in front of some alter looking thing lined with seven silver chalices. Though we might have been identical once, he's done everything possible to individualize himself. From dying his hair darker, getting tattoos on almost every inch of his skin, and even the piercings. I shudder thinking of the Jacob's Ladder he got this summer before we'd headed off to college. No one would be coming near my dick with a needle, thank you very much.

A hooded figure emerges from the shadows. The voices stop their chanting and the seven of us wait on our knees, not knowing what to expect.

"Welcome Freshman. Tonight, you will be initiated. The vow you take here binds you to this school, your new brothers, and the island. You've been chosen amongst the masses, weeded out, and tested. If you've made it this far, the dead of Hell House have deemed you worthy."

I shift on my knees, not sure what he means by the dead of Hell House, but I try to pay attention.

"Brothers, hand them their chalices." Seven seniors step forward, obeying, each grabbing the cup as they stand directly in front of us.

"Pledges, repeat after me: I hereby pledge my body and soul, my very blood, heart, and essence to become a brother of Hell House. Should I break this pledge I will accept the consequences of my actions." We all repeat his words, the chant starts up again in a language I don't understand. The guy in front of me steps forward, his hand holding the challis out to me. He brings it to my lips, and I see from the corner of my eye that the seven others are doing the same.

The hooded figure raises his arms, "Drink!" He demands, so we do.

The liquid burns the back of my throat like no alcohol I've ever had. I clutch my stomach and feel it roil inside of me. Was this some kind of sick hazing prank? Blood whooshes in my ears, my heart hammering against my rib cage. What the fuck was happening to me? I writhe on the floor and see the other new pledges doing the same. I start convulsing, my head smacking into the ground. I can't see, I can't think.

A scream wretches out of my mouth and then my body goes limp.

I watch through blurred vision. My head laying flat on the cave floor as the hooded figure reveals his face. My eyes clear as I blink fast. Headmaster Hayden is gleaming down on us, a wicked smile coating his lips.

"Welcome back to Hell House, Sins." Pride rises in my chest at his words, making me brush myself off and stand up to my full height. My throat burns with smoke, but I push down the discomfort. I wasn't about to let my new fraternity brothers see me looking weak. I'm overcome with the knowledge that I was now a part of the most exclusive fraternity in the US. The Ledger legacy would be continued through me, through my name, and I'd make sure the world would remember it.

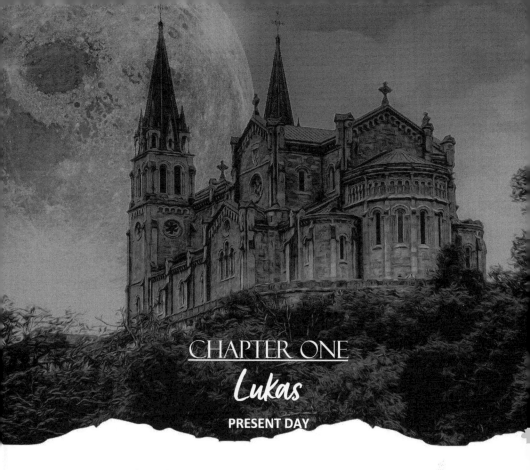

CHAPTER ONE
Lukas
PRESENT DAY

My headboard is pounding the walls with each thrust I dish out. Whatever her name is below me is screeching in my ear, and I'm bored as fuck and slightly deaf after all her screaming. Either she really is enjoying herself that much or she's an overeager actress, and by this last thrust I'm leaning toward the latter. She licks my ear and mistakes my shudder of repulsion for pleasure. "You like that, Daddy?" She purrs. Daddy? What the messed-up fuck is that? I flip her over so I don't have to have her hot beer breath in my face. It's gotten far too easy luring people into my bed, that she's just become another name to add to my list of one-night stands. I pound into her from behind as she arches her back, her badly dyed red hair hangs limply over her shoulder, her hands grip the rails between my headboard. I try clamping my hand around her mouth to get her to shut the fuck up so I can find my release already, but she's slobbering all over it. Fuck this, my hand would have been a better lay. I pull out of her and give myself a few pumps trying to picture anyone but the girl below me until I'm coming, filling up the condom.

She sits up and tries kissing me, but I pull back throwing a washcloth at her. "Clean yourself up and get out of my room." I practically bark at her. I know I'm being a dick, but I'm beyond caring at this point. She knew what she was signing up for the minute she pulled me off of the dance floor. I'm not exactly known for my chivalry. She scrambles for her clothes and tumbles out of my bed. I sit off to the side and take a swig of water. I carefully peel off the condom making sure it doesn't snag on my piercings, and toss it in the trash.

"Will I see you later Lukas?" Whatshername asks, fully dressed now and holding her gold heels in her hands. I give her a once over with my eyes like I'm really considering it.

"Not a chance in Hell, sweetheart," I say with a smirk. I get up from the bed and give her a little shove out the door, music from the back-to-school party my fraternity was throwing assaults my ears. I grip my tattooed hand around the door frame making sure to slam it shut for extra emphasis. I catch the red head's shocked face before she disappears behind the door.

I stalk back to my bed, a frown pulling at my brows noticing the wet spot on my sheets. I yank them off, tossing them to a pile on my already cluttered floor. My posters that are tacked on the wall rustle from how hard I throw the dank sheets. My room is full of expensive wallpaper and crown molding, boasting of the wealth and history this house holds. It gives me a twisted sense of pleasure to see my band posters tacked up, debasing its value and sticking a middle finger up to it.

Just as I plop back down onto my bed, still fully naked, a knock comes at my door, I swear to God if it's that girl, I'll make her regret it. I let out a grunt, as the rapping continues. "LukASS." I roll my eyes. It was just my brother Pierce. He doesn't wait for my response before opening the door. He's visibly plastered, swaying as he holds onto a red solo cup. He points a finger at me, "Woah dude, cover your junk." He says covering his eyes dramatically.

I laugh and grab my blankets, covering myself up. "It's my room, asshole." I grab my vape pen from off the nightstand and take a puff, the smell of vanilla and sex swirl around me.

"Stop being such a dick and come back to the party." A riot of laughter can be heard coming from downstairs.

"Nah, I'm done for the night." I say taking another puff. The girl had quieted this demand in me, but she didn't light my soul on fire, and I wondered if anyone ever would, or if I was destined for a life of boring as fuck sex.

Graham pops his head in from behind my brother, munching on an open bag of Cheetos, his hand coated in orange dust as he brings one to his mouth to chomp on loudly. "Whatcha doin in here, let's go. I made snacks." I roll my eyes. Graham was either perpetually eating or cooking. I knew now that the two of these fuckers had started bothering me, that they wouldn't leave me alone. I inhale one last jolt, letting it coat my lungs before sitting up. I yank on my briefs and see the two goons who'd interrupted my plans for spending my night sketching out more tattoo designs smile widely with victory.

"Let's get fucked up," I say spreading my arms wide.

They answer with a "Hell yes!" Graham says, pumping his orange hand up in the air.

Once dressed, I rejoin the party that's in full swing. Sweaty bodies sway back and forth while I weave my way to the kitchen. If I'm going to be here, I'm going to need alcohol. I hated crowds. Inevitably someone would throw themselves at me and the Lust inside of me would demand to be released. If I drank enough though, I could keep that instinct down. It was a temporary fix to this endless battle that raged inside of me. I push past a few stragglers clogging up the space in front of the keg. I glare and it's enough to send them skittering. *The Bad Touch 2K20* by DJ Gollum pulses through the speakers, a chorus of drunken voices sings along as they grind on each other. A set of Christmas lights that had been left up, blink haphazardly, making the room look like a small rave.

I spray the keg contents into a plastic cup, filling it to the brim. I tilt my head back, guzzling the room temperature alcohol. It was disgusting but it would get the job done. I fill up another cup, my veins already buzzing. I see Walker sitting out on the porch tuning his guitar. He looks alone, which looks fuckin' perfect to me. I head outside, the warm air stirring with the breeze. The noise from the party is much quieter out here, though there are a few party goers strewn around the lawn. I take a seat opposite of Walker, who doesn't acknowledge my arrival, too engrossed in strumming the strings of his guitar. His

14

backward baseball cap sits low on his brow hiding part of the diagonal scar that runs from the top of his hairline and into his eyebrow, barely missing his eye. If you asked him how he got it, he would give you just another made-up story that was more outrageous than the next.

"You think they'll leave soon?" His gravel-full voice asks. I sip my beer and chuckle.

"Not a chance." He scowls at my answer. We'd both bonded over our dislike of other people. If we weren't required to join this fraternity by our parents, we wouldn't have. My father and brother had nagged the shit out of me until I relented. Walker's father was also a former pledge and threatened to not fund his college education should he not become a part of the fraternity. I wondered, not for the first time, if they knew the truth. If they knew what exactly they'd signed us up for. The living hell we'd been shackled to. I tend to drown my sinful instincts by overindulging in alcohol and keeping my hands busy with sketches or tattoos. Walker fights back his Wrath by either toting his guitar around or decimating the shit out of his punching bag. He'd already gone through several guitars and punching bags this last year alone, so I wasn't sure it helped him much. These things inside of us were powerful, they demanded to be obeyed, and sometimes that twisted part inside of me enjoyed it. There were times I found myself relishing in the Lust I'd been saddled with. Buried deep in pussy or playing with a cock, it didn't matter. But lately that feeling had been waning. I found myself wanting more- needing more than the screams of pleasure a stranger gave me. I wanted- fuck I don't even know what it was I wanted, but it no longer aligned with the urges the demon inside of me demanded. I felt more and more like a puppet on a string. I was desperate to cut my ties with it, but I knew the consequences would be far more devastating than I could even imagine.

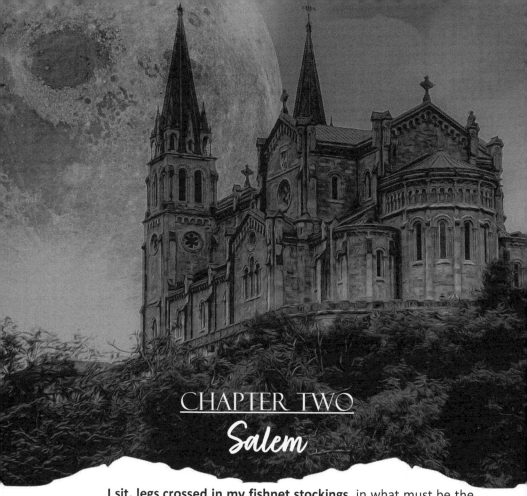

CHAPTER TWO
Salem

I sit, legs crossed in my fishnet stockings, in what must be the most uncomfortable chair known to man. My black Converse covered feet are bouncing with anxiety. I pop my gum, completely bored out of my mind. Whoever was in charge of decorating this office absolutely knew what they were doing when picking out the furniture. Whereas the Headmaster's chair looked like you could curl up in it and take a nap like it was a cloud made of angel feathers, this chair felt like they'd found it at a Medieval torture store with extra knives thrown in just for fun. What did they do? Go into a store and say, "Yes, please give me one that feels like nails are going straight up my ass." Kinky fuckers.

I pick at my black nail polish while waiting for Headmaster Hayden to show up. I'd received an email that my presence was required at 10 am sharp and it was now 10:15. I let out a loud sigh of irritation, wondering what the fuck he could want to meet with me about and come up with nothing. I'd only been at the school for a total of 14 hours, so there was no way I'd fucked up already... was there?

I count the ornate tiles that line the headmaster's ceiling trying to pass the time, impressed with the amount of detail and gold foiled figures that are etched into each one. This ceiling would have even impressed Michelangelo. Though one could never be too sure, it wasn't like I knew the dude personally to ask him.

When the headmaster finally shows up, I'm sitting upside down, my fishnet stocking legs hung over the back of the chair. I was just one row away from finishing my riveting tile count. 1,523 tiles so far.

The headmaster clears his throat and I pop a bubble from the gum I was chewing.

"Ms. Knox, sorry to keep you waiting." My eyes lock with his, and I find a disapproving scowl meeting my annoyed stare. I let out a sigh and turn myself right side up.

"So, what's all this about?" I ask cutting right to the chase. This bozo has already eaten up an hour of my time that I could have spent sleeping in my new dorm room. It was far too early to be jerked around. Especially after attending the 'Welcome Back to School' frat party I'd wandered into last night. My head was still pounding from that extra shot of tequila.

The headmaster makes his way to his desk and takes a seat. When he sits, a brief look of comfort swipes across his face before shifting into one of seriousness. The smug fucker with his comfy chair. Was I being salty about this Godforsaken torture chair he had students sit in? Yes, yes, I was. My ass was going numb after the hour I'd sat here waiting for him. If I were the hexing type, he'd be on that list for sure.

"As you know, your grandmother, Clementine Knox, has been a huge contributor to Kildale Academy and she made it crystal clear that your attendance here to this prestigious Academy was to be given special attention. She called me just last night to remind me that you were to be offered every opportunity."

Of all the pompous and nepotistic things... THAT'S why I'd spent my morning in this torture chamber?

"Well, if that's all-" I go to stand up, but am interrupted by the Headmaster who makes a gesture for me to halt.

"Not exactly. See, while you are from an impeccable family line, and one that donates frequently, this is still a prestigious Academy and any... shenanigans will not be tolerated."

"Shenanigans?" My eyebrows raise at his insinuation. I mean, he's not wrong. I do love a good shenanigan.

"Your file was quite the read Ms. Knox, and it took some convincing from Clem to get the board to agree to your acceptance. I hope that all of those childhood antics stay where they belong- in the past."

I bristle at his words, shifting uncomfortably in the chair. My ass was tingling, and I wanted nothing more than to be out of this room and away from this man's overinflated sense of authority. I'd known men like him all my life, and this one seemed no different. The same brand of assholery, just in a new zip code.

I tilt my lips up into an appeasing smile, one I'd used countless times to get myself out of a tight jam.

"I thank you so much sir, for the concern. But like you said, those were childish antics. I swear, totally in the past. I so appreciate you taking the time out of your busy schedule to meet with me." He couldn't see my crossed fingers I had behind my back.

He gives me another once over, displeasure pursing his puckered lips. "Yes, well... One more thing. Since you are a legacy, you'll be expected to attend the alumni ball that takes place next month." I feel my eyes begin to roll and try to stop them mid movement. A ball? Just great. Being in a room full of stuffed up egotistical people sounded like one of my nightmares come to life. Kill me now.

I smile tightly, "Can't wait, sir." He nods and I grab my black purse that I'd bedazzled in spikes. It was cute as hell and doubled as weapon should I ever need it. A smack with this purse would definitely do some damage. Maybe even take an eye or puncture a testicle.

"Oh, and Ms. Knox, don't forget the school uniform. We have a dress code to adhere to."

My back went ramrod straight. Who does he think he is? Miranda Priestly? Fashion Police? School wasn't even in session yet, and I know you can wear whatever the fuck you wanted to during non-school times. I'd read the damn student handbook front to back.

"I wouldn't dream of it, sir." I turn on my heel, and jog back to my dorm room. I felt like I'd just painted a giant target on my back. Fan-fucking-tastic.

CHAPTER THREE
Pierce

Last night's debauchery is still clinging to my skin as I slowly, achingly sit up from the couch I passed out on. I stretch my arms above my head to work out the kink that's lodged itself into my back. As I bring my arms down, I rack my hands down my face. My fingers brush against something slimy plastered onto my stubble. I go to peel it off and, "AH! Fuck!" The shiny foil wrapper glistens in my hand and I drop it like it's a venomous snake intent on injecting me with STDs. I throw the thing on the ground. I just had an open condom wrapper stuck to my face. A fucking open condom wrapper ON MY FACE. I stumble over my own feet trying to get to the nearest bathroom to wash my face and hands off- or maybe just set myself on fire. Sick. I hope to Hell it's not a used one, but

I didn't stay around long enough to check. I scrub my face until it's raw. When I assess my reflection in the mirror, I notice a square imprinted onto my left cheek. God how plastered was I to not notice I fell asleep on something like that? My mind wanders to the princess and the pea story.

Obviously, I was no prince.

I wash my hands off for a final time and tread through the house, careful not to step on the strewn bodies that liter the floor. I'm intent on finding some coffee and aspirin for the splitting headache that was starting to burrow beneath my skull. Garrison has already beaten me to the kitchen and is currently sitting in the school uniform, perfectly pressed and alert, sipping on his tea.

"How are you this awake after last night, Gare?"

He pauses the tea that he was about to take a sip of, "What the hell happened to that pretty face of yours Pierce?"

"I don't want to talk about it." I glare at the coffee machine. Why were there so many buttons? I haphazardly stick the coffee in and press one of the buttons. The machine makes an angry whirring noise and then turns off. I smack it and try turning it back on and off again.

"You need some help, brother?" Garrison asks, an amused expression crosses his face. He runs a hand over his neatly trimmed goatee.

"I got it." I might have been an okay student, but I was the captain of the football team, I could figure out some piece of junk coffee machine. Garrison smirks at me and continues to sip his tea as he scrolls on his phone.

"Tell me someone has made coffee." Emmet's voice calls out, his southern accent comes in thick as he stumbles through the back door. He scans the counter, his gaze landing on me punching the coffee machine's buttons.

"Where were you?" Garrison asks, taking in Emmet's disheveled appearance. Was that grass stuck in his black curly hair?

"I passed out on the lawn." He says with a yawn as he scratches his stomach. I let out a chuckle, then push another button on this Godforsaken machine. Last night's party was even more epic than the two years prior. It's a shame my brother Lukas had been in such a melancholy mood, he really missed out. He kept retreating to his room or went off to sulk with the house recluse, Walker. I don't know why he enjoyed that guy's company so much. He was one scary motherfucker.

Finally, whatever combination of buttons I'd just punched in gets the coffee sputtering out in a thick black rope of caffeine. I chug the hot liquid, black and bitter, and slap my face with my two hands- a habit I'd picked up during football to get my head in the game. I had a meeting with the headmaster at 11:15, and he'd chew my ass if I was late. I ran upstairs leaving my fraternity brothers in the kitchen and suited up. Our school uniforms were black, white, and gold, with the school insignia located over the left breast pocket. A large KA, in white lettering, complete with a golden shield surrounding it. The girls were required to wear black and white plaid skirts with black tights or black knee-high socks. I secretly preferred the socks. Fuck tights. Those things restricted easy access when you wanted a quick fuck in the bathrooms.

I check my Rolex and note I'm ten minutes early. I straighten my tie as my dress shoes smack against the black and white checkered tiles in the main office building that houses all the faculty's offices and conference rooms. The tiles remind me of a high stakes chess game about to be played. I pad up the giant staircase, my legs protesting with each stair I ascend. I partied way too fucking hard last night. I turn the corner to where the headmaster's office is located and am met with the sight of a girl who's jogging down the corridor, wearing fishnet stockings- fuck me, she was hot as sin. Not the typical girl I would go for at all, but something in the way she moves and looks has my cock stirring to attention. As she gets closer, my eyes take in her curves, blood red pouty lips, and her black hair that's done up in two high pigtails. I stand straighter, the Pride in my chest beginning to rear its head in demand. I want her to look at me, but she keeps her eyes down until we're about to pass each other. What I would do to play with those pigtails. A vision of her kneeling before me as I yank her pigtails while she sucks me off fills my mind. Pride grabs at my throat and my hands start to sweat. She's so close to me, my heartbeat hammers in my chest. I find myself knocking into her, my body acting before my mind can even catch up. This Pride inside me demands that she look at me- appreciate me. She stumbles over her converse, and I grab onto her arm to steady her.

"I'm sorry." I say giving her my most charming smile and run my fingers through my dirty blonde hair. She looks up at me with pure annoyance coating her deep green eyes. Fuck, it's like she could see straight into my soul, and I feel Pride writhe beneath my skin. I let go of her arm but don't back away.

"Fucking asshole." She murmurs.

I see red. "What did you just say?" My chest trips over itself in anger. No one ever talks to me that way.

She turns to face me, hands on her hips. She licks her lips, and my eyes track the movement. "Fucking ass-hole." She says this time more slowly, annunciating each letter. Before I know what I'm doing, I find myself grabbing her, and pressing her her up against the wall, our chests mere centimeters away from each other. I have her arms pinned above her body. She blows a bubble with her gum, sage green eyes staring at me with defiance. I fight the urge to pop the bubble with my teeth.

"I'm sorry I didn't hear you. What did you just say to me?" Her gum pops loudly in my face and she flicks her dark eyelashes down my body in annoyance. She takes a breath and I feel my body moving to close the space between us. I move my head a fraction of an inch forward, and her eyes widen, and she sucks in a breath- fucking yes, she wants this. My cock thickens in my pants, and I'm so lost in my excitement that I don't see her knee raise up before she kicks me square in the balls.

I yelp, hunching over and grabbing at my privates. I felt that zing of pain all the way to my bones... Fucking hell, that hurt like a bitch.

As I'm hunched over, I glance over at her in disbelief only to find that pouty mouth quirked up in a smirk.

"Don't ever touch me again asshole, or next time I'll use this." She shows me a black studded purse before she saunters away, hips swaying. Those fishnet tights clinging to her alabaster legs.

My chest rages with the insult. Fucking nobody ever talked to me that way. I was Pierce Ledger, and I'd make her remember my fucking name. I'd have her screaming it and worshiping it before I was through.

∎∎

"You wanted to see me?" I ask as I slink into the headmaster's office. My balls still feel like they're on fire and the aspirin I took doesn't seem to be touching my hangover. I was in a foul mood and ready to get this meeting over with so I could get some fucking sleep and ice my nut sack.

"Ah, Pierce, yes thank you for- what's that on your face?" Fuck- the condom imprint was still imbedded on my cheek.

"Oh, uh- nothing. Just fell asleep on something." His wrinkled face pulls down into a deeper scowl, which should be impossible because his face seems permanently etched in disapproval. His jowls pull his mouth down like he was the unhappy tragic Melpomene from the famous Sock and Buskin theater masks. He'd been headmaster at the school for years and had a reputation of being ruthless. Knowing him like I do now, those rumors aren't unfounded.

"Please, sit." I try not to grimace as I sit in the world's most uncomfortable chair, and I feel a pang from the injury I'd just sustained. I hate this room. My thoughts slide to the girl in the hallway, how she's spun my head. How she was so unlike anyone I'd been attracted to and yet here I was having this visceral of a reaction to her and fuck me, what an impression I had made on her. Condom wrapper imprint and acted

27

like a total insane asshole, real nice Pierce. I get lost in my spiraling thoughts, my headache pushing from behind my eyeballs that I miss what the headmaster said. I try to play it off like I heard the whole thing and nod my head.

"New year, same rules, do you think you and your fraternity brothers can handle that?" I fight rolling my eyes.

"Yes, sir."

"Now, listen about that special job I mentioned..."

My head snaps to attention. Special job? I must have been lost in my thoughts. I sit up straighter. Headmaster Hayden knocks his gnarled knuckles on the mahogany desk.

As he goes into detail on what he expects of me, I feel at war within myself. The Pride part of me that lives in my chest, swells with excitement, desperate to prove itself, but my human side? My human side is raging, making my heart hammer and palms sweat. I know that I don't have a choice. That I'll be forced to do whatever it is he asks of me. Especially with the threats he has hanging over my head, over all seven of our heads. I can't disregard his wishes and a voice that sounds like mine screams from inside of my head, trapped.

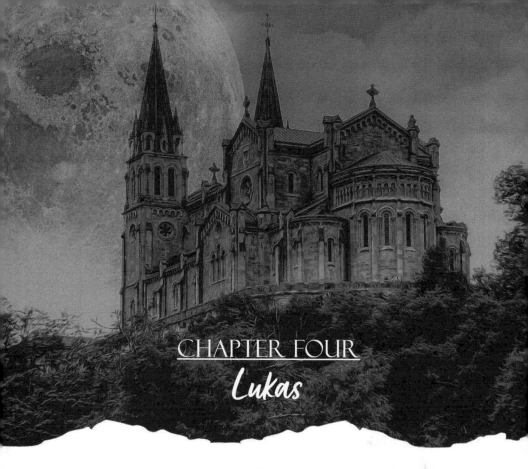

CHAPTER FOUR
Lukas

My twin was up to something. I know him like I know the back of my hand, each intricate tattooed rose petal. He'd come back from his meeting with the headmaster acting jittery, which was unlike him. When I tried asking him what was up, he shrugged me off and locked himself into his room. I scratch at my scruff and pile a huge helping of eggs onto my plate. Graham had insisted on feeding everyone that was home, and I wasn't complaining. Graham makes the best food- the things I'd do for his lasagna alone was downright obscene.

"Hey Graham Cracker, do you have any more of that special hot sauce you make?" Emmet asks, mopping up his eggs with the remnants of the hot sauce Graham makes. The red liquid coats his dark skin as he messily shoves the food in his mouth, his face scrunching up into a scowl. We'd broken into fights over the hot sauce before, and if Graham ever fails at taking over his family's restaurant business, the dude could make a fortune bottling this shit up.

"Nah, man. I gave the last of it to Lukas." I feel Emmet's eyes boring into my plate. Shit. I avoid his envious stare as I shovel the last few bites of eggs accompanied with the coveted sauce into my mouth. He slams his plate into the sink, the rest of his eggs flying.

"Yo, calm down or I won't make anymore." Graham says, one hand on his aproned hip and the other pointing his spatula at Emmet, who is still glowering at me. I lick my fork and see the green of Emmet's eyes flash in envy. He's probably coming up with some retaliation, but fuck it was so worth it. I stifle a smirk from gracing my lips by biting down on my lip. That smirk would for sure send Emmet overboard and I was far too hung over to deal with his bullshit this morning.

My mind floods with images that are begging me to sketch them out despite my lingering hangover. My father's requirement of my education demanded that I earn a business degree like my twin, which didn't leave much room to pursue my true passions in my school schedule. However, I had worked out a deal with the art department for me to sit in on the classes I wasn't technically signed up to take. I could attend one advanced art class per week, in exchange for some modeling. It was cold as fuck sitting in a room full of students that were sketching my bare ass, their eyes calculating every brush stroke. As uncomfortable as it was initially, I'd grown not to give a fuck since it granted me access to what I truly desired. And shit, did it feel good to be able to thwart my father's wishes. He hated anything that he deemed frivolous, and art fell into that category with him. Especially my art.

I remember the moment I stopped trying to show him what I was working on. I was five and I'd just drawn my mother as she sipped her tea. I ran clutching the parchment in my tiny fists as I flew into my father's office, feet bounding with excitement. I didn't get her nose right, but I still thought it was so cool. I couldn't wait to show him. He'd been on the phone, as usual, and when I waved the paper in front of him- he yanked it from my hands, not even bothering to look at it before he crumpled the paper I had spent so much time on and tossed it into the trash. That was the last time I allowed myself to be naïve enough to think he cared about what I did. He cared about his bottom line. He cared about his business, his yacht and his many stock holdings. He cared most of all for his legacy and the insistence that Pierce and I follow in his footsteps. He sure as shit didn't care about my mom, or what she wanted, and I'd go to my grave blaming him for what happened to her. I feel my teeth grinding in frustration with the turn my thoughts had taken. I'd play along with his demands- biding my time while I earned my degree and then I'd be gone.

In my room hunched over my art desk, my fingers strain. They're covered in smudges and are cramping from the hours spent creating, getting everything perfect. I swipe my charcoal over the page- shading and bringing the images in my mind to life. Everything gets quiet in my mind for a while and the pressure inside my chest dulls as I work. I miss lunch and ignore the dull ache that's taken up residence in my stomach. The groaning it makes only spurring me on. It isn't until around 3pm that

I'm interrupted by Sloan, who has misplaced his weed stash. Knowing him, he was probably just getting up. He usually stayed up late smoking, playing video games, and he never woke up before noon. Sloan had figured out a way to take all his required classes in the evening, and he usually slept through most of the lectures.

"You know I don't touch that shit Sloan." I make a final stroke around the intricately designed wrought iron fence I'd been sketching all day. I'd woven skulls and roses throughout the design and finished with a flourish of my signature down in the corner. My floor is littered with bunched up papers I'd tossed trying to get it right.

"Yeah, but have you seen it?" I rub at my cramping shoulder, smudging a bit of the charcoal as I massage my aching muscle. "You know I need it to relax."

"I haven't, but if I do, I'll let you know." He nods at my response then heads downstairs to bother the rest of our frat brothers. I stand stretching out my lower back, determined to grab some food. Pierce's weird behavior from this morning nags at my mind, but I push it away reasoning that it was probably just him coping with a hangover.

When I enter the kitchen, I find it empty, giving me full access to the refrigerator. I pile some meat on bread and smear a bit of mayo on. When I squirt the mustard, it shoots out at me from the bottom. "What the FUCK!" I roar. That shit almost hit me square in the eye, missing by a millimeter.

I hear a dark chuckle coming from behind me. Fucking Emmet. I should have known. I wipe my mustard filled face with a paper towel.

"We even now, asshole?" He leans against the doorway with his arms crossed over his chest, a wicked smile playing on his lips. He nods assessing the damage he'd done with his prank.

"I guess we'll see." He says before knocking his knuckles on the door frame as he leaves the kitchen.

Fucking Emmet. I rip into my sandwich, sans mustard. I need a shower.

When I finish my food, I toss the plate into the sink then head up to the second level where the communal bathroom was located. The school had renovated the old mansion to make it fit for a fraternity. I walked into one of the shower stalls and turned on the water waiting for it to warm up. As I let the tepid water flow over me, I felt the tug of Lust grabbing at my chest. Fucking hell, not again.

I look down to see my pierced cock rock hard and aching. The pressure in my chest increases, demanding I give in. I wrap my hand around my length, obeying as I stroke it. Images of people I'd fucked playing in my mind as I satisfied the Lust that lives in me, controlling me. When I finally come, I let out a loud groan. For once I'd like to remember what it was like to feel this way without the pull of the demon I'd been saddled with.

CHAPTER FIVE
Pierce

The Pacific Northwest is in a mood swing, the temperature plummeting fast after the summer months, just in time for school to start. A chilled fog hangs in the air as I trudge down the wooded path from Hell House to Paladin Hall where I have my first class of the day. My mind has been a fucking mess since meeting with the headmaster, my thoughts sparring against what he expects of me. The consequences of not following through with his request.

Wind whips at my face, biting into my skin while I make the five-minute walk to class. Though the frat house isn't far, it's still eerie and no one else is on the path as most of my fraternity brothers opt for classes that start later in the day. The Douglas Firs that surround the path creak while the bitter wind batters the miserable island. By the time I arrive at the hall, my skin is pebbled with goosebumps and the chill from the wind has settled in my bones. It takes me a moment of rubbing my hands together to get some feeling back into them.

My first two years at Kildale Academy were spent getting all my prerequisites out of the way, which means I'll finally be able to focus on the classes that are specialized to my degree.

I'm about to enter Intro to Business when a flash of creamy white legs covered in fishnet stockings catches my attention. A smirk graces my lips at seeing the hellion that I'd run into the other day on my way to the headmaster's office. Judging by the disgusted look on her face, she's seen me too. I check my watch and see I've got some time to spare before class starts. I slink over to where she's sipping on a coffee cup. Maybe the early start won't be so bad.

"Fancy seeing you here." I lean against the wall, hands pushed deep into my pockets.

"Drop dead." She says, looking down into her cup, not sparing me even a glance.

I feel a rustling in my chest of displeasure, but then an idea hits me. I pat my body in confusion and finally get her to raise an eyebrow at my overt display.

"What are you doing?" Annoyance laces her husky voice.

"Yep, that's what I thought." She looks at me confused. I finish patting my body. "I'm still here, so I guess you aren't a witch like I thought." She scowls at me. "You'll have to work harder than that to get rid of me." I smirk at her, knowing I won this round. Something about knowing I rile her up has my blood pumping with excitement.

"Hey, Salem, you coming?" Her short brown-haired friend calls over and I see my girl stand up straight. She flits her sage green eyes over me in a dismissal.

Before she saunters off to join her friend, I say, "Salem? Guess I was wrong, you are a witch after all." She scowls at me and grabs her friend's arm.

It's not until after they disappear into the classroom that my mind snags on the importance of her name. Salem. Shit.

My mind whirls with the knowledge of what the headmaster asked of me, and my heart stutters putting two and two together. How many Salems could there be at this Academy?

I amble into the room that's steadily filling with students, my eyes snagging on Salem, who sits in the front row, legs crossed as she picks her black nail polish. She's sitting next to her short friend who'd called her over chatting about something. I notice the seat next to her is wide open. Before I'm able to grab it, a smarmy looking dude snatches the seat, leaving me with the next best option. I head up a step and settle into the seat directly behind her.

Just as I'm settling into my chair, a man in his mid-50's enters the classroom, commanding the room's attention with his tweed ensemble, complete with elbow pads. He plops his briefcase down onto his desk and snatches up a piece of chalk. "My name is Professor Crane, and this is Intro to Business. If you are not supposed to be in Intro to Business, please leave, otherwise welcome." He goes into detail about the expectations of the class, his wirey looking TA passes out the syllabus as he talks. The TA is of medium build and seems to have taken all his fashion advice from *Harry Potter*. He even has the round glasses. I wouldn't be surprised if I found out he had a lightning bolt tattooed onto his forehead.

"Now, if you will take a look at this last bullet point, you'll notice the group project accounts for 20% of your grade. You'll be expected to work as a team and come up with a business plan for a made-up company. You have from now until the end of the semester to work on it, so I will be assigning those groups now." The class visibly shifts with unease. He counts people off into groups of four and five when he finally lands on me. He counts to four, grouping me in with Salem, her friend and the guy sitting next to her. I cock a smile and lean forward, "See, I told you, you wouldn't be able to get rid of me that easy." I whisper into Salem's ear, her dark hair pulled to the side in an intricate braid. I fight the urge to yank on it as my breath tickles against the bare side of her neck. Her body stiffens, but she keeps her eyes facing forward ignoring me.

I sit back in my chair with a chuckle, not hating the turn of events this day has taken.

I push down the headmaster's request, the Pride in my chest struggling against me. He'd have to godsdamn wait for when I carried out his wishes and I'd do it when I was good and ready. And now having met Salem, I was even more at war with what he expected from me. The girl had no idea what was coming. I'd still carry out the headmaster's request, but I was going to have some fun with her along the way.

CHAPTER SIX
Salem

It'd been a day from Hell. Not only did I get put into a group that would determine a huge chunk of my grade with that asshole from the hallway, but I'd just found out that my credit card was maxed out. Meaning my mom hadn't paid the bill and I needed to get to the bottom of it. Thankfully my meals were covered so I wouldn't starve, but any other expenses...? I sent off another text to my mom, while I waited for her reply. To round out my day, I'd gone to drink out of a water fountain only to have it spray in my face. I could feel the beginnings of a headache creeping in, probably from the change in barometric pressure. Leave it to me to end up in a place with constant weather fluctuations. I let out a sigh, slinging back an aspirin and rubbing my temples.

I was expecting my new roommate to show up at any minute. I hoped to God it was someone I would get along with and I was dreading having to relinquish my privacy. I'd taken special care to leave room for her things in the small closet and dresser we were to share, making sure my stuff didn't spill over. The box sized room barely fit the two twin beds comfortably. I'd decorated my side with a few wrought iron black shelves that I'd placed a few candles on and a handful of my favorite books. I tended to gravitate to the fantasy genre as a way to escape the clutches of reality. I'd even made sure to bring my special edition of *The Hobbit* that my grandmother had gifted to me as a young girl. I couldn't bear the thought of parting with it when it came time to pack.

Our room was the last one down the corridor on the top floor of the gothic building. The outside of the dormitory looked like someone had transported it from Edinburgh with its gargoyles carved into the stone façade and twisted ivy that slithered its way up and around the weathered brick. Just looking at it made me feel like I'd been accidentally sent back in time.

A tentative knock brakes my concentration and in pops a blonde-haired girl, who'd swept her hair into two disheveled space buns. She's wearing a tie-dye crop top and bell bottom jeans that hug her curvy figure. "Hey, are you Salem?" her voice calls from the doorway.

I pop my gum giving her a once over.

"Yeah, that's me. Are you Skye?"

She drags in a large duffle and heaves it down onto the empty bed then collapses next to it. "I sure hope this is the right room, because

I cannot move another muscle." I let out a chuckle as she breathes deeply. "Those stairs are a killer and I thought I was in such good shape."

"Twelve flights will do that to you. I thought they'd have to call an ambulance for me when I moved in over the weekend." Skye turns her head to look at me with a wide grin.

"You'd think with all the money that goes into this school they could have put in an elevator." I nod my head in agreement. The building was definitely due for some major renovations.

"I better check on my dad and make sure he didn't pass out on the stairs." Skye says struggling to sit up from her prone position on her bed.

"Do you need any help?" I offer.

Surprise flashes across Skye's face before she smiles shaking her head.

"I only have one more bag but thank you. I have a feeling we're going to be good friends. I have a sense about people you know." Her dad knocks and Skye lets him into the cramped room. He has a receding blonde hairline and seems pretty in shape for his age. Skye and her dad share the same bright smile and deep tan like they were the kind of people that spent a lot of time outdoors. He takes in the small space, his shoulders tense with the anxiety.

"So, this is your room, sunbeam? Seems small even for a dorm." He laughs uncomfortably.

I stand and stick out my hand, "I'm Salem." I say taking pity on him. He's obviously struggling with letting his daughter go, which is more than I could say for my own family. They didn't so much as drop me off at the Boston airport. My mother was off on some cruise with husband number three, and my dad and I haven't talked in years.

"Hank Dannon." He says gripping my hand back. I let Skye and her dad go through the motions before he heads out with an unsure wave that warms even my ice-cold heart. I push down the sharp pang of jealousy I get when I see families that care for each other.

"He seems nice." I say once he's gone while Skye is unpacking her belongings.

"He's the best. I'm all he has left so this is hard for him. Well, hard for us both I guess." She says clutching a piece of her clothing to her chest before finding a space for it. "So, tell me about campus. What are you studying?"

I chew on my gum that's now lost its flavor. "I'm majoring in business as requested by my family but minoring in English Literature. So far, I haven't met too many people, but I do have plans to meet up with my new acquaintance Javelynn later tonight. Are you down for coming out with us? We're going to check out the campus theater, I guess they're showing *Friday the 13th*." Skye seems like she's in need of a good friend, same as me. I'd met Javelynn at the party and we'd hit it off instantly. They were laid back and seemed kind. I was excited to find out we were in the same business class and at least I'd have them in my group for the project.

"Um... sure. I'm not really into horror movies, but it could be fun to go and meet some new people and see more of the campus. I've only seen pictures online."

"Well that settles it, you're coming." She gives me a tentative smile. I was determined to turn around this shit day, and thankfully the aspirin I'd taken had kicked in. I swing my legs off my bed and grab my new roommate by the hand. "Let's go conquer those stairs, and I'll show you around campus.

CHAPTER SEVEN
Skye

Salem had taken my need to see the campus seriously and dragged me to every corner imaginable before meeting up with her friend Javelynn, who explained that their name was due to their parents' affinity for King Arthur. They grimaced when telling Salem and I about how they nearly missed being called Merlin.

"I mean they could have always gone with Excalibur." Salem quips, earning a lopsided smile from Javelynn, who's dark hair is pulled into a low bun extenuating their slim neck.

I thought back on my mom telling me the story of how she and my dad had decided on the name Skye. They'd been married for three years when I came along. They'd gone through list after list of baby names, but nothing had fit. When my mom went into labor, she had been working out in the garden. My father was working, and she'd left her phone in the house. The contraction rendered her unable to walk as her knees sunk into the dirt. She laid down trying to breathe. All she was able to do was cradle her stomach and look up to the sky as she waited for the contraction to pass. As she laid there delirious with pain, she started to slip into unconsciousness. Before she went under, she thought she had never seen a more beautiful blue sky in her life. Thankfully a neighbor had seen her go down and had called 911. They were able to get her to the hospital in time. Apparently, her blood pressure had plummeted which caused her to pass out. They performed an emergency c-section, and both my mom and me were fine.

After I was born, she looked into my eyes and said that the color matched the sky she'd seen so perfectly, that it had offered her a peace she hadn't felt before. She knew instinctively in that moment what my name was.

The memory of her recanting that story seems so close that I can almost smell her floral perfume and it leaves a twinge of pain right in my heart. That never seems to get easier. The waves of grief creep up in the most unexpected moments. I turn my focus back onto my new friends, feeling guilty about being swept into my own thoughts.

As Salem and I walk together we discover that Javelynn is originally from South Korea and had moved to the US when they were 2 years old, their father worked his way up in a multi-national company and now held the CEO position. They were a business major, just like Salem and they insisted we attend the open mic night in town that was coming up soon. There wasn't much to do on this tiny island other than hang out on campus or go into the small harbor town. The only town on the island where most of the custodial staff lived with a few small business owners. There was one grocery store that looked more like a stop and shop, and two competing bars. The locals were either loyal to O'Malley's or Diablo's.

I was grateful my first class wasn't until tomorrow, since I'd missed orientation due to our camper getting a flat tire. Dad and I had to wait a whole day until the tire shop could get a replacement for us.

I had English Literature first thing in the morning, which I found was with Salem, thankfully, so at least I would know someone in my class.

The movie Javelynn and Salem brought me to was cringy from what parts I saw between my fingers that I held over my face. The song was haunting more than anything and I hoped that I didn't have nightmares. Actually, I hoped I'd be able to fall asleep at all. I was a huge chicken when it came to scary movies.

As we climb the steps back in our dorm, Salem bumps my shoulder with hers.

"You good, Dannon?" I notice she has a habit of calling people by their last name.

I smile, "Totally. Just a bit out of breath." She leaves me to my panting as I continue my trek up these torturous stairs.

My legs are Jell-O by the time I finally crest the top floor, miles behind Salem who'd taken the stairs like she was a professional stair climbing champion. It doesn't take much for me to fall asleep after the long day I've had, but I'm feeling optimistic for the first time in a while. Maybe things will be good here.

CHAPTER EIGHT
Pierce

"And you're doing well in all your classes?" My father's voice booms through the speaker of my phone.

"Dad, classes just started. I'm doing fine." Irritation rubs at me, wondering what the purpose of this call is. I flick at the metal part of my pen making a satisfying clink as it slaps back down onto the base. I flick it over and over again in a steady rhythm, feeding my anxiety into this one action.

"Your brother isn't answering my calls. Tell him to call me back if he wants me to keep footing the bill for his education." The line clicks off, and an empty tone fills my ear. I let out a sigh, removing the phone from my ear and stifling the urge to chuck my phone. I could easily replace it, God knew money wasn't an object, but I didn't want the hassle of having to program it. I clench my jaw instead, my molars crunching bone on bone against each other.

I set my shoulders back, shoving down the interaction with my father. I'll relay my father's pleasant message to Lukas later. I gather my things for class and grab a power bar on the way out. I had football practice all this week and I looked forward to the challenge. I might have been a mediocre student, but football was where I shined- and I took every opportunity to bathe in that limelight.

Being the star quarterback meant there was no shortage of pussy, but it also was a fucking rush to do something like it was second nature. When I was out on that field, it was just me and the ball, and I made that ball fucking sing every time. I hike my shoulders up to my ears then shake them out, anticipation warming my belly.

I go hard all practice. My arm throwing out one perfectly placed spiral after another. The frigid air only spurs me on as sweat beads down my brow, chilling my skin instantly. I'm high off the adrenaline by the time we're headed off to the locker room showers, my fingers buzzing with a phantom ache around the leather ball. As I'm about to enter the building, Coach Thompson pulls me aside before I have a chance to follow my teammates.

"Looking great out there Ledger." He says in a firm Midwestern accent. "I need you to keep that level of focus in check. Our first game right off the bat is against Faulkner University."

I suck in a breath. I was hoping we wouldn't have to deal with those assholes until later in the season. Last year they kept going for my knees until Coach was forced to replace me. That moment when I was hauled off the field clutching my shin plays back in my mind more times than I'd like to admit. The Pride inside of my chest grows tight with the memory. Faulkner's linebacker, Phillip Jenkins, had a hard-on for my kneecaps and their refs tended to turn a blind eye to their many penalties. I ended that game caked in mud, bruises and the bitter taste of defeat.

"You'll be fine, just keep doing what you're doing." Coach says, slapping me square on the shoulder. I give him a nod then head off to the showers. Most everyone is done, and I check the time seeing I only have a few minutes to get myself ready before Intro to Business starts.

I run the water, a cold stream of icy liquid pelts my skin slick with sweat, washing off all the muck from practice. I hear a girlish giggle echo from behind me as I wipe down my body with soap. A firm naked body presses against my back, the mystery woman's breasts skimming across me. Normally, I wouldn't even think twice about turning around and taking a dip in some pussy, but I can't find it inside me to even muster a quick fuck. I shrug her off, spinning around and seeing Katie Torrance, one of my regular quickies. She gives me a pout.

"Not today, Katie." She lets out a scoff placing her hands on her wet hips.

"You've got to be kidding me, Pierce." Her voice grates against my eardrums.

I walk out of the shower, grabbing a towel with Katie quick on my heels.

"I've got class."

"That's never stopped you before." She says trying to slide up to me, her fingers dancing along my biceps.

I snatch her hand, gripping it a touch harder than I should.

"I said no, Katie, and if you ever fucking touch me again without my permission, I'll break each pretty little finger that you touch me with."

She reels back clutching her hand, tears spilling over her lashes, and scrambles away, grabbing her clothes on her way out.

I run my fingers through my damp hair. What the fuck was going on with me? I rubbed absently at my chest a low rumble answers, pumping me full of righteous indignation. Who did she think she was trying to pull that on me?

I get dressed, making sure my tie is in the perfect position, my hair styled within an inch of its life. I feel a deep appreciation as I look in the mirror, happy with the reflection staring back at me. I'm not blind, I know I'm good looking and I know how to work that to my advantage. I give the mirror a little wink and my chest heaves with Pride. I have plans for a certain little witch today, and I wouldn't be distracted by a little side piece.

CHAPTER NINE
Salem

I make a bubble with my gum as I doodle on my notepad. The temperature in the room is downright glacial, barely better than outside. My skin pimples with goosebumps at the chill. I'm surprised my breath doesn't show. I grasp my hot chocolate cup willing the warmth from the cup to worm its way into my fingers- to no avail. My hot chocolate is now tepid chocolate. I chug the room temperature chocolatey remains and get up to toss the container into the trash. As I pass in front of the door, Pierce, bane of my existence, Ledger almost collides with me. His stupidly handsome face breaks out in a predatory grin as he grabs my wrist. I pull back on instinct, but that only brings him closer. His hand is surprisingly warm as it sits wrapped around me, his skin sending a bolt of lightning down my spine. I shove down the unwelcome feeling. Not a chance in hell is my body going to betray me for a cute as fuck smirk. Not today, Satan's Spawn.

I glare at him and make another bubble with my gum that pops right in his face. His eyes flare, along with his nostrils and he clenches his jaw glaring down at my mouth like he's not sure if it offends him or he wants to kiss me. That thought sends a jolt of confusion through me and I frown, wrenching my wrist from him. I definitely didn't want Pierce's filthy mouth on mine. Definitely not. Nope. Nope. Nope.

I wipe my hand down my skirt and take a step back.

"Witch." Pierce says with a smirk.

"Bottom feeder."

"Only if you ask nicely."

I scoff, of course he would make that into a sexual innuendo.

A cough comes from behind me, and I note the Professor is staring at us, along with the rest of class. I frown, tossing the cup I was holding into the bin like I intended, and try to pretend I don't feel the flame of embarrassment climbing over my cheeks. Pierce, however, looks as arrogant as ever, striding to his seat behind mine. I glower at him, to which he just winks. Insufferable.

I sink down in my chair, crossing my fishnet stocking legs beneath the small desk. Technically, I'm not supposed to be wearing these tights, but no one's said anything yet. The Professor glares at me and then up to Pierce before starting his lecture. I ignore Javelynn's concerned stare tuning out everything around me, completely focused on the glowing PowerPoint on the board. I especially tune out my hyper awareness of Pierce's legs directly behind me. His body warmth pummeling into my back.

I feel a flare of that heat seep into my body, almost as if I'm somehow leeching it from him. I frown feeling an electric tingle at his audible gasp. All thoughts of the lecture empty from my head as my focus turns to follow the odd sensation that's taking over my body.

I fight the urge to turn around and look at him.

What is this?

Heat courses throughout me, when just moments before I was freezing. My limbs shake with the sudden urge to release this pent-up heat that's taken over my body. Panic grips me as I look around the room to see if anyone else is experiencing the same surge of heat. Then as soon as it came on, the feeling drops, and Pierce lets out a groan loud enough that the Professor gives him another disapproving glare. The cold comes roaring back and I shiver. Javelynn looks over at me with a frown and I just shake my head, pursing my lips, not sure what just happened. They shake their head in response and return to typing notes into their laptop.

I was too young for hot flashes, wasn't I? Maybe the heat had tried to kick on above me? I mean it was an old building. Maybe I was getting sick with something?

Thankfully the rest of class passes quickly, no more weird surges of heat.

I completely forget about the incident while sitting in my English class listening to the Professor drone on about Pride and Prejudice. I'd only read that book like a thousand times, so she wasn't really telling me anything new. I sit next to my new roommate as she diligently takes notes. Skye oozes good girl vibes. I was itching to take a crack at her, make her loosen up a bit.

Professor Cranston passes out the syllabus, her wild brown curls of hair bouncing over her cream-colored sweater with each step. She was a tiny woman, whose hair was two times the size of her head. I wondered if her neck hurt with that much weight.

I glance over the syllabus, noting that we have several chapters assigned in Pride and Prejudice as well as essay questions due by the next class. I type out a reminder on my phone, which the Professor mistakes for texting in her class. I have to show her what I wrote just to get her off my back, but I don't miss the untrusting sneer she gives me. I let out a breath of frustration. Yeah, we're off to a great start.

Skye looks at me with sympathy which I brush off. I'm used to people's snap judgements.

My phone buzzes, and fuck it, the teacher already thinks I'm trouble, so I sneak a glance at it seeing a group chat between my Intro to Business group. Javelynn sent us all a meet up time to discuss our project. I had to admire their go-getter attitude. I see three tiny dots pop up and then Pierce's response that he'll be there with a winky face. A fucking winky face. That guy was so full of himself that it even came through in a text.

Jackson follows with his affirmation that he'd be there, and I glance over to the Professor whose back was turned as she finished doling out the syllabus to the rest of the class. I quickly send a thumb emoji, even though I hated those and slide my phone back into my black studded purse. I shake my leg absentmindedly, ready for this class to be over. Sure, I loved English Literature, but I wanted more than just the bland same old tirade. I wanted something that sent my mind on fire with inspiration. Memorizing Jane Austin's birthdate wasn't it.

Dread fills me as I think of spending the evening with my business group. As much as I liked Javelynn and I didn't know anything about Jackson other than he was cute in a preppy sort of way, the thought of spending any time around Pierce sent me glowering. I push away the dread by imagining I was smacking him with my black studded purse. I snort under my breath, *that* would wipe off his stupid smirk for sure. I would never really do something like that unless I was in danger, but still imagining it brought me a wicked sense of joy. If I had to suffer through his presence, at least I found a way to keep myself entertained.

CHAPTER TEN
Skye

The art room was set up in a circle with canvas holders and stools placed around a circular stage that held one wooden stool and several props. I stare at the fake apple that sits on the desk next to a pile of grapes and my stomach clenches with nerves. I have to show the professor that I belong here. My scholarship depends on her approval. The pieces I'd produced to the scholarship committee had been enough to get me in the door but holding onto my position was a whole other beast. Art was subjective and I hoped my style translated to the professor that I was worth keeping around. I shift my weight on the padded stool that I'd claimed for myself. I arrived early wanting to scope out the classroom before everyone else. I'd never taken an actual art class before. Everything that I'd learned was self-taught, with spurts of YouTube videos.

A few fellow art students trickle in, selecting their seats and fiddling with their stand's height. I take out my roll of brushes, feeling the fine hair tips fanning against the pads of my fingers. The feather light brush of them calms my nerves, letting me breath a bit more freely.

The professor waddles in at 10 on the dot. She has short, white tufted hair that's bound with a bright purple scarf. Her ears hold two large turquoise gemstone earrings that jingle against her smaller silver hoops that go up the length of both her ears. Her arms are covered by a matching purple shall that's covered in turquoise flowers. As she shuffles to the middle of the room, she passes my stand and I notice her brown shoes are paint speckled and well worn. She raps her elaborate silver cane on the stand, getting the attention of student's who were caught up in their conversations.

"Hello, hello. I am Professor Whitelsbee. I am the primary art teacher here at Kildale. We will be getting right in the thick of it, because there's no time like the present! I want you to whip out your paints, grab a canvas from the back of the room and make me something beautiful. Something that shows me who you are."

We sit stunned for a moment until Professor Whitelsbee bangs her cane on the ground. "Go!" We spring into action, scrambling for a canvas to bring back to our stations.

I pick the closest one to me and unpack my paints, uncapping the ones I want to use and squirting the malleable colors onto a painter's pallet. I stare at my canvas thinking of what to put together, but nothing comes. What is something that shows who I am?

I mix a few colors together as I think. A loose idea starts to form in my mind.

Professor Whitelsbee moves staggering around the room, studying our movements. Several students seem well underway, but I've yet to even mar my canvas with a splotch of paint. She shuffles behind me and lets out a sound of disappointment as her eyes flick over my blank canvas, she doesn't stick around, but I can feel the knots of nervousness tightening around my chest. I pick up my paint brush and pack on a light glob of blue paint.

The color matches my eyes, so I decide to paint the scene my mother always talked about, the story of my name. I flick my paintbrush over the white canvas, the colors blending together until it starts to take shape in front of me. It always feels like a magical experience when I transfer the ideas in my head into something tangible.

I lose myself in the painting and before I know it, the hour is up, and people are packing away their supplies and cleaning off their paint brushes. I step back from my work, admiring what I have so far when I catch the Professor scowling at me. My heart rate picks up as I hurriedly join the rest of my class in the cleanup and set my canvas on a drying rack stationed in the back. Professor Whitelsbee bids us farewell, her words not mine, as we file out of the classroom. I wave goodbye as I leave, but the Professor is already hobbling in the other direction. I wince, thinking back on her disapproving looks all throughout class and my stomach churns at the possibility of not living up to her expectations.

I have plans to meet up with Salem and Javelynn at lunch, and hurriedly walk down the dimly lit corridor. The cafeteria is on the opposite side of campus and my stomach is already screaming with hunger.

When I finally find my new friends they're deep in conversations and questionably made burritos. Salem's laughing at something while Javelynn chews their food with a smile.

"Hey! Skye, listen to this. So, I'm running late to my Speech class and I'm booking it so I can make it on time. When I get there, the door is locked! I try jiggling it and pull thinking, maybe it's just stuck, when my professor opens the door and I fall back, my feet going right over my head, flashing my Speech teacher my underwear."

"That's one way to try and get an A." Javelynn says wiping their mouth with a napkin. Salem shoves their shoulder, with a grin on her face.

"I can't believe he saw my underwear. His whole face got red, and he looked up at the ceiling when he asked if I was okay."

"Were they cute underwear at least, or was it a granny panty situation?" I ask, digging into my soggy looking burrito. Oh God, this tasted like wet sand.

"They were plain black and full coverage at least, but still I had to sit there the whole class knowing that my teacher had seen my nether region."

"Next time maybe wear something that says, 'I heart Speech'." Javelynn says with a snicker and tossing their trash like it's a basketball.

It sinks straight into the open hole, and a few people nearby let out a small clap.

"I hope there won't be a next time. Ugh, how am I going to get through a whole semester in this class?"

"Maybe sit in the back... or wear pants like me." Javelynn says pointing down at their outfit.

"I wish this school was more progressive and then they would allow us to wear pants. My legs are already freezing and we're not even in winter yet."

"What are we doing this weekend?" I ask, taking a sip of my water wishing I had picked something different to wash this taste away.

"There's a pool night at Diablos." Javelynn mentions, scrolling on their phone. "There's also a yoga meet up at the top of Possession Hill or a group hike that starts at the lighthouse and takes you around the island. The weather looks like it might be clear enough for kayaking."

We settle on doing some yoga since our legs are sore from all the stairs in our dorm. I, for one. could use some deep stretches after I've had to hobble up the stairs the last few days.

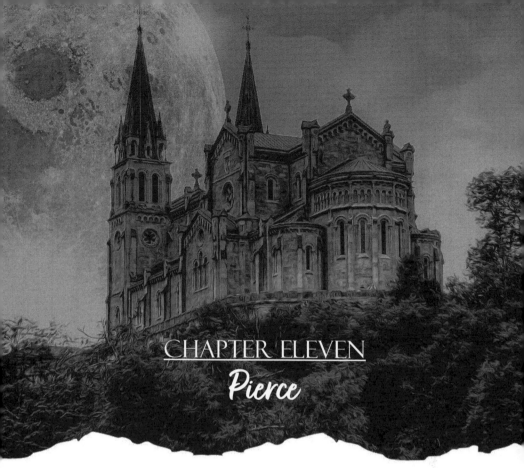

CHAPTER ELEVEN
Pierce

My plans for Salem were derailed this morning, by none other than the little witch herself. Bumping into her threw me off my game and distracted me from my goal of messing with her. And then there was that weird moment during class when I felt like all my body heat was being sucked out of me. I chalked it up to the coldness of the day, but the sensation threw me enough to make me forget about my plans. Thankfully, Javelynn had called a group meeting and I could exact some torture on my prey while we worked on the project. Who said guys couldn't multitask?

I slap my hands against the sides of my face.

Time to focus.

I stride into the library, and the faux gaslights that sit right outside the doors flicker as I pass. All these buildings were old, weather worn from the salty sea air that saw over a few decades of use. Tiny tufts of moss cling to the sides of the stone having to be scraped off or power washed by the groundskeeping staff, but I personally preferred it when they left it alone.

My steps squelch loudly against the marbled floor, echoing against the arched entryway, which earns me a scowl from the dowdy librarian. She looks like the cranky loud one from that old show *All That*, only much older. I half expected her to pull out a bull horn and yell at me for my shoe noise, but instead she returned to scanning her pile of books.

I swivel my head looking for the group I'd been saddled with for this project and landed on the back of Salem's head. She'd ditched the braid from earlier and thrown her raven hair up into a high ponytail that made my hand itch to yank on it. I crack my knuckles, walking up to the table with a bounce in my step.

Time to play.

I feel my smirk slip into place, tugging my cheek up in amusement.

"Well look who finally made it." Javelynn says, clicking their pen in annoyance.

I pull out a chair and flip it around, straddling my legs around it and clutch the back with my hands. I tap my fingers out the wood in a rat-a-tat rhythm, earning me a scowl from Salem, making me smirk even harder.

This is going to be fun.

Jackson pushes his round wire frames up his nose, glancing nervously at all of us before clearing his throat.

His voice comes out in a posh accent that I can't really place. Like a male Anna Delvy. I wonder if his glasses are even real or if he wears them as a fashion statement.

"We should divide this project into four parts, don't you think?" I feel my eyebrows raise as he talks.

I'm about to make a quip back, but Javelynn gets there first.

"That's a great idea, Jackson, but how about first we come up with what we're even working on, then we can focus on who does what."

Jackson's cheeks pink, but he nods his agreement.

I lean back slightly admiring Javelynn's natural leadership skills.

We look over the project requirements, the grade percentage glares at me as I flick over the instructions. Javelynn is saying something to the group, but I've tuned out. Focusing on that grade percentage makes my palms start to sweat. My father's voice reverberates in my mind. His expectations feel like a noose around my neck, pushing me towards goals that he's set in stone since I was in the womb. The Pride inside my chest roils with the desire to be seen as the best. It yearns for me to fulfill the Ledger Legacy, choking me about the neck into compliance. I feel my eyes briefly flutter, the sense of Pride settling, but not fast enough that it's escaped Salem's notice. She frowns at me, her pen resting smack in the middle of her lower lip as she looks at me with confusion. I bristle, brushing her off and refocusing on Javelynn, who thankfully is still talking.

I flick out my phone under the table while my group is otherwise engaged in what Javelynn is saying. I send off a quick text to Emmet, letting him know I'm in place, using our agreed upon poop emoji as the signal. Innocent enough that it looks like the two of us are shooting the shit with each other without giving away our true intentions. I figured that to make sure my plan goes off without a hitch, I'd need reinforcements. No one can pull off a prank like Emmet, and that's partly due to how well he knows his prey. He was the king of pranks, and his expertise was one I required when dealing with my little witch.

The headmaster was adamant that I carry out his plans for her, but in order to do that, I needed to know her. Our interactions thus far showed me that I wasn't about to become best friends with her anytime soon… my chest rolls in disapproval. My Pride was still sulking from her flat-out dismissal of me. I'd make her pay for that eventually.

I catch a flash of movement in my periphery as I nod my head at Javelynn's business ideas. Emmet had arrived. I tilt my chin at him as he slinks through the library, his wet feet squeaking against the tiles. Salem turns to face the noise.

She's easily distracted, I note taking that moment to swipe her phone from her bag that lays slightly ajar. Jesus, her bag could cause some serious damage, I think, as I snatch the phone from the spiked purse without raising suspicion.

Salem turns her attention back to Javelynn, blowing a bubble with her gum. Emmet comes close enough to our table that I'm able to hand off the phone to him behind my back.

Emmet's dad was the CEO of some tech company that specialized in security, which was just code for talented hackers that charged you a lot of money to stop other hackers.

It took Emmet only a moment before he was looping back around to put the phone back in my hand.

I feel the cool kiss of the phone slipping into my palm. Emmet uses this moment to knock into Salem, giving me a moment to place it back into Salem's spiked purse while she glowers at Emmet.

"Oh! I'm so sorry." He drawls, laying on the southern gentleman accent and earning a forgiving smile from Salem. I feel myself frown at seeing how easily she interacts with everyone else.

"No problem. I'm alright."

"Maybe you should watch where you're going." The words tumble out of my mouth before I realize I've said them. Both Salem and Emmet, swivel their heads towards me. Emmet with a stare that clearly says, 'what the fuck' and Salem looks about ready to set me on fire.

"What's your issue? He said he's sorry."

I feel myself flare with irritation. Her sassy fuckin' mouth.

"No issue, just annoyed by the distraction from working on our project." I force the lie out between my clenched teeth. I don't know why she can get me so riled up like this. My emotions tumbling out of control.

"Oh, please. Like you've even been paying attention." Shit. She's good.

I smirk, "What makes you think I haven't been paying attention?"

"What's the business name then?"

I stare at her as her face takes on a triumphant glow. Fuck, she's caught me, but then I realize she's far too pleased with herself.

Javelynn raises their eyebrow, while Jackson looks like the smug little shit he is.

I lean into Salem's space, catching her by surprise as a waft of vanilla and caramel hits me.

"We haven't named the business yet, little witch."

Her eyes go wide with surprise. Gotcha.

"Can we focus on the project? I really want to get as much done as possible since this accounts for a large chunk of our grade." Javelynn breaks Salem's and my stare and I nod, picking up the project paper.

Emmet stands awkwardly off to the side taking in the scene, before giving a wave as he heads out of the library.

"Asshole." I hear Salem whisper as she writes something on her paper.

"Hag." I retort.

She glares at me, her jade-colored eyes flashing with contempt. I glare right back, the world quieting around us as we're locked into another staring match. The electricity flowing between us is almost palpable.

"Seriously?" Javelynn's voice cuts through to us again and I shake myself.

"Sorry, Jave." Salem sounds full of remorse which irritates me.

"Well, this has been fun, but unfortunately I have another engagement." Jackson says his voice sounding like a new accent entirely as he gathers his things and pushing his glasses up the bridge of his nose.

"Great." Javelynn throws up their hands in annoyance. "You two better get your shit together so we don't fail this project. I'm not risking an F because you two couldn't stop making goo goo eyes at each other."

"Goo goo?" Salem practically shrieks.

"Shhh!" The librarian directs at our table mid book scan.

"I was not giving him goo goo eyes." Salem whispers, turning to Javelynn. "If anything, they were my 'I hope I don't murder you' eyes."

Javelynn rolls their eyes. "Whatever. It's obvious you two need to just have a little hate sex so we can get back on track."

I let out a low laugh while Salem stares at her friend with an open mouth. I press my finger on her chin helping her to close that perfect little mouth of hers. She whips her head away from me, which only makes me laugh more.

"Be quiet or get out!" The librarian whisper shouts.

"We were just leaving." Javelynn says. They point their index finger at both Salem and I. "Get your shit together."

Javelynn leaves us both, Salem sitting there stunned and irritated and I'm enjoying seeing her squirm.

"So..." I venture, rubbing the stubble that's coming in on my chin.

"Shut up, this is all your fault."

"My fault?"

"Yes you! Irritating me and distracting me from the project! Now we lost valuable time to work on a huge part of our grade."

"Relax princess, we have plenty of time." I bop the back of the chair with my hands before I push myself up to standing, spinning the chair back to the proper place. I grab my bag then stride toward the archway doors.

"How can you be so dismissive?" She says her shoes clipping fast behind me. I catch the scowl of the librarian on our way passed her desk.

"How can you be this uptight?"

"I am not uptight."

I hold the door open for her to which she squints her eyes at me before walking through in a huff. I follow after her towards the dorms even though it's in the opposite direction from Hell House.

"You are. Is that why you reacted the way you did when Javelynn suggested we fuck each other?"

She turns on her heel to face me, but I'm closer than she anticipated because I smack right into her by her abrupt change in direction.

"Fuck!" Her purse of death gouged my arm. "Why do you have this thing? It's a weapon."

"I did warn you that I would hit you with this the next time you tried to touch me. Also, not that it's your business but I have it to keep people like you away."

"I didn't try to touch you, you changed directions and hit me. Besides, why would you want to keep me away when you're so obviously drawn to me."

"Get over yourself Pierce. I would never be drawn to someone who spends more time looking in the mirror than on their homework assignments."

"So, you think I'm good looking?"

She rolls her eyes then turns to start walking again, shoving her hands into her skirt pockets.

"The problem with people like you, is that you know you're good looking and you think the world should bow at your feet for just gracing us with your genetic lottery face."

"There's nothing wrong with being born beautiful. I just happen to be blessed that way, and also, I hate to break it to you, but I spend equal amounts of time in front of the mirror and on my homework. Guess that means you can allow yourself to admit you're into me."

"Never." She trudges along the path her shoulders set near her ears, her footsteps stomp at the gravel with each step.

"Why are you following me? Isn't your house that way?" She points in the direction of the woods.

I tsk, "You're not doing a good job of convincing me that you're not into me since you know where I live."

"Everyone knows where you live Pierce. That doesn't prove that I'm into you."

I reach out and grab her elbow, spinning her into me, careful not to impale myself on her Medieval torture purse. "Maybe not, but everything else about you gives you away."

Her body is pressed against mine, molding perfectly to me, she lets out a small shuddering breath of surprise. "What gives you away, little witch, are your eyes. The way they dilate when you look at me, like you're undressing me in that wicked little head of yours." I trail my fingers down her spine and feel her arch up into me. "Your breathing hitches just a little when you talk to me, which means you either have asthma, or I make you nervous. And one other thing?" I glance down at her lips, noticing her tongue flicking out across her bottom lip. "You're fucking shaking in my arms."

She sets her jaw, her brows pulling down into a frown before she pushes her hand against my chest, taking a step back. "That's because it's cold outside."

"And the other things?"

"You're clearly delusional."

I let out a laugh, something about her spunk has me intrigued.

"You're clearly in denial."

"You know what they say about denial?"

"What's that?"

"It's a river in Egypt."

"Oh my God, that was such a dad joke." I break out into a full-on smile.

"You're easily the most annoying person I've ever met." A smile tugs at her full lips, I flick my gaze down for a brief second.

"I'll take that as a compliment." Her breath hitches as I look back into her piercing jade eyes. I feel myself leaning into her when I suddenly feel a buzzing coming from my pants pocket. She hears the buzzing then takes a step back, her frown slipping back into place with a shudder.

"Aren't you going to see what that is?" She asks as my phone buzzes again.

I slip my phone out to see a few missed texts from Emmet.

E: Stop flirting and get your ass back to the house already.

E: Headmaster Hayden is asking for an update.

E: Did a quick sweep of her phone, looks like she's single.

Her eyes fill with mistrust as she assesses me for a moment, taking in my tense shoulders. "Bad news?"

"Nah, just my housemate bugging me."

She nods her head, her pony bouncing with the movement. My hand itches to bring her closer so I can play with it, but I force myself to head back to the house.

"I'll see you around, witch."

She frowns at me, "Later, douchebag." I chuckle as I peel myself away from her. I have the oddest feeling that I could have spent all night exchanging barbs with her. I feel a pang of regret at what I have to do to her, but I don't have a choice. Everything hangs on carrying out the headmaster's demands. Everything.

CHAPTER TWELVE
Emmet

I sift through Salem's digital footprint while I wait for Pierce to get his ass home. My father had developed several discreet pieces of tech that afforded us the life I'd grown up in, but it also served us well when we were gathering intel on those in our lives. This wasn't the first time I'd swiped someone's phone for access to their most intimate details, and it wouldn't be the last.

It's the reason Pierce opened up to me about his deal with Headmaster Hayden, because I already knew. There was nothing that went on with my housemates that I didn't know about. I take a sip of whiskey, as I go through Salem's messages. It was clear she had a strained relationship with her family. Her mother seemed flighty at best, forgetting she had a daughter. My jaw twitches with irritation reading the last text between the two.

Salem: Mom? My card keeps getting declined. Did you pay the bill??

Mom: Fuck if I know. Don't bother me with trivial details.

Salem: … ok. But if I can't buy anything that's not a trivial detail, that's a huge detail.

Mom: What more could you possibly need? All your meals are taken care of at that school of yours that we paid for.

Salem: Mom, could you please just look into paying the card?

Salem: Mom?

Salem: Mom…?

I take another sip of whiskey, the liquid burning my throat as it goes down.

"Dude, did you get anything good?" Pierce plops down on the couch across from me. I swivel the liquid in my cup around as I continue scrolling through Salem's information.

"Nothing yet." I lie. I've learned plenty about our little witch while he was busy chasing after her. I learned she's been kicked out of three schools, she doesn't have many friends, her family comes from a long line of money, she went through an adorable boy band phase when she was younger before finding that she enjoys listening to Lana Del Ray with an occasional Taylor Swift binge. She'd rather be reading or listening to music than interacting with people, and she's been arrested

73

at least once that I could find for protesting. It warmed my cold heart to see that she'd been marching in the streets for someone like me. Though I was privileged with money, sometimes people couldn't look past the color of my skin. While we moved through affluent circles, when I put a hoodie on and went jogging, I was so fucking aware of my surroundings. There's nothing quite like the blind hatred of stranger who professes they're acting out of a moral compass for the good of the community.

I knock back the last of my drink, thoughts swirling with what to do with this information. I tend to keep my cards close to my chest. I learned at a young age that it didn't take much for people to betray you.

"Let me know if you find anything good." Pierce says pushing up from the couch before heading off to the kitchen. He was far too prideful. It would be his downfall, being arrogant enough to rely on his last name and his looks. He figured people wouldn't dare cross a Ledger, so he gave his trust freely and easily. He smiled frequently, unburdened by the crushing anxiety I felt daily.

I wondered what that must be like, to feel free from the crushing weight that I carried with me wherever I went. I felt the Envy rise in my chest. I welcomed my old friend, basking in the emotions letting them flow over me.

I knew my fellow fraternity brothers hated the sins we'd been shackled to, but I relished it. It felt like I was finally awake. It allowed me to become the person I'd been too weak to be before. That night we drank out of the challises was the night I was fucking born. The Emmet from before was timid, scared, a fucking pussy. I'd vowed to never go back to that person. No matter what.

A ping on my phone notifies me of an incoming text message Salem had. I'd programed all of Salem notifications to have a different sound so I could differentiate between my own messages and hers. No one ever paid enough attention to notice I'd done this every time I'd hacked into a new phone. I immersed myself in their life for a week or two, before moving onto someone else. I'd occasionally circle back around to people I'd spied on before, especially my house mates. Couldn't be too careful with people who lived in the same building as you.

Skye: Wanna meet up for burgers?

A read receipt appears. I sit up straight, watching as my phone mirrors Salem's, her response coming to life before my eyes as she types back.

Salem: Sure. Cafeteria in 15?
Skye: See you there 😬

I feel my lips pull up into a smile. Looks like I was about to bump into Salem once again this evening.

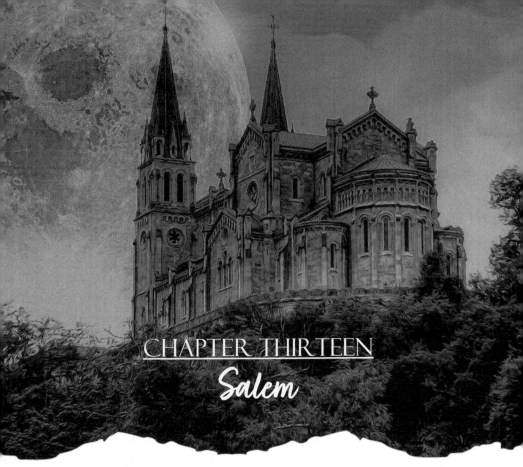

CHAPTER THIRTEEN
Salem

I'm early, burger already in hand while I wait at a free table in the cafeteria. I wished that I could have headed off campus to one of the pubs for something other than this sludge they'd called food. My stomach rumbles with hunger, but I'm resolved to wait for Skye to arrive before I tear into my burger. Those Knox manners my family drilled into me as a kid must have stuck.

I see a flash of blonde space-buns walking towards the table. I wave to catch her attention. She spots me, a smile forming across her face.

For the first time in maybe years, I felt like I was finally finding my footing. I didn't usually make friends easily, and both Skye and

Javelynn had been more than welcoming. We slid into our friendship naturally, as if we'd always known each other.

"Javelynn has class until 7, so they won't be joining us." She says as she sits daintily next to me, tucking her long legs into a proper leg cross. She dips a fry into a side of mayo.

"So, I have no idea what my art professor wants from me." She says between bites.

"What do you mean?"

"Well, every time she sees me, she scowls." Skye mimics her teacher's face which makes me laugh.

"Oh God, that's terrifying. Never make that face again."

"Now you know my pain. Every day it's just this glaring."

"No please. I can't" I say laughing, trying to close my eyes.

"If I have to suffer then I'm taking you with me." She tries to pull my hands away from my eyes.

"Am I interrupting?" A deep southern drawl as soft as honey says from behind us. I drop my hands and see the guy from earlier who'd knocked into me. Skye looks up at him with interest, but the stranger keeps his eyes glued to me.

"Um, no not at all." I say finding myself playing with the ends of my ponytail. Oh my god, Salem pull yourself together- I mentally chide forcing myself to stop twirling my hair like a lovesick teenager.

"I wanted to apologize for earlier." I could listen to his voice all day that I almost forget to respond, until I feel Skye's elbow poking into my rib.

"Oh! Yeah, no- no problem." I feel my cheeks warm with embarrassment.

"I'm Emmet." He says, offering his hand. I look up into his deep green eyes that stand out against his dark bronzed skin. I give my hand in return, feeling our fingers lock together.

"Salem." I manage to squeak out. He gives me a smile that's full of intensity. God, this guy is so hot, I almost feel the need to fan myself. I feel like I'm ten seconds away from needing a fainting couch.

"I'll see you around campus then?" he asks.

"Yeah! Absolutely. Let me give you my number." Oh my god this is so embarrassing, I feel like I'm falling all over myself, but his voice does something to my insides that makes me feel all mushy.

I give him my digits and he texts me from his phone so I can save his number.

When he turns to leave, I lean into Skye for support.

"Oh. My. God." She whispers. "There's no way that it's legal for someone to be THAT pretty. I mean, did you see his eyelashes? I would kill for those eyelashes. Are you going to text him?"

"I don't know! I wouldn't even know what to say. Besides, he has my number. He can text me."

Skye bumps me on the shoulder with hers, "I love it. Make him work for it."

CHAPTER FOURTEEN
Skye

All week, Professor Whitelsbee has been breathing down my neck about my work. She stands over my shoulder, her free hand on her hip and a scowl permanently etched on her face as she looks at me as I paint. I came to the art room tonight on her suggestion that I rework my piece. I've slowly become acclimated to classes and found it ironic that the one class I came to Kildale for was the one giving me the most trouble.

I splatter paint across my canvas as my earbuds pulse loudly against my eardrums. The wicked vibes are driving my inspiration. I grab black paint going darker- edgier- layered. I'd evoke emotions from this piece and prove my art teacher wrong. Professor Whitelsbee was 'deeply unhappy' with my piece I'd produced and was making me redo it, hence the violent paint strokes and pulsing mood music I found myself swaying to as I worked. I wasn't about to let this one Professor's taste ruin everything I'd worked for. My very position at this school could be in jeopardy and I refused to be sent packing already.

Paint flecks and flicks, spraying me as I push the colors around. It clings to my blonde space-buns and splatters my cheeks. I'd recently dyed the tips of my hair lilac, which made my space buns look like they were surrounded by tiny purple halos- or so Salem said when I revealed my new do last night. I tended to change up my hair whenever I was feeling extra stressed, and with this new school, being separated from my dad, and Professor Whitelsbee's constant scrutiny, my stress was palpable. I notice a few globs of paint splattered across my favorite AC/DC oversized t-shirt. It's one I usually wear when painting, and no stranger to a rogue paint fleck. It hits me mid-thigh, covering my shorts underneath. Though it was cold outside, I usually got overheated when painting, so I opted for breathability figuring that when it came time to go back to the dorms, I would walk as fast as I could.

A shuffling sound fills the room as I stand there examining my work. I remove an earbud with my paint-stained hand, looking around for the source of the noise. It was late and I was pretty sure I had the art room all to myself. The noise starts again, this time closer. It sounds like the shuffling of shoes against a canvas drop cloth. I step around the piece I'm working on and come face to chest with a tall dark-haired student. I let out a squeak of surprise as I crane my neck to see who just interrupted my paint session. I'm met with the sight of tattoos peeking up his black shirt collar and an eyebrow piercing which was currently raised in surprise. As my eyes lock onto his I feel my chest tighten.

"Sorry." He grunts out and adjusts his skintight jeans. My cheeks heat as he notices me following his movement down his body. This guy oozes sex and danger. He lifts a tattooed finger to my chin, closing my opened mouth, the contact sending a shiver down my spine. I look up into his green eyes, forcing myself to take a breath. He lets out a dark chuckle, perfectly aware of how he was affecting me, and wholly unsurprised like this kind of reaction was normal for him. I yank my head back and straighten my spine. His eyebrows shoot up as he regards me for a moment, both of us standing there without saying a word before he turns back in the direction he had come from. My stomach clenches in a riot of butterflies. That one small touch had ignited in me a clawing desperate desire for more.

Once he's gone from the room, I shake myself out of the stupor I found myself in. I had no idea what had just happened, and I was left wondering who the hell that was. He easily was the hottest guy I'd ever seen in my life, and made me feel as if my insides had turned to Jell-O.

I walk back around to my canvas more determined than ever to just finish this so I can get the heck out of here and back to my dorm. I can't afford to be distracted by a walking sex-god.

"You ran into Lukas Ledger?" My roommate, Salem screeches at me when I tell her of my bizarre run in at the art room. I almost trip over my white and teal roller skates that I'd forgotten to put away while walking over to our small closet. I snatch them up before anyone breaks an ankle and toss them in. My paint-stained hands start rummaging through my side of the closet we shared, and I grab out some clothes to change into.

"Who?" I ask distractedly as I pull on my pajama shorts. They're my favorites, white with tiny cherries printed all over them, hugging my bottom comfortably if not a tad tight.

Salem rolls her eyes and throws a pillow at me.

"How have you been here a week already and not know of Lukas Ledger from Hell House?" I just stare at her blankly. I have no idea what she's talking about.

She gives me an exasperated sigh. "The guys who live at the Tartarus Fraternity? It's literally the first thing I heard about when I got on campus. I went to their 'Welcome back to school' party my first night here. His twin brother is an asshole though."

"Why do they call it Hell House?" I crinkle up my nose. And dear God, that man has a TWIN? I can't imagine that much hotness walking around campus.

She gets a gleam in her eyes, "Because, legend says that when this place was first built, the settlers discovered that it served as a portal into purgatory. That all of these souls would find a way through the veil on a full moon, and they would possess the settlers, but a clan of witches were able to cast a spell trapping them behind the veil. But rumor has it that they missed some- and those missing souls were said to be the inhabitants of the Tartarus Mansion. One day the owner of the mansion murdered his whole family and servants before killing himself. Now the

Mansion is the site of our schools only fraternity and they're said to act out the sins those lost souls left behind." She wiggles her fingers to emphasize the spookiness.

"That sounds like the most elaborate way to excuse their bad behavior." I toss the pillow back at her.

"You have to admit, it makes for a pretty cool story though." She props herself up on her bed with the pillow and props her book back up that she'd been reading when I came back to the room and interrupted her.

I was lucky to be housed with Salem as my roommate. She gave all the witchy vibes but underneath her hard exterior, she was pretty chill, and we got along well. I'd never had many friends since my Dad and I moved around so much. When my mom died, my dad and I packed up our house, selling anything that was worth something, and we set off on the road in a mobile home my dad purchased off of one of his work buddies. We flitted from place to place, never staying for an extended amount of time. As long as they had working Wi-Fi, we were set. Dad worked remotely, and I took classes and worked on my art. We'd seen most of the US and Canada over the last few years of our nomadic existence, which made for an amazing Instagram feed, but also had left me lonely. This time away at college would be the first time in years that I would be putting down some real roots, and hopefully I'd be making some new friends during my time here.

We fall into an easy silence as Salem reads her book. I type in 'Hell House' into my search bar on my phone, my curiosity peaked.

As I scroll, I'm met with pictures of some of the hottest guys I've ever seen, until I find one of the man I'd run into tonight. His picture is just as breathtaking as he was when I saw him in person. I swallow hard remembering his intense stare and the heat his touch left on my skin. I find myself touching my chin where his finger had been then shake myself mentally. The last thing I needed right now was to become distracted by some bad boy wannabe. I'd promised the school when they'd issued my hard-earned scholarship that I would be worth the investment. That I'd make the most of the opportunity they were giving me. And those dangerous green eyes that belonged to Lukas Ledger with his tattoos and dark hair, looked like a one-way ticket to expulsion. No matter how much he'd make my skin tingle with desire. I switched off my phone, determined to ignore all things Lukas and the sinful boys of Hell House.

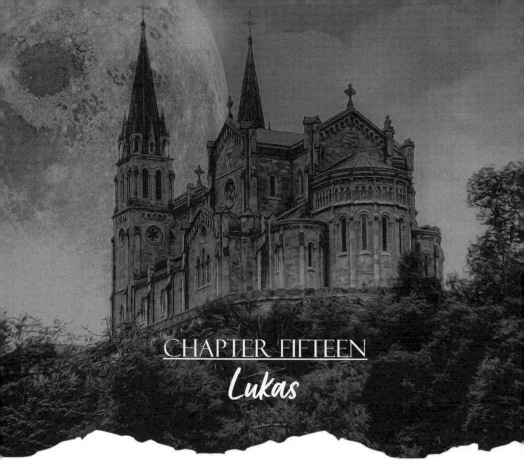

CHAPTER FIFTEEN
Lukas

I'd been looking forward to using the art room all day. My fraternity was throwing yet another party, and I wanted nothing to do with it. Hiding up in my room wasn't an option, and I had zero interest in going to town. The halls were devoid of any human life, knowing most of the student population were probably at the two places I was actively avoiding.

But, when I arrived at the art room, I'd found it occupied by a paint splattered menace with pigtails. I flex my hand trying to shove the feel of her skin off of my fingers. Touching her had sent a jolt of desire straight to my groin. Usually, Lust woke that part of me, but this? This happened all on its own for the first time in I couldn't even remember. Maybe before we'd all been possessed on Initiation Night.

I rub absently at my chest, scowling as I rush out of the building trying to make sense of what just happened. Were the demons losing its clutch on us finally? Or had I started gaining more control over it? I reign in the hope I feel bubbling up inside of me. I can't let my thoughts run away with me.

I wrestle with what to do, and decide I need to talk to Pierce. My twin usually knew what to make of things. I just hope I can catch him before he's too many beers down for the night.

■■■

The house practically glows against the setting sun, making the tall spires cast a long shadow against the grass. The tower sits in the center, jutting out like a middle finger to the heavens. I tuck the image away in my brain to sketch it later. The gravel path crackles beneath my long strides as I jog up to the house, passing several revelers who are already swaggering with some kind of substance. I can already hear the thumping bass that rattles the panes, scaring off any small creatures that might hang around this end of the woods.

"LUKASS!!" Pierce calls out as he hangs off of the porch, his arm wrapped around a beam as he balances precariously on the black painted rail, his outstretched hand clutching a red solo cup. Yeah, he was already wasted.

Pierce wobbles then jumps off the railing into the grass without spilling his beer.

"DUUUUDE! Did-ja seeee that? Not evena drop on me!" As he goes to put the beer to his lips, he misses, spilling the contents down his shirt, to which he just frowns patting it in confusion.

"My God, how much have you had?" I laugh shaking my head at him as I take his arm directing him back into the house.

He dismisses me still patting his drenched shirt like it will magically dry if he keeps pushing at it. Pierce is ridiculous when he's drunk. He can go from being the life of the party to having an all-out fight with whoever's "insulted" him in a matter of seconds. Hopefully he stays in more of the life of the party mode because I'm in no mood to break up any of his fights tonight. In fact, I was beginning to wish I hadn't come back to the house at all as several people start eye fucking me. They're not even subtle about it.

"Let's get you some water." I say, pulling him with me into the house, eager to get away from all the leering. The music is pulsing through my body as Pierce stumbles against me, his breath reeking of stale beer as he pulls on my shirt for balance. You'd think with how much money all of our families had combined, we'd at least be able to have quality beer shipped out here, but I guess that's what made it college. Crap beer and weekly parties while we stumbled blindly towards becoming adults.

"LuKAAASSS!" Graham says as we stagger through the door. He pops a cheese ball into his mouth as he sways his hips to the beat of the techno pulsing out of our speakers. A gaggle of girls circle him as he tosses one of his cheese balls at a girl wearing what looks like a disco ball for a dress. She catches the ball easily in her mouth, doing a little victory dance that causes the flashing lights to bounce straight off of her. Jesus, that dress was a fucking hazard. My eyes burned just from briefly watching them as we pushed our way through to the kitchen.

Pierce follows me without complaint, more occupied by his wet shirt than the surroundings of the party.

I prop him down on one of the stools. "Sit." I command, seeing him slouch over the table, his ass barely staying on the stool. I roll my eyes, grabbing a water from the fridge and plopping it in front of Pierce.

He makes a cheers gesture at me with a smirk before pounding it back like he's taking a shot.

The music pulses on, becoming louder. I can barely hear myself think.

"You good?" I ask Pierce, making sure he doesn't slip off the stool and crack his head open. He stands up suddenly and pulls me into a hug so tight that it squeezes my lungs. He holds me for a second slapping my back several times before pulling away. He points his finger at me.

"You're like a mirror, but like... I can hug you." I can't help but bust out laughing.

"Yeah, man. That's what happens when you have a twin." He's more wasted than I thought.

"DUDE! Let's go play poooool. You know. Likes we usssed to." He hiccups.

"Yeah, I don't think..." but he's already weaving through the crowd. "Shit."

I go after him, dodging arms that are raised up as they dance to the music. I barely miss being whacked by a rogue elbow that belongs to one of the frat brothers. He looks like he's attempting to do the chicken dance while a few girls giggle at his antics.

I see a flash of blonde pigtails and immediately feel my pulse speed up wondering if it belonged to the girl I'd run into earlier. Was she here? I scan the room feeling my heart in my ears, but I see nothing but sweaty bodies belonging to the same people who usually frequent our parties. I let out a note of frustration before heading into the billiard room where I find my brother standing on top of the pool table with a stick in his hand.

"DUUUUDE. You made it!"

Several eyes swivel in my direction, and I feel Lust begin to stretch out in my chest, taking note of the interest that surrounds me.

"Here!" Pierce tosses the stick down at me, and I catch it easily, wrapping my fingers one by one around the well-worn wood.

"Fine. One game."

Pierce jumps down, managing to land on his feet like a goddamn cat, and I can't help but shake my head at him letting a small laugh out at his crazy ass.

"You won't regret it." He says, snatching the pole from my hands with a smirk plastered on his face.

Guess I'm playing pool with my brother. I resolve to talk to him about my encounter later, the feeling leaving me unsettled, like that moment you go down the stairs and forget that there's one more step.

I push it down, focusing on Pierce attempting to gather all the pool balls at one time and failing miserably.

I shake my head again. This is going to be a long ass night.

CHAPTER SIXTEEN
Pierce

My head is pounding. I let out a groan as I crack an eye open and find myself sprawled across the billiard table in nothing but my briefs. My hands fly up to my face remembering our last party and the fucking open condom. I pat my skin, afraid of what I'll find, but thankfully all that seems to be there is a small spot where my cheek was pressed into the green felt of the table. I let out a sigh of relief, stretching out my body. My toe brushes against the 8 ball, plopping it into the corner pocket.

"Nice shot." Lukas's voice grumbles from the corner chair completely immersed in the dark.

"Jesus Christ!" I cover my pounding heart with my hand.

Lukas lets out a deep chuckle, leaning forward in the chair resting his tattooed arms over his knees bringing him partly into the light.

"Need some coffee?" He asks, knowing full well that I don't function without it. I let out an irritated grumble as my head continues to pound.

"How bad was I last night?"

"You were able to get one shot off before you decided the pool table was a great place to take a nap. I think your exact words were 'mmm looks just like grass' right before you swiped the balls with your forearm, quite gracefully might I add, then you snuggled up in the fetal position and passed out.

I let out a groan, pressing the palms of my hands into my eyes.

"What time is it?" I mumble. "And when did I lose my clothes?" I scan the area finding my clothes crumpled next to the pool table on the ground.

Lukas tracks my gaze, "Yeah, I wouldn't put those back on. They landed in someone's vomit."

I grimace.

"Think you can pull yourself together for a little hike over near Possession Cove?"

I eye my twin, realizing he must need to talk to me about something. "Get me some coffee, then we can talk."

He rolls his eyes standing up, "Fine, but you better go get some clothes on your ass because no one wants to see that."

I come downstairs after throwing on a black shirt and jeans. The kitchen smells like coffee, which has me hurrying my steps. I enter the kitchen seeing a few of the guys eating scrambled eggs that Graham has whipped up. He stands off to the side with a whisk and a bowl as he spins the egg yolks into submission.

"Wow, you look like shit Pierce." Emmet drawls from the stool he's perched on.

"Thanks man, you're looking like a peach yourself." He raises a bite of eggs slathered in hot sauce into his mouth while he winks at me.

"Ready?" Lukas asks.

"Coffee."

"Got you covered." He hands me a thermos, which I grab greedily.

"Where are you two headed?" Graham asks holding his whisk as he points at me and Lukas.

"Going for a walk."

"Without my eggs?" He asks, sounding offended.

"I couldn't eat anything right now. My stomach feels like I could throw up at any second."

"Oh, but you can tolerate that sludge you call coffee? No. Sit down, I'm making you a plate of eggs. You'll have a bite."

"Graham, you're acting like your mom again." Garrison says as he makes himself some tea.

Graham's mouth opens like he wants to argue, but then changes his mind. "Fine, you want to starve? Starve. Everyone else loves my eggs."

"I do love your eggs Graham Cracker. I just can't eat anything right now." I slap him on the shoulder as I move past. I see a flicker of hostility like he wants to shove that whisk up somewhere, but he just nods his head, going back to the eggs.

Lukas looks ready to burst into laughter at our exchange, but I don't want to piss off Graham any further. I didn't need him spitting in my lasagna later.

Lukas and I trudge up the hill that takes us over to Possession Cove. The morning air feels crisp against my skin, waking me up and making me feel invigorated. I take a sip of the thermos Lukas made for me, grateful for the hit of caffeine. The warm liquid snakes its way down, warming up my cold extremities.

"So, what's with this spontaneous hike Lukas?"

He looks around, continuing up the steep incline.

"Lukas?"

"I'll tell you when we get there."

I let out a grumble, too hungover to argue. But if he wasn't my brother there's no way I'd be trailing after his ass. For once it's not raining, the sky is clear, and the wind isn't biting at my face.

As we crest the top, I hear a low gong ringing out.

"What the fuck was that?"

The sound chimes again, and Lukas and I look at each other in confusion.

"Now BREATHE IN 2, 3, HOLD! GOOD! RELEASE." Comes a feminine voice through the trees.

As we break through the tree line, we're greeted by a bunch of spandex asses pointed to the sky. I smirk at my brother. "Is this what you wanted me to see? Because I am no longer complaining."

He lets out a laugh, "No, but it's a good surprise."

My eyes wander across the group, finding a certain raven-haired witch. She's wearing a matching lavender sports bra and legging set that hugs her every curve, leaving little to the imagination. Shit, seeing her bent over like that makes me want to come up from behind her and let her know just how much I like seeing her bent over like that.

I see my brother is similarly distracted, staring at the girl next to Salem, her hair thrown up in two messy pigtails. I recognize her as Salem's roommate.

"Either join us or stop your ogling." The instructor calls out. She looks likes she stepped out of an early 90's workout video with her neon leotard, complete with matching scrunchie.

I put my hands up, "No thanks." Which catches Salem's attention. She stands up, putting her hands on her hips. She looks like she could either stab me or kiss me and I'm here for it.

I tip my chin up at her as Lukas and I walk around the contorting yoga class continuing down the other side of the trail.

"Who was that?" Lukas asks.

"Just some girl from my business class."

"Mhmm."

"What?"

"You like her."

"Whatever, she's hot. I wouldn't mind getting a little piece of that."

He studies me for a second as we trek down the dirt path. One thing I loved about our time here at Kildale, was the time my brother and I were able to bond without our father's overbearing presence. Though, he frequently called to check in on us and make his usual 'stay in line' threats, it felt freeing- like I could finally breathe being out of that house. I don't know how our mother put up with his bullshit for so many years, well... until she didn't. I feel the familiar sting of grief when I found my thoughts have strayed to my mother.

As if he knows where my mind has wandered, I feel Lukas's hand clap onto my shoulder as we both navigate our way around a moss-covered boulder. Lukas was the one that found her all those years ago. I honestly don't know how he was as functional as he was.

The closer we get to the beach, the louder the waves and seagulls become. The rocks become more like gravel as we continue down the sloping hill. The air around us feels eerily still.

As we hit the clearing, I stop to catch my breath. Though it's not a hard hike, I'm still recovering from my bender and feel like someone has socked me in the stomach. Maybe I should have eaten those eggs.

"So, what did you drag me all the way out here for, then?" I ask Lukas who tosses me his water.

"I wanted to make sure we weren't overheard." I raise my eyebrow to that.

"What's going on?"

He takes a breath, glancing around. "I think... I'm starting to be able to control it."

"What do you mean?"

"I mean I was able to feel lust without that thing driving me to feel it."

I look at him for a moment and see the earnest expression in his face.

"Maybe it was just a one-time thing. Besides none of us are able to keep them at bay for long."

"It has to mean something though, right?"

"Yeah... that you found someone you want to stick your dick into."

"Shut up, you know what I mean."

"I do. I want you to be right. I mean I fucking hate being stuck together with this thing inside of me. Sometimes I don't even notice when I'm acting like me or when I'm letting Pride take the driver's seat. You have to trust me that we will find a way out of this though."

"Yeah, but how?"

"You let me worry about that. What are older brothers for?"

"You're only 14 minutes older, Pierce."

"Doesn't matter, I'll figure this out. I swear it. Even if it kills me." I smile trying to reassure him. If he only knew the lengths I was already going to. The dark shit I'd already done to free us all. It gutted me not to share this with my brother, but the further away I could keep him from this, the better.

"Don't joke like that."

"Enough of this horseshit. I'll race you to the water. Ready? Set? GO!"

I'm off before he has a chance to register that we're supposed to be racing. I make it to the water easily, not bothering to take off my shoes before jumping in. The water is freezing as it sloshes up my legs, saturating my skin with tiny pinpricks.

"You asshole." Lukas says, running up behind me. He splashes me, then tackles me into the water. I come up sputtering, wrestling him into the water. This is what I'm fighting for. More moments like this that are completely normal where these demons we're tethered to aren't controlling our lives- tethering us to this godsdamn island.

Lukas and I wrestle for a few more minutes, before coming out of the frigid water. My clothes are dripping and I'm instantly grateful there's no wind today. As we wring out our clothes, I contemplate telling him about the headmaster's plans. We've always shared everything, and it kills me not to open up about this to him. Had the Headmaster not expressly instructed me to keep it under wraps, I would have told him already. But then I think of the threats he levied against me and my fraternity brothers should I step out of line, and decide against it. No matter how much I want to share, it's not worth being stuck like this forever. I fucking hate feeling like a puppet on a string. I vowed to get us out this and I intend to do anything within my power to keep that promise.

Chapter Seventeen
Lukas

My nuts are fucking freezing up here, and the stool I'm sitting on has one half of my ass numb, but I can't move because good art models are still. Just as I take a steadying breath, the tip of my nose starts to itch. I feel the eyes of the room picking me apart as they sketch my naked form and the urge to scratch my nose intensifies.

Fuck.

I wiggle it as best I can without being obvious to Professor Whitelsbee, who's crotchety disposition would be more than happy to renege on our agreement. I feel like the girl from *Bewitched* trying to get this itch off of me. I try and distract myself, thinking of Pierce's and my discussion this last weekend. He didn't seem convinced that I might be able to start controlling my Lust, though I hadn't wanted to test out my theory. I had a nagging feeling that he was hiding something from me, which was unlike him even though he seemed to be in good spirits after our hike. I spent the rest of the weekend holed up in my room sketching the girl who'd captured my attention Friday night. Filling up page after page with her wide eyes and lush bottom lip, but never getting it quite right. It had been only a moment that we'd bumped into each other, but that moment was long enough to etch itself into my mind.

Imagine my surprise when I found out that she was to be sketching me today as I sit here in nothing but a thin white sheet- and sometimes not even that.

My eyes drift over to the clock that sits above her blonde and purple tipped messy pigtails. My thoughts snag on what I'd like to do with those pigtails, and I make the mistake of locking eyes with her. My heart catches in my throat and I feel my cock jump to attention. My cheeks flame and I quickly flit my eyes down to the ground. I don't need to be getting a hard on while I'm naked in front of the entire Freshman art class. Think of anything other than her mouth. Anything else- I tell myself. But my mind doesn't listen, instead replaying the image I'd conjured up of her down on her knees for me, my hands gripping her by the hair working her down my shaft, that's now playing on a loop over and over again making my Lust groan with need. I take a chance and shift on the stool trying to cover up my growing problem.

"Mr. Ledger!" Professor Whitelsbee snaps and I instantly stop moving. "Do you not understand what the words 'still as a statue' means?"

I don't respond, instead forcing myself back into the proper model position, this time locking my eyes with a fuzz on the floor. I bore my eyes into it, muscles cramping with each second that passes. Lust knocks against my chest, angry that it's being interrupted, and I feel a jolt work its way down my spine and into my cock. My mind assaulted with images of her and me together.

Shit, shit, shit. Maybe Pierce was right-my control is nothing more than a fool's hope.

I need to get out of here, before everyone in here gets more of an eyeful than they bargained for. I feel my control slipping at Lust pushes against me.

I clear my throat, "Professor, I need a break really quick." I murmur, loud enough for her to hear and several students to stop their sketching.

She glares at me, "Fine. Students, keep working on what you can without our model present." She flicks her neon orange hair wrap over her shoulder clicking her tongue as she dismisses me. I grab the white sheet and wrap it around myself, careful not to knock into my ever growing semi. Most of the students busy themselves with their art-thankfully they're too wrapped up in what they're doing than to pay attention to my clumsy retreat, except when I pass the object of my desire. Her eyes flit down to where my hand is holding the white cloth, and her cheeks hold two bright red spots. She licks her cherry red painted lips and my Lust roars to attention tenting my cock straight up behind the sheet. I want nothing more than to grab her by the neck and drag her with me to the bathroom and fuck her senseless to get rid of this obsession I've seemed to develop.

I need to take care of this problem- fast. I almost stumble over the fabric dragging on the floor of my makeshift toga, which garners a few snickers. I rush to the changing area near the back and scramble for my underwear, my cock painful with how engorged it is. Shit.

I shrug on my clothes, leaving my fly undone and sneak out to the hallway, covering my crotch by crossing my arms over the area as if I'm about to check someone in basketball.

I finally make it to the nearest bathroom, noting it's empty thankfully. I fling myself into a stall, whipping out my aching cock, wasting no time to wrap my hand around its length. Expertly working myself over every piercing while the images of that blonde beauty on her knees for me flicker in my mind. Those luscious red lips taking me all the way to the back of her throat. I was desperate for her in a way I hadn't ever felt before. Sure, I had my passing attractions, especially with Lust trying to drive some of the time. But this? This fucking need to be inside of her with a mere look?

Fuck me, I wanted to get inside of her.

A hot jolt of pleasure worms its way down my spine as my balls tighten and a thick stream of my cum pelts into the toilet. Shit, what was wrong with me? Needing to jerk off in the middle of class just from her looking at me. That was virgin behavior, and I was far from one.

I tuck myself into my pants and flush. I needed to get laid. Maybe that would tamper down this ridiculous crush and I'll be able to look at her without getting an embarrassing hard on. For fucks sake, I didn't even know her name.

I make sure to wash my hands before heading back to the art room to apologize to the Professor. I didn't want her snatching my time away, because she was just the sort of crotchety old bag that would- just because she could.

CHAPTER EIGHTEEN
Skye

My face feels like it's on fire. I totally just saw Lukas's hard cock poking through the white sheet, and he was huge. AND PIERCED. I feel my mind malfunction a bit at that piece of knowledge, especially since I started wondering what those piercing would feel like.

He'd covered most of it during the art session and curiosity pricked at me as I sketched each muscle of his, lower and lower until I was right at the cusp of where it was hidden. My fingers made steady strokes, filling in his intricate tattoos that spanned almost the entirety of his body- I couldn't help but think about what it would be like to lick my way down those tattoos.

Thankfully, by the time he'd abruptly gotten up after locking eyes with me, I was almost done with the sketch and was working on shading and filling in the rest of his tattoos. Although, I wanted to rework the rose that covered his hand, not getting the petals the way I wanted them.

It was a special kind of hell having to sit here sketching the hottest guy I'd ever seen, especially when he spent a lot of that time scowling at me. I'm not sure why, or how I pissed him off, but my God when that man smolders... he might as well be melting my panties off with the amount of heat he gives off with it.

I spent the entire class period trying to calm myself down and avoid his confusing panty melting gaze while trying to make my sketch as flawless as possible for Professor Whitelsbee. It seemed my status here as a scholarship student infuriated her, making her ten times more critical of me than the rest of my peers- at least that's the impression I got when she talked about me getting a 'free ride' to one of the best schools.

I clean up my supplies, avoiding the frowning face of the Professor, who's tapping her boney ringed finger on her cane. I wish I knew what I could do to get her approval.

I peel myself away from the classroom, wondering what I could do to earn her favor. I'm so lost in my head that I don't notice I'm about to careen straight into Lukas barreling right for me. Our bodies collide, before I get a chance to stop my momentum. His body is pressed against mine for a split second, before we bounce back. But that moment was enough for me to feel just how well he fit pushed against me. His muscles taunt against my chest making my nipples pucker. His face pulls into that beautiful smolder as he stares down at me. His towering form making me feel small next to him.

"Lukas." I say in surprise.

His eyes flash with heat for a moment as he looks down at me. "You know my name?"

I tuck a stray hair that's fallen out of my pigtails behind my ear. "Um, yeah the professor introduced you at the beginning of class." I wasn't about to admit that my roommate told me who he was and had been googling things about him since I ran into him the other night.

"Right." He says almost looking embarrassed.

"I'm Skye. Skye Dannon."

"We really have to stop bumping into each other like this Skye, Skye Dannon."

I feel myself let out a giggle, *shit.* This guy was too hot, I couldn't think straight. Was he flirting?

"So, art room stalker to art model?"

He lets out a little laugh, "Yeah, I have a standing arrangement with Whitelsbee."

"Any ideas on how to get on her good side?"

He rubs his tattooed hands together. "You really want to know?"

"Yes, I'm desperate. She absolutely hates me."

"She hates her own shadow. There's no getting out of that one, sorry to break the bad news."

I feel my shoulders droop.

"Don't let her get to you." He chucks his hand under my chin, and I'm immediately filled with a riot of butterflies again. Damn this man's magic touch.

"I wish I didn't care so much, but my scholarship depends on her approval."

"Yikes, that's quiet the pickle." He scratches at his chin. "I might be able to help. Maybe you could show me some of your work?"

My mind panics thinking of the last thing I was just working on... Lukas' naked chest and I feel my face heat.

"Um... yeah, sure." I pull out my sketchbook from my bag. He takes the book, flipping through my art, a scowl similar to the Professor's crosses his face as he scans the pages. My stomach clenches, wondering what he could be thinking.

"You've got a unique style, Skye." He clears his throat.

"But?"

He lets out a sigh, "Well knowing Whitelsbee as I do... I'm thinking she's far more traditional than you or I could ever be. I mean look here at this sketch you did." He flips to one of a man sitting on a park bench that I'd done over the summer when we were passing through Venice Beach. "These harsh lines bring out a darkness in an otherwise serene picture. It's like you're capturing something beneath the surface." I remembered that day, why I'd chosen that man over the countless others. There was something broken about him that called to me, that made my hands itch with the need to sketch him.

"And this one?" He flips to the next page when I'd done a portrait of a little girl and her dad. She had fat tears staining her cheeks after skinning her knee, but it was the dad's face that looked almost angry that made me sit there and draw what I'd seen. I remember hoping that the little girl was alright as they walked away. "This is captivating, but not necessarily Whitelsbee style. She loves flowers and bright colors if you haven't noticed from her wardrobe."

"I'm not really that kind of girl."

"I can see that."

We stand there for a moment looking at each other. The way he looks at me and my work makes me feel almost naked. I feel seen in a way that no one else has ever come close. When they see me, they see my blonde hair and big boobs, my long legs and bright smile- but they never look closer. Most never bother to see past my exterior. I've done my fair share of playing to those expectations, being the good girl I knew everyone wanted me to be. But something about the way Lukas looks at me, makes me want to shed that exterior and embrace the darkness I'm so obviously drawn to.

"I better head to my next class." I say taking my sketch book back. I catch a hint of disappointment from Lukas, or maybe I'm just seeing what I want to see. As I put my book back into my bag, my hair comes loose from behind my ear. I stand straight up to see Lukas has taken a step closer. He reaches his tattooed hand up around my stray hair, tucking it behind my ear as he searches my face. My heart feels like it gets lodged in my throat. I swallow thickly, my body erupting in nerves at that small touch. He steps away opening and closing his hand that just touched me. His face contorts for a moment becoming serious like he's seconds away from devouring me. I feel a wave of lust shoot through me. I gasp, which makes Lukas's green eyes dilate. His eyes look almost pitch black from how large his pupil has become.

"I- I'll see you around." I manage to say, forcing my feet to carry me away to my next class.

Really Skye? Gasping from how turned on you felt in front of him? Ugh. I feel the embarrassment clinging to me as I sink into my Chemistry seat. Why was I even entertaining ideas of Lukas Ledger? I didn't have time to be distracted by his royal hotness. That guy was a walking red flag, but then I think about how easily we were able to talk. I mean I could always be his friend? I mulled the idea around, wondering if I could be friends with someone like Lukas. He'd really seen me, and that alone makes me wonder if I'd been too quick to judge him. Seeing his exterior like people saw mine. I bit down on my lower lip as I got lost in my thoughts. Friends with Lukas Ledger? Crazier things had happened.

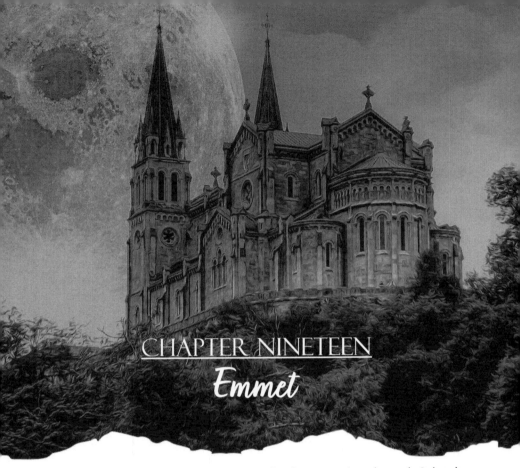

CHAPTER NINETEEN
Emmet

It'd been one week. One week of me pouring through Salem's phone, learning everything I could. It was surprising how much of ourselves we left on our phones. Her mother still hadn't fixed her credit card issues, she played it off to her friends like she'd rather stay on campus, but I knew the truth. She couldn't afford to buy even one book, which after getting to know her through her digital trail, I knew must have bothered her. The girl loved to read.

I'd memorized her school schedule. She usually spent time with Skye and Javelynn, and though she was friendly with people in her classes, she didn't establish anything deeper.

I'd contemplated texting her but needed to wait until our plan was in motion. The headmaster wanted full control of her, and it was proving difficult to keep eyes on her while she lived off in the dorm. I could feel our demons becoming stronger the closer we drew to Samhain, when the veil would be the thinnest. I knew that the headmaster had demanded that Pierce take point and had instructed him not to tell anyone other than me. Little did Pierce know the Headmaster and I had our own deal should he fail.

"It needs to be tonight." Headmaster Hayden instructed us in his office.

"But I thought we were making good progress- I mean we got information off of her phone and know where she's at most days."

"That's not good enough." The headmaster's voice boomed, echoing off his high ceilings.

"We need her, Pierce. This is not up for debate. You know what will happen if you don't follow through. Do it tonight. End of discussion."

"But-"

"Do I need to remind you of what I am capable of?" His eyes flash as he lifts his hand. A choking sound fills the room. Pierce claws at his neck as a thick black liquid escapes his mouth, staining his shirt as it slides down his face and neck. He tries to breathe but instead a gurgling sound from the ink wretches out of his mouth. The headmaster has cut off Pierces oxygen completely as I stood idly by examining my cuticles, bored of the theatrics. I really needed to go into town and have Regina take care of my nails, they were becoming unseemly.

Pierce comes crashing to his knees as he continues clawing at his neck. I let out an exasperated sigh, "I think he understands your point headmaster."

The headmaster glares at me a moment before releasing Pierce from his hold. Pierce vomits out the black liquid, tears tracking down his red face, his lips stained black.

"Clean yourself up. I trust that you'll follow through with the plan tonight?"

Pierce hangs his head, nodding with a shudder that wracks through his body.

Salem would regret the day she arrived on this island. We'd make sure of it.

CHAPTER TWENTY
Salem

I wake with a startled scream lodged in my throat. It felt like someone had been shaking me awake. My heart is hammering so loud that I can hear it in my ears. I'd been having my recurring nightmare, one that I'd had since I was a little girl. Every time I thought I'd outgrow it, it would rear its ugly head, leaving me in a pile of sweat and anxiety. My lungs burn as I take in a breath to steady myself. I sluggishly try to piece together why I smell smoke. Why I suddenly find myself coughing. I wonder briefly if I'm still stuck in my nightmare, my heart thrashes wildly as I continue coughing.

"Wake up Salem." A distant voice calls to me.

My eyes are still bleary with sleep, I try to wrench them open but my lashes cling together. I knew falling asleep without taking my makeup off was a mistake. I rub at my face, my chest burning as my diaphragm convulses against my lungs forcing the deep smoke-filled coughs from my throat. I manage to pry my eyes open and kick my too hot blanket off when I hear the shrill screams of my roommate, Skye. As I look over a blinding light sears my vision, I could have sworn I saw a woman floating right above me. She looked eerily like a young version of my grandmother.

"Oh my God our room is on fire! Salem. Salem!" Skye screams as she scrambles over to me holding her shirt against her nose and mouth. My eyes finally adjust to see the blaze creeping up our wall and onto our ceiling.

"What the f-- " She grabs me by my arm, and I'm sprawled out of bed, my bare knees slamming into the floor. I barely remember to grab my phone before fleeing our flame engulfed room.

The moment we land in the hallway we scramble to search for the fire alarm, my fingers are flying across my phone screen dialing 911. While I wait for my phone to connect, I bang on the doors that we pass. "There's a fire!" I scream, my fist slamming into the next door. It dawns on me that I don't have any pants or shoes on, but I'm beyond caring. We need to get out and get out now.

The hallway begins to fill with confused students as smoke billows out from our room. A blaring siren rings and strobe lights fill my vision before the hallway becomes utter chaos. Students slamming their bodies into each other as they push their way out of the quickly filling area.

"Oh my god! I'm too young to die!" One of the students cries as they shove other people out of their way.

The sprinklers are triggered, sputtering thick cold globs of wetness down on us. My phone beeps still struggling to connect to emergency services. My body is quickly soaked from above and I register my white tank as I'm shuffled along, my fists pounding on any closed doors that I pass before I'm being swept away by the surging crowd. We don't have a large school, but the dorms are packed full of most of the student population, the exception being the fraternity and sorority houses.

"Move! Move!" An authoritative woman's voice cuts through the chaos as we part, making way for one of the professors. A woman in her mid-fifties comes through with rollers clinging to her gray flecked brunette hair. "Everyone out!" She takes in the sight of the flames cresting up the ceiling, when a few guys wearing nothing, but their briefs come barreling through holding buckets sloshing with water. I find Skye and put my hand in hers as we scramble to make our way out of the burning dormitory. The night air envelops us, the wind carrying a chill from the ocean. My body shivers with goosebumps as my wet shirt clings to my body offering no warmth. I feel a pair of strong hands being placed on my shoulders, making me jump with surprise. Pierce stands behind me with his hands up. "You look frozen." If I didn't know any better, I'd say I caught a glimmer of concern in those deep green eyes, before it's shoved down, replaced by an impassive glare. At least those eyes of his didn't dip down to my overexposed chest. I cross my arms remembering my transparent white shirt, my hand still clutching my phone which beeps incessantly with a busy signal.

Pierce rolls his eyes and shrugs out of his hoodie, leaving him in a black tank. I glare at his outstretched hand with the balled-up hoodie.

"For gods sakes take it, Salem." I stand there debating for another moment, but when my teeth start chattering, I snatch it from him and shove my frozen limbs through. God dammit this shit smelled like Pierce's arrogant ass. All woodsy and warm. I scowl and mumble a thank you, though every instinct inside of me roars to stomp away from him.

He takes a step towards me, "What was that witch? I didn't hear you." If my arms weren't so frozen, I'd throat punch him. Fuck this guy. I was shivering out here in my underwear after my dorm room had gone up in flames and he had the audacity to try me.

"I said fuck off."

"No, you didn't."

"Fine. I said thank you." His eyes dip to my exposed legs.

"We should get you some pants." I'm fully shivering now, too cold to argue so I just nod my head.

"Shit, Salem, your lips are turning blue." His thumb comes up to my bottom lip and I almost bite him from how hard I'm shivering. I can't even feel my feet anymore. I feel my knees buckle, before Pierce grabs onto me by the hoodie I'd just put on.

"Woah. Okay, Salem? Salem, I'm going to lift you up now, okay?" I nod, feeling his arms wrap around me as he sweeps me up into his chest. I'm immediately grateful that Pierce is a such a meat head with his workouts as he lifts me easily.

"I'm getting you out of here."

"Skye."

He nods, looking for Skye amongst the crowd. "I don't see her. We can just shoot her a text letting her know where you went."

He shuffles my weight in his arms before heading to Paladin Hall, the closest building to where we are. He tries the first door only to find it's locked. "Shit. Okay, wait there's- there's another set of doors here."

I bounce against his rock-hard chest, letting my head rest on his large shoulders. The wind whips against us as he carries me over to the second set of doors which thankfully are unlocked.

Once inside, he sets me down, wrapping his massive hands around my frozen feet. He starts rubbing the length of my legs getting blood flow back into them.

"My god, it's like touching an icicle." He murmurs, working his hands up and down my legs.

"How do you feel about using my socks?" I scrunch up my nose, but don't have much room to protest.

"I promise they don't smell." He sits next to me, ripping his shoes off, his socks coming right after.

"Here, put these on your feet." He shoves his sock-less feet back into his shoes while I shrug on his warm socks.

After I have the socks on, I text Skye, telling her where I am. A read receipt quickly follows.

Skye: I'll be right there.

"Skye's on her way." Pierce nods, gathering me into his arms. I tell myself it's only for the warmth. I'm not a big hugger but after that experience, I'm glad to have someone holding me.

"The flames were just everywhere." I feel Pierce go ridged around me before he rubs his hand up and down my arm.

"I'm glad you got out okay."

"It was weird, like I had a guardian angel or something, waking me up in time." I shake my head, remembering the face of the woman yelling my name before Skye and I fled the room.

"Do you believe in angels Pierce?"

"I think anything's possible." We fall into a comfortable silence, taking each other's body heat as we wait for Skye to show up. I never in a million years would have thought Pierce Ledger would help me like he was.

"Thank you." I say, feeling Pierce's hand still against me.

"Yeah, well... couldn't have you turning into an icicle. Then who would I annoy."

"Ah, there he is. Douchebag Ledger, in all his glory."

"Need I remind you that I just saved you from hypothermia?"

"Mmm, but it sounds like it was for purely selfish reasons."

"I never claimed to have pure intentions Salem."

He glances down at my lips, and I feel myself move into him. His eyes go wide, licking his lips as he moves in towards me. We're a breath away from each other when Skye comes barreling in through the door.

"Oh my god, Salem. Are you okay? I'm freezing and was wearing more clothes than you." She stops taking in Pierce and I on the floor.

"Oh good, you were able to warm up." Her blue eyes twinkle with laughter. She knows just how much I loathe Pierce Ledger. She just saved me from making a huge mistake. What was I thinking about to kiss Pierce? God, I must have been delusional from losing my body heat.

"I'll see you later, Salem." Pierce says letting go of my arm as he brings himself up to standing.

"Wait. You're leaving?" He looks down at me, wrapped up in his hoodie. He swallows, his Adam's apple bobbing with the motion.

"I need to go find my brother."

"Lukas?" Skye asks. "I saw him over by the dorm building with Emmet."

He nods, then leaves- the doors wafting in a blast of cool air as he walks through them.

"Asshole."

Skye examines me for a moment. "Are you good?"

I let out a breath. "I mean we're alive, thankfully. But shit our stuff." She looks at me her eyes filling with tears.

"Yeah. I had a bunch of pictures of me and my mom." A few tears spill over.

"I wonder what started it?"

"You know these old buildings. Probably faulty wiring."

"We should probably find some clothing." Skye grabs my hand, pulling me up. My legs feel like tiny needles are stabbing my skin as we walk down the hall towards the main hall.

"We're okay." Skye says, more to herself than to me, but I nod.

"We're okay."

CHAPTER TWENTY-ONE
Skye

Salem and I sit buried under a mountain of blankets while we wait outside Dean Camden's office. My fingers wrap around a styrofoam cup of hot chocolate that I find myself mindlessly sipping. I had such little possessions as it was, and I wondered if I'd just lost everything I had in the fire. My heart stutters thinking of my photo album carrying some of the only pictures I had of my mother. I feel my eyes begin to water with exhaustion and a tiny bit grief for my things that I was certain were ruined. I should have left the album with dad, but stupidly I'd thought it would be safe with me. We'd been up all night since fleeing our room. The fire happened around 2 am. Prime rem sleeping time. We're lucky to have woken up when we did.

A familiar woman's voice cuts through my wandering thoughts.

"Salem, Skye. Would you mind coming into my office?" She asks, and I recognize her as the woman who was running down our hallway with rollers in her hair, although they were missing now. Her jaw is tightly clenched, and she has deep purple bruises under her eyes that scream of a lack of sleep. She ushers us both into her office which is cozily decorated and thankfully she has a space heater pumping warmth throughout the small space.

"Take a seat please." She gestures to two tattered thread bare upholstered chairs that have a dark floral pattern. Upon closer inspection what I'd assumed were vines, were actually snakes. Creepy.

"Thankfully, those quick-thinking boys with the buckets of water were able to contain the fire to your room, but unfortunately that leaves your room completely uninhabitable. According to the fire department, you'll be allowed to go and see if there's anything salvageable, but in the meantime I'm afraid we don't have any extra dorm rooms."

"So where will we stay?" Salem asks, pulling the blankets around her tighter.

Dean Camden shifts in her seat and clears her throat. "It seems the only place on campus with rooms to spare is the fraternity house. Now, normally you'd need to be a pledge to live there, but these are extenuating circumstances. The boys have already been made aware of your situation and were most agreeable to accommodate you both."

Salem and I lock eyes, silently communicating our worry. We were supposed to move into Hell House. My stomach clenches with anxiety thinking of all the rumors surrounding that place and now we were supposed to live there? Fuck my life.

My thought snag on having to coexist in the same space as Lukas Ledger. Our few interactions had proven that I was an utter disaster anywhere near his proximity, but now we had to live in the same house? I fanned my face, suddenly feeling overheated. Salem shared my same panicked expression. I'm sure that close embrace I found her and Pierce in earlier was eating at her.

Salem HATED Pierce, but the way they looked at each other? I felt like they were about to tear each other's clothes off and go at it on the floor. I set down my hot chocolate and rub at my temples, feeling the bloom of a headache starting to manifest. This is not how I imagined this day would go. I had plans to work on my piece for Professor Whitelsbee, maybe do some sketching to practice, then study for my Chemistry test in between attending my regularly scheduled classes. Life had a way of laughing at your plans before sprinkling some chaos around like a maniacal evil genius. I'm pretty sure it had the matching villain mustache to twirl as it fucked up people's well laid plans.

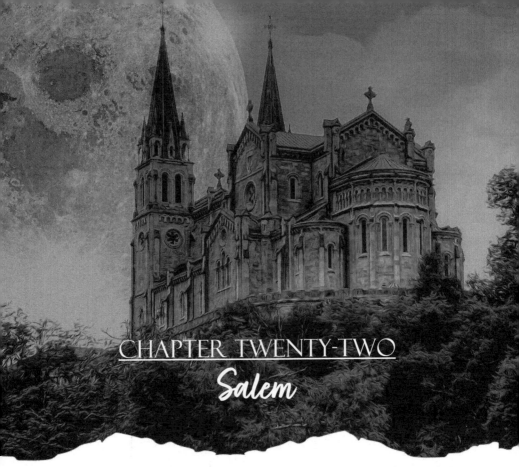

CHAPTER TWENTY-TWO
Salem

Skye and I pick over our charred belongings. My side of the room was worse, I'd found only a few clothing items that made it unscathed due to the fact that they were squished with Skye's. My bed was turned to ash which made my stomach roil. I had just been sleeping there. What would have happened if I didn't wake up in time?

"Did you find anything?" I ask clutching my few belongings and the burned entrails of my special edition of *The Hobbit*. I couldn't bring myself to let it go just yet, even though it was falling apart in my hands.

"My album thankfully escaped. It's a little burned on the outside and there's some water damage but I think I can salvage the pictures." She says in a small voice sniffling, "And my roller skates seem to be okay, I'd stashed them under my bed." We'd borrowed some clothes from

Javelynn but both Skye and I were having a hard time fitting into them. I drop down to my knees, looking under my ruined bed and find the pink vibrator I'd stashed there. It was burnt rubber now.

A knock on the doorframe jolts me out of my reverie. Pierce's large frame eats up all the light pouring in from the hallway like my very own unwelcome black hole.

"What do you want Ledger?" I say clutching my charred book to my chest and hiding the vibrator behind my back. I remembered how he left abruptly after almost kissing me last night. Out of all the people to deal with at the moment, he sits firmly at the bottom of the list. Which is saying something. My mother used to hold that rank. He stands awkwardly for a moment taking in the damage before clearing his throat and fixing his face up into a smirk. That goddamn smirk.

"Headmaster sent me to help you both settle into your new digs. I'm supposed to carry anything you need help with." He looks down at my arms. "What's that behind your back?"

"Nothing." I say clutching the vibrator harder, but as I do, my thumb presses the on button and it begins to vibrate in my hand.

Pierce's eyes go wide with amusement. "Nothing?"

I nod my head yes, even though we both know I'm lying.

"That nothing wouldn't happen to be a toy shaped like an eggplant, would it?"

"A burnt eggplant maybe." Skye says, and I shoot her a look, which only makes her chuckle.

"So, you don't need help with... anything there?"

"Thanks, but I think I got it." I bite out in no mood for his barbs. I stand up, removing the still vibrating burnt toy from behind my back and click it off. Thankfully, Pierce doesn't say anything, but his face gives away how amusing he finds this.

Skye hands him a suitcase that he takes without complaint, and we all trudge down the 12 flights of steps. At least we won't have to make that trek every day, even if I loved what it was doing to my backside.

By the time we make it across campus, my clothes are damp with a mix of perspiration and rain. Hell House jumps out from behind the densely packed foliage just as dark and foreboding as I remember. The house is eerily empty, but then I remember that most everyone is in class. We'd been excused due to our special circumstances.

We take the front stairs. As we ascend, I notice that each rail is intricately carved with a cherub figurine. Creepy. It felt like they were staring at me as we ascend to the second level. Pierce stops at a room that doubles ours. My mouth drops open a fraction at how ornate and detailed the room is. It houses two twin beds, but half of the room seems to be decorated already with several band posters tacked up around the walls and an art desk strewn with sketches.

"This one looks occupied." Skye says dropping her things down. Her space-buns are a tangled mess, and she has purple smudges under her usually bright sky-blue eyes.

Pierce drops her bag and leans up against the doorframe, his damp blonde hair sweeping against his forehead. "This is Lukas's room."

I see Skye's eyes widen and I have a feeling that mine look similar right now.

"It's this or the servant's room. It's small but those are the only options, unless you want to take the communal couch." I scrunch up my nose thinking of all the grinding I'd seen going on the night of their back-to-school party.

"We'll take the servant's room." Skye says, going to pick up her items.

Pierce rubs his chin. "Well see, the problem with that is the servant's room only has space for one twin bed."

I catch Skye's panicked eyes. "It's fine, I'll take this one."

Pierce seems to glare at me for a split second, before I catch Skye shaking her head. "No, no it's fine. You deserve to have a space to yourself. You lost more things than I did."

"Are you sure, Skye? We can see if there's somewhere else for us to stay. Maybe somewhere off campus."

Pierce lets out a chuckle. "Good luck with that. This is a small island witch, unless you can conjure up a house with some sticks and whatever voodoo magic you hold in that black heart of yours, you're stuck here."

I fix him with what I hope is a withering stare, but with how tired I am it could probably pass for mild annoyance. "Fine." I say too tired to argue. "Show me to my room."

He gestures opening his arms wide and I leave Skye to settle into her new digs. I wonder if Lukas is any better than his asshole twin.

We pass through a dank corridor that rivals the west wing in the Beast's castle. I take in several cobwebs, a musty smell hangs in the air. I follow close behind and up around a spiral staircase that leads to a room at the top. By the time we crest the last step, I'm ready to pass out. Taking in my new room, I feel like I'm Rapunzel tucked up away in her tower. There's one tiny window that looks over the back of the house. I can faintly make out the ocean in the distance.

"This is it. The guys come in and out all day, but at least up here, they shouldn't bother you too much. Graham usually makes us dinner around 7, if you're brave enough to join us for it. It's some of the best food and there's never leftovers." He's being far too nice for my liking, making me feel on edge, like he's up to something. I let go of my mere possessions and my knees crumple beneath me as I reach the bed.

"Get some rest witch." He says gripping the door on his way out.

"You're not going to lock me in here, are you?" I mumble to Pierce, sleep already clawing at me as I lay down, not even bothering to take off my borrowed clothes.

"I make no promises." Pierce says his face is full of mischief as he closes the door behind him. I let out a groan of frustration. I guess I lived here now.

CHAPTER TWENTY-THREE
Lukas

"You're fucking kidding me?"

"What? Yours was the only room with an extra bed." Pierce says shoving a burger in his mouth with a messy chomp, making crumbles of food dribble down his chin.

"You're telling me I have to share a room with Skye Dannon? There's no where else for her to go?" Fuck my life. How was I supposed to share a room with her? I couldn't even be in the same room without getting hard or having my mind imagine the filthiest scenarios- all of which involved having her naked in one way or another.

Normally I'd be jumping at the chance to make my desires come to fruition, but something about this insane attraction I felt towards her scared me.

"What are you worried about? Her finding your stash of porn you keep under the bed?"

I clip him on the back of the head.

"Ow. Motherfucker. What was that for?"

I bite into my own burger. "I haven't had to hide porn since we were kids, moron. It's all on the internet now."

He chuckles, an evil glint in his eyes makes me wonder if he knows I've been obsessively drawing her. There's no way she hasn't found those already since Pierce let her into my fucking room. I feel panic clawing at me. How do I play this off like I'm not some crazy stalker?

"You like her."

"What? No." I shove down the pull of Lust that's trying to fight its way up at the hint of my straying thoughts. Just one mention of her name seems to have it rearing to go. Not that I blame it. I don't even seem to need it's influence when it comes to my attraction to her.

"Ohhh. Protesting too much brother?"

"Brother, why would I saddle myself with liking just one person. You know I could get anyone I wanted."

That's what I need to do. Focus on getting with someone else and hope she had some ridiculous flaw that would make her immediately undesirable. That kind of shit had to show up while being forced to share a room with her.

"So, you don't mind if I ask her out then?" Garrison says having listened to our whole conversation, quietly eating.

I regard him for a moment before grinning like I don't give a shit-a look I've perfected growing up the way Pierce and I did. "Why would I mind?" I ignore the squeeze of jealousy that instantly settles in my stomach.

"I don't mind at all." I'll make that my truth even it I don't feel it right now. Skye Dannon won't control me like this. I've had enough of people and things trying to control me and some hot girl that managed to snare my attention momentarily won't be one of them.

CHAPTER TWENTY-FOUR
Skye

Okay. I'm not going to panic. I'm going to be a mature adult about rooming with arguably the hottest guy I've ever seen. Oh god, what if he masturbates while I'm in here? What if he has a girl in here at some point? How am I supposed to get dressed? My thoughts spiral, each one more anxious than the next. I feel a stab of regret at not choosing the servant's room, but it wouldn't be fair to Salem. She'd lost almost everything in that fire, whereas my things remained mostly unscathed. I'm exhausted, but I feel a nervous energy coursing beneath my skin that won't let me rest just yet. I take in my new accommodations, putting my things where I want them. I clutch my photo album of my mom to my chest, inhaling the scent of smoke and thumb through the pictures. I wish I could reach through the photo and curl up on her lap, telling her everything that she's missed. I heave out a sigh and place it under my new bed. I'm so exhausted that I feel sleep clawing at me. I go to turn off the light, and my vision snags on Lukas's desk. I glance around wondering when he'll get here and decide to take a peek while the room is still vacated. I tentatively pick up a crumbled paper that sits on the corner of his desk, unfolding the edges of the paper, when my breath catches in my throat making me let out a strangled gasp. I take in the picture in front of me, the dark sweeping lines that make up the art and my hand shakes, my heart hammering as I stare in disbelief.

It's me.

I'm looking at a detailed up-close portrait of myself. He's captured even the most minute parts of myself down to the small bump on my nose. In the picture, I'm mid laugh, eyes dancing with joy, tiny freckles dotting the sides of my nose. My hair is swept up into two messy space buns, and I have one earbud hanging down onto my shoulder. I'm lost in examining the picture that I almost don't hear an exaggerated cough from behind me. I quickly drop the paper and turn around, a fierce blush creeping up my neck at being caught.

"Already making yourself at home I see." Lukas says in almost a drawl that sends my already hammering pulse skyrocketing. Jesus, did he get better looking every time I laid my eyes on him? I feel my legs clench together and I silently chide myself. He's going to be my roommate.

"Sorry." I manage to say, slinking back over to my side of the room. I sit tentatively on the edge of the bed, aware that Javelynn's skirt they'd leant me was a smidge too small and showed off a ridiculous amount of my legs. Lukas doesn't seem to notice though and strides over to the piece of paper that I'd dropped. My stomach knots up when I see him give the paper that same scowl he'd had when I showed him my artwork the other day.

He crumples the paper up without a word, kicking off his shoes and laying down on top of his covers. I feel awkward wondering if we're going to talk about roommate rules and expectations. My leg starts bouncing of its own volition while I churn over my thoughts. My mind fills with all different scenarios until I'm practically sending myself into a panic attack.

"Spit it out already, I can practically hear your anxiety from here." He says, his arm slung across his eyes blocking out the light.

"Well... I ... what..." I bite my bottom lip then steady myself before I ask, "What are you expecting?" He dips his arm down, arching his eyebrow piercing in a question.

"With this roommate situation." I clarify. "I've never shared a room before Salem, and well especially never shared one with a guy. I'm not sure what the rules are. Are you going to change in here? Have girls in here?" I swallow nervously.

His mouth quirks up, "Well it's my room Tails, so I'll be changing in here. And I tend to bring all kinds of people up."

"Oh." I say before my mind snags on that word he just called me. "Tails?" I ask confused.

He gestures at my hair, "Pigtails."

"Oh. My space buns?" I touch my hair self-consciously.

"Whatever. I'll leave a sock or something on the door handle. Feel free to do the same." I feel my eyebrows shoot up. I had absolutely no intention of using that, but good to know where Lukas stood. It didn't escape my attention that he'd said he brought all kinds of people up here. A image of him with another guy flashes in my mind and fuck me why did he have to be so hot. I shove the thought out no matter how tempting it was and gather my clothes from my bag.

"Is there a bathroom I could use?"

He crooks a finger up to the right, "Four doors down on the left."

I scurry out to follow his directions and try to calm myself down. When I enter the bathroom, my stomach plummets. Oh god. We were sharing a bathroom too? Oh God, oh God. I feel like I'd just stepped into the set of *New Girl*, only larger and with more urinals. Thankfully I clock two stalls and several showers that I'm glad have a modicum of privacy to them. I was half tempted to turn around and ask Lukas if there was another bathroom I could use. Pierce hadn't given us much of a tour, only dropping us at our rooms before he disappeared. I'm sure Salem's fast asleep by now. She looked dead on her feet, and I wasn't far behind truth be told. I decide to woman up and head into an empty stall, peeling off my borrowed clothes and putting on my cherry pajamas. Dean Camden had taken pity on us and helped me clean what clothes I could salvage from my room over in the campus laundromat. Thankfully they didn't reek of smoke anymore. I was grateful for something familiar and comforting. Being apart from my dad for the first time was hard enough, but throw in a roommate, then a fire, and a new hot distracting roommate? I knew dad would freak out about the fire and the roommate switch, but I just wasn't in the headspace to deal with that right now. I resolve to call him tomorrow. I'm sure he's going to be more than thrilled about my change in living situation. I wince inwardly wondering if I should keep that part out. I didn't need him causing a fuss and have him jeopardize my scholarship. I was determined to keep my spot here whatever it took. Even it took rooming with the world's hottest, most distracting man alive.

When I come back from the bathroom, I collapse on top of the bed while Lukas sketches at his desk. Not even bothering to get beneath the covers, I lay there listening to the sounds of Lukas's charcoal pencil scratching across the parchment. It quickly soothes me into a dreamless sleep.

When I wake, I hear muffled laughs coming from downstairs. The room is dim, the sun just starting to set off in the distance. I blink my eyes, clearing them of the sleep that still clings to my lashes. My stomach rumbles and I realize I haven't eaten much of anything all day. I tumble out of bed, change my outfit, and re-tie my hair into neat pigtails, opting to leave them swinging instead of thrown up into a bun.

I make my way downstairs and pick up on the conversation going on. I slow my steps, intent on listening to these guys I now lived with.

"They won't want your man meat Graham Cracker."

"Let him enjoy his shark coochie."

"It's charcuterie! Everyone likes charcuterie." A deep voice with a hint of Italian accent answers.

"We won't judge you for wanting your man meat on a little cooch, Graham."

"Who doesn't like Italian Sausage, huh?" A riot of laughter erupts at this.

"I bet you want them to eat your Italian Sausage Graham."

"They could be vegetarian." A grumbly voice chimes in.

"Well then, they can eat the cheese and grapes!" The one who must be Graham answers.

"Or vegan."

"Then just the grapes." Graham says slamming something down that sounds like he just threw a salami on the counter.

I see Salem walk up next to me looking slightly more rested, if still a little disheveled. I give her a signal to be quiet and come over by me. She joins me in my corner, listening.

"Not another shark coochie." A new voice grumbles.

"IT'S PRONOUNCED CHARCUTERIE! CHAR-CU-TERIE!" Salem and I look at each other stifling our laughs.

"Should we put them out of their misery?" Salem whispers.

A large hand comes around my shoulder, making me jump as I let out a shriek.

"It's rude to eavesdrop." Lukas's twin brother whispers, his arms slung around mine and Salem's bunched up shoulders. The scent of soap and something woodsy envelops us.

"Ugh, hands off Pierce." Salem says, shrugging out of his grasp. He lets us both go, putting his hands in his pockets and smirking down at Salem. She stands with her arms crossed over her chest and pops a gum bubble looking at him with disdain. The two of them looking at each other have enough heat to start a wildfire. Pierce looks like he's seconds away from devouring her, and as much as Salem tries to seem annoyed by him, there's a spark of desire dancing across her eyes.

My eyes bounce between the two of them.

"Liking your new home?" Pierce says, not taking his gaze off of Salem.

"Oh yeah, I've always wanted to live in a super creepy frozen tower."

"I'd call you Rapunzel, but maybe Mother Gothel is more appropriate."

"I'm going to-" I start but get interrupted by Salem stepping closer to Pierce.

"And what would that make you? The bad guy with the goiter and six toes?"

He feigns being hurt by holding his heart. "Obviously I'm the good looking one on all the Wanted signs." He flashes his smirk, and even I have to admit it's effective. It's weird that it doesn't have the same effect as when Lukas looks at me though. While they're twins, the vibes each of them gives off are vastly different.

Salem swallows hard, scowling at him before snatching my wrist. "Let's go get some food Skye."

"Gladly."

CHAPTER TWENTY-FIVE
Lukas

I'm lying in my bed, with Skye just a few feet away wrapped up in her blankets. Every noise she makes is torture. I had to find a different spot to eat at dinner, so I didn't stare at her like some creep as she licked the homemade ice cream Graham had made for our new guests. Double chocolate flavored with whipped cream on top. I don't know where the dude found cherries, he was a freaking food genius, and was able to obtain whatever food he desired on our remote island. I guess with his family's restaurant connections it wasn't too surprising.

I try and still my thoughts, letting darkness sweep me into sleep, but I'm unsuccessful. Instead, I find myself tuning into the low moaning sound Skye keeps making. Fuck it's so hot.

I wrack my hands down my face. Having her within reach and not be able to do anything about it is killing me.

I don't know what it is about this girl that has me so captivated. Besides her obvious beauty, there's a goodness to her that follows her around, but there's a darkness too. Like she's been hurt but made it through to the other side, and damn if that doesn't intrigue me. I'd been hurt more times than I could count but felt like I was drowning in it.

Ever since I'd found Mom... no I couldn't think about that tonight, even though that was the moment that forever changed me. Sometimes I wondered what it would have been like if she had chosen different, and not left us. Sometimes, I was ashamed to admit, I wondered what I would have been like if Pierce had been the one to find her. Or Dad. I rub the rose on my hand, feeling the sense of guilt eat at me. If I had gotten there just a little earlier. Had I noticed the signs, just maybe she'd be here still, and I wouldn't be so broken.

Shit, I promised myself I wasn't going to go there tonight.

"Lukas..."

My entire body goes rigid hearing my name out of Skye's mouth. The room is too dark to see anything, but I hold my breath to see if she says it again.

I swallow, my heart hammering against my chest. "Skye?"

I wait to hear her response, but only hear the soft whine of an inhale. I let out a grumble. It's only night one, how am I supposed to do this for the rest of the year? Maybe I could desensitize myself...

Skye lets out another moan, and my head snaps to the side trying to make out if she's awake, but it's too goddamn dark in here. Is she dreaming about me?

I hear a rustling in her sheets and some mumbling that I can't make out.

Great. Just great.

"Are you awake?" I venture, holding my breath for her response. I hear more rustling.

"Don't you feel weird sharing a room with someone you don't even know?" Her light voice asks and its music to my ears. I inhale, turning in the dark to face her.

"What do you want to know?"

"I don't know." She thinks for a moment. "What's your favorite color?"

"Black."

She lets out a laugh. "Figures."

"Why what's yours?"

"Blue." She sounds exhausted. "Together we'd make a bruise. Black and blue."

"Eh. That's not so bad."

"Why not?"

"Bruises are a reminder that you survived the pain."

"That's incredibly insightful for this late at night."

"Get some sleep, Skye."

I wait, listening as her breathing becomes steady. She lets out a little moan and Lust takes notice. The sound takes me from zero to a hundred. I can feel the sensation of desire spreading from me to the room around me. It overwhelms me to the point where I need to grip my cock to release this pressure.

"Ugh oh my god, Lukas yes." I hear her whisper and it sends me over the edge.

My lips tug up into a smirk, I knew she wanted me. Maybe this wouldn't be so bad after all.

CHAPTER TWENTY-SIX
Salem

It's the middle of the night and I find myself thrashing against my threadbare blankets. A scream is lodged in my throat only this time thankfully, there's no smoke. A light sheen of sweat clings to my skin even though my room in this god-awful tower is freezing. The nightmare was the same as it always was but since arriving on campus, they'd become more intense. I try to brush it off as stress, but I can't stop the images from replaying in my mind.

A woman, who looks like a younger version of my grandma is wearing a long white dress and a crown of flowers. She gestures for me to follow her. I do without question, stepping through a tucked away path in the dense woods. She moves gracefully, smiling back at me with reassurance, checking to see if I'm still following. I feel an icy chill as we make our way to a hidden cave. I know what awaits me here, but still my feet keep moving of their own volition. A low thump fills the air around me that matches the steady beat of my heart. We reach the back of the cave, the cold seeping into my bones.

"Fix it Salem." My grandmother's voice pleads. Her scent of rosewater and lavender envelops me as I walk past. I step until I'm almost flush with the back of the cavern wall. It's dark, staring down at me like it knows a secret I haven't been privy to. I ignore the sense of foreboding and do what I know I must, what my body urges me to do. My hands reach up to touch the wall and a flash of light jolts out, searing my hand. My flesh burns, and I let out a scream. The scent of charred meat fills the air as a pattern emerges on my palm.

"You have to fix it Salem!" My grandmother's voice calls again, this time more insistent, laced with fear. But I don't know what to do. I cradle my burnt hand.

"What do I need to do?" I yell out, but my words are eaten away by a whooshing noise.

Suddenly a hooded figure is standing before me, gripping me by my wrist. I can't make out their face, but they're strong. The thump thump thumping becomes more frantic as I try to yank myself away from this man.

"You cannot win this fight, Salem. Yield!" The man yells, the deep growling of his voice so familiar but I can't seem to place where I've heard it before. He kicks me from behind my kneecap and I falter. He lets out a cruel laugh as he places my palm against the cavern's wall.

A loud boom pierces my ears and I see a crack forming from the bottom of the wall, making the earth quake beneath us. The man releases my wrist and slams my head into the jagged rock so hard I see black spots before collapsing. It's then that I notice the cavern is filling with water, but my body is unable to move. I wake right as my mouth begins to fill with salt water, entering my lungs as I struggle to breath.

I wrap my arms around myself and try to take a deep breath, it was just a dream. I could still feel the man's boney fingers wrapped around my wrist. I run my own frozen fingers over the area, desperate to rid myself of the night terror. I flip my hand over tentatively half afraid that I'll find my skin burned into whatever pattern that was. I let out a sigh of relief at seeing my unblemished skin with its familiar lines right where they should be.

A knock comes from my door and has me gathering the tiny slip of a blanket up around my body before I shuffle to open it. My hand shakes ever so slightly that I chide myself for letting my nightmare rattle me. When I open the door, a shirtless Pierce, bane of my existence, is standing there arms crossed over his sculpted chest. My God, did everyone in this house have to be so damn attractive? I could barely get through dinner without drooling over the multiple men that were surrounding us. But this asshole? He was getting my body reacting in a way that was making me mad. Out of all the people, I had to be attracted to this one.

"I heard a scream, are you okay? Holy fuck it's freezing up here!"

"No kidding." I say clutching the blanket tighter. It wasn't this bad when I first went to bed, but the temperature dropped drastically in the night.

He scratches at his slight dirty blonde scruff on his chin before responding. "I could invite you to my room, but Garrison snores, I don't think we have any extra blankets right now."

I scoff at the thought of going into his room.

"Or I could keep you warm?" He says, his lips curled up into a smirk.

My mouth drops open at his suggestion. On the one hand I hate him. On the other I don't want to end up with hypothermia again and I'm still feeling shaky after that nightmare. I squint my eyes at him. "Ok, Ledger, on one condition."

"Name it." His grin spreads wider like I just told him I bought him his favorite candy.

"You keep your hands to yourself."

"Afraid I'm going to feel you up in your sleep, witch?"

I scowl. "Never mind, I'll freeze." I say, going to close the door, but he catches it in his strong fingers.

"I promise, I won't touch you. Pinkie swear." He removes his hand from the door and lifts a pinky to me. It should be illegal how well manicured this man's nails are. I let out a noise of frustration, still frowning at him, but I lift my own pinky the black polish chipping at the ends. He wraps his pinkie around mine and stares down at me, his eyes gleaming with mischief.

"I'm just going to go grab my blanket and I'll be right back." He leaves me standing in my room alone. Goosebumps dot my flesh as I settle back into my bed. Was I really letting Pierce Ledger sleep with me in my bed? I briefly thought about finding Skye and asking her to keep me company, but I didn't want to bother her, or subject her to the frozen tundra that had become my room. Pierce might be an asshole, but he could have just let me freeze... both times. And, fine if he wants to offer me some body heat, who am I to turn that down? I'd pass on the frostbite look, thanks.

He's only gone a few minutes, but it seems even colder when he gets back.

"Jesus, how were you sleeping in here? Forget the Rapunzel idea, I'm going to have to start calling you Elsa." He sits on the edge of the bed, making it dip where his weight settles. He covers us both with a thick quilted blanket that is so soft I have to stop myself from caressing it.

"Really like those Disney references, huh?"

"What can I say, I have great taste."

"I thought the end of that sentence was going to end differently."

"What did you think I was going to say?"

"Another Disney movie reference."

"Nah, I think I'll cap it at those two. Don't need you knowing how big of a nerd I am. It'd hurt my reputation."

"Well, we can't have that."

I turn facing the brick wall, my back to Pierce. It feels significantly warmer now that I'm tucked in against Pierce. I push away the fact that he's still shirtless and now snuggled in next to me. In my bed. Shit.

"Goodnight, witch."

I let out an exasperated sigh, "Sweet nightmares, Ledger."

It doesn't take long for me to fall asleep as I'm nestled up to the one person that irritates me the most.

■■■

My mouth feels like it's full of cotton. I try moving my body but am unable to. My eyes fly open as I realize I'm still in bed with Pierce, and he's holding me flush against him. My every curve lining up with him. Not only that, but I feel a slight rocking against my clit by his very erect cock. I let out a moan, not meaning to but holy fucking shit. He rocks again and it sends a shot of warmth up my spine.

All thoughts of why this is such a horrible idea empty from my head when I feel Pierce's fingers slide down my front and grab a handful of my breast, flicking my nipple. I have no idea why I'm allowing this other than it feels so good. I arch myself back against him and hear a grunt escape his lips.

"Fuck, Salem." He says grinding his full length down my wet slit. My underwear is completely drenched but it seems to be the only scrap of fabric separating us from having him thrust inside of me.

My breaths are coming in fast as I feel his lips on my neck. The sensation of his lips on my skin snaps whatever this fever dream I'm locked in and I shrug out of his embrace, clutching my heart and running my fingers through my messy hair.

"I said ONE rule, Pierce!"

"You seemed to be enjoying it though." He says, reaching for me, but I shove his hand away before he can pull me back in. He runs his hand up and down his erection that has freed itself from his pajama pants and fuck me it's huge. I can't seem to tear my eyes away from it and find myself licking my lips.

"That's it baby, I can see how much you want this."

My eyes snap up to his, "Never in a million years." I spit out.

He lets out a groan, still working himself over, "Never?" He cocks a smile at me, and goddamn him I don't know if I want to slap him or kiss him. I feel a surge of anger over the confusion he's making me feel. I shove him, this time off the bed. He lets out a yelp and stands up with a menacing stare. I meet him with an equally fierce glare, one that hopefully says, "Take your enormous cock out of here and fuck right off."

"You wanna play like that baby girl?" He says hooking a hand around my ankle as he yanks me forward, I'm lined up against him before I even know what's hit me. He slams his lips against mine, and for some reason, I open for him. I stroke my tongue over his as he grinds his hips down into me. The friction of our bodies sends a delicious heady warmth down into my clit. My body is screaming at me to have him and have him right the fuck now. I wrap my legs around him and pull him closer, even though my head whispers at me to push him away- my clit has other plans. All of which include getting an orgasm from Pierce. He leans back suddenly and slaps my inner thigh.

"What the fuck?" I seethe embarrassed by how needy he's made me and missing his body against mine. He lets out a dark chuckle as he looks down at me with satisfaction.

He stands up and tucks his cock back into his pants, grinning at me. "Never, huh?"

"Get out, asshole!" I feel my face burn with anger, lust, and disappointment. Feelings I don't want to explore further because I'm too busy launching myself onto my feet to shove Pierce out of my room.

"I'm keeping your blanket by the way." A look of surprise crosses his face before I'm slamming the door.

Fuck Pierce Ledger.

CHAPTER TWENTY-SEVEN
Skye

I could barely sleep last night. Lukas may be hot as hell, but he snored like a lawn mower that was running all night and I was pretty sure I'd heard him jerking off at some point, although that could have just been my imagination, but damn did I feel all kinds of turned on laying mere feet from him.

I was feeling extra grumpy this morning from my lack of sleep for the second night in a row. Dark circles replaced my usually bright skin, making them look puffy with exhaustion. No amount of concealer was working on those babies this morning.

The air in the house felt crisp this morning, and I pulled on an extra pair of knee socks as quietly as I could so I wouldn't disturb Lukas who's engine-like snore was still revving away. Lucky jackass. I slightly envied his ability to sleep that deeply.

I wish the school's dress code wasn't so archaic and would allow girls to wear pants if they wanted. It seemed that no matter how many steps we'd made as women, there were people determined to keep us rooted in the past. I fix my plaid skirt in place and button up my wrinkled white shirt. I originally planned to get dressed in the bathroom, but it was full of guys this morning. I'd have to work out what schedule everyone kept to avoid accidentally stepping in on a hoard of nude dudes. I sweep my hair up into my space-buns and finish applying my makeup in a handheld mirror. I skip doing a cat eye since I can't really see well in the dim lit room and tiny mirror.

I make my way down the stairs avoiding the gaze of the creepy cherubs that stare at me from the railing. The closer I get to the kitchen, the stronger the smell of bacon gets. My mouth is already salivating by the time I reach the bottom stair.

The guy cooking, who I think is named Graham, is dancing around the kitchen singing into the spatula. I stand back watching the performance with a smile. I'm rapt by his easy movements and sheer joy he has as he moves around the kitchen wielding his spatula. He does an air guitar movement in his big finish, and I let out a clap, practically bouncing on my toes with enthusiasm.

He turns taking me in with an easy smile, complete with two dimples on either side of his scruffy cheeks.

"That was quiet the performance." He puts down his spatula and puts his hands on his hips which are covered by an apron that says, 'Kiss the chef'.

"Are you hungry?" He asks, going to remove the pan of bacon from the oven. He speaks with a hint of an Italian accent that sends my heart fluttering. Damn all these guys for being too cute for my own good.

My stomach lets out a loud rumble, sending heat straight to my face. I clutch at my middle and his dark brown eyes dance with amusement.

"I'll take that as a yes."

"You caught me. It's Graham, right?" I ask, giving him an embarrassed smile. He nods pushing some buttons on a machine that starts to spit out coffee. "Can I help you with anything? It all smells so good."

He looks surprised for a moment before flashing me his dimples, "Everything is pretty much done right now, but I'll keep your offer in mind for the future."

He divvies up the food onto some plates and a few guys I'm not familiar with straggle in half awake.

Graham hands me a plate with the most delicious looking frittata I've ever seen. If I was the food picture taking kind of person, this is exactly the sort of food I'd have to capture and post. He garnishes the side with some pancetta which I realize I had mistaken for bacon.

"Do you do this every morning?" I ask, taking a bite that makes me let out a throaty moan without my permission.

He shrugs. "I don't mind." He pops in a bite of frittata into his mouth, and I watch his throat as he swallows.

I realize I'm staring and quickly avert my eyes. I look around trying to decide where I should go and sit down.

I feel Graham's eyes tracking me as I sit at the bar stools that line the side of the kitchen. I tug at my skirt that has slid up and notice a few of the conversations behind me feel stilted.

I eat in silence, scrolling on my phone looking over my schedule for the day.

"You're in my spot." A deep grumble comes from behind me. I know that voice.

I sigh, turning around. "I didn't see your name on it."

Lukas glares down at me, he's shirtless and showing off every inch of his tattooed sculpted chest. It takes everything inside of me, to keep my scowl glued to his piercing green colored eyes.

His nostrils flare, and he looks to be two seconds away from shoving me off the stool.

"Dude, leave her alone." Graham says, holding out a plate of food.

Lukas shifts his glare over to Graham yanking the plate from him, but Graham just smiles back unfazed. My eyes bounce between the two guys before Lukas finally relents, sitting on the stool directly next to me. He's so close that his arm brushes mine as he eats. I shift in my chair, but there's nowhere to go.

I take a breath. Fine if he wants to play this game, I'll make him regret it.

I shovel the frittata into my mouth, the succulent taste exploding on my tongue. I let out a little noise of satisfaction, crossing my legs as I eat, my skirt hiking up my thighs. I lick my fork for every last piece, working my tongue over the prongs.

I sense Lukas's eyes on me, and I do my damnedest to ignore him as I take one final bite, fluttering my eyes closed enjoying the sensation of my food melting in my mouth.

I jump off the stool, noting a fire lingering in Lukas's eyes as he covers his crotch. I smirk with the heady knowledge that I just won the little game he threw down. I take my plate to the sink, and then go over to Graham.

"That was the best breakfast I've ever had in my life." I say truthfully.

He coughs, two little dots of red appear on his cheeks above his adorable dimples. "No problem."

"Thank you." I say, leaning in to give him a hug. He stiffens for a moment, surprised, but then wraps his strong tattooed arms around me. I catch Lukas glaring at us, his hands balled up into fists. The roses tattooed on his hands stretching over the clenched skin. I kiss Graham on the cheek, directly on top of his dimple before pulling away. I feel his hand grip tight around my low back at the contact. When we pull apart, he scratches at the back of his neck.

"Maybe you can help me make dinner later." He says, and I gift him with a wide smile.

155

"I would love that." I say truthfully. My Dad and I were on the road so much, I never learned how to cook properly. Other than being proficient at the microwave, I'm useless in the kitchen.

I look at the time, noting I don't have long before my first class begins.

"I'll see you later." I say to Graham turning to leave. I will myself not to look behind me, but I feel more than one pair of eyes on me as I exit the room. So much for not getting involved in any guys this year. It looks like I'm neck deep and its only day one of living here.

CHAPTER TWENTY-EIGHT
Pierce

The headmaster summoned me first thing this morning. My arms can still feel the pressure of Salem's lithe body snuggled against them. I rub at one arm with a frown. I don't even know what compelled me to go up to her room last night. Or even what made me stay. I was supposed to be following the headmaster's orders when it came to her, or my brothers and I would pay the price. But I'd felt the unwelcome sting of guilt when I saw how cold she was.

Because of me.

I was the reason she was here, and I hoped she never found out. If she was mad this morning, then she really would be pissed if she found out the truth. Find out what I did. Who I was.

She'd never talk to me again, and I wasn't entirely sure why that thought bothered me as much as it did. I was Pierce Mother-fucking Ledger. I didn't need anyone, and certainly could get any girl I fucking wanted. I didn't need Salem and her bewitching eyes, and her pillowy lips that I wanted to sink my teeth into.

My body let out an involuntary shudder remembering how I'd been so close to shoving my cock into her this morning. I let out a frustrated groan finding my cock ramrod straight pushing against my pants.

I needed to get laid. I should have taken Katie up on her offer. But the thought of Katie had my erection deflating faster than a balloon being poked with a needle. The fuck was wrong with me? Maybe I was getting sick with something.

I hurry down the path, the sun barely a sliver over the water, the ever-present fog surprisingly less dense this morning. Maybe we'd get a lucky break in the weather and be able to head down to the beach this weekend. I pick up my already fast pace to get this meeting over with, dread gnawing at my stomach with each step closer.

When I arrive, Headmaster Hayden is already waiting for me, his pronounced jowls looking even more droopy today- like his face was attempting to melt right off of him. I hoped I never looked like that when I was older. Maybe some light plastic surgery would save my face from looking like a melted wax candle that was precariously attached to a skull.

"You took your time getting here this morning." He growls.

The sweat dripping down my back disagrees, but instead of arguing I know the old fucker wants nothing more than a good ass kissing, so I respond, "Sorry, sir." I didn't want a repeat of last time's antics. Who knows when he would have stopped drowning me in that inky goo if it wasn't for Emmet.

He assesses me for a moment before sinking into his chair, gesturing at me to do the same. I brace myself for the pins and needles that are about to assault my backside from sitting in his guest chair. I wince as I lower myself down, then wait for him to continue.

He clears his throat with a wet crackling that sounds more like he's about to hawk a loogie instead of have a conversation with me.

"Now that we have the girl where we want her, I need you to get closer. Make her trust you. Use your proximity. We don't have much time until we can open the veil at Samhain and reunite the souls with this world."

"And if I do that, you'll free us from the seven's possession?"

Anger flares in his eyes, and then is gone in a flash, his face working hard to contain his rage.

"Of course. That goes without saying, and you know what will happen if you fail." He says it as a statement, not a question. Like I need reminding that we would be stuck like this forever if I didn't help him succeed. I was reminded of it every time Pride rose in my chest, making me fall more and more into someone I didn't recognize. I push the memory of me standing over Salem with a match as I tossed it in the corner out of my head. The way the flames blazed so suddenly on the gasoline I'd poured per the headmaster's instruction. I could have killed

159

her. The thought strangles my mind, before I'm reminded that she got out alright. That I shook her awake before barreling out of the room, her scream reverberating against my eardrums as I fled the building. Each step reminding me what a fucking coward I was. Reminding me of just how far from myself I'd become because of this curse.

I rub at my chest, like that will make it go away, as the headmaster prattles on about prying information from Salem.

She was in for a rough Freshman year with the headmaster determined to break down the gate that separated us from the souls trapped in purgatory. They used to run amok on this island until Salem's ancestors created a spell that would keep them contained. Only, they missed one. They missed a big one, and he'd been biding his time for years, hiding in unsuspecting people until the time was right.

The headmaster was his latest puppet, but there seemed to be no distinction from the demon and the man. I wondered if that would happen to the seven of us if we didn't extricate ourselves from the sins the headmaster had bound us to on initiation night. God, how I wish I didn't drink from that fucking challis.

How many people would have to pay for my choice? How many was I willing to let suffer to get what I wanted? And worst of all, how much of this was me deciding for myself and not the demon that lived in me?

CHAPTER TWENTY-NINE
Salem

All day, people I didn't even know before, have been coming up to me and asking about the fire. It's exhausting. I don't like to people on my good days and today isn't one of those. I've been displaced, frozen, tired, woken up by a nightmare, turned on by the most annoying person in the world, and I was stuck going to classes in an outfit that was far too tight for my liking. Add on not being able to buy anything new and pelt me with incessant questions I didn't know the answer to, you just guaranteed I was being an absolute peach.

I chug down a watery tepid cappuccino because of course it is, but at this point I need the caffeine. I don't need to add caffeine withdrawal to my list of ever-growing complaints.

Someone more positive minded might say to look on the bright side, and thankfully that person wasn't here, or I might just accidentally throat punch them. Well not really, but I'd glare and imagine it in my head. After everything that I'd been through within the last 24 hours, it was okay to fucking wallow for a minute.

I finally am able to break away from a crowd of people who'd heard that I received 3rd degree burns from the fire and catch up with Javelynn and Skye for lunch.

"Oh my God, hide me from the mob please."

Javelynn chuckles sitting at the table next to me. "You're being dramatic. Our school isn't big enough to be considered a mob."

"Always so literal Javey." I say bumping my shoulder into theirs. "Thank you for the clothes by the way."

"Well, it was that or have you show up to class naked, so really I'm saving everyone."

"Are you saying I don't look good naked? I'm offended."

"Well, if you thought people couldn't leave you alone today, just imagine what that would be like sans clothes."

"Good point." I tip my water bottle at them, and we clink our water bottles together.

"Is everyone hounding you today?" Skye says looking disheveled and tired as she sits down.

"Yes." Both Javelynn and I answer at the same time.

"I just had to prove to a group of people that I, in fact, did not receive 3rd degree burns."

Skye takes a sip of her lemonade. "People thought that we burned down our room on purpose, so we'd have to stay at Hell House. Someone literally said they were jealous they hadn't thought of it first."

"That's insane."

"Well, the guys at the fraternity are a hot commodity." Javelynn states. I glare at them. "What? I have eyes. They're gorgeous. I don't know how you're not drooling everywhere having to be in that house with them."

"Oh, trust me, it's a struggle." Skye says. "The bathroom was overrun by a bunch of naked dudes this morning, I had to change in my room and I'm in desperate need of a shower."

"I'll second that." Javelynn says laughing into their sandwich.

"Hey." Skye scolds frowning into her bag of chips.

"I'm kidding, you look amazing."

"I hardly got any sleep last night. Lukas was snoring all night and it was so loud. I'm going to have to get some of those ear stopper things, what are they called?"

"Noise canceling headphones?"

"No, no- the little squishy things that you shove into your ears. They're like bright orange. I need those."

"Oh, um... you know I have no idea what those are called. Why can't I think of it? I have no trouble reciting the periodic table, but THIS is the thing that stumps me?"

"I think they're just called earplugs. We should stop by the school store and see if they have any. With as many of us that have roommates here, I don't see why they wouldn't stock them."

"Good idea. We should see if they have any uniforms in our sizes too."

I shift uncomfortably in my chair, "Um, yeah. Sounds great." I take a bite of my turkey sandwich, as I swallow it feels like a rock settling into my stomach. I needed to fix my money situation, and soon, which meant I would have to contact Grandma Clementine. Ah. The cherry on top of my clusterfuck of a week.

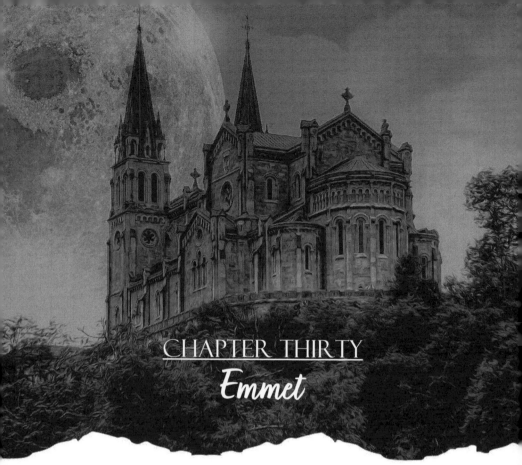

CHAPTER THIRTY
Emmet

The headmaster's living room is flush with a roaring fire to stave off this ungodly cold front. It's far too early in the season for it to be this cold. We sit in wingback chairs that face the fire. The flames cast dancing shadows around the dimly lit room. The wind howls against the windows, rattling them with a furious force.

"I'm worried about Pierce. While he did what I asked him to, he resisted. Even with all of my influence, he's too stubborn for his own good."

"What would you like me to do about it, sir?"

"Keep watching him like you have been. If he slips up, or starts developing feelings for that girl, let me know. We've worked far too hard to be thwarted by some stupid frat boy"

I nod my head, standing to leave.

"And Envy?"

"Yes?"

"Don't fail me."

▪▪

I walk, setting a brisk pace through the woods. The headmaster's house sits directly above the cliffs on the far side of campus. More than one person has jumped from that very area, so they decided to have a teacher in residence to dismay anyone from making that decision. So far as I know, it's worked.

I shove my hands in my pockets, listening to the sounds around me, remembering my father's instruction. His number one rule was to always be aware of my surroundings. He'd go so far as to create different scenarios to catch my off guard. Honing my skills.

While other kids were playing with toys, I was learning how to assemble a computer and take it apart again. With my father's business being only somewhat legitimate, being targeted was a constant possibility- even all the way out here on this island. He'd drilled into my head that you never let your guard down. The moment that you do? Death. Or worse. He'd shown me the letters he'd received on what someone would do to my mother and I if he didn't comply with their demands. Those people never lasted long. My father's reach was too wide.

"Information is power, Emmet." My father would frequently say, as we sat side by side building his latest piece of tech. His tattooed covered arms hunched over the tiny wires. "And how do we get that information?"

"By listening?"

"That's right."

So, I learned to listen, blending into the background. I became the king of observation, learning what made people tick, what secrets they were holding onto behind their easy smiles and bright laughter. The more I watched, the more I learned. I became the ultimate chameleon gathering secrets that could blow up an entire life if I so chose.

All of that now prepared me for what I had to do now. Who I had to become to get what I wanted.

CHAPTER THIRTY-ONE
Skye

"Okay so you need to crack the egg into this bowl." I raise the egg, bringing it down on the edge of the bowl like Graham showed me, only I end up smashing it, the pieces crumbling in a wet gooey mess on my hand.

"Dio mio. How have you never cracked eggs before?" Graham sasks, laughing so hard his dimples pierce into his cheeks.

"I know, I'm hopeless." I say, matching his laughter. He grabs me by my forearms and drags me over to the sink.

"Nah, I've seen worse." He says turning on the sink and sticking my hands under the water.

I wash the egg goo off of my fingers, making sure to pick off the tiny white shell pieces that are stuck in the slime.

Once my hands are dry, Graham hands me another egg. "Try again."

"Seriously? You're going to trust me with this thing?"

He leans back on the counter, arms crossed over his chest. His dimples on full display. Damn his cuteness.

"I trust you came here to help me make some food. So, help."

I let out a sigh of frustration before squaring my shoulders in determination. "Okay. I've got this."

I take a breath, then swing my hand down fast, this time the egg cracks right in two.

"Oh my god! I did it."

Graham comes up from behind me, placing his hands on mine.

"Now, you pull it apart, like this." I'm trying to pay attention to his words, but all I can think about is how his body is pressed against my back, his hands on mine. I manage to follow his movements breaking the egg yolk into the bowl.

"What are you two making in here?" A scraggly bearded guy asks as he lazily scratches at his stomach. If rolled out of bed was a look, he nailed it.

Graham backs away from me, washing his hands off.

"We're making a cake for later, Sloan."

"You must be one of the new girls." Sloan says yawning at the end. He looks like a raccoon in human form, all scruffy and adorable.

"I'm Skye." I go to the sink washing the egg off of my hands.

Sloan gives me a lazy smile, grabbing a bag of chips and a container of cookies out of the cabinet before he heads back downstairs.

169

"So, you want to combine these eggs with the milk and give it a good stir." Graham says walking me through the rest of the steps. He already had dinner cooking by the time I got back from classes, so he offered to make a desert with me. He didn't even seem to mind that I had no idea what I was doing, instead taking the time to walk me through each step. It made my heart melt a little. Graham's company felt easy and fun, even if I found myself wanting to poke him right in the dimples the entire time.

"We combine the dry ingredients with the wet ones." Graham says pointing at my bowl. I bring it over and pour the contents into the one he's holding. As I pour, I accidentally get part of it on Graham's shirt.

"The one time I don't wear an apron!" He laughs.

"Oh, I'm so sorry." My cheeks flame with embarrassment.

"No, it's fine." We set our bowls down, and before I have a moment to start stirring, Graham is taking his ruined shirt off. Holy shit- abs.

"See, no problem."

"Mmhm. Yep. I see." Oh my god, Skye- keep it together.

"You okay, amore?" Oh, dear baby Jesus, that accent.

"Yep, fine. Just a little overheated." My face feels like it's on fire. I'm trying not to stare at Graham's sculpted chest.

"Well, well, well. What do we have here?" Lukas' voice cuts in.

"We're making cake." Graham answers, picking up a large wooden spoon and begins stirring. The image of this chiseled man stirring cake batter should not be such a turn on, but it's doing all kinds of things to my insides.

"And you don't need a shirt for that?" Lukas says getting a drink out of the stainless-steel fridge.

"It's my fault, I splashed ingredients all over him."

Lukas raises his eyebrow ring.

"What's for dinner? Whatever it is, it smells amazing." Salem says breezing into the kitchen. "Oh, wow. What's with the shirtless chef?"

"Skye decided to relieve Graham of his shirt."

"Nice job, Skye." Salem winks.

"It was an accident."

"Happy accident." Salem says for only me to hear.

"Alright, alright. Too many people in my kitchen. Out. Out. Out." Graham says.

"You're acting like your mom again, Graham." Lukas says, taking a swig of his pop as he leaves the kitchen, but not before I catch his furious glare he casts in my direction. I stare after the mind-fuck that is Lukas Ledger before returning to my sloppy cake batter bowl.

Graham slides up next to me, his dimples on full display as he hands me a spatula.

"Now, for this type of cake you want to use gentle movements. None of that beating nonsense the fancy gadgets that splatter this masterpiece everywhere."

I feel myself leaning into him as he shows me how to spin the mixture.

"Here." He comes around me, his large hand swallowing mine as we churn the batter. He moves my hand with his as his free hand

171

holds onto my waist. I grip the handle of the spatula tightly trying to calm myself down. "There. Perfecto." I turn around and smile, he looks down at me, mirroring my joy.

We stand there for a beat, his eyes trailing down to my lips before he backs away checking the clock timer.

He gathers a cake pan and I struggle to not stare at his shirtless chest again, picturing myself painting some of this chocolate cake batter all down his abs while I lick it off.

Yeah, my plan to not get involved with any guys and just focus on school was off to a great start.

CHAPTER THIRTY-TWO
Salem

Tiny furious droplets pummel against my thin glass window with a consistent loud pinging, waking me from my dreamless sleep. I was grateful for the reprieve from the nightmare that had been plaguing me since I got here.

I have no classes this morning I realize as I stretch my cold limbs out trying to get circulation to my extremities. I'd slept hard, pinning my arms under my head resulting in a knot at the base of my neck. I tentatively rub the spot, trying to work out the kink.

I still haven't bought my own blanket, since my mom hasn't answered any of my phone calls, so Pierce's stolen red one had to suffice for the meantime. I almost felt bad about depriving him of his blanket but then I remembered his quips at me, and the feeling was gone almost as quickly as it had arrived. He could shiver all night long for all I cared.

I'd spent the night alone. I woke this morning feeling refreshed with a hint of curiosity nagging at me. I'd been living at Hell House for the past two days and had yet to explore anything further than the kitchen and my own bedroom.

I could feel that internal nudging for me to poke around a bit more. One thing I never ignored was my gut feeling. I shrug off the blanket, bracing my limbs for the onslaught of cold air. I hurriedly throw on a donated well-worn Kildale Academy black hoodie complete with the wildcat mascot, as the chill pimples up my bare arms before I'm fully covered. I find a pair of black fleece leggings that Skye leant me and step into them, pulling their warm fabric over my skin. The hoodie hangs loosely around me as I throw my hair up into a ponytail, securing it with a white scrunchie.

There's a tiny mirror hung up in the corner of my tower that gives me just enough space to see one full eye and eyebrow, sometimes part of my nose if I'm at the right angle. I check to see if I removed all the sleep from my eyes, and from what I can see I got it. I slip on some Converse shoes and tread carefully down the spiral staircase, clutching hard to the rail for balance. Each step bows, creaking with my weight as I creep cautiously. These stairs are long overdue for replacement, I think as my mind conjures up scenarios of me falling through one of these dilapidated steps.

I finally make it down, my hand aching from how hard I was clutching the wooden railing. I shake it out running my thumb across the joints. It's warmer down here as I walk down the hallway, the vents blowing warm air through my pony as I pass under. I really could use one of those in my room.

I walk to the stairs and continue down the hall, noting the few paintings that line the walls. It feels like a mix between a museum and a haunted house, taking in the opulent gold frames that house each painting. The eyes of the painted figures practically follow me like I'm in a Scooby Doo rerun.

The house is quiet, I note checking the time on my phone. Mid-morning. The guys were probably off to class. I knew Skye probably was off in the art studio working on her latest piece. She'd been obsessing over her art professor's disapproval. Honestly, I didn't know what issues her professor saw when she looked at Skye's work. I was no art expert, but everything Skye had shown me was absolutely amazing.

I trail my fingers along the wall as I walk, following the dust-filled crevice on top of the trim that spans the length of the hallway, intricately carved with floral decals sitting half-way between the floor and ceiling. The dust gathers on my fingertip, sloughing off the smooth wood and drifts slowly to the ground.

My Converse drag lazily along the wood floor as I take in the gothic opulence surrounding me. It makes me feel out of place. Like I should be wearing a ball gown instead of a worn-down hoodie and leggings.

By the time I'm nearing the stairs to the basement after throughly poking around the different levels, I'm feeling ravenous. I wonder if Graham has any food stowed away in the refrigerator, or if the vultures that are my new housemates devoured it all already. I don't really blame them. Graham can cook as well as a five-star chef.

I debate making my way to the kitchen when a low mournful strumming breaks the silence. I strain my ears, listening to the echo of the song reverberating up the stairs. I can't seem to place the melody, though it sounds familiar. I decide to pop in a piece of gum to stave off my hunger for the time being and investigate where the song is coming from.

I place my hand on the cool metal rail that lines the wall headed to the basement. It's dark, but the light from upstairs gives enough of a shine that I can see well enough. The angle of the light makes all the shadows seem elongated, making the stairs to the basement feel ominous. My heart rate picks up. I try to squash this irrational fear. It's just a basement. I'm an adult, I should be over this ridiculous anxiety over just venturing into a basement.

The music becomes louder the closer to the bottom I get. It's sadness and anger all wrapped together, and I finally place the notes being strung together as *House of the Rising Sun,* by the Animals.

I step cautiously, the music luring me like a siren's song. My curiosity drives me forward leading me to a propped open door. Inside are two disheveled full-sized beds, a punching bag and a man plucking at a fire engine red Fender Strat, playing like he was born with this instrument in his hands.

Why in the hell are all the men who live here unbearably hot?

This man is so caught up in his song, that he doesn't register me standing here like some groupie creep. But he has a leather jacket on with no shirt and I can see every single defined ab. He even has a sexy as fuck scar running across his eyebrow. Kill me now.

As I try to back up, my heel brushes against a stray can of pop and I freeze. The rockstar God in front of me pauses mid rif, the loss of his fingers against the strings creates a fuzzy sharp sound in the amp that grates against my eardrums.

"What are you doing in here?" His voice sends a shiver of hot lava down my spine. It's all gravely like someone threw a handful of rocks into his voice box- and it just made him ten times hotter. I mean imagine if he came out and sounded like fucking Elmo. Disaster. But thankfully his voice matches his looks.

"I... uh. I heard the music." He sets down the guitar, switching off the amp and leans forward on his knees.

"And you would be...?"

"Salem... my um... Dorm room burned down so I'm staying here, up in the tower." I chide myself for getting all flustered by another hot dude. I missed my vibrator, at least that kept my crazy libido in check... most of the time.

He assesses me for a moment, his eyes dragging down my body in a lazy perusal that has my stomach clenching in a bundle of nerves. "You know how to play?" He asks.

"Oh, no. I wish."

He tips his chin up at me. "No time like the present."

My heart stutters. "Are you serious?"

"As a heart attack." He growls, but what should scare me only has me moving towards him. The closer I get I notice his knuckles are coated with dried blood. He has several scars on his chest, a few that slice into the tattooed skull he has laying over his heart. My fingers itch to touch it, but I clench my fists into balls instead. I can't trust them at the moment to not roam over his bare, hot as fuck chest.

"Here." He gestures to the empty stool next to him, handing me the guitar. I settle onto the wooden stool, lifting my feet to sit on the bottom rung. He stands up, placing the strap around my neck from behind.

"Rule number one? Always support your instrument." His fingers linger for a moment on my shoulder before he moves around to the front of me. A guitar pick sits between his teeth, as he talks around it, his voice coming out clenched. I look up into his whiskey-colored eyes and bite my lip, feeling nervous under his scrutiny.

"I'm going to teach you a chord, okay?" I nod, watching as he places my hands where they need to go.

"You want to hold right here, putting enough pressure on the strings right here and.." he lifts my finger pushing it against the biting metal, "...here. Now you want to take this." He removes the pick and holds it out for me to take. I grip it between my fingers, and he laughs, readjusting how I'm supposed to hold it.

"Like this little wildcat."

I scrunch up my nose. "Wildcat?"

"The shirt." I look down at my borrowed sweater registering the university mascot. "Now strum your pick across the strings." He pops on the amp, and I try but the chord sounds more like a strangled cat than an epic guitar wail.

He frowns down at me, moving behind me. He places his hand around mine as I keep my fingers pressed into the chord.

"You want to push a little harder, like this." His words tickle against my ear, sending a shiver throughout my body.

"Again." He demands, keeping his hand firmly on mine, his fingers pressing down on where the chord needs to go. I feel his warmth coming through my back as his scent of cinnamon cloves envelops me. I feel myself clench, wondering what those hands of his could do to me, before I shake myself out of it and strum the strings. This time, the chord is beautiful, echoing an almost ethereal sound around the room.

He releases me and takes the guitar with him. I feel the loss of both instantly.

"What's your name?" I ask, realizing I was too caught up in the moment.

"Walker."

"Like Texas Ranger?"

"If I had a nickel."

"How many nickels would you have?"

"Probably a million. But yes. Unfortunately, just like Texas Ranger."

"Don't tell me your middle name is Texas." He barks out a laugh. It sounds dark and warm, like honey. It's a sound I want to hear over and over again.

"No, thankfully my parents spared me that fate. But it's close enough."

"What is your middle name then?" I ask raising my eyebrow and turning in the stool so I can face him more fully.

"You're just full of all kinds of questions, aren't you?"

"What can I say, I'm full of curiosity."

He scratches his scruff on his chin. "Well, I'd hate to see that curiosity kill you like it did the cat."

"So, maybe don't keep calling me wildcat."

"Maybe don't be so curious." He says his whiskey eyes dancing with amusement.

"If I wasn't so curious, I would have never learned... whatever chord that was."

"How can you say you learned the chord, if you don't even know the name of it?"

"Well, will you tell me the name of it?"

He looks at me for a second, his dark eyebrows furrowed together in contemplation. "I could tell you, but what fun would that be?"

I shove his knee, but it barely moves.

"Then I'd know the chord. Duh."

"If I tell you the chord now, how do I get you to come back?"

"Luring me with your siren song guitar worked the first time, maybe try that again."

"Is that all it would take to get you to come back to my lair? Play some tunes on my guitar and you'll come running? Wouldn't that make you, my groupie?"

I roll my eyes. "I am not a groupie. Why are you down here in the basement like a troll dungeon anyway?"

"Why are you up in the tower like a forgotten princess?"

"Touché."

"This house only has so many bedrooms, so we took which ones were available. I got the short straw and ended up down here with my roommate Sloan. Hence all the wrappers and cans." He gestures to the mess around us.

"Well, I have a project for business that I need to work on soon, thanks for teaching me whatever chord that was." I stand up and head for the door, careful to not knock into the small pile of cans that I'd hit earlier.

"Salem?" The way his gravely voice calls my name has me stopping straight in my tracks. I turn facing him and see a vulnerable look cross his scarred face. I hitch my eyebrow waiting for him to speak. He rubs his scruffed up cheeks.

"Do you by any chance sing?"

"Sing?"

"You know the thing where you make music with your mouth?" What a fucking smart ass, but two can play this game.

I tap my black polished finger against my chin. "Can't say I've ever heard of it."

He stands up to his full height, his head mere inches from the low ceiling. He prowls closer to me, and I feel my heart speed up. He leans over me, bracing his muscled forearms above my head boxing me into the wall. He grips my chin in his marred-up hand and looks down at me.

"You've got a sassy fucking tongue on you."

"All the better to lick with." I say starring directly into his whiskey-colored eyes. I see the moment my words register, his pupils darkening with desire. He takes a step closer, his Doc Martins hitting the tips of my Converse.

"And what exactly would you be licking?"

I grab him by the jacket and tug him down to me, lining my mouth up to his ear and whisper, "Ice cream."

I push him square in the chest surprising him enough that he steps back.

I send him a wink as I exit his room. I see his mouth drop before I leave, my steps carrying me halfway up the stairs as I smirk to myself before I hear him calling after me.

"Hey, wildcat?"

"Yeah?"

"What siren song should I play to get you to come back down here again?"

I smile to myself, "How about, *My Guitar Gently Weeps*."

"Done."

I run up the stairs, heading to my tower room to put on something different. I wonder briefly why he was so interested if I could sing, and if I should tell him the answer is yes. I fucking love to sing, but usually only do so in the privacy of a shower, or alone in a car with only me to hear. The tower stairs wind up, narrow and creaking.

I groan, remembering that I have to deal with Pierce today for our project. I wonder if he'll bring up our little cuddling session that had me in knots for the rest of the day. To be honest, I'm still in knots and all worked up, especially after that encounter with Walker. The way he leaned over me, had my insides fluttering. Damn my broken vibrator.

My legs burn by the time I get up to my room, but then I'd rather it be this than the million flights I had in the dorm room. I go through my small possessions trying to decide what to wear. I'd put off talking to my grandmother, feigning a headache to Skye the other day when she went shopping for new school outfits and ear plugs. Thankfully, she didn't inquire further, but it only bought me a day or two of putting off this conversation. I sigh, leaving my leggings on and pull on a maroon thermal long sleeved shirt that I'd borrowed from Skye. She is slightly more booby than me, but it still clings to my frame outlining my curves. I make sure my hair is still up and head off to deal with Pierce and our business group. This should be all kinds of great fun.

CHAPTER THIRTY-THREE
Pierce

I wiggle my pen in the air until it looks rubbery. I'm fucking bored as hell waiting for the group to arrive. How I'm the first one here today boggles my mind. The rain is coming down hard echoing off the high dome shaped ceiling of the library. There are not many people here this morning, but at least my favorite sunshine librarian is here and she looks about two seconds away from chucking a hardback at anyone that talks above a tolerable decibel.

"Hey. Am I late?" Javelynn looks at their smartwatch as they shake off the rain from their coat and hanging it on the back of the chair.

"I'm just early." Javelynn doesn't hide their shock, before sitting on the opposite side of the table. Maybe I came here wanting to catch Salem after my morning football practice. We had a home game tonight, and coach wanted us to work on some last-minute plays. I hadn't been able to get the feel of her body out of my mind, and she'd been avoiding me since I woke up, cock nestled right up against her throbbing clit. I might have had to take an extra-long shower to release some pent-up tension she'd made me feel.

Jackson breezes in, his glasses nearly all the way fogged up. It's a miracle he hasn't run into something already. Just as I think he's managed to get to his seat unscathed, he knocks straight into Javelynn causing them to become a tangle of limbs while Jackson's glasses go flying.

"What the hell happened here?" Salem asks, popping a bubble, her dark eyebrow raised as she scrutinizes the scene in front of her.

Jackson has managed to grab ahold of his glasses that have landed on the table without breaking. He places them on his nose slightly askew, clearing his throat. "Sorry about that Javelynn."

Javelynn's face looks flushed as they lick their lips and readjust their shirt back into place. They flick their hand in the air like it's no big deal.

Salem takes the available seat next to me, and immediately my entire body is tuned into hers. The smell of her minty gum with an undercurrent of vanilla hits me square in the chest.

Never in a million years.

Her words circle around my head, taunting me like my own personal version of hell. I hadn't been able to stop thinking of how good it felt to wake up next to her, my body draped around hers.

Javelynn passes a laminated portfolio to each of us. I leaf through it, more than impressed. This looks professional as hell.

"Jave, when did you get time to do all of this?" Salem asks, her fingers skimming over the shiny pages.

"I like to be thorough." They reply like this isn't weeks worth of work. I feel a sense of inadequacy filling up in my stomach. I pull at my shirt collar, knowing I'll need to put more effort into this project, and I sit up straighter. I paw through the contents. It's good. Real good. Javelynn obviously knows the inner workings of what makes a company tick. I bristle at that. As much as my father drilled into us about the company, he never actually showed either Lukas or I anything about what it will take to be successful in taking over the family business. He's always made it look easy, like coasting on our name alone would be enough, but looking down at this packet in my hand I realize just how out of my depth I am. And fuck, isn't that a tough pill to swallow. My Pride shifts uncomfortably within me, clearly displeased at not being the best.

We work diligently together in silence this time and manage to make some progress- the project is really starting to take shape. My leg closest to Salem bounces and I find myself wishing she'd brush up against it for a fraction of a second. God, I was pathetic. Is this what I'd been reduced to? I cuddle a girl for one night, something I never fucking did, and I was salivating over mere scraps of her attention.

I run my hand over my chin, setting my pen down. The words are starting to blend together, and I need to get my ass ready for tonight's game.

I slap the sides of my face, which earns me a glare from both the librarian and Salem.

I note the injustice of the librarian saving her glare for me, but Jackson nearly tackles Javelynn and not a peep of disapproval. I see how it is lady. I see how it is. I rap my knuckles against the table before standing to leave.

"Anyone coming to the game later?" Salem hadn't so much as grunted in my direction and I was feeling desperate for any reaction. I'm not above yanking her hair at this point just to get her sage green eyes to look at me. I'm met with tired grumbles and Salem doesn't even look up at me, which makes my hand flex just a touch. I force my Pride down, barely able to grasp it before it leaks out of me. I can feel it fighting inside of me, trying to overtake me. I hurriedly grab my stuff and am out the door before it can spill out as it takes control of me. The longer it's in me, the less and less I'm able to get a handle on it and I'm afraid if I don't get it out of me, I won't know where the demon begins, and I end.

Mud clings to me from my toes up to my neck. I'm pretty sure I resemble a fucking swamp monster right now with the rain pelting the field making it into a literal mud bath. We're down by three and have only 2 minutes left of the 4th quarter. The roar of the crowd assaults my ears as hard as the pelting rain pinging off my helmet. My head's not in the fucking game, instead I've been preoccupied with getting control of this thing inside of my chest and trying not to think about Salem and wonder if she's here, wondering if I'm doing the right thing by listening to the headmaster, not being able to even tell my brother. I needed to pull myself together and win this game.

"Where's your head at Ledger?" Coach yells at me during our last time out.

My team looks to me as we huddle together. We have one last chance to get some points up on the board and close out this shit show of a game.

"What are we doin' Ledge?" Hunter asks.

"You ready to run, Hunt?"

He gives me a sharp nod and I tell him the play. We break and line up in formation. I feel a mix of sweat and rain rolling down my back as I wait for the ball to snap. I flex my fingers readying them to catch the ball and breathe out, my teeth clamping down hard on my mouth guard. Before I know it, the ball is spiraling into my hands, and they clamp down working on muscle memory from years of practice.

I scan the field waiting for Hunter to get free of the defense. My arm winds up ready to let the football fly. As my fingertips let go, I turn my head to look in the stands, a rookie mistake to take your eye off the ball, but as I lock eyes with someone who looks a lot like Salem, the sky erupts in a flash. A bolt of lightning cracks open from the sky hitting the ground next to me knocking me straight on my ass.

The rain smacks my face as I stare up at the sky, unable to move. That shit threw me harder than all the times I'd been hit tonight. I let out a groan trying to raise myself off the ground. As I prop myself up on my elbow, I overhear the announcer directing people to leave the stadium amongst several loud screams. The deep authoritative voice crackles over the loudspeaker. Thunder and the sound of hundreds of people fleeing the bleachers reverberates around me. I tilt my head to look at the downpour and see another flash of light coming straight towards me. I don't even have time to move out of the way as it barrels straight down towards me.

CHAPTER THIRTY-FOUR
Salem

"**You've got to be kidding me**. Why did you drag us here Javelynn?" Rain pelts at us as we climb the bleacher steps. The entire school has turned out for the first at home football game, despite the inclement weather. We're lost in a sea of black and white clad spirit wear, with several large wildcat foam claws waving haphazardly around us. I lean away from a clearly drunk attendee who almost gets a foam claw right in my eye. This is why I consistently avoided sporting events at all costs.

"It wouldn't kill you to have some school spirit." Javelynn says, sipping from their thermos.

"You don't know that." I grumble, wishing I was back in my freezing room curled up with a book. Today had been exhausting and confusing. I put all of my energy into ignoring Pierce at the library, though his constant intense focus was eating me alive. I felt his eyes on me and was more aware of him than I cared to admit. And, fine, I secretly liked that he seemed to be struggling. It gave me a heady sort of power that I was content to relish in. We'd been like a lit match held aloft from gasoline from our very first encounter, if we ever came together- we'd be explosive. I didn't have time for that kind of all consuming passion. I had goals, schoolwork. Did I really want to be distracting myself with someone who drove me crazy? Ugh, I knew the answer was a hell yes and I loathed myself for it. I wanted Pierce, and that terrified me. Especially since I found myself having the same sort of pull to Walker today. I bit down on my lip thinking of how hot he looked strumming his guitar. I was a sucker for a tattooed brooding musician and fuck me, he had that entire vibe down like the stereotype was made because of him. I couldn't deny that I'd felt a genuine attraction there. Our banter coming easily. He made me feel... happy. I fought the urge to drag my finger along his scar. What was it about something that was meant to mar you forever that made you look even more beautiful? He had the look of a survivor who'd fought hell itself and came out the winner, and damn that did things to my insides.

Skye bumps my elbow distracting me from my thoughts. She seems wholly at home watching the teams tackle each other.

I have no idea what's going on as we sit watching the game. We arrived while the game was already well underway. I feel like a drowned rat, thankful that Javelynn had spare ponchos. I don't care how uncool I look sitting here wrapped in literal plastic. It's keeping this rain from drenching me to the bone and I already dealt with being mildly hypothermic enough times at this school.

The clouds are rolling in, making it look darker- fast. The crowd around us doesn't seem phased, but I feel an urging inside of me to get out of here.

"We should go." I say, right as the crowd roars, drowning my words out. I shake Skye's arm, but she's too busy jumping up and down cheering with the crowd.

"Skye." I say looking at the gathering clouds. She turns her head to me with a full smile on her face.

"We're going to win. I just know it!" She yells.

The players are lined up, readying for another play. They move synchronized, each muddied body rushing to their predetermined positions, shoulder pads and helmets coming to blows. As I watch the game, a tingle works its way up my spine. I don't know how I know, but I'm slick with fear in an instant, with a clawing feeling that I need to warn someone of the impending danger.

"Watch out!" I scream a second before lightning rips out of the sky. I swear I see one of the players look up at the stands right at me as the lightning smashes into the ground right next to the players, scattering them like a game of jacks. *Pierce.*

My heart jumps up into my throat as the hundreds of people in the stand around us all start to rush down at the same time, shrieking and shoving. I look around frantically trying to find a way to not be trampled.

The drunk man from earlier body slams me, his hot beer breath rakes over my face as he lets out a bellowing scream.

"Get off of me!" I shove him backwards, his arms windmill for a moment as he loses his balance slipping on the slick bench. The chaos envelops him as Skye and Javelynn are swept into the retreating hoard.

The eerie sensation works its way up my spine again this time with a steady thump against my chest and I glance up. I know without a doubt, the lightning is about to strike again.

The entire stadium is in chaos, the announcer's crackling voice penetrates above the shrieks, urging people to use caution and leave the area in a calm manner, but no one is listening.

I see Pierce's body trying to get up from the ground, the other players already running off the field for cover. I don't know how I know it's him other than this sixth sense that's manifested during the last few minutes. I'm too wrapped up in worrying about the next lightning strike to give the why a moment of thought.

The wind whips at my body rustling the damp plastic poncho.

Move Pierce. I urge, my feet carrying me toward an opening in the crowd. I vault myself over a chain link fence, the metal digging into my flesh. I'm up and over landing hard on my Converse. If I die for trying to save Pierce Fucking Ledger, I swear to god I'll come back and haunt his ass.

My feet barely touch the muddied field before I can feel the danger spike in my chest. The sky brightens, a long-jagged bolt reaches directly to where Pierce is struggling to get up.

I reach my hand out instinctually and scream. "NO!"

193

I feel a part of myself latch onto the bolt as it barrels down to Earth. I have the sense that I can direct it and I fling my arm off to the side. The motion sends it careening into the metal goal posts. I crumple feeling drained.

What the ever-living fuck was that?

"Salem?" Pierce is on me in a moment. Grabbing me up by the waist. His mud-covered jersey slides against my poncho, making it difficult for him to find purchase.

"Fuck, Salem?" He wrenches the poncho off of me, tossing it to the wind. I burry my fingers into his bicep, trying to keep myself steady. We lean on each other, of all people to trust to get me to safety I can't believe I'm relying on him again, but I have no choice. My feet slip in a mud puddle, but he doesn't let me fall. Instead, he scoops me into his arms like he did on the night of the fire and runs us off the field and into the home team's hallway that connects the stadium to the locker rooms. The hallway is empty, rain and thunder echos off the walls. It's quieter here, but I can still hear the sounds of people screaming.

He sets me down ripping off his helmet, dropping it on the floor with a thwack. He's on me in an instant running his dirty hands down my drenched hair, like he's making sure I'm okay.

I look down and notice I've wound my fingers around his jersey in the center of his chest. I've never been into sports but there's something unbelievably hot about this man in his football uniform standing in front of me that has my heart stuttering.

"You're okay." He says stepping closer, dipping his head so that we're pressed together, his forehead resting on mine. I manage to nod, my thoughts spinning out of control. The contact lasts for a moment before he stands straight up his eyes roam over my body like he's looking for injuries. Ridiculous, he was the one that was almost hit by a fucking bolt of lightning.

Did I direct the lightning or was that just coincidence? I've heard of people having a sixth sense before, but I've never felt so certain of anything in my life like I was aware of what was going to happen. I didn't even know what specifically was about to happen just that there was incoming danger.

I stare up into Pierce's eyes, his face is streaked with mud and rain drips down over his mouth. My eyes look down tracking the falling water over his mouth briefly remembering how thoroughly he'd kissed me the other morning with those lips, then force myself to look away, but not fast enough as I notice a heat come over Pierce's features. He pushes me back against the wall. My hand snakes up from his chest and wraps around his neck. I don't know who moves first, but all of a sudden, his lips are on mine, my mouth opening eagerly for him tangling our tongues together.

I feel the urge to rip off everything he's wearing but don't even know where to start there's so much padding. He breaks the kiss, clearly having the same idea as he effortlessly removes his jersey over his head in one swift motion. I run my fingers over his shoulder pads, yanking him forward by the strings dangling in the front and kiss him with everything inside of me. He bangs his forearms above my head, the shoulder pads dig into my body, but I don't care. I need him closer.

"Ow, fuck." He grimaces, pulling at his pants.

I glance down and see him reach down into his pants and shuck out his playing cup, tossing it next to his helmet. "It was getting a little tight in there." He chuckles, wrapping his hand around my neck, using it to pull me forward, taking my lips again in a fevered kiss, pressing his hard length against my damp leggings. I can feel every inch of him as he dominates my mouth, pushing his hips against mine. I'm a fucking puddle of desire, ready to climb him and take exactly what I want.

"Ledger!" An authoritative voice calls from down the hall, making us break apart. We're both gasping for breath as we stare at each other, the desire between us clear as day.

"Get your ass in here." The voice calls again, each word clipped and angry.

"I have to…"

"Yeah, of course. No problem." It takes a moment for my body to calm down from the surge of adrenaline. I run my fingers through my wet tangled hair. "Go." I urge.

He stares at me a moment like he doesn't want to leave.

"Ledger, if you make me wait any longer, I'm adding laps to your next practice."

"Fuck." He curses, scooping up his equipment. He places a kiss on my lips surprising me, before he trots down the hall, disappearing around the corner.

What the actual fuck was all of that?

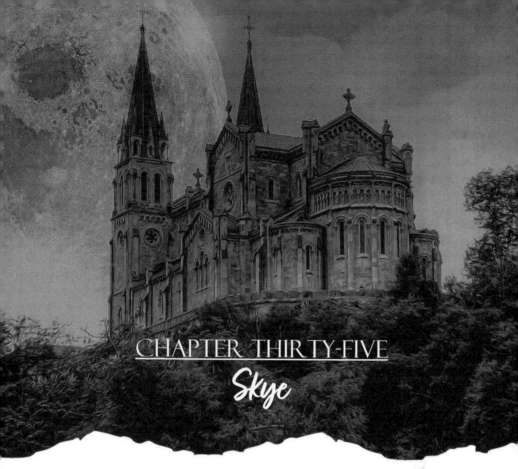

CHAPTER THIRTY-FIVE
Skye

"Crap!" The phone beeps in my hand, no service. I've been trying to get ahold of Salem since we were separated at the game. The storm lifted enough for Javelynn and I to be able to head back to our prospective residences, and now I'm curled up on the living room couch wrapped in a tattered blanket.

One of the guys started a fire, so at least I'm starting to dry off and am relatively warm. I press the call button again.

"You know what they say the definition of insanity is?" Lukas strides into the room, all dark and dangerous and stupidly hot. I glare at him as he sinks into the seat next to me.

"Trying the same thing over and over again, expecting different results." He yanks the phone out of my hands.

"Oh my god, give that back."

He smirks down at me, his dark hair falling across his brow. "Make me."

He lifts my phone above his head, his tattooed biceps flex with the motion making me swallow thickly.

"I need that. I can't get ahold of Salem." I try reaching for the phone but he's too fast, yanking it out of reach. He tips up his mouth into a smirk, spreading his legs wider as he leans back keeping the phone from my outstretched fingers.

"Seriously, Lukas. Come on." He lets out a laugh as I decide to hell with it. I shrug out of the blanket and swing my leg over his lap bringing my chest directly in front of his face. He falters for a moment, his face full of shock as he stares straight at my breasts. I feel his free hand grip into my hip while I lean over him to grab my phone. The motion presses him straight into my cleavage, but I'm finally able to get my hand around his.

"Give it to me Lukas."

"If you insist." His muffled voice calls out. He pulls my lower half closer bringing my hips against him. I can feel something rub against me. A flash of his pierced cock pops into my brain, remembering that time in art class when we had to sketch him. My face heats and all thoughts empty out of my brain but one big inappropriate fantasy that I definitely shouldn't be thinking about while straddling Lukas' lap. It takes everything in me not move my hips like my body is screaming at me to do.

I'm not inexperienced by any means, but something about Lukas has me feeling out of my depth.

"You better move or I'm going to suffocate in these things."

"Not a bad way to go." I hear Graham grumble as he walks into the room glaring at Lukas and me.

I ease myself away from Lukas and when I see his face, it's lit up with a shit eating grin.

"Jealous, Graham Cracker?" He says bucking his hips up gently rocking me into him. Oh, my goodness, I think I've just short circuited.

Graham angrily stalks off and I smack Lukas straight in the chest. "Asshole."

I wrench myself off of him and place a hand on my chest to catch my breath like I didn't almost consider letting him guide me on his lap like that. I stomp off snatching the blanket I'd discarded, and head for the kitchen. I yank open the refrigerator door grabbing a water more forcefully than I need to. I'm a mix of emotions as I sling back the water to cool me off.

Lukas walks in quietly, hands pushed deep into his pockets. He pulls out one of his hands and holds out my phone to me. "You know I was just messing with you right?" He looks down at me with an unreadable expression. I can't quite seem to make him out. "Service is down for the whole island right now."

"Oh." I frown down at my phone noting the icon in the corner that I didn't notice before.

"I'm sure Salem is alright."

"You don't know that for sure." I mumble back.

He assesses me for a moment. "You've lost someone." He says it like a statement and not a question, his words hitting me like a ton of bricks.

"Am I that obvious?" I sneer, building up my defense mechanisms ready to retreat from this conversation.

"Maybe not to the average person."

"What does that mean? That super special Lukas Ledger is able to read people?" I scoff. I know I'm being nasty, but he's picking at an old scab that I thought was long healed.

He works his bottom lip into his mouth, making him look as vulnerable as I feel. "No." He answers softly. "But maybe I recognize my own pain in you." I can't help it-my mouth drops open in surprise.

"You..." I clear my throat. "You've lost someone?"

He nods his head sharply. All playfulness from earlier is gone, instead he looks moments away from crying- and something about that makes me want to hug him. *I recognize my own pain in you.*

I don't know why I hadn't seen it before, but it's so clear in the way he carries himself wearing his pain like armor, whereas I tended to stuff mine down- pretending it didn't exist.

"My Mom." His voice cracks on the word *Mom* like it breaks him to even utter the word. That's all it takes for me to latch onto him. I pull him against me, feeling his shoulders shudder against me. I burry my face against his neck, and he does the same to me.

"I lost my mom too." I whisper, ripping open the scar I'd buried for him to see.

His hand rests on my lower back, and this moment that passes between us feels like we're communicating our pain, our trauma into this one hug. He stands up and wipes a stray tear from my cheek, one that I didn't even realize I'd shed.

"Skye?" His green eyes blaze down at me as he cups my cheek, his thumb rubbing against my skin gently.

"Oh, my fucking God, Skye, please tell me the heat is working in here." Salem says bursting in through the back door, her hair and clothes are drenched. I break away from Lukas, going to the mud room to grab a bunch of towels to throw at Salem. I notice she's missing the poncho Javelynn had given to each of us.

"What happened? I've been trying to call you, but the service is knocked out." I say dumping the towels in Salem's arms. I catch Lukas' amused look before he leaves the two of us, I assume he's heading to our shared room. Fuck. I'll have to deal with that later.

Salem wraps a towel around her shoulders and uses another one to wring out the moisture in her hair.

"We need alcohol for this conversation."

"Tequila or Whiskey?"

"Both. Trust me."

I grab two bottles and two cups, trailing Salem up to her tower room. "Okay, what happened?" I ask plopping down on her bed. It's suspiciously warmer than I remember it being before.

"Drinks first." I pour us each a drink. I picked the whiskey because it feels like she's about to spill something serious. I hand her the cup and she tilts it into her mouth in one quick shot.

"Goddamn." She coughs. "Another." I diligently pour her another one and watch as she downs that one too.

"Okay, spill Salem." I feel a sense of unease. I've never seen her so worked up before. We haven't been friends long, but still she wasn't even this worked up after our room burned down.

"This is going to sound crazy. I mean maybe I am crazy. Maybe I'm just imagining things." She lets out a laugh that sounds devoid of any humor. "Okay, have you ever had like this... sixth sense before? Like you knew what was going to happen before it happened?"

"Um... not that I can really think of offhand." Her shoulders crumple a bit at my response. "I mean, maybe? I'm not sure." She covers her face in her hands and lets out a groan.

"Wait. Why is it so warm in here?" She stands up letting the towels fall off of her as she looks around the cramped room. When she crouches down, she shrieks. "A space heater? Who the hell...? Skye?"

"Nope, not me." I sip at my whiskey, letting it burn my throat and coat my stomach. There's been too many emotions pelting at me tonight and I want to feel the sweet nothings that alcohol gives me.

She sits up on her heels staring at it for a moment. She shakes her head. "I don't have the emotional capacity to deal with this right now."

She stands up, swaying a little, those two shots hitting her fast and hard. A knock comes from her door, and we look at each other wondering who it could be. She goes to open the door and an incredibly wet Pierce is standing on the other side. He's leaning against the doorframe, wracking his eyes over Salem like he's ready to devour her whole, water dripping from his hair. I swear being in the vicinity of these two feels like I'm about to witness a spontaneous combustion.

"Um, I'm going to head out." I say pushing myself off of the bed.

"No, Skye. Stay." Salem implores, not taking her gaze off of Pierce. He frowns, his jaw ticking with irritation. "Did you need something, Pierce?"

"I thought we could finish our conversation from earlier." He grumbles, clearly frustrated and I'm feeling all kinds of uncomfortable wishing I could vacate the room so they could work out whatever is going on between them.

"I can go if you want?" This small room is feeling immensely smaller by the second.

"Stay-Go." Pierce and Salem say at the same time.

His green eyes that are a shade lighter than Lukas' flash with anger before he puffs out a frustrated sigh. "Fine. We'll talk later." He runs down the winding staircase, his steps pounding all the way down.

"Okay. Spill it."

Salem groans, sinking down the wall she's leaned up against, then sprawls her legs out.

"I kissed Pierce tonight and I'm pretty sure if we hadn't gotten interrupted there might have been *more*."

"Yeah, I'm going to need more alcohol." I top off my drink and sit on her bed. This red comforter on here was so freaking comfortable.

She laughs. "That's not even the crazy part."

"What do you mean?"

She chews on a stray cuticle. "Okay. I could be completely out of my mind, Skye, so promise me what I say doesn't leave this room."

"I swear." She levels a serious glare my way that makes me feel like I'm a toddler in trouble. "I swear, Salem." I say again. I would never betray her trust.

"When we were at the game, I felt like... I don't know, like I knew that something bad was going to happen before it did."

"How do you mean?"

"I can't really explain it, but before that first lightning strike hit the ground, I got the oddest sensation that danger was approaching."

"That's not sooo weird. I've heard of people experiencing that before."

"Right, but when the second one was about to hit, after you, Javelynn and I were separated, it happened again. I found myself leaping over the fence to get to Pierce, and then... Fuck."

I hand her another drink because whatever she's about to tell me has her unsettled, no unsettled is too kind of a word, she seems freaked out and scared.

"I... Skye. I think I might have been able to direct the bolt of lightning away from Pierce."

I shake my head no. "That's impossible. It probably just ricocheted or something."

She scrambles up on to her knees, her eyes wide. "Skye, I don't know how else to explain it, but I felt this tug from in here and I raised my arm like this and threw it. I felt it latch onto me before I threw it."

I stare at her, mouth agape. "I don't know what to say."

"I don't know what to think!" She cries. "And then the stuff with Pierce in the hallway, I'm such a mess. Out of all the people, why am I drawn to that one."

"Something about those Ledger boys."

Salem assesses me, and even with three shots down her throat she's too sharp to miss my meaning.

"Lukas?"

I nod filling her in on what transpired earlier and even what I'd seen in the art room.

"Pierced? As in like a Jacob's Ladder?"

"I don't know what it's called!" I cry, feeling immediately embarrassed confessing my darkest fantasies aloud. I can't help that I'm curious about what it would feel like to have him inside of me, his piercings rubbing up and down as he fucked me.

"You're too much of a good girl sometimes, Skye! You should be down there in your room right now finding out how great that would feel."

"No way. I'm here with you. You needed me."

"You know, I think you might be my first real friend." She says, her eye shining with sleep.

I get off the bed and grab her by her wrists, hauling her up. She stumbles into me. "Come on, time for bed." She lets me lead her to her bed. "You're my first real friend too." I say as she snuggles down into the blanket. I make sure she's propped the right way, just in case she had too much alcohol and tie her hair back. As I finish the final swoop through the hair tie, she grabs my wrist.

"Promise you won't say anything?" My heart breaks that she even feels the need to ask.

"Promise."

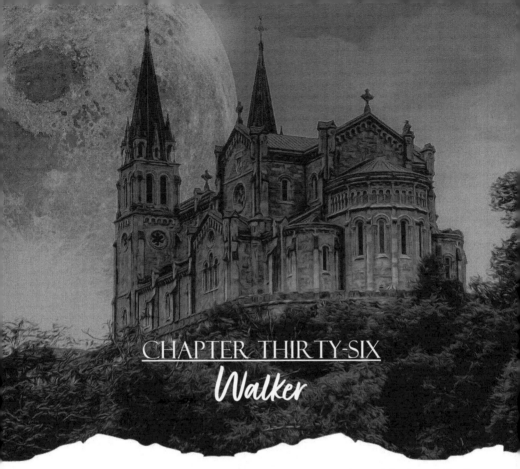

CHAPTER THIRTY-SIX
Walker

Diablos is hosting a Battle of the Bands night and I've yet to find a replacement for my singer. I take out my frustrations by beating the absolute shit out of my punching bag jabbing it with my bare fists. Yeah, it's fucking stupid seeing as I play guitar with these hands, but nothing else will quell this rage inside of me. Nothing that I want to do anyways. The guilt eats at me enough when someone has been on the receiving end of my Wrath.

Sweat drips off my nose. I swing my arms in a quick one-two jab over and over again until I'm drenched and shaking. I grip the bag for stability, my head resting on the leather exterior. Fuck. What are we going to do? A bunch of local bands from nearby islands and Seattle were coming into town to preform and my band had been practicing all summer. We were ready- that was until Helena up and quit the band after finding out our drummer and her boyfriend, Gary, had cheated on her. And not just a casual kind of cheat, this guy had escorts numbers saved underneath the name Taco Bell in his phone. Who the fuck actually calls Taco Bell? The island didn't even have one. She was gone before we could even vote fucking Gary out, which is what I would have opted for. Fucking stupid ass Gary. The only thing saving him from being tossed out was the fact that he was the only townie who knew how to play drums.

"Knock, knock." Salem's voice calls from the doorway and just like that, my rage is back. Fucking hell, I wasn't in the mood to be around anyone right now. The guys in the house knew better than to be around me while I was like this, you'd think someone would have warned her. I bet she didn't even have a clue to who she'd been unlucky enough to have to live with. It's not every little girl's dream to grow up and move in with a bunch of frat guys and seven demons.

"What do you want, wildcat?" She looks taken aback by my rough greeting, and I hate that. I clench my jaw and flex my aching hands.

"I was wondering if you had thought about the name of the chord yet?" She chews on the bottom of her lip and goddamn, she couldn't look more like a sex kitten if she tried. Her hair is down in loose wavy black curls that look like they're begging to have me run my bloodied-up hands through them. Her big green eyes sparkling with a hint of mischief as she stares me down, not taking any of my bullshit. She steps closer to me, not sensing the danger lurking within me. I'd let myself get carried away with her the other day, but she'd looked so edible I couldn't help myself. And the way she'd responded to my touch? Shit, I'm half hard just thinking about how good she felt against me. It'd been a long ass time since I'd let anyone get close to me. I was constantly toeing the line, keeping this Wrath inside of me in check. I didn't want to accidentally have it go haywire on someone that actually meant something to me, and this girl in front of me had the potential to fit that description.

"And what if I told you, I couldn't remember the name of the chord?"

"I'd call bullshit." She's grinning at me and fuck me if it doesn't do something funny to my insides. I see the red flag but the way she's looking at me, has me ignoring the shit out of it. My favorite color has always been red anyway, I'm like a bull running straight ahead at it. I walk towards her, aware that I should keep my distance but still, I find my feet taking one step in front of the other- almost like a magnet pulling me in.

"Why are you here, really?" My hands ache and not just from punching the shit out of my punching bag. No, they ache because I want to grab onto her and pull her into me. I want to wrap them in her wild hair and pull her lips up to mine. But instead of doing what I want, I shove my hands into the pockets of my gray sweatpants.

"I needed to get away from all the commotion upstairs." Interesting. She didn't like the party preparations.

"Will you be going?"

"I mean... I live here and really don't have much else going on."

"What would you say about coming out with me to Diablos?" I don't realize I've said the words until it's too late. They're already out there, inviting her to be around me more.

She perks up, "For what?"

"They're hosting a Battle of the Bands."

"Get out!" She squeals, and something about it makes me wonder if she'd sound like that in bed.

"My band was supposed to perform, but our singer dropped out last minute."

"Is THAT why you asked if I could sing the other day?"

"You caught me."

She taps her plump lips with her finger. "What if I said that I could sing?"

Hope surges in my chest. "Really?"

"Mmm. But if I do this favor, I want one in return."

"Anything." I breathe out, realizing I mean that. She could probably ask me for the moon and my dumb ass would try and get it for her. Anything to keep her looking at me like that.

She laughs, a dangerous twinkling sparks in her green eyes. "I want you to teach me guitar, all the chords *and* their real names."

"Hmm. I mean I guess, I could do that, but before I agree I want to know if you really have what it takes to sing."

She places her hands on her hips, and damn she looks adorable.

"Give me a song."

"Well, we're preforming *Sex and Candy* the Alexander Jean version. Do you know it?"

She quirks up her mouth into a sexy smirk and starts singing. Holy fucking shit, this girl is ten times better than I could have imagined. She's all smoke and gravel as she belts out the lyrics. She sounds like a 1920's jazz singer made a baby with Janis Joplin and threw in a dash of Adele. It's fucking magic. I'm rapt, unable to move as she hits the notes with practiced ease. Her eyes are closed as she pours her whole heart into the melody, the sound wrapping itself around my chest. We're going to kill it tonight if she agrees to come with. As she comes to the second chorus, I join my voice with hers. Her eyes snap open in surprise, but she doesn't falter for a moment. Our voices meld together in a harmonious crescendo that has my knees weak.

"That was…" she says looking at me like she's seeing me for the first time again.

"…magic." I manage to say, clearing my throat.

Her face falls, and I'm desperate to bring back the smile she'd had just a moment ago. What did I say?

"Right. Well. What time is it at?" Her tone sounds clipped. Flat.

I search her face, wondering what just happened to make her shut down so fast. "Uh, we have to be there by 6 if you're going to perform with us?"

"Okay. Yeah, see you then."

As she leaves the room, I'm left feeling unsettled. I send off a quick text to my band mates, letting them know we're still on for tonight, at least I hoped so. I didn't know much about Salem, but she didn't seem like the type of person to go back on their word.

I stretch out my hands, my knuckles burn. Fuck, I need to ice my hands so I don't cramp up playing tonight.

I allow myself to feel that kernel of happiness. We were playing tonight. A wicked smile splays over my face. We were fucking playing tonight, and we were going to win. I felt it in my bones.

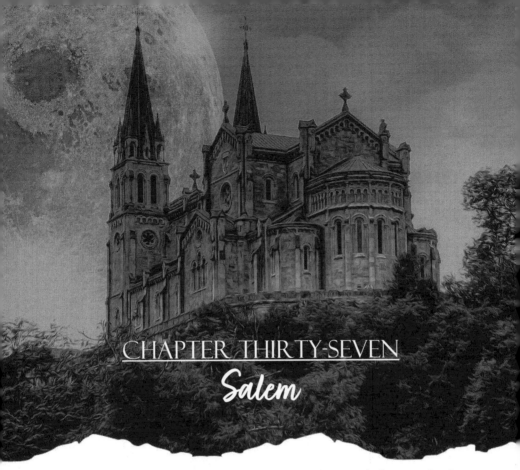

CHAPTER THIRTY-SEVEN
Salem

"How's your head?" Skye asks, her legs curled up under her butt.

"I'm fine. I took a shower and spent some time doing my hair today before everyone else woke up."

"Would that be for a certain twin who came barreling in here yesterday wanting to ravage you?"

"Pfft. No. It's for me. I was feeling shitty and wanted to make myself feel better. It sounds stupid, but I felt like it was something small that I could control while feeling out of control."

"That's not stupid, Salem."

"Anyways, while you were sleeping, I went to visit the basement troll and got invited to sing at Diablos tonight."

"What basement troll?"

"The guy who lives down there, I ran into him yesterday and hadn't had a chance to tell you about him yet. Yesterday was a clusterfuck."

"Are you still feeling... you know, confused about the lightning stuff."

I shift uncomfortably on the bed. "I'm trying not to think about it."

She nods. "So, Diablos?"

"I have to be there at 6, want to come cheer me on?"

"As if you even have to ask. God how is it already early afternoon? I need to get ready, oh and I have an outfit that you can borrow for tonight. It'll look super cute."

Skye leaves me alone, and I fall back down on my bed, staring at the arched ceiling. I had a hard time sleeping, my mind replaying the moment on the football field. It couldn't be... magic. That was preposterous and total grounds for throwing me into a psych ward just like my Aunt Vickie that no one dared talk about. My family was incredibly tight-lipped revolving the circumstances that lead to the loss of my mother's sister. We didn't even have pictures of her up in the house. The only explanation I'd ever received is that she'd 'gone mad' and died shortly after Grandma Clementine and Mom took her to get help. I wondered if whatever happened to her was happening to me now.

I'd gone down to the basement needing to feel something other than fear over what I'd experienced, and I especially wanted to avoid Pierce. I wasn't ready to deal with all the confusing emotions he made me feel, on top of grappling with whatever happened last night. Some trick of the imagination, or maybe I was just tired?

I grab my phone and check my messages, surprise- my mom left my messages unread. I quickly invite Javelynn out for the night then resolve to call Grandma Clementine. I'd put it off long enough and couldn't keep borrowing clothes from Skye and Javelynn.

I press call before I can lose my nerve and steel my nerves against whatever things are going to pop out of her mouth.

"Saaaalem." She coos in my ear. "What took you so long? I haven't heard a peep from you since you started school."

"Hey Grams."

"Now, tell me, why didn't you tell me about this fire? I had to hear about it from the Headmaster, I mean really. How embarrassing to not hear it from my own granddaughter."

"It's been really crazy here with trying to acclimate to the new school and all, um anyways..."

"Now, your cousin Delano always calls to check in, although there were those murmurings that he'd went and got himself a boyfriend."

"Grandma."

"Don't chide me child, I was speaking."

"Okay, yes, but it doesn't matter if Delano has a boyfriend if that's what makes him happy."

I can feel the disappointment radiating straight into the phone. "Salem, I'll never understand you young people."

I let out an exasperated sigh, no matter how many times I tried talking to her about important issues, I was always told to be quiet. That I didn't know the way of the world. She loved to make me feel unimportant and silly for voicing my opinions, especially when it came to the offensive things she frequently said without consequence.

"Grams, have you heard from Mom? I've been trying to text her, and she hasn't paid the latest credit card bill."

"Money? Of course, it's always about money. Not like my children and grandchildren can call to actually call to talk to me."

"Grams?"

"No, I haven't heard from her, but I have the account particulars and can have Marino pay it. Is that all?"

"Um, yes. That would be helpful, thanks. I haven't been able to replace anything I lost in the fire."

"Well, if you'd called me earlier, I would have been able to help you then. Honestly, Salem. Sometimes you're just like your mother."

I let in a sharp breath, "Okay, I have to get going. I have some homework to do. I'll talk to you later." I quickly get out and hang up before she can get more jabs in. God, that was exhausting.

Aware that the conversation was mild compared to how offensive she can get, I breathe a sigh of relief over having handled the credit card situation. I'm in desperate need of some new underwear. I escaped the fire with the ones on my butt and one other pair that didn't go up in flames.

A sharp rapping comes from my door. It must be Skye with the outfit she said I could borrow, I think, but when I open the door, an exhausted looking Pierce is standing on the other side. Shit.

"What's up, Pierce?"

He smirks, "You didn't call me an asshole right off the bat this time, we're making progress."

"Is there something you came here for?"

"Other than you?" He moves towards me, his hands grabbing my hips hard as he pushes me back against the wall, surprising me. I can't say that I hated it, no I felt like I went from existing to being set on fire all in the matter of a moment. His breath hits me, smelling of mint.

"I had a raging hard on all night, Salem. Do you feel this? What you do to me?" He grabs my hand and places it on his erection. I feel it twitch against my palm, begging for me to play with it.

"I've been going out of my mind, needing to feel you." He places a soft kiss on my lips, that contrasts how hard his hands are holding onto me- hard enough to leave a bruise. "Need your lips on mine." Those words are all it takes for me to wrap my hand in his shirt and yank his lips down on mine again, hard. He opens his lips. A smile plays at the corner of his mouth as I dive my tongue in to meet his. He rolls his hips against me, and I snake my fingers up into his hair. I can't help the moan that leaves my mouth, as he finds just the right spot to piston his hips into.

"Lock the door." I manage to say as he kisses his way down my neck. He doesn't waste a moment, flying to the door, making sure it closes with a snick of the lock. He's back on me in an instant, walking me back to my bed. It sinks with our combined weight, the coils groaning as he lays me back, his body flush against mine. God, I need this.

He rips off his shirt, and I immediately run my fingers down taking in all of his muscles. They seem to have a mind of their own with the way my fingers hungerly trace the divots of his defined six pack, taking time to follow the outline of his v. He shivers against my touch. "You're killing me, baby."

"How do you kill someone with no heart?" I say laughing against his mouth. I push down the little flip I felt in my heart at hearing Pierce call me 'baby'.

"Cruel woman. You wound me." He snatches one of my hands and places it on his chest. "Do you feel how hard it's beating for you?" I stare up into his eyes and feel my breath hitch as a riot of butterflies churn low in my stomach. Oh, no. Not feelings.

CHAPTER THIRTY-EIGHT
Pierce

Salem's hand rests on my chest, my heart beating erratically from her touch. I had to take an extra-long cold shower last night after she'd turned me away. I'd never been this worked up over someone before. Girls had always come easy, but Salem was making me work for it.

I dip my nose down and trace her slim neck with the tip, taking in her sweet vanilla scent. "Did you happen to notice it's warmer in here?" I ask, nibbling her dainty ear. It's almost pointed like an elf, making her look like my *Lord of the Rings*, Liv Tyler fantasy come to life.

"That was you?" She shrieks, pushing me up so she can look straight at me. Her sage green eyes bounce back and forth as she roams my face.

"Guilty." I smirk, peppering her body with kisses. I cup her full breasts and tweak her nipples. Goddamn, this girl was undoing me. She wasn't even wearing a bra.

"I don't know if I should find it sweet or creepy that you broke into my room."

"Definitely sweet. I wouldn't risk a felony for just anyone." I bit her nipple through her shirt, making her arch into me.

"Spoken like a man who's familiar with breaking the law." If she only knew.

A loud knock comes from her door. "Nooo." I groan into her cleavage. "I haven't even started with you yet."

"It's Skye with my outfit for tonight."

"For the party? Let's skip it. We can stay here and keep doing this." I peck her lips and roam my hands down her curves.

She bites her lip, looking guilty. "What?"

"Uh, I'm not going to the party." I sit up off of her and grab my shirt. My erection strains against my sweatpants. I'm thankful I'm not wearing something tighter.

"Salem?" Skye's muffled voice calls.

"Just a second." Salem calls back, her fingers comb out her hair that I'd mussed up. "I'm going to Diablos tonight. Walker asked me to sing for the Battle of the Bands."

Fucking, what? "Oh. I didn't know you knew him." I stand up yanking my shirt back on and push my fingers into my hair, as I pace the small room. I'm trying and failing to keep my cool.

She looks at me warily, "Yeah, I just met him."

"You need to be careful around him Salem. The guys got anger issues." She rolls her eyes at me, going to open the door for her friend. I grab her by the arm and turn her towards me. "I mean it Salem. I'm not being an alpha asshole right now. He's been known to fly off the handle."

She fixes me with a cool glare. "I can handle myself."

"It's not that- "

"Hey, are you guys going to open the door? I have to get ready too."

"Sorry, Skye." Salem shrugs out of my grip and opens the door. Skye's holding a slim black dress and I want nothing more than to snatch it away, so she'll have to go in what she's wearing. But shit she still looks hot in whatever she wears.

"This is so cute."

"Right? Totally you." Skye says, twisting the knife right into my chest.

"What time is this Battle of the Bands at?"

Skye and Salem turn to look at me. "I think 7. I have to be there at 6 to warm up with the band."

Fucking Walker and his bad boy rocker catnip ways. "I'll be there."

Skye and Salem exchange a meaningful look that I can't fucking decipher. I feel out of my depth here, not that I would ever admit it. I rub at my chest. Looks like I was going to Diablos tonight.

CHAPTER THIRTY-NINE
Lukas

Skye's fucking intoxicating scent was everywhere. Although she kept her side of the room we shared relatively clean, she still left a mark on where she'd been and it was driving me crazy. I could sense her presence like a ghost intent on haunting me. Tormenting me. I wanted to take that good girl exterior that she exudes and mar her up, just like I did to this house. I wanted to break her open and dirty up her soul to match mine, even though I knew she deserved better- I didn't fucking care. I didn't care because I was more than fine with being selfish. I wanted her for myself. I wanted her sweet cunt dripping all over my cock as she screamed my name.

I saw the way the other guys in the house looked at her, and I wanted to stake my claim on that hot body of hers. Make her beg for me and drive her as crazy as she was driving me. I couldn't stop thinking of how amazing she'd felt pressed up against me as she straddled me on the couch. It filled my mind with all kinds of dark fantasies, and it took everything in me not to wrap my hand around her slim neck and squeeze. I wonder if that good little girl would enjoy something like that. I ached to be the one to find out.

A scrap of red fabric was peeking out from under her bed. I feel my nostrils flare. Was that... was that her underwear? My heart picks up its pace as I stand frozen to my side of the room. I hesitate for a moment, chewing on my bottom lip before striding over and snatching up the pair of red lace panties and shoving them into my pants pocket. Lust surges in my chest so hard that I feel its effects seeping out.

Shit, shit, shit! No! Get back here! I think, but it's too late. I'm rock hard from fingering these red satin panties in my pocket.

"Hey!" Skye says brightly, breezing in like a ray of fucking sunshine. "What are you doing?" She asks, her head tilting to the side as she eyes me on her side of the room. I angle my body away so she doesn't notice how hard I am from thinking of her.

"Uh... I was just, you know..." I gesture and fucking hell, the panties are still in my hand stuck on my fingers and waving in the air like a red flag.

Her mouth drops open with a gasp. "Are those my underwear?" She goes to snatch them, and I move on pure instinct. I raise my arm up and out of her reach.

"No. Oh my God, Lukas. Not again."

"What, you don't like this game? I think it might be my favorite." She shoves me, trying to catch me off balance as she jumps for her underwear. It's so fucking cute it hurts. I laugh at her pitiful attempt, wanting nothing more than for her to get closer to me.

"Come on, those are mine."

"Are you sure? It's my room too. I could totally pull off some silky red panties."

"Those wouldn't even fit an inch of you." She slaps a hand over her mouth, and I let out a barking laugh.

"You dirty girl. You checking out my package during art class?" She moves to tickle at my armpit, wrenching a sound from my mouth that sounds like a tortured emu. Oh, it is on. I wrap my free arm around her middle and hoist her up easily, maneuvering her away from my outstretched arm.

"I… it was right there." I almost drop her. She *looked* and that knowledge fills me with a smug satisfaction. I wonder if she's thought about it while she lays in the bed next to me. I wonder if she wants to lick around my piercings, and the thought makes my already hard dick twitch.

"You *did* look." She covers her face with her hands, and I plop her down onto her bed, lowering my hand behind my back, making sure my grip on the panties is tight.

"It was hard not to!" She removes her hands, and her face is bright red as she stares up at me from the edge of her bed. I love that I can rattle her, and it makes me want to keep pushing at her to see what kind of reaction I can get out of her.

I see the moment before she tries to strike, her delicate paint covered fingers twitch right as she lunges for my hand. I move easily, swatting her arm. She's dangerously close to my hard on and I'm desperate for her to pay it attention.

"You'll have to do better than that." I taunt, the gleam in her eyes giving away how much she's enjoying this. Fuck, I just want to shove her down on top of me, those big baby blue eyes looking up at me as I ram my cock to the back of her throat over and over again, until tears were staining her rosy cheeks.

"Fine. Keep them." She says standing to her full height, her eyebrow arches in a dare as she stares me down. If she were to take a centimeter of a step closer, she'd feel me poking her straight into her belly. I look down at her full bottom lip, wishing I could sink my teeth into it.

"What did you think of it, Skye?"

"Wh-what?" I close the distance between our bodies. She sucks in a breath, her gaze not leaving my face. I lean down and pull her against me. I'm about to press my mouth against hers, when I feel her yank the panties out of my hand. She shoves me hard in the chest, a look of triumph crosses her features as she sashays out of the room, red panties in hand.

"Better luck next time." She waves her paint covered fingers at me as she leaves the room, leaving me hard and frustrated. Rooming with Skye was going to be the death of me.

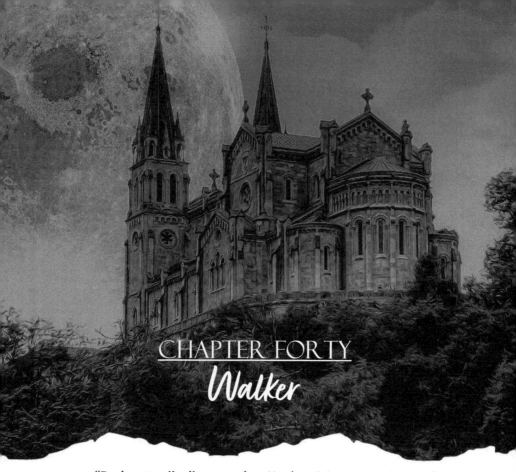

CHAPTER FORTY
Walker

"**Dude, stop jiggling your leg.** You're giving me anxiety and you know I have to be fuckin' zen before a show." I shoot Gary a look. Fucking Gary is the whole reason we're in this mess. He's too zen, maybe he needs a dash of anxiety after everything he did.

"She'll show." Damien, our bass player says. He's cradling his bass, the instrument slung low across his middle. Gary pretends to be the zen one, but in reality, it's Damien. He exudes a natural 'I don't give a fuck' energy. That all goes to hell the moment he gets on stage and shreds the shit out of those strings.

The bar is filling with a few bands, all exuding nervous energy readying their instruments for the upcoming show. A few regulars are spread out, downing their beers and ignoring the people filling up the room. I palm my guitar pick out of my pocket and roll it between my fingers, transferring some of this pent-up energy into it.

"Are you sure she can sing?" Gary asks.

I fix him with another glare. "Yes, she can sing." Salem's voice cuts through the conversations happening around us. I turn to take her in and am practically knocked sideways with how hot she looks. Her raven hair is down and curled like earlier, and she's wearing a tight-fitting black dress that looks like it's painted on her body. I fight the urge to grab her to me and claim her with my lips, but I feel the urge linger percolating under my skin. I see my band mates are equally as floored by her as I feel. Gary stumbles over himself extending a sweaty hand to her. She grips it and tries to hide her grimace unsuccessfully as he vigorously pumps their hands up and down.

"I'm Gary. Drums." He attempts a smolder.

"Which one is the cheater?" She asks me. I point straight at Gary. She casually flicks her gaze over him from top to bottom and back up again, removing her hand from his and wiping the sweat off against her dress.

Gary immediately looks sulky and put out. "Come on man, you told her?"

"Was it a secret?"

"That kind of shit is private, no need to ruin my chances over it." He sits back down looking dejected.

"Your reputation is your own to make with your actions." Salem says. "Salem." She says moving over to Damien. He swallows hard, and grabs her hand, planting a kiss on her knuckles.

"Damien" he growls, looking at her like his next meal. I narrow my eyes at him, grabbing Salem by her hip and yanking her backwards. She turns around to face me, my hand still lingering on her hip.

"I see we're feeling a little caveman tonight." She pulls away and I miss the feel of her immediately. "So, we doing this thing?"

"This thing, is something we've been working on for weeks." Gary snips.

She stands ramrod straight, towering over him on her heels as she peers down her cute as a button nose at him, hands on hips. "It's my understanding that you need me to even go on tonight, so maybe cut the attitude."

Fuck this girl was a firecracker and I fucking loved it. "How many acts are there tonight?" She asks me.

"Ten. We're going on third." She lets out a shaky breath. "You nervous?" I ask, aching to bring her closer to me.

"Yeah, I don't really sing in public. Ever." I tuck a stray hair behind her ear.

"You'll be great. Once the lights hit you, it's like the crowd isn't even there. Just pretend it's you and me, like earlier. You blew me away."

She lights up at my praise, and sports two bright red circles staining her porcelain cheeks.

"Hey Salem." A tall curvy blonde calls out, I see my band mate's attention snap to her direction. She's beautiful in that good girl kind of way. Good, maybe they'd leave Salem alone.

"Skye! This is Walker, the basement troll. And this is Gary the cheater and Damien the hand kisser."

The blonde known as Skye assess us.

"Basement troll?" I ask leaning down to her ear.

She arches her dark eyebrow, readying to answer when she stops. I follow her line of sight and see Pierce Ledger with his fists clenched at his sides staring at us. I feel my Wrath rise in my chest, readying for a fight, but the sensation is quickly doused when I feel Salem's slim hand press directly over my heart.

He shakes his head and heads off to the bar.

"Something I should know about?" Pierce would rather be five drinks deep at the frat party then at a place like this, and the way he looked at Salem as if he had a right to has the bitter taste of jealousy swirling in my mouth.

She shakes her head back and forth, her curls bouncing. "Nothing official."

I mull over what that could mean in my head. "Come on, let's get warmed up." She lets me lead her away by the crook of her elbow. I glance back meeting Pierce's stare before he slings back a beer, not lifting his gaze from where I'm touching Salem. I frown, wondering what his problem is. Salem squeezes my hand bringing me back. This moment right here could be the one that changes the trajectory of my music career, making all my aspirations of putting out my own music a reality. No pressure.

CHAPTER FORTY-ONE
Salem

My tongue feels like sandpaper inside of my mouth. Seriously, where did all the moisture go? I find a pop machine in a dimly lit corner of the bar situated off to the side of the stage. The first act has finished their set, and my body is shaking with nerves. We were able to run through the song a few times, finding our rhythm together before the Battle of the Bands started. The place is packed, making me sweat.

I feed the machine my card with a shaky hand, only to have it spit it back out with an error message. "Goddammit." I say kicking the machine with my borrowed heels that are a half size too small. That decision is going to haunt me later, I can already feel the beginnings of a blister starting to form on my heel. I lean my forehead against the cool plastic. What was I doing here?

A familiar scent hits me as Pierce crowds me from behind, feeding the machine a crisp dollar. I turn and am struck stupid by him. Why did he have to be this good looking? I'd been keeping myself busy all day, avoiding any thought of what happened to me last night at the football game and every time I saw Pierce, brought me right back to that moment of insanity. That's what it had to be. I'd heard of college students succumbing to the pressures of campus life and I had just survived escaping a fire. Maybe my brain was catching up to the trauma.

"Which one?" He asks with his stupid smirk gesturing at the options on the pop machine. I fought the urge to kiss it right off his handsome face.

"Water." He presses the button on the bottom, scooping out the bottle out as the machine spit it out of the slot. "Thanks."

"Oh, you want this?" He holds the water. I'm too weary and amped up with nerves to play this game. I sigh, turning on my heel only to have him catch me by the crook of my elbow.

"Wait, Salem. Here, I was just kidding." I snatch the water, breaking the seal and drink a few gulps, coating my parched tongue. He watches me, a nervous energy clinging to him, but I meant what I said to Walker. Pierce and I weren't anything official, and while I felt drawn to him, he was a walking red flag- a disaster in the making. We'd exchanged a few heated moments and here he was acting like a jealous boyfriend. I didn't know what to make of that.

"Salem?"

"I have to go on."

"Knock 'em dead." He rubs his hand down my bare arm sending my stomach into even more of a fit of nerves than I'd been feeling. Great.

"Salem?" Walker's deep gravel full voices calls over to me. "You ready?" His eyes bounce between Pierce and I. I walk over to where he's waiting.

"Yep. Let's do this." I give him a smile that I hope masks how scared I'm truly feeling. Walker places both hands square on my shoulders looking me straight in the eyes. "You've got this. You're going to bring this place to their fucking knees, wildcat." He manages to take my nervousness down a few notches that is until I feel Pierce's gaze following me with every step I take up to the stage.

The crowd erupts into applause at our appearance. We're only the third act, so most are relatively sober still. My body shakes with anticipation. I'm really doing this. My knees wobble as I put one heel in front of the other, blinking hard against the blinding spotlights. Pierce elbows his way to the front, and I swallow thickly as he stares up at me, hands pushed deep in his jacket pocket, his jaw clenched. I place a hand over my eyes shadowing them from the unforgiving lights. I scan the crowd and spot Skye standing next to Javelynn who's looking up over at Jackson. He gives Javelynn a shy smile, which brings one to my own lips. Go Javelynn.

I drop my hand and catch Walker striding up to one of the mics out of my periphery. Damien and Gary also take their places easily like this is just another day for them. Walker speaks into the mic, "Thanks for having us Possession Bay! We're the Hateful Hydras with special guest Salem Knox." Hearing my name boom from the speakers makes my heart drop to my toes. *Oh shit.*

I look around frantically, maybe I can get out of here. Walker has a great voice. They don't need me.

A low note plays across the speakers, and I know it's too late. Walker arches his scarred eyebrow at me, nodding his head in reassurance. Fuck me, I grab the microphone, my freshly polished black nails gleam at me and my heart hammers so hard in my ears that I miss my cue. I lick my lips and see Pierce smirking at me. I narrow my eyes and give the signal to go again. This time, I nail my cue and let the lyrics fly. The crowd goes silent as Walker, Damien and Gary build the song behind me, weaving the melody around my voice. I lose myself, pouring every ounce of pent-up emotion into the song. Walker joins me, and it's just as magical as when we sang together earlier, only now there's witnesses to our harmony. Our voices blend easily and then he's right there, singing next to me into my microphone. He's so close that I can smell the sweat coming off of him, he looks so good as he works his fingers down the neck of the guitar, gifting the song an impromptu guitar solo that rivals the genius of Jimi Hendrix. The crowd goes absolutely wild, jumping up and down and screaming so loud I can hardly hear when I'm supposed to sing again. But I make it, finishing in time with Walker. The air turns positively electric between us. I find myself pulled to him unable to look away from him as we sing the suggestive lyrics.

As the song ends, I throw my arms around Walker's slick neck and beam up at him. "You did it." He says looking at me with awe.

"We did it." My breath is coming in hard, my adrenaline coursing through my veins making me feel giddy. We make our way off the stage, and I'm met with the screams of Skye and Javelynn.

"Oh my God, girl! I didn't know you could sing like *that!*"

"I'm sorry I doubted you girlie." Gary says, and I can tell he means it.

"Thanks." I'm grinning from ear to ear, that is until I spot the back of Pierce leaving the bar in a hurry.

I feel a low tug in my gut to go after him, but then decide no. Fuck him, I'm not letting him and his mood ruin this for me.

"Let's go celebrate!" Javelynn says grabbing us away from the bottom of the stage so the next group can preform. I latch my hand onto Walker's forearm and pull him with us. He follows without resistance. I catch him grinning back at me with the same joy I'm feeling.

When we get to the bar, he pulls me to him in another hug. "That was fucking epic, wildcat."

"I can't believe I did that."

"I can."

I can't help it. I wind my fingers through his hair. "Thank you."

"Babe, I should be thanking you. We might have a chance at winning this thing because of you."

"I forgot to ask, what's the prize for winning?"

"$5,000 and some recording equipment. It would be a total game changer for us."

I frown, thinking of the school we go to, the privilege it's dripping with. "My family doesn't support my 'bad habits' as they call it.

I have to make my own way for the things I want." He's still holding me against him, and I can feel each ridge of his muscles. He moves my hair, baring my neck. His breath tickling my skin as the faintest press of his lips linger on my skin.

"Here!" Skye says handing me a beer. I break away from Walker's embrace a jumble of emotions.

"How did you get this?"

"Javelynn has their ways." I tip my beer bottle, clinking it against Skye's.

"To an amazing performance and even better night!" She says before we both drink.

"To an even better night!"

CHAPTER FORTY-TWO
Emmet

"And no one else has seen this video?" Headmaster Hayden asks, his face flickering with the light of the fireplace's flames.

"No one. I've searched the internet and school servers to see if anyone's even mentioned it. It seems that people were too busy fleeing the area." The guys at the house are too busy throwing a party or attending the Battle of the Bands to notice I've slipped out for this meeting.

He presses play again, watching as Salem lifts her hand to the sky, stopping the lightning bolt midair, before directing it away from Pierce's fallen form.

"Incredible." The headmaster murmurs. "She must have been hiding her powers all this time. You haven't seen any mention of magic in her messages? Her internet searches."

"Not a word. Are we sure she knows?"

"How could she not?" He scoffs angrily. "Look how she walks with purpose like she knows exactly what she's doing. No, she knows. Now to get her on our side. It's time you come out of shadows with her, Envy. I don't trust Pierce's head is clear enough for this, especially after those pictures you showed me of them kissing in the hall after this. Pity." He tsks. "Can I trust that you'll see this to completion? The clock is ticking."

"I know what's at stake. You can count on me, sir."

"This body is becoming uncomfortable." He complains, rubbing over his knobby gnarled knuckles.

I take a sip of whiskey letting the burn work its way down into my chest.

"How much do you think she knows?" I ask.

"Hard to tell just by this video, which is why I need you to feel her out. It's unlikely that she knows who any of you truly are. What you harbor inside of you. What's the status of Emmet's father? Were you able to get your hands on the signal blocker?"

"He's been busy. He's supposed to come down in a week to take me out to dinner in Seattle to discuss the business. I can ask him then."

"Good."

We sit in silence, on each side of the burning fire. Everything was coming into place. Now, all we needed was to get Salem on our side. Get her to open the portal no questions asked. Then I could be free to remain in this form forever. If I failed, we'd all be ripped back into purgatory. That was something the others weren't aware of. When Pierce made his deal with the headmaster, he wasn't told our fate would result in freeing all seven of us from our demons should we fail. The headmaster was aware of how much the others resented him and the demons they'd been saddled with, he was no fool. And neither was I.

They'd have to drag me back to that hell hole, and I wasn't going without a fight. I'd play as dirty and dark as I had to, to get what I wanted.

CHAPTER FORTY-THREE
Walker

I'm on fucking cloud nine with this wildcat swaying to the music in front of me. We stay to listen to the other bands performances. None hold a candle to our set, I'm sure of it. But we won't know the judge's decision until tomorrow. I'm feeling the buzz of alcohol coursing through my veins. I usually don't indulge, careful to keep a tight leash on the Wrath inside of me, but all it took was a beaming smile from the beauty in my arms to make me break. I cap my drink limit at two beers, enjoying the feeling of my hands holding Salem's lush hips. She has the body of a witchy vixen, and I ache to bend her to my will. I wonder what she'd feel like wrapped around my cock. The body part in question, likes the direction of my thinking and stirs to life against Salem's full ass. I can tell the moment she feels me, her swaying halts for a moment before she arches into it, making me release a groan.

Shit. I'm rock hard in a sea of people. She rolls her hips on me, and it takes everything inside of me not to bend her over and take her right here. I notice a few guys eyeing her with interest. I shoot them my best 'fuck off' glare, wrapping my arms around her front as she grinds on me to the rhythm of the music. I never want this song to fucking end. I lean into her whole heartedly, running my hands up and down her sides, hitting the swell of her breasts.

"Let's get out of here." I whisper against her ear. She nods, grabbing my arm.

"Skye! Javelynn! It's getting hot in here." They stop dancing and I spot Graham behind Skye.

"Hey." I tilt my chin up at our house's temperamental chef. He could throw around as much attitude as he wanted for the type of meals he created. Fuck, if he turned into Gordon Ramsey himself, I'm sure we'd all just eat in gratitude. He returns the gesture of the chin tilt and drinks from his beer, still dancing against Skye.

"We're going to head out." Salem tells her friends, waving goodbye as she drags me through the crowd. I grab my jacket deciding to come back for my equipment later. I know the owner will keep it safe. As soon as we're outside, we're hit with a cool wind that smells like sea. The air does nothing to quell this fiery need that's blazing inside me with one thought in mind. I want to take Salem back to my room and make her mine, but then I remember that stupid fucking party.

I slip my hand into Salem's amazed at how well it fits and pull her towards the docks with the intention of taking her for a walk.

"I don't want to go back just yet." She falls into step next to me, with a wince.

"What's the matter?"

"It's just… these shoes are a little tight. I lost most of my things in the fire and I've been borrowing clothes from Skye and Javelynn to make sure I'm not walking around campus naked."

"That would be a travesty. Well, Bambi, how do you feel about riding on the back of my motorcycle?"

Her whole face lights up. "I parked over here."

"Wildcat, and now Bambi?"

"You're walking like a newborn deer." She rolls her eyes then lets out a gasp as she spots my bike.

"How have I not seen this?" She runs her fingers over the sleek exterior.

"You like it?" A smile plays at the corner of her lips. I hand her my helmet and watch as she locks it beneath her chin. "Damn, that looks good on you. Put this on too." I hold my jacket out for her to slip her arms through. It dwarves her, but looks so fucking hot on her voluptuous frame.

I hike my leg and straddle my bike. "Hop on."

She looks down at her dress contemplating, before she says, "Fuck it." She sits herself behind me, her dress riding up her thighs as she buries herself into my back, her slim hands wrap around my middle. I reach behind me, placing my hand on her thigh.

"Hold on tight, wildcat." I bring the engine to life, the vibrations working through my body and hers. I feel her clench her thighs tightly as I peel out of the parking lot.

The wind whips at my face as I take the road into town. We pass the rival bar, that's not as busy as Diablo's. There are several stores dotting what's considered the downtown. All closed at this time of night. The gas station and a few restaurants are still open, the lights looking fuzzy in the mild fog.

The sound of my motorcycle eats up the quiet with a steady rumble. It's a relatively small island with a road that wraps around the entirety, and I decide to follow it. We dip into the dense forest, passing the scattered dwellings of the locals. This view during a clear day is beautiful, but at night there's a sense of danger, and knowing what I do about what lies in a cave not far off I'd say that's an accurate assessment. I mean the town is literally named Possession, as are the beaches and caves around here. I was just too stupid to see it for what it was, following along with what my family wanted for me.

I take the turns up and around the hills easily with Salem gripping me tightly. We pass through the school gates, the lights still on in a bunch of the dorms and the library.

When I pull into the house's gravel road, I take care to keep the bike steady. I pull off to the small stable that serves as a carport and park the bike.

She grips me for a moment longer, lingering and it shoots a dart of desire down to my cock.

Salem gets off the bike and removes the helmet, her hair falling around her face with a hint of static. I tuck her hair behind her ear and her eyes lock onto mine. They're filled with the same heat that I feel coursing through my veins. Fuck.

"I didn't even notice this was over here." She says gesturing at the crude building around us. It'd been gutted for those of us who had transportation on the island. Mostly people walked everywhere, but it was convenient for when you wanted to take the ferry down to Seattle or another island nearby. I can hear that the party is still in full swing. I grab onto Salem's hand, and she rests her head on my arm, her legs still wobbly.

"Need me to carry you?"

"Nah, I can manage." She says. I spin her into me as we lean against my bike, my hands digging into her hips.

"I had fun tonight."

She bites her lip, pressing her body into mine. Her legs are slightly parted, making room for mine to sit directly between them. I move my hands down cupping her full ass, pressing her into me where I want most. I shove down my worries and focus on this. Us. Her. The way she feels against me.

"Walker." Her lips part, and I don't hesitate. I lean down, taking those luscious lips with mine. I groan into her mouth as she weaves her fingers up into my wind-blown hair. She breaks the kiss and gives me the widest smile that hits me right in the stomach.

I tuck her against my side, my fingers weaving into hers as we walk up the path to the house. It's there that I spot Pierce and Lukas sitting on the steps both with a drink in their hands.

I feel my body tense, my Wrath gathering in my chest readying for whatever bullshit Pierce is going to pull. He's a stupid drunk, and by the looks of him, he's ready to tear off someone's head.

"Hey, Pierce." Salem says, trying to get past. He sneers at our entwined hands.

Salem grips my hand tighter at his assessment.

"So, this is how it is?" He spits out, his words sounding like they're laced with pure venom.

Lukas sits back looking between his twin and us.

"It isn't like *anything,* Pierce. Why are you mad at me right now, Ledger?"

"You've got to be fucking kidding me." He stands with a slight sway.

"I'm not doing this with you when you're clearly intoxicated." She goes to move around him, her hand still digging into mine while I fight the urge to punch Pierce straight in the face for making her upset.

"Let me pass. I'm tired."

"What so you can go to his bed, and let him fuck you the way I want to?" Rage claws up my throat. Fuck this guy. It's then that she lets go of my hand and I feel like I've been punched in the chest. They clearly have something going on, something I don't want to get in the middle of, despite how amazing I feel being around Salem. She deserves better than me anyways. I should have never indulged myself or fed the hope I'd felt blooming from her attention.

"I'll see you later." I say going up around the other side of Lukas. He lets me by still watching Pierce warily.

This is not how I pictured the evening going. I'd wanted her in my bed, screaming my name and marking up my back with those nails of hers. I let out a sigh of frustration, edging my body through the same crowd of people that keeps coming over for the frat's parties.

When I'm finally tucked away downstairs, my roommate, Sloan, nowhere to be found as usual, I swipe open my phone and stare down at a picture Gary sent me. It's Salem and I locked in an adoring stare off, singing together. I'd never experienced anything like that in all my years of making music. It was fucking magic. Her and I fit in a way that had me regretting my decision to leave her up there with Pierce. I didn't do messy. I didn't do people, period. I kept mostly to myself, and a few select people, but she's somehow wormed her way in within the span of two days. There was chemistry there. A spark of something that had me giving her a glimpse of myself that I'd tucked away for a long time. And damn did I like her bringing it out in me. It felt like I could breathe again. But I'd walked away.

She let go of your hand.

I push the thought away. I wasn't stupid. I saw the way Pierce was losing his mind over her, which is something he never does. He has a string of women at his disposal, and the fact that he'd shown up at the bar for her instead of partying like he usually would speaks volumes. But was it really even fair for Salem to get involved with any of us in the house while we were chained to these fucking sins?

I stare at the picture again, tracing Salems face with the pad of my finger. Pierce might want Salem, but there was no denying the way Salem had looked at *me.*

I throw down my phone, frustrated and pent up with desire. I decide to take a few swings at my punching bag, despite the soreness I feel from going so hard at it earlier. I'm afraid of what I'll become if I don't release some of this energy. I pound into the bag with my bruised-up knuckles until fatigue sets in.

I collapse into my bed and am asleep before I can even get under the covers.

A sudden scream wakes me from my dreamless sleep and has me falling out of my bed. *What the fuck?*

I blink my eyes trying to see, but the room around me is shrouded in darkness. The scream pierces my eardrums again and I'm scrambling off the floor, knees burning. I feel my Wrath whir to life, ready to attack. The scream sounded like it was coming from right outside my door. I yank open the door, my hand slipping with sweat and glance around the corridor. The lights flicker with a low buzzing. I rub my hand across my eyes as I stumble towards the stairs.

"I can't. I won't!" The voice yells from behind me. I whip myself around and head in the direction of the voice.

"Salem?" She doesn't answer me. I see her outline near the entrance to the storage room that no one uses. She appears to be alone- her body shakes almost violently.

"Salem? Salem, are you okay?" I wrap my arms around her as her eyes flutter behind her lids. Her skin is ice cold, I tuck her against me caressing her hair. "Hey. It's okay, I've got you."

She lets out a loud gasp, then crumples against me with a shriek.

"Salem? Babe? I pull her back to look her in the eyes, her knees weak and wobbling as I hold her steady. 'I'm right here, you're okay." Her jade green eyes latch onto mine just as the lights stop flickering.

"It was just a dream, you're alright."

She shakes her head back and forth, clinging to my black t-shirt. "I've got you." I soothe, desperate to battle away her fears.

"They were everywhere. Walker-I... it felt so real."

"Why don't you come with me, you can tell me about it. Can you walk?"

She nods her head, finding her strength while she lets out a sharp breath. I take her hand in mine, noting her thin cami and boyfriend fit black underwear that she's wearing. No wonder why she's cold. She follows me into my room and curls up in the chair facing my bed.

"You can have my blanket if you want." I offer, gathering the heavy comforter from my bed. I hand her the rolled-up bundle to which she takes gratefully, dripping it around herself like she's a Sith Lord. "Do you want me to get you anything? Water?" She reaches out for my wrist and shakes her head.

"Please, don't leave me right now."

I sit across from her and hold onto her hand, letting her wrap her frigid fingers around my warm ones.

"I'm not going anywhere. Do you want to talk about it?"

She hesitates, her eyes looking unfocused as she decides. I squeeze her hands, letting her know I'm there and that's all it takes for her to snap back, clear and focused.

"I've had nightmares for as long as I can remember, but I've never woken up somewhere other than my bed until tonight. The night of the fire, I was having another episode. I woke up screaming like... like someone shook me awake. They've gotten more intense since I've arrived here."

I run my thumbs across the backs of her hands. "I know that stress can trigger them, and I'm sure that's probably what it is." She says dismissively. But, her haunted look, the screams that tore at her throat plague my mind. "I'm- I'm so embarrassed. Thank you for this."

"Salem, it's fine."

"I just need a moment and I'll be out of your hair."

"You don't need to leave. You can stay here, if you want. I can take Sloan's bed, he's never here anyway."

"Where is he, I never see him around."

"He stays up in the game room. He tends to pass out on the couch up there."

"I don't want to kick you out of your bed."

I smile, pulling her over to me, tucking her close to my body. "If you insist."

She lets herself smile a soft, tired flickering of a smile. I boop her on her button nose.

"Let's get you some sleep." She lays back, tucked in tight under my blanket. I lay next to her and smooth her hair down, looking in her heavy-lidded gaze. Her warm vanilla scent hits me as she snuggles in close.

"Thank you, Walker."

I kiss her on her forehead. "Anytime, wildcat."

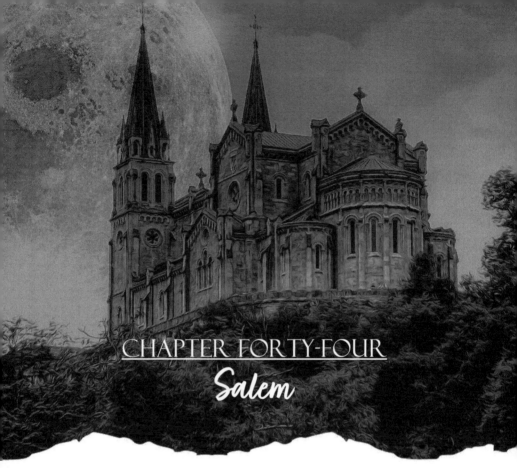

CHAPTER FORTY-FOUR
Salem

I wake, weighed down. The scent of leather and cedar surround me. *Where am I?* My eyes feel heavy with sleep, but I know that is not my ceiling. I turn my head and take in Walker's sleeping form. His arm thrown across my middle.

The nightmare slams into me, reminding me how I woke trembling in Walker's grip. His hands holding me up, while my knees buckled beneath me.

It's different this time. I'm in the house. Hell House. The remnants of a party are scattered around me. I walk through the empty room and it's eerily quiet. I follow the urging sensation to go to the basement, passing the carved cherubs on the stairs who's features look animated, almost like they're talking to each other.

"They're waiting for you." A distant voice says.

"Who?" I ask. My voice sounding far away and strangled.

"Come."

My legs carry me over strewn sleeping bodies. I'm careful to not wake them, stepping carefully as my weight creaks against the wooden boards. I come to the precipice of the stairs, my body stalls, wanting to stay up here, where it's warm. Safe.

"Come." The voice urges and I can't help but obey.

My bare feet slap against the steep stairs that lead to the basement. I pass Walker's door and I ache to go inside to the musician that makes me feel seen. But, in this dream I can't do anything but follow this distance voice.

I come to a doorway and that's when the illusion fades away and I'm standing in a cave looking at a wall of broken up rock. There's a large split in the wall, black and writhing with bodies. Or what used to be bodies.

One reaches for me, scratching me on my forearm. I let out a scream and try to double back but my feet are rooted to the spot. What I thought was broken rock turns out to be a wall of skulls embedded into the rock. Some missing jaw bones. Some cracked down the middle. Up and up and up they sit, glaring at me with their missing eye sockets.

"Help us, Salem." A few of the voices scream. Their demonic faces writhe against the opening.

"Salem, they need you. Put your hand on the opening."

"No! I can't. I won't!"

"DO IT, SALEM!"

The bodies are getting more restless, reaching for me, pulling at my hair, their nails dig into my face as I scream out in pain.

I run my hands over my face and down my arms. Safe. I'm safe. It was just a dream. I'm desperate for a drink of water or something to help calm me down. I gently lift Walker's arm off of me and tip toe out of his room, careful not to wake him. When I make it up the stairs, I realize I have no pants on. Fuck. Maybe I should go upstairs first.

"Salem?" I jump and spin around finding Pierce staring at me. Last night he was acting like a drunk jealous boyfriend. I wondered if he even remembered. "So, you *were* with Walker last night?" his scruffed up jaw ticks.

I could correct him. Hell, I could defend myself, but this arrogant mother fucker thinks he has some claim on me, just because we kissed a few times? I am not in the mood for alpha male bullshit. I decide to grab a water out of the fridge just when I see the man I met in the library a while back emerge from the living room, looking freshly put together and extra delicious.

"Emmet?" I squeak out as he peruses my bare legs. I feel my face flame with embarrassment as he stalks closer.

"Salem, Salem, Salem. What happened to the rest of your clothes?" His buttery southern voice growls out and it takes everything in me to remain cool and collected like I didn't just have a mini orgasm from the way he said my name.

"I had a rough night."

Pierce scoffs audibly to which I roll my eyes at him.

"I was wondering if you'd like to take a hike with me today? Maybe down to the beach? They have kayaks available to rent." Emmet asks.

"Oh dude, that sounds like an awesome time." The elusive Sloan says as he wanders into the quickly overcrowded kitchen. "We should definitely go before the weather turns." He yawns out.

Pierces's eyes bore into me, waiting for my answer.

"Hey, wildcat." Walker says, wrapping his arms around me from the back and giving me a hug. Kill me now. Emmet tracks the familiarity of Walker's movements with a frown puckering his beautiful face.

"We're going kayaking?" Graham says maneuvering his way to the stove. "Why so many people in my kitchen, huh?"

"Hey, Graham, do you need any help with that? Oh, hey Salem!" Skye says walking up to me. "Where are your pants?"

"I had a nightmare last night and slept walked into the basement. I was just heading up to get some pants on when all this chaos decided to stop me." I say. Pierce overhears me and flashes me a look of surprise before he excuses himself from the room.

"Well, run upstairs. I'll save you some eggs and then we can talk about last night."

"So... kayaking?" Emmet asks, looking like he's lost his footing.

"Sounds great!"

"Kayaking!" The guys around us cheer. I look to Skye, and we share a laugh. I hightail it up to my room and change.

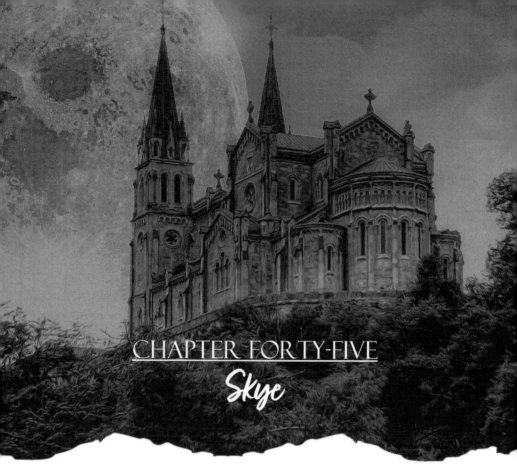

CHAPTER FORTY-FIVE
Skye

On all my adventures with my dad, we never once tried kayaking. Salem is just as lost as I am, while several of the guys grab all the gear. I'd helped Graham pack snacks into something the guys were calling a 'snacklebox' which looked suspiciously a lot like a fishing tackle box stuffed with charcuterie like snacks.

Sloan drops his gear and begins stretching out in several yoga poses.

"What are you doing?" Emmet asks, clearly agitated that his idea to go kayaking was hijacked. He fits himself with a lifejacket, accentuating the broadness of his shoulders.

"You ready for this?" Salem asks holding onto her paddle that ends above her head. She's wearing some borrowed sweats and her hair is tied up in a high pony.

"Not in the least." I tug at my lifejacket that wraps around me like a corset, pushing my boobs up uncomfortably.

Walker comes around putting his arm around Salem's shoulders. "Do you want to ride with me?"

"Oh! Um."

"Actually, I invited her out and was hoping she'd accompany me." Salem looks between the two devilishly handsome males who are vying for her attention.

"You riding with me, blue eyes?" Graham asks, juggling his backpack full of food.

I give him a smile, "Sure."

I was surprised when he'd shown up last night at the Battle of the Bands, asking to dance with me instead of being at the frat party. We'd had so much fun, laughing and dancing together until my legs could no longer handle even one more song. He'd graciously walked me back to the house, making sure I had a piece of cake before I went up to bed. Lukas was fast asleep in his bed by the time I crept in.

Things with Graham were fun and easy as opposed to how crazy Lukas drove me sometimes. I mean he had my panties in his hands! I feel my face warm as I think about how he felt with his hands on me, teasing me, violating my personal space. I didn't exactly hate it. Gah. I shut down my thoughts about Lukas and focused on the man in front of me.

We carry our two-person kayak down to the water meeting up with the group. Salem chose to go in a single instead of choosing between Emmet and Walker. That girl had so many eggplants pointed in her direction it was unreal.

We get into the kayaks and follow the guide who sets an easy pace for beginners like Salem and I. She takes to it easily, whereas I send Graham and I into a circle before finally finding a good rhythm. The sky is thankfully clear today, devoid of its usual doom and gloom I was slowly becoming accustomed to. The wind was absent, making for an easier time on the water. My shoulders and arms start to burn the longer we paddle along the coast. Since the day is clear, I'm granted a gorgeous view of the high cliffs dotted with foliage. There are several twisted trees with bright orange bark that a younger version of myself would have loved to climb. The group is quiet considering how boisterous they tended to be. They each seem lost in their own thoughts the closer we get to the first stop. Possession hosts tons of caves and inlets that are hidden from plain sight. Rumor has it that pirates used them to their advantage as hideouts and a place to bury their treasure. The guide fills us in on local lore while pointing out several groups of wildlife. An eagle dips into the ocean ahead of us, snatching a large fish that fights with all of its strength to be dropped. But the talons are in too deep and the fish stops flailing as the eagle flies off into the trees with its prize. The sight fills me with sadness, even though I know it's the way of the world. As we paddle closer to one of the caves the guide begins to tell us of a local legend, similar to the one Salem told me about a few weeks ago.

The guys seem to shift uncomfortably as he talks.

"We could skip this stop, don't you think?" Sloan pipes up.

"Yeah, I second that. I'm not tired, we can keep going." Graham agrees from behind me.

The guys all nod in agreement, but the guide isn't budging. "Sorry guys, you might not need a break, but we have two first timers here and I'm not as young as I used to be."

They seem to silently communicate to each other across the water, I catch Salem's annoyed expression.

"Well, I'm down for a break. My arms are shaking."

That seems to settle it, all of us working to push our kayaks up to a flat part of the beach that sits right outside of a massive cave. I pull out my phone from my waterproof pocket and snap a picture. I'm already picturing how I could recreate this on canvas. The deep gray spikes hang precariously from the mouth of the cave almost resembling a large monster's teeth. I can see why a place like this would garner a host of myths around it. It looks perfectly ominous.

We pull our boats out, setting our oars down out of the way of the incoming tide. I join Sloan in his stretches no longer finding them so crazy now that my back and arms burn. This place had a habit of pointing out all the ways I wasn't as fit as I thought I was.

"The trick is to use your breaths." Sloan says, coming over to adjust my poor attempt in copying his yoga stance. "Now really sink into it here. Tighten your core. Yes. Now breathe in. See the difference?" His hands linger on my hips as I stretch. I catch Graham's eyes on me, taking in Sloan's hands on me. I stand up and thank him for his help, smiling at him. He's cute in a hipster woodsman kind of way. It was absolutely working for him. He goes to lay down next to a patch of sandy grass, putting his hat over his face like an old man. I join Salem on a picnic blanket, Graham lays out the box of snacks he packed having the other guys hovering close by. They seem deep in conversation, Emmet and Walker giving several glances at the mouth of the cave.

Salem too, seems unsettled. Giving the same area a look of concern. I feel like I'm missing something. I pop a salty olive in my mouth with a frown. This outing is far more subdued than I thought it would be. Maybe they're all just tired from the past couple of days. I know I'm still a little sluggish from last night's excursion.

"What's up with you, Salem?" I ask taking a piece of cheese spread and placing it on a cracker.

"This place. I don't know. It feels weird."

"How so?" Emmet says taking a spot next to Salem on the blanket and snatching a small sandwich.

She shifts, biting her lip. "I don't know, it just... It feels like I've been here before."

I don't miss the way Graham, Walker and Emmet all seem to zone in on her. I look at the guys wondering what's up with them and why they wanted to avoid this place so much. Almost like... this place meant something to them. And maybe not in a good way.

CHAPTER FORTY-SIX
Salem

I'm lightly sunburned and completely wiped out by the time we make it back to the house. The guys perked up after that weird stop at the cave. That place made my skin crawl, but also it almost called to me, like I needed to walk straight into the darkness and see what was waiting for me. I couldn't shake the sense that I 'd been there before, as crazy as that sounds.

I climb up the steps to my room, feeling dead on my feet. I wish this place had a bathtub that I could sit and soak in and forget about the craziness of the last few weeks. But no. All that awaits me in the bathroom is a sausage fest that I'd learned how to avoid seeing surprise penises. It was worse than the DM section of my Instagram in there. If I woke up early enough, I could sneak in a shower before it became eggplant city. But now? I need a shower desperately after kayaking around the island. My arms and back feel like they've been put through a meat shredder, then sewn back onto my body. I want nothing more than to pelt my skin with hot water until it's an angry pink and my fingers are pruned.

I peel off my sweaty clothes and pile them into the small laundry basket I have stacked next to my bed. I wrap myself in a white fluffy towel and head down to the bathroom. I listen at the door, thankful that it seems empty. Most everyone else is still downstairs talking about the pod of whales that popped up next to our boats. I was slightly worried we would have a *Moby Dick* moment, but they passed us without taking us down. The wake they left though had managed to flip the guide's kayak. Thankfully Walker and Emmet were able to turn him right side up. And fine, yes, I absolutely ogled their muscles as they worked him right side up. It was hot. But I was starting to feel like a shiny new toy amongst some of the guys. All testosterone and seconds away from peeing on me to mark their territory. No thank you. I made my own rules. I wasn't one to be tied down to one guy.

I start the shower up letting the water fall over me, my towel hung up on the hook outside the stall. The soft consistent pelting of warm water over my skin is just what I need. I let myself drift, not paying attention to how long I've been here, just the sensation of water running over me.

"Salem." My eyes fly open at the sound of Pierce's voice on the other side of the curtain. I can see his outline as he drags a finger along the seam of the plastic. I'm certain the opaque covering isn't hiding much of my naked outline.

"What are you doing here, Pierce?" I ask, far breathier than I intend. He grips the edge of the curtain with his fingers. My heart races wondering if he's going to yank it open.

"I want to see you." His voice sounds tortured, and shit does it affect me. He's waiting, I notice, for my response.

I wait a beat before I croak out, "Okay." I'm not sure he heard me, when he rips open the curtain, eyes roaming over my wet naked body. He steps in, closing the curtain behind him, crowding me against the wall of water cascading over me.

"You're beautiful." He exhales.

"And you're fully clothed." His socks are soaked through. I spot a large bulge straining against his gray sweatpants, obviously happy by what he sees.

"Can I touch you, Salem? I feel like if I don't, I'm going to die."

"That would be a tragedy." I say working my fingers over my body, spending time to circle my pert nipples. He follows the movement.

"Please." He growls, his green eyes almost eaten up entirely by his blown-out pupils.

"I'm not your girlfriend." I say, waiting for his agreement.

"What would you rather be?"

"Not sure. What can you offer me?"

He palms his cock, pulling it out for me to see it's length in its entirety. The sight of it makes me salivate, but I don't dare admit that

I've thought about what it would be like to have that in my mouth. In my body.

He's bigger than I've ever seen, and I don't know if I could handle how girthy and long he is. I wasn't just appeasing him by telling him he had a monster cock. It was an accurate assessment that has me missing my vibrator.

"I'll let you touch me, on one condition…"

His eyes flare, "Anything."

"You can only use your mouth and hands."

He scowls at me, but yanks his clothes off, tossing them over the top. His socks land with a wet thwap onto the tile. He moves towards me like a predator, joining me under the shower head, making his dark blonde hair look almost brunette.

"This doesn't make me yours." He growls at my declaration before slamming his lips on mine. I feel the length of him bobbing against my stomach as he tilts my head back, deepening our kiss. God, he drives me fucking crazy. I already feel myself getting wet and not from the shower. He cups my breasts leaving nibbling kisses down my neck until he sucks in one of my pink nipples.

"You're fucking driving me insane." He says as he drops my breasts, cupping my ass with one hand and spreading my slit with his other hand. "Is this all wet for me, baby?"

I nod, aching for him to touch me. He drops to his knees.

"I don't kneel for anyone, Salem." He licks my clit with a rough sweep of his tongue.

"Then what are you doing down there for me?"

"Fucking worshipping your pretty cunt." He sticks a finger into my sex as he lays a sloppy kiss over my sensitive clit, pulling it into his mouth by his teeth.

"Oh fuck." I hitch one of my legs over his shoulder, letting him have better access which he makes perfect use of by slipping in two more fingers and assaulting my clit with his talented tongue.

"Come for me, Salem. Come on my face." He says slapping my ass as he buries his face right between my legs. I work my fingers through his wet hair, as my orgasm builds. I squeeze my legs around his head as he sucks my clit right as I'm about to explode, he slips in a fourth finger and has my entire body shaking with release. I scream out, lights flickering above us as I come hard all over his tongue. He lets go, and I'm a puddle of sensations. Barely able to stand up. He grips my hips as he stands up, kissing my stomach on his way.

"Baby." He says leaning over me. His mussed hair dripping small water droplets down. He takes my mouth, coating the taste of me over my tongue. It's tastes sweet and I'm suddenly wishing I hadn't drawn the line at just his mouth and fingers. He pecks my lips one more time, before stepping back, taking his rock-hard cock away with him. I watch as he lifts my towel off the hanger and wraps it around his bottom half. He's scooped up his clothes and is out the door before I have a chance to run after him.

"Fuck you, Pierce!" I yell after him, standing there completely wet and naked and confused. *Shit.*

I look around the bathroom, and thankfully there's a few towels inside one of the cabinets. I wrap myself in its freshly laundered comfort and stalk off up the stairs. Goddamn fucking Pierce Ledger and his mind-blowing orgasms and the way he can kiss me stupid. Well fuck him, two could play that game.

I fling my towel into the laundry basket and find my leggings and oversized t-shirt that I'd stolen. I go over to my phone and see a few missed notifications. Skye sent me a bunch of pictures from our outing. I make a note to save these, noting the way that Graham stares at Skye in some of these. I'd need to feel her out later to see what she thought about that. I was all for a man who could cook, and those dimples? Please.

I see another notification from my Grams, alerting me that my card was paid, and she even upped the limit. Thank God. I decide to do some online shopping, first stop underwear.

I'm several carts into my online shopping spree, when I get another notification from Headmaster Hayden. My stomach sours. Something was off about that man, I could feel it.

I press open, scanning the email requesting a meeting with me tomorrow morning. Ugh. I hit reply wishing I could come up with some sassy remark, but I'm too tired to care. Fuck it. I hit accept to the meeting and put the time into my planner, wondering what the hell he could possibly want to see me for. I wonder if I can take a pillow with me to sit on, instead of having to wait in that god-awful torture chair.

CHAPTER FORTY-SEVEN
Lukas

I'd slept in to find most of the house empty, including my roommate. Did she even come home last night?

The thought makes my stomach drop. Who would she have been out with? I decide a little light internet stalking was in order. She kept her Instagram as public, so it wasn't really stalking, was it?

I pull up her handle and flip down to her stories. I had an anonymous username, and never posted anything. Enjoying my outsider perspective to the social media site, it allowed for me to interact without giving away any personal details. As a Ledger, I was expected to keep a certain public standard which included not sharing any personal details. As much as I might not share though, plenty of others did. Tagging the famous heir Lukas Ledger in a lust filled haze.

Her stories load with pictures of her out at Diablos last night. She's swaying to the music, having the time of her life with Graham behind her. Graham? My chest constricts. I put down the phone, not wanting to see any more even though there's several more posted.

When we'd first been possessed by our sins, Graham was my first conquest. We pretended it didn't happen, but I'd be lying if I still didn't think about how good it felt.

I decide to take out my frustrations on some sketching. Professor Whitelsbee was being stingy with how many classes I could sit in, claiming I wasn't being a good model. One screw up was all it took with her, and I was feeling the brunt of that.

I lose myself in my art, until my hands start to resemble claws, and I'm sore from the hours I've been hunched over. Maybe I should take Sloan up on his stretching instruction he's always offering. My stomach rumbles loudly, reminding me that I need to eat. This is why I couldn't have plants. I'd kill them all by forgetting to water them. At least my body spoke up to me loudly when I got too in my head, as I often did. The real world was fucking insane, but in my art, I could control the chaos.

I emerge from my room to the sounds of laughter. They must be back.

"The fucking whale almost took you right out with it! I don't know how we all managed to stay upright, and the guide was the one who got flipped." Sloan's voice booms up the stairs.

They all look wind whipped and tanned. Skye is perched on the edge of the couches arm next to Graham's splayed-out form. I wonder what it would be like to be sandwiched between them. Fucking Lust, rearing its head again. I push it down waving to the group gathered in the living room.

"Hey Luk-ass." Sloan calls out. "You missed an awesome day."

Skye looks like she's avoiding looking in my direction. From guilt or attraction, I can't decipher her reasonings. Not for the first time I wish I was saddled with something like mind reading or flying. That would be a hell of a lot more useful.

I grab some cheese and meat from the fully stocked fridge and throw together a sandwich, careful of the mustard that I'd made sure to replace. You could never tell with Emmet though, the little fucker was too good at sticking to the shadows, pulling off pranks and spying on people. The apple didn't fall far from the tree with that one. His dad had come by the house several times sweeping it for bugs. And not the creepy crawly kind. I didn't give a fuck how Emmet's family made their money, just as long as it didn't affect me. Despite their less than legal dealings, they were generous- giving to several charities, including domestic violence survivors which earned them some points in my book. Maybe if my mom had a place like that... Fuck. I shoot down that line of thinking, aware of where thoughts like that tended to take me.

I shove the sandwich in my mouth, putting the ingredients back where they belong. One thing Graham cared about the most was this kitchen and his food. You never fucked with Graham's food. He'd go zero to angry Nonna in seconds. He hated when his mother's influence leaked out of him like that, but the rest of us just found it funny. I especially liked when he waved his spatula around scolding us.

I join them all back in the living room, sitting in the only empty chair across from Skye and Graham. I listen as they recount their day.

"I just hated stopping by that fucking cave." Sloan says. Everyone goes still and I can tell Sloan wishes the words never left his mouth.

"What is it with you guys and that cave?" Fuck. She was far too smart, and we were far too obvious. Of course, she would pick up on our weird vibe.

"Seriously? No one wants to answer?" she glances around the room, but no one meets her in the eye.

"Ugh, whatever. Be weird. I need to go take a shower anyway." I don't miss the way Graham stares after her, like he's considering joining her.

Shit. Are they already at that point? I rub my chest feeling dejected.

I head upstairs and barre myself in my room. I finish a homework assignment while Skye showers. I fill out the last problem, right as Skye bursts in clearly agitated and dripping wet. She's wearing a terry cloth robe, and I ache to find out if she has any clothes on underneath. I watch as several drops of water run down her bare legs. I stifle the desire to trace my tongue along the same path of the water droplets.

"Ugh, you're here."

"Yeah, I kinda live here."

"Why is everyone being so weird about that cave, Lukas? Seriously. It's maddening." She sits on the edge of her bed, her wet blonde hair cascading over her shoulder. She's bare faced and fucking beautiful. I feel this attraction to her, beyond the Lust, beyond surface level bullshit. It's like I'm seeing straight to her soul, wanting a chance for ours to entwine.

I sit back on my stool and face her. "Everyone has secrets, Skye."

"Not me."

I arch my eyebrow ring. "None?"

"None." She clips. I push off of my stool and walk over to her.

"So, you'll tell me anything I want to know?"

She squares her shoulders and sets her jaw, pointing those baby blues straight at me. I sit next to her, only to see she pulls her robe closed. Interesting. I run my thumb over my bottom lip, thinking she has to be naked under there for that kind of reaction.

"Maybe." She answers.

"Well, that's not fair. You said you don't have secrets."

Her dainty little nostril flare and it's the cutest fucking thing. I can't help it- I love riling her up.

"Fine, what do you want to know?"

I give her a devilish smile. "How often have you thought about my cock since you saw it?"

She flushes tomato red, her breaths coming in labored. She licks her lips, avoiding my gaze.

"How many?"

"That's right, Skye."

She gulps, "N-none."

"I'd believe you more if you didn't just stutter."

"None!" She says with more conviction.

"Are you sure?"

"Y-yes."

"Sounds like you're not sure." I tug at her robe belt and her eyes go wide. I see the tell-tale signs of desire flash across her features. I snatch her hand and hover it over my raging cock. "Are you sure, you've not thought about it once?"

"I think about it every night before I go to sleep." She confesses.

The warmth of her hand so close beats down on me and I ache for her to close the distance, but I won't force her. Most everyone else throws themselves at me, but not her.

"Aren't you tired of being a good girl, Skye?" My cock twitches upwards begging to be played with.

"Yes." She breathes out, her hand wrapping around my length as she presses her mouth against mine.

CHAPTER FORTY-EIGHT
Skye

I'm beating myself up for not doing this sooner. I find myself straddling Lukas' lap on my bed as we kiss, and I have no idea how I got here. I must have done it without thinking, I just needed to be closer to him. He's rough, exploring my body with furious intent. He rips the belt of my robe off, exposing my nakedness to him. My breasts feel heavy, aching for his attention.

"I fucking knew it." He says with a smirk as he lays back looking at me with appreciation through a lust heavy gaze.

"Knew what?" I say, grinding my hips into him. I can't seem to stop myself, from relieving me of this building pressure that's been with me since I met him.

"Knew you'd be naked under here." He sits up on his elbows, taking a nipple into his mouth. He releases it with a loud pop. "Knew you'd be this perfect." I blush, looking down at my cellulite speckled stomach. I was no size two. He kisses my stomach right where I'm most insecure like he knows I need reassurance that he finds me attractive.

"Fuck. Skye." He holds my hips as he juts up into me. I'm completely bare, soaking the front of his black sweatpants. "Condom. Now." He gestures to his bedside table, and I hop off him. I grab one of the many condoms and toss it to him, shrugging out of my robe and making sure to lock the door. And try not to think about why he has so many. At least he takes precautions.

He tears of his clothes and sheaths his length laying straight back in my bed. He grips his cock in one hand while the other rests behind his head. He's fully on display, every intricate tattoo laid out for me to see.

Holy moly. He's so hot. Seeing him like this in my bed has me ready to go feral on him.

"Come here, baby." I stride over to him without hesitation, desperate to cover up and feeling embarrassed, but the way his eyes roam over my body has me stepping with more courage the closer I get. I lay down next to him and he runs his tattooed hands over my face.

"So fucking beautiful." He places tender kisses against my lips while I wrap my hand around his length, feeling the barbells of his piercings against my fingers.

"Does it hurt?"

"No, it feels fucking good. Keep doing that." He guides my hand, showing me just how he wants to be touched. His kisses turn heated, nipping my bottom lip and tangling his tongue with mine. My entire body flushes with need. He works me until I'm a mess of desire. I can feel myself clenching in anticipation, feeling desperate for him to take me.

He flips over me, caging my face with his elbows as he lines himself up with my entrance.

"Fuck, Skye, please. I need to be inside you right now, baby."

I feel his desperation matching mine. I nod, gripping his ass and lifting my hips up to welcome him.

He works himself in, inch by inch until he's fully seated inside of me. I feel so full it's almost painful.

"You, okay?" He dips his forehead down to mine, his arms shaking, sweat coats his chest.

"Yes. Lukas, it feels so good." He edges himself out letting out a groan as he pushes back in. I clench around him, feeling every inch, his piercings heightening every slight movement. I roll my hips, letting my legs spread as wide as they could go.

"Oh fuck. Yes." He shoves in deeper, his body shaking against mine. I run my fingers down his back urging him on. He kisses me, and I lose myself in him completely. I turn us so that I'm on top, which takes him by surprise. I ride him as he grips onto my ass, guiding me.

"I've wanted this since I first saw you." He confesses, breaking our kiss. I sit up, letting him watch me ride him. My breasts bounce with each thrust. He grips onto them, squeezing them hard enough to leave bruises, unable to get his full hand around them.

"These are so fucking perfect." He grunts, pulsing up into me.

"Turn around." I arch my eyebrow at him but do it anyway.

"Just like that. Ride my cock, baby." I settle back down onto his length, with a gasp. From this angle he's hitting me in a spot I didn't even know I had.

"Oh, fuck!" I yell out.

He laughs. "I don't think I've ever heard you swear. I fucking love it. My dirty girl."

I am so close to spilling over the edge as I bounce up and down Lukas' enormous cock.

"Oh shit, yes. I'm going to come, baby get there." He wraps a hand around my front, rubbing my clit as I ride us straight into simultaneous orgasms. I can feel his heat the moment he erupts inside of me, I'm right there with him, clamping down as it shoots through my whole body. We stay like that for a moment, almost like we're both too stunned to move. I finally find it in me to go and clean myself off. I wordlessly stalk off to change into some clothes.

Oh my God, I'd just slept with Lukas. My roommate! What was I thinking?

He watches me with a guarded expression.

"I'm sorry. I don't- "

"Don't you dare apologize for that." He bites out, standing up and yanking off the condom. Chucking the evidence of what we'd done in the trash.

"I shouldn't-"

"Did you not feel what I was fucking feeling?" He's still shaking, only now it looks like it's because he's angry. "I'm sorry if I messed with your good girl persona, but that wasn't a mistake so don't try and write me off as one."

He storms out of the room, butt naked. I crumple to the floor, holding my chest. It hurts.

Why does it hurt?

"Skye?" Graham's voice comes from the door. Dread coils in my stomach. Did he hear what went on in here. "I made dinner. Do you want some?"

I pick myself off the floor, nodding my head. "That sounds nice." I shove down my feelings and join the guys downstairs, like it never happened. Like I didn't feel my soul link up with Lukas in the most earth-shattering sex I'd ever had and that scared me more than anything. Offering Lukas a piece of me would only result in making me a broken mess.

CHAPTER FORTY-NINE
Salem

Headmaster Hayden was fifteen minutes late and counting. I really should have brought my pillow with me- I think as I shift in the god-awful chair. Fucking sadist.

I'd been able to stop by the school store earlier this morning and grab a few new school outfits. I mourned the loss of my fishnet stockings, wishing I could individualize the monotony of this boring uniform. I pop a piece of gum, grateful to replenish my stash.

"Ms. Knox." Hmm twenty-two minutes late, I guess that's an improvement. It's on the tip of my tongue to spit out exactly what I'm thinking, but I refrain, deciding he's not worth the headache.

"Headmaster."

"Well, the fire department has come back with some leads regarding your room fire and I'm afraid it's looking grim." He sits in his chair, his jowls shaking with each word he utters.

"How do you mean?"

"Well, they did mention possible arson."

"Arson?" I screech. "How is that possible. Both Skye and I were dead asleep."

"So you say."

"Sir? Are you seriously accusing me of setting my own room on fire?"

"People would do a lot less to be moved into a house full of, oh what are all the ladies calling them now, hotties?"

I stand gathering my things, feeling my anger rise. It was one thing to hear those rumors floating around school, but to hear it from your headmaster?

"We didn't start that fire."

"Well, since there's no proof, no charges have been filed... yet."

"Charges?"

"Yes, you can't just go about setting rooms on fire without consequences."

"We didn't-"

"Yes, yes. I heard you. Now, as for the other matter I called you in here about, I wanted to remind you that your presence is required at the alumni ball this Saturday."

Shit, I'd forgotten all about that.

"You really want the girl you're accusing of arson to attend the alumni ball."

He levels me with a glare. "We will be seeing you this Saturday. And Ms. Knox, it's a masquerade, so dress appropriately."

I storm out of his office. How fucking dare he? He'd basically said he believed Skye and I had intentionally set a fire to our room. Like a bunch of Hell House groupies. Fuck.

My Converse slap loudly against the marble floor with each frustrated step I take.

I round the corner, frown pulling at my brow, when I see Pierce striding up the hallway. It hits me that this is exactly how we met, and I wonder why the hell he's here seeing the headmaster.

"Beautiful, where you off to this morning."

"Not now Pierce, I have class." He wraps his hand around my wrist and spins me into him easily, placing his nose in my hair. I wore it down today, with a few beach waved curls to frame my face.

"I can't stop thinking about the taste of your pussy on my tongue." He whispers into my ear making my knees shake.

"Sounds like a personal problem." He gives me his signature smirk that's the perfect mix of asshole and handsome motherfucker.

"What do you say, we meet up later?" He trails his nose down my neck

"Are you not coming to class?" I hitch my eyebrows up.

"Why, are you going to miss me?"

I shove him in the chest, taking a step back, still tethered to him by my wrist. "Never."

"Where have I heard that word before?"

"Asshole. Why are you meeting with the headmaster anyway?"

His spine goes ramrod straight, dropping my wrist like it's shocked him. "Frat stuff. Alumni ball. Which by the way, are you going? Maybe I can take you?"

Is he... lying? Stalling? My internal alarms are going off and I don't like it. I narrow my eyes at him as he shifts from one foot to the other. Interesting.

"I think I can take myself, thanks." I spin on my heel and stomp down the hallway.

I make it almost completely out of the building when my phone buzzes with a notification from Pierce:

Pain in my ass: Forgot to mention how fuckable you look this morning.

Me: As opposed to when?

Pain in my ass: Don't be like that, baby. Let me take you to the ball.

Me: Pass.

I fire off a text to Skye informing her of my insane meeting and ignore the incoming ones from Pierce. I go through the motions of moving from one class to the next until lunch when I drop my bag and lay my head on the table. Skye sits down with the same kind of mood I'm feeling. Maybe even more so.

"What is with you two?" Javelynn asks as they set their tray down, joining us.

"Life." I sigh, picking open a yogurt and stabbing the contents with my spoon. "Headmaster Hayden is demanding I go to the Alumni Ball this weekend."

"That's an amazing opportunity to network." Javelynn says slugging back a sweet tea.

"But it's also dancing and handshaking and people-ing. I need to order a dress."

"I see you were able to get some new clothes finally." Javelynn says pointing to my bag.

"Yes, I'll return the ones I borrowed tomorrow. Thank you so much for helping us out, seriously. You're a life saver."

"Yes, seriously. Thank you, Javelynn." Skye pipes up squeezing their hand in gratitude.

"Don't sweat it."

"So why are you in a funk today, Skye."

"Ughh, I don't even want to talk about it. I did something stupid."

"Something or someone." Javelynn quips and it makes me bark out a laugh.

By the expression on Skye's face, I'd say it's the latter. "Oh my God, Skye."

She covers her face with her hands. "Ugh I know!"

"Let's talk about something else. Javelynn, you looked pretty cozy with Jackson." Skye says deflecting.

Javelynn's face pinks. "We may have shared a dance or two."

"Anything else you want to share?"

Javelynn bites into their sandwich. "Other than I think he's super cute and nice. He's got that whole Clark Kent thing going for him."

"We love a hot a nerd." I click my drink with their's.

"I second that." Skye says, joining our cheers.

We eat discussing our classes. Skye still can't seem to get her art professor to appreciate her work, and our English Professor has been breathing down my neck about the quality of my essays. I'm about to go on a tirade about it, when I spot a leather clad, tattooed mirror of Pierce heading straight towards us.

"Would that someone you didn't want to talk about earlier be headed over this way right now, Skye?" I ask, noting that Lukas looks anything but happy to see us.

"Oh, shit. He looks mad." Javelynn says and I agree, he looks ready to knock off someone's head. Maybe Skye's. Shit is right.

"No, oh my god. Is it too late to hide me?"

"Definitely, too late." Lukas says taking the seat opposite Skye.

"Lukasss." She hisses.

"Sssskkye" He hisses right back. "What did you turn into a snake since the last time I saw you?"

"You want us to stay or leave?" I ask, not sure what this energy between the two of them means.

"Stay." Her eyes are locked with Lukas's as they stare off communicating silently with each other.

Oh yeah, they definitely did something.

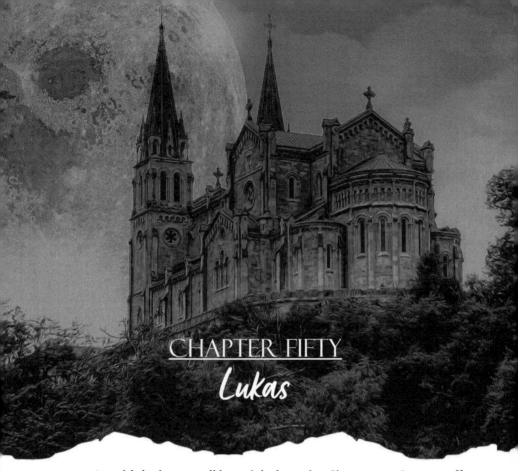

CHAPTER FIFTY
Lukas

I couldn't sleep at all last night knowing Skye was trying to stuff me in a box labeled 'mistakes' while she laid mere feet away after what we did. I ached to go to her, hold her against me and kiss her lips stupid. And fuck me did it suck to be on the other side of this, where typically I was the one brushing people off and upright ghosting them, to the point of cruelty, this time I was being brushed aside like yesterday's lunch. Karma was a fucking bitch. I could do without this twisted feeling that's settled in my core, ripping apart my insides. I want her to declare that last night meant as much to her as it did to me. It was different to me. *She* was different to me, but she's been avoiding me all night and ducked out early this morning. We were going to have this out right the fuck now.

"You can't pretend that last night didn't happen." I hear the audible gasp of her friends but ignore it.

"You can't be serious, right now."

"I'm not fucking joking." I clench my hands, nails biting into the fleshy parts of my palms.

"I don't want to talk about this here."

"I haven't been able to get you to talk about it anywhere, Skye."

"Just, drop it would you?"

"You're not a bone and I'm not a dog, so no I can't just 'drop it'. We need to talk about this."

"Why?"

"Because it meant something to me."

She gapes at me, tears gathering in her eyes making her baby blue eyes look bright and broken. Dammit. I go to reach out across the table to wipe them, but she rears back shaking her head no. The rejection stings. I feel eyes on us, while we make a scene, but I don't care. Let them look.

"I can't do this now." She goes to gather her things.

"Skye." She shakes her head shooting me down again, and I feel the sharp stab of defeat.

"Give her some space, Lukas." Salem says. I nod, stuffing my hands into my leather jacket as I watch Skye walk away from me without even a glance in my direction. I'm left alone, hearing the sound of murmurs start up around me.

Did she not get it? That I wasn't this person? I'd had sex a countless number of times, but it was never like that. I wasn't gentle, but yet I found myself being so for her. Maybe that was the problem. If I'd wrapped my hands around her pretty little neck and pounded her pussy like I was punishing it, maybe she wouldn't have run away so easy. I shake my head, remembering how she felt with me though. Being with Skye was life altering in a way that made my soul feel like it'd been set on fire. She'd held onto me. Not my Lust or all the trapping that came with that. Me. I'd damn well remind her of it too.

CHAPTER FIFTY-ONE
Salem

"**Ugh. I hate all of these.**" I say flopping down on my bed and laying flat on my stomach as I scroll through the store's online boutique site. I kick my legs up behind me, feeling too tired to change out of my school uniform. Headmaster Hayden reminded me that my presence is required at the alumni ball that takes place this Saturday. Since there's no malls on this tiny island, I'll have to have it shipped as soon as it can get here, but I haven't found anything that I wouldn't be caught dead in. That is until I switch over to this site that Javelynn recommended to me.

Pierce had blown up my phone the rest of the day, sending me flirty eggplant emojis with peaches and winkie faces. As much as I found myself liking some of the time we spent together, I couldn't ignore that niggling feeling after seeing him going to the headmaster's office. He could fuck right off with whatever lies he fed me this morning.

The site Javelynn recommended was a pure gold mine. I didn't even know where to start. For as much money as my family has, we'd never been one for formal balls or charity fundraisers. Even my own prom experience was cancelled due to a global pandemic, so I had never actually had a need to buy a fancy dress. I feel a foreign flutter of excitement stretch across my abdomen as I zero in on the most perfect dress I've ever seen. It has a corseted bodice, with black lace and interwoven beading all down the front. The bottom fans out in black glitter tulle that fades into an ombre of silver then white at the bottom. It was perfect. I check the price and size before adding to cart. Thankfully the website had suggestions for accessories and shoes which made it easy to complete the look. I check out, smiling to myself. Everything else might have been going to shit, but at least I had this. Funny how things change, because when I first heard I would be required to attend, everything inside of me screamed hell no. But now?

Now, I was feeling excited about dressing up in something that devastatingly gorgeous. When the actual heck did, I become this person? I still wasn't happy about attending and especially the demand to be there. If there's one thing that irked me the most was having to obey crotchety old men with a god complex.

I bite my bottom lip then close out my tabs when I hear a knock outside my door. A tentative rap, tap, smack.

"Who is it?" I call out, feeling too tired to go to the door.

"Walker." His deep voice travels through the door and straight into my stomach.

I feel instantly sweaty with anticipation before I call for him to come in. I stifle the stirring of butterflies that churn inside my gut. He's changed out of his school issued uniform, a knit cap sitting snuggly across his head covering most of his scar. His hair curls out at the bottom of his hat and I suddenly feel the urge to run my fingers over the edges that are poking out. I bite my lip seeing him with his guitar slung across his back and remember the way his fingers felt against mine as he held me, showing me how to pluck the strings, and how he looked at me as we sang together, and especially the way he comforted me after my nightmare. Yep, I had a huge crush on this man who was sucking all the air out of the room with his very presence. I feel a smile edging up, battling away my grumpy mood.

"What's up?"

"We got it, babe."

"The Battle of the Bands?"

He nods and I shriek, jumping off the bed and flinging myself around him, wrapping my arms around his neck.

"Oh my god, oh my god! That's amazing, congratulations!"

"Don't act like you didn't have anything to do with it, we won because of you. The judges deliberated a day longer because of the band at the end, but they were swayed by, and I quote, 'the raw chemistry and effortless ethereal harmony made by the two singers'."

"They really said that?"

"Yeah, wildcat. Can you blame them? That was fuckin' magical."
His whiskey-colored eyes shine down at me perusing my body lazily with
heated intent. I feel the trace of his gaze on my skin, making me realize
that I have my ass on full display with my school skirt pushed up and
showing the edges of my undies.

"Did you bring your guitar up here to teach me some chords?" I
sit up, crossing my legs. Walker tracks the movement with a lick of his
lips. My eyes catch on a flash of metal. Was that... was his tongue
pierced?

"A deal's a deal, but I didn't realize how small it would be up
here."

"What you never explored the house?"

"Not all of us are as curious as you, angel."

"That's a new one."

"What is?"

"Angel."

He tucks a strand of my hair behind my ear as he settles on the
bed next to me moving the guitar from behind his back up and over to
the front of his chest. "That's because you have a voice like one." He
makes the breath in my chest catch, letting loose a string of butterflies
deep in my core. He lifts the strap off of his neck and hands me the
guitar, letting me get used to its weight as I slide my fingers around its
neck and flick my fingers down the strings. He adjusts the strap, hooking
it over my head, moving my hair out of the way. I don't miss the way his
calloused fingers linger on my skin, sending a shiver down my spine.

He angles himself so that I'm settled in front of him, his legs spread wide allowing me into the opening. He wraps his hands around me from behind and pushes my fingers into the strings. The sensation is familiar, like the day we first met, but this time I'm more aware of the wall of muscle that sits behind me.

"I want your fingers, here. Here. And here." His gravel voice whispers into my ear.

I smile, moving my fingers away from where he placed them which makes him bark out a laugh.

"You are such a handful." He places my fingers back where they should be and instructs me to pluck the strings one at a time.

"Why do I know that?" I say, plucking it again.

"It's the opening to *Stairway to Heaven.* A guitarist's rite of passage is to learn that beginning."

I pluck them again and he moves my fingers for the next notes in the song. It's beautiful and haunting, even with my clumsy attempt to play, the music reverberates off my arched ceiling making me lose myself in the sensation of Walker and I and this song.

We get lost in the music as he teaches me actual chords that he insists I study. I hand him back the guitar, not wanting him to leave yet, even though it's late and I have homework to do.

"Will you play something for me before you go?"

He smiles, strumming out a familiar tune before adding his voice to the song. He plays *Sweet Creature,* by Harry Styles and it floors me. Though it's not the first time I've heard him preform, it still hits me like it is. He's insanely talented. I feel a sudden anger sweep over me, quick and steady. I want to punch something, rip my very bed apart seam by seam and I don't know why.

Walker jerks up mid song, his hands clenched into twin fists, his jaw clenched and eyes turning to pitch.

"I have to go." He practically runs out of my room, and as soon as he clears the first step the feeling of rage dissipates, leaving me empty and utterly exhausted. I rub my temples with my fingers, wondering what the hell that was. But I've gotten good at ignoring things lately, choosing to rather shove them in a box.

I tap open my phone and send a text off to Walker, wondering what made him run off like that. I thought we were having fun together.

Me: Thx for the lesson

I wait a moment and see three dots appear and then disappear, twisting my insides as I wait for his reply. The dots appear again and a whoosh fills my hand as his text emoji pops up. A smilie face. Fine. Okay. I'm not going to read into it. It'll just drive me crazy. I sit back and decide to get my homework out of the way. Fucking boys of Hell House and their twisted ways.

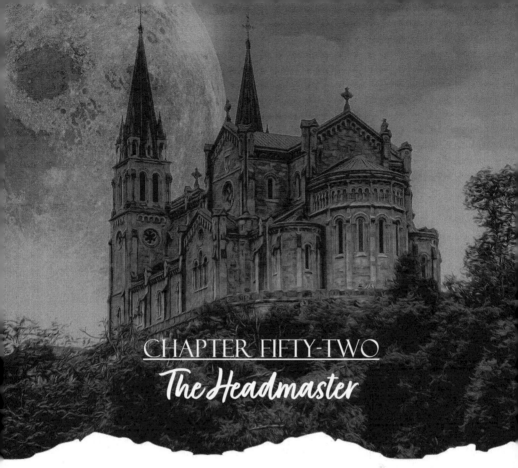

CHAPTER FIFTY-TWO
The Headmaster

This body was cumbersome. I felt it in every creak of his joints as he walked with such effort in every step. It was tedious, but there was nothing to be done about it. We were stuck together, until the time came where I could be free. Just a little bit longer. I urge him across the hidden path, carefully, aware that one wrong step could send his gnarled bones careening toward the twisted rocks below. Then he would be useless to me, and we couldn't have that. I'd waited far too many years to see my plans be foiled by a twisted ankle.

We finally crest the opening of the cave and I feel my host's heart speed up in anticipation. I do so love when they're this willing and obedient. It makes my job that much easier. He absentmindedly checks his watch and I shove down my irritation. What could possibly be more important that what we're doing. I swear the living had no sense of priorities. I tug hard at the bond tethering us, and he snaps to attention.

That's right asshole, don't forget who's in charge.

He'd recently made the mistake of thinking he could get involved with a woman romantically. As if I'd allow for this sack of sallow skin and bones to be taken out by a sex induced heart attack. Not that she was even remotely interested anyway. His health was skating on thin ice as it was, and I didn't have time to possess someone so completely and perfectly positioned as he was. He unfortunately was my only option at present who could do what it was I needed. I make a mental note to have him order more green juices with kale.

The time was fast approaching. I let myself feel a wave of excitement, envisioning all my carefully laid plans coming to fruition.

We creep through the cavern, the tide out leaving behind a soft pliant sandy floor. When the tide came back, it would wash away our footprints like we'd never been here.

The girl would never see us coming until it was too late. Getting her to the island had been easy but getting her to fulfill the rest of the spell would take some work.

He checks his watch again and it takes everything in me not to tug on something more vital than our bond.

It really was a tragedy at how people couldn't seem to hold onto their attention span anymore. I blamed the smartphones. And people thought I was evil. It's like they've never seen social media.

I take over completely, pushing him from front and center, which expels some of my energy, but it can't be helped. He's dragging his feet much too much for my liking. I make this body place his hand on the back of the cave wall and lean his head against where I knew the crack existed. I strain his ears to see if I can hear them, but like all the times before, they're silent. Anger stirs inside of me. I'd make those witches pay for what they'd done to us. They would pay for the years we'd been forced to be separate. The years I'd been left alone in this place.

Through all of my time here scouring the archives, I was able to find a potion that would allow for seven of the strongest to break through the veil. We'd timed it perfectly, but now their hold was weakening. Their time was running out, and if we didn't succeed in breaking down the veil permanently, they'd be ripped back to purgatory once again. Once we got that little witch to do what she was here for, we'd finally be free.

We make quick work, or as quick as his gnarled hands allow us, sprinkling the rosemary and salt concoction in a perfect circle. We draw a star in the center, connecting the edges of the circle to the star's points.

Just a little longer, I have the man whisper to the middle of the star. Just a little longer, my loves.

CHAPTER FIFTY-THREE
Salem

I feel my thoughts circling back to that eerie cave. I haven't been able to stop thinking about it since our kayaking trip, nor shake the feeling that I'd been there before. I pull out my phone and press the map app open, zooming in on its location. It's not that far of a hike and I could probably make it there and back before dark.

I tuck my phone into my hoodie's front pocket. I'm wearing it with a black skort and some fishnet stockings that I'd ordered online replacing the ones I'd lost in the fire. I decide to wear a pair of Doc Martins for the walk instead of my Converse that I loved so much. I pop in an earbud, cueing up some music while I slip out of the house intent on putting this cave thing to rest.

I pass some of the guys in the kitchen arguing about how much basil is too much basil, while Graham wields his spatula like it's an extension of his arm. Skye is laughing at the scene unfolding as she chops up some garlic. I nod to her, gesturing that I'm going out. She smiles, nodding back then goes back to her garlic chopping shaking her head at the guys surrounding her.

The air is cool, but not uncomfortable making me feel invigorated as I stride through the woods. There's a path that winds from the house, up a steep incline and down to the beach where we had stopped the other day. I focus on my breath, getting lost in the lyrics of my music, humming to myself. God, that time up on stage had been everything. I ached to do it again and wondered if Walker would ever ask me. He'd made himself scarce all week, only sending me an occasional text here and there. His absence ate at me in a way that didn't make sense. We'd only shared a kiss, but it was electric. Plus, things with Pierce had been more than rocky. I never knew where I stood with him. I push the boys from my thoughts and focus on my footing, avoiding the divots and tangles of roots that line the trail.

I get to the top, noting that we'd been there for morning yoga not that long ago, remembering that Pierce and Lukas had crashed our session, leering at our asses in downward dog like the assholes they were. They'd been hiking this same trail, I realize.

The way down was infinitely more difficult, and I silently pat myself on the back for choosing the Doc Martins for this. I carefully hoist myself over a fallen tree, barely missing its jagged bark that leaves a light scratch mark up my arm. Shit.

The trail leads out to a hidden cove near where we'd picnicked. The same sense of familiarity niggles at the base of my skull. Getting down the path took longer than I anticipated, and the sun is already starting to dip down in the sky. I hurry my pace along the beach, coming to the opening of the cave.

A shiver worms down my spine, stealing me of all my warmth. I'm filled with the sense of foreboding like the very ground I'm standing on is evil.

My toe has barely crossed the threshold when I hear a voice calling me from behind.

"What are you doing here, Pierce?"

"I could ask you the same thing." He looks good. Too good. His dark blonde hair flutters in the breeze, sweeping across his forehead making me want to reach out and push it back, but I don't. I pretend that I haven't seen every inch of this heartthrob in front of me.

"Come on, let's go back to the house. Tide is coming in."

I narrow my eyes at him. "I'll leave when I'm ready." I turn on my heel and head into the dark cave with Pierce boring his angry green eyes into me.

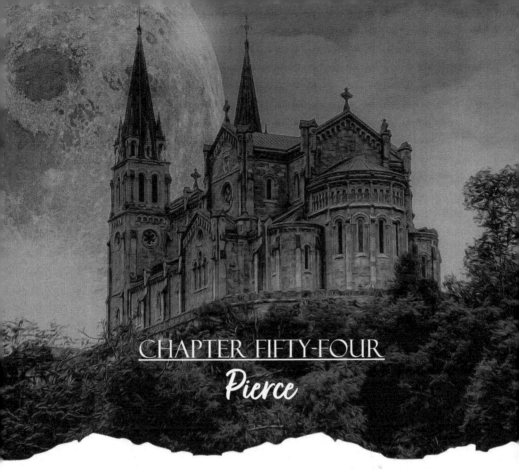

CHAPTER FIFTY-FOUR
Pierce

This fucking girl. I don't know how I'd gotten so attached to her so quickly, but I need to protect her from what she was about to stumble upon in this place. I was addicted, even though I shouldn't be. She didn't know who I really was. What I'd done. Sometimes I could forget that I'd done it at all, but the knowledge was always right there, waiting to eat me alive. Threatening to have me removed from her forever. She didn't know I was her enemy, needing her for whatever power lay in her veins.

"Salem." She ignores me, swinging out her phone as a flashlight, illuminating the darkness of the cave. The light reflects off the puddles and rocks that line the ground.

I look back at the mouth of the cave and notice that the sun is quickly approaching the horizon.

"Salem." I say with more urgency, scrambling to keep up with her pace.

"What the fuck is this?" She stumbles backwards, coming to a halt.

I grab her by the arms and look at what has her so shaken.

Her toe sits just outside a crudely carved out circle in the sand complete with a pentagon and several large rocks dotting each point. It looks fresh enough that whoever made this, must have just been here. Or maybe still be here. I scan the area, listening for anything that could be out of the ordinary.

"Salem, let's go." I pull her by the arms hoping she follows me, but as she takes a step back her flashlight collides with the cave wall. She shrieks, dropping the phone, cracking the screen with a loud crash.

"Why are there skulls?" Her entire body is shaking. I pick up her phone and slide it into my pocket.

"Baby, let's go." I urge, feeling a surge of power washing over me that quakes my knees.

She finally snaps out of it, and grabs my hand, rushing us towards the cave entrance. The waves are breaking through quickly, the tide coming in and covering a part of the beach. If we waste any more time, we'll be completely shut in. The sun has set, and a chill lingers in the air, the harsh wind biting into my face.

She's close behind me, Doc Martians slapping loudly as we step through the current. We're almost there when Salem slips, bringing me down with her. My knees hit stone and the water rushes at us wrapping around our legs and attempting to drag us out to sea.

"Hold onto me." I yell, gripping her by the forearm and hoisting her up. She's completely drenched and shivering, sputtering sea water out of her mouth.

"My phone!" She whips her head back to the cave.

"I've got it." I assure her, trying to hurry her stubborn ass out of here. Being trapped here could be deadly in more ways than one. We manage to hit a dry part of beach and haul ass up the path and out of the stronghold of the ocean waves.

"Are you alright?" I wrap my body around her soaking wet one. She's shivering and here I am again, offering her my warmth.

"F-f-fine."

"Goddammit, baby. Let's get you warmed up."

"I d-don't need your help." I push her back looking straight into her glassy jade eyes.

"I'm not letting you drown, or freeze, although it seems that's the way you want to go since you've tried that several times since I met you." She lets out a little laugh, wringing out the wetness of her sweatshirt.

"Come on, let's get you back to the house." She lets me put my arms around her as we hurriedly trek up the dark path. We make it back in record time. The house has died down some, with most everyone up in their respective rooms or playing games in the game room. I wrap a blanket off the couch around her and set about making her some hot chocolate.

She has a faraway look as I hand her the piping hot liquid. I sit next to her, but she's lost in her thoughts. We're silent, both too focused inwardly. I feel out of place. If she had touched that wall of skulls tonight... I shudder at the thought.

I'm in so deep with her that I don't know what my role in this plan is anymore. Do I fulfill the headmaster's wishes, using the girl I care for as a pawn to open a veil into purgatory just to free me and my fraternity brothers from this curse, or do I choose Salem? Choose to stay locked with this demon inside of me for eternity.

"Goodnight, witch." I say leaving her as I turn my thoughts inside out. I don't know how to fix this. I don't know how to choose, and that kills me.

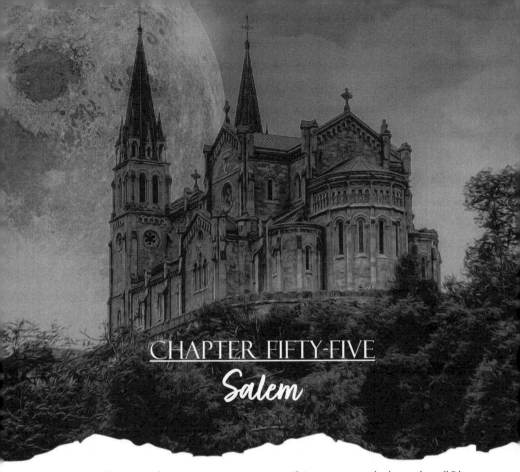

CHAPTER FIFTY-FIVE
Salem

Skye cinches up my corset, until I can scarcely breathe. "Oh-my- God, not- so- tight." I say gasping between words. After Pierce and I got back from the cave, he let me go to sleep off the shitty night. I've avoided him since. Those skulls and pentagon gave me a feeling of dread that settled deep in my stomach. It didn't help that since then, my nightmares had been plaguing me, becoming more intense. I was sure that the cave was the one from my dreams, I just didn't know why. What did it all mean if anything?

"Whoops. Sorry." Skye says attempting to loosen the black ribbon so I can breathe. "I've never done this before. Okay. How's that?" She asks, stepping back putting her hands on her hips, studying me.

I take a tentative breath in and am happy to find that my diaphragm is allowed to move this time.

"Much better. Blue isn't really my color- I like my oxygen too much." She laughs, stepping closer wielding a deep red lipstick in her hands.

"Pucker." She says. I obey, letting her apply this last touch to my look. She hands me a tissue to blot my lips together. Once I feel that I'm sufficiently blotted and not in danger of swiping my lipstick into an accidental Joker look. I stand taking a glimpse at Skye's phone she's holding out for me to get the full effect.

"Wow." I say, taking a step forward. The dress is heavy, but even more beautiful than it was online. It could have gone the other way. I was no stranger to online shopping disappointment.

Skye takes a few pictures from different angles before I fix my mask to my face with some adhesive. Its black lace matches the lace on my corset and is sprinkled with several rhinestones so that it glitters when the light catches it.

"Looks like there's a blood moon tonight." Skye says as she scrolls on her phone. I tug at the top of my dress, not paying attention.

"Do you think this will hold, or will the girls come popping out if I do one too many hops in *The Cha Cha Slide*?"

"I doubt this is the kind of event where you'll be doing *The Cha Cha Slide.*"

"Well, that's the only dance I know, so maybe I'll get lucky and just graze the snack table until I can slip out."

"Don't act like you're not excited. I could tell by the look on your face when you put on the dress. You owe it to this amazing dress to take it for a spin around the dance floor at least once."

"Well, I can't argue with that logic." I give a little twirl and can't help that it makes me feel all kinds of girly. Shit, I didn't know I had it in me.

It'd been a bear of a week, crammed full of tests and papers drowning me in schoolwork. I'd successfully avoided Pierce and hadn't heard much from Walker other than to keep practicing my chords, and only saw Emmet in passing while grabbing breakfast. I'd have to face at least two of them tonight, which made my stomach knot with nerves. Those two certainly knew how to work my emotions. I found myself almost missing them.

"What are you going to do?" I ask Skye.

"Probably just study or hang out in the common room."

"Thanks for coming up and helping me get ready, the mirror in here is a joke and the bathroom was overflowing with testosterone."

"Ugh, don't I know it. I'm holding my bladder right now, waiting for them all to leave."

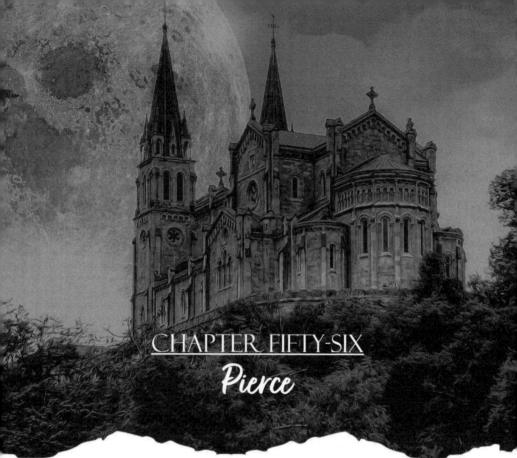

CHAPTER FIFTY-SIX
Pierce

"Luk-ASS! Let's go, or you're going to make us late." I knock on the door and fiddle with my bowtie, wishing I could chuck the thing in the fire. Only ventriloquists and pedophiles should wear bow ties. I knock again, only to have Lukas yank the door open on my second knock making me stumble. My body ached from the away game we'd played last night. Our field and stadium were still torn up from the freak lightning storm. We'd been forced to forfeit that game, putting us at a disadvantage. It ate at me knowing I would never find out if we could have scored those last needed points. Our coach was taking the loss out on us by having us run extra drills in the gymnasium.

"Bro, chill." He says, his vape hanging from his lips.

"Dad is going to kill you." I say, yanking the vape out of his mouth.

"Hey! I was using that."

"I'm saving you from Dad's criticism. Don't say I never did anything for you." Lukas's bow tie still sits around his neck limp and untied. I sigh, grabbing the fabric and making a quick and tidy knot. I could fold these in my sleep for how many black-tie events we'd been forced to attend growing up.

"Ready to get this over with" he says pulling at the tie back and forth across his Adam's apple. I let out a breath of frustration.

"Don't ruin that." I say crooking my finger at him. I push my hair back off of my forehead, as he rolls his eyes at me.

I'd offered to accompany Salem, but she was back to not speaking to me. I'd wear her down before the night was over though. I felt like shit after the cave. I needed to know she was okay.

Most of our housemates, except for Skye, Emmet and Sloan were headed to the alumni ball since we were all legacies. I didn't understand the school's archaic rules about it, but here we were following tradition. I take a trip to the bathroom before we head out, ensuring that ever strand of hair is in place. I don't want to give the old fucker anything to bitch about tonight. I fix my black devil horned mask in place and sweep my tongue over my teeth.

■■

We arrive at the ball and wait in a line of the academy's most prestigious alumni and current student legacies. Helicopters and ferries have been running all evening, making sure that everyone arrives on time and in style. My cummerbund digs into my side as we wait outside Bracken Hall, the air heavy with a cool mist.

"Stop fidgeting." Lukas says, his hands shoved in his pockets. He's wearing a matching devil horned mask, only his has faint roses carved into it.

"How long is this thing again anyways?" He asks, bouncing gently on the balls of his heels. The line moves, allowing us a glimpse inside. My eyes scan the crowd, snagging on the drink table. Well, I know where I'll be headed first. We're finally let through and are blasted with a whoosh of hot air as we walk through the vestibule into the ballroom.

I make a beeline for the flutes of champagne only, as I'm about to sweep one off the table, a large foreboding figure steps in front of me. "Pierce." The deep timbre of my father's voice hits me.

"Father." I say, lips tight.

"Ah and your elusive twin. Where have you been hiding Lukas?" His words sound light to anyone listening, but the gleam in his eyes looks murderous.

"Nowhere." Lukas says, walking around him to swipe the goblets of wine that sit on the other side of the table. He swirls the deep red liquid around before slugging it back in one large gulp.

"Really Lukas, must you make such a scene." Our father's voice scolds, his grey bushy eyebrows pulling together to form a deep frown of disapproval.

"I expect you two to be on your best behavior."

"We know the drill by now." Lukas spits out. He'd been moodier lately, and I made a mental note to ask him why later.

"Don't embarrass me. Mark my words." He stalks off, plastering a fake as fuck smile on as he greets some similarly important former alumni who look just as fake as he does. Is this our future?

I pull at my bowtie wishing I could rip it right off my neck. The sensation of having it around my throat feels more suffocating by the moment. I can't wait to get this evening over with.

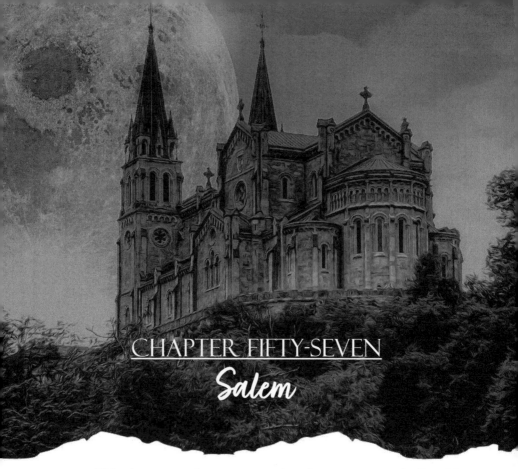

CHAPTER FIFTY-SEVEN
Salem

This dress may be gorgeous, but it was not made for this weather. The trek amongst the graveled path while wearing heels was not the best decision. I almost twist my ankle at least four times as the mist turns into a light sprinkle, then quickly changes to fat droplets that saturate my skin. I pick up my pace, knowing that my hair is ruined. I should have brought an umbrella, but I'm too far down the path to turn around now. I silently chide my stubbornness at not taking Pierce up on his offer to accompany me to the ball. I'd be irritated, but at least I'd be dry.

I'm thoroughly chilled by the time I make it to Bracken Hall. The doors have been closed and I rap my frozen knuckles on the ornate wood. A few minutes pass when someone opens the door in a fit of giggles.

The party seems well underway as I squeeze past the woman and her beau that are so lost in each other that they don't pay me any mind.

I'm welcomed by a gust of hot air that warms me to my numb toes. I look around wondering where the closest bathroom might be. I don't have any classes in Bracken Hall, so it takes me a minute to find my way through the throng of people milling about the entry and hallway areas.

I take in my appearance and attempt to fix my water whipped hair. Ugh, Skye and I spent so much time on that. A few girls funnel into the bathroom behind me, loud and obviously several drinks in.

"Aren't you the girl who burned her room down, so she'd have to live at Hell House?" A high-pitched voice asks. My hand stops midway through combing. I can't believe people are still spreading that stupid rumor.

"I didn't burn it down." I say, not turning to face the girls and continuing to detangle my hair. I was almost done. Just a few more strands and I could leave this bathroom.

"Not that I blame you, I mean I don't judge. Those guys ARE hotter than sin." Her friends snicker behind her. My fingers release the final knot and I squeeze my hands around the bottom of my limp hair, expressing several drops of water on the ground.

I must not be giving this girl the reaction she wants because she continues, "But, come to think of it, I'm not sure why you think they'd go for someone like you. Seems like a waste."

I'm reminded of all the high school bullies I'd endured over the years. The ones who'd giggle that I was named Salem in the town of Salem. That my hair was darker, that I dressed how I wanted. As much as I acted like their words didn't hurt, they did. This girl's needless attack opens up those wounds I'd thought long buried. Instead of folding in on myself and ignoring her like I want to, I stand up straight and turn on my heel. I tower over the petite bully who's red hair is done up in an elaborate braided crown, her white mask affixed on top of her cerulean eyes. I had absolutely no tolerance for mean girl energy.

"Actually, my room burning down on accident, ended up for the best. I really enjoy all the sex those hot guys have been giving me. I didn't know that their cocks would be that big, or generous in bed." Her crimson painted lips pop open, and I exit the bathroom as fast as my aching feet will carry me, my lies licking at my heels. If she wants to spread rumors, she could have at it.

"Big cocks, huh?" Pierce's voice makes me jump. I instinctively put my hand over my heart, then scowl at him. Of course, he had to overhear me saying that. He takes in my appearance with a lazy flick of his eyes down and my traitorous body lights up underneath his intense gaze.

"What did you do? Jump in the ocean on the way here?" He lifts his black devil mask, setting it on top of his head with a frown as he grabs my damp hair with his free hand, tucking it behind my ear. His close proximity to me sends a shudder down my spine, remembering how his hands felt on me, the imprint of his lips.

"No, moron. It's raining."

"Well, if you had come with me, you could have avoided that." A challenge lies flickering behind his eyes, and I square off in front of him, nearly toe to toe, chest to chest. We're so close that my breath mingles with his and a waft of champagne and mint simmers between us... His eyes go from challenging to a hint of lust, heating with desire as I lick my bottom lip.

"If you weren't such an asshole, maybe I would have." I put my mask on, determined to not show how much he affects me. This night seems destined for a lot of annoying interactions, I might as well get it over with. As I go to walk around him, Pierce grabs me gently by my elbow.

"Wait, Salem." My mouth opens at him using my name instead of calling me witch or some other stupid nickname.

"What do you want Pierce?" His eyes briefly settle on my lips before snapping them up to my eyes.

"I want to dance with you." He expertly places his large hand on the small of my back and before I know it, he's leading me off to the large ballroom that's bursting with couples that are just ending their current dance.

Panic claws up my neck, and I shake my head. "I don't know how."

He pulls his mask down and gives me a smile befitting his devilish charade. "Don't worry, I'll catch you if you fall." For some reason, I feel my stomach flip at that, not hating the way his hand fits perfectly into the arch of my lower back, flirting dangerously with the top of my butt. I feel myself leaning into his touch, hoping that he might just graze lower. Dear God, what is wrong with me? This is Pierce Ledger of all people! But that bitch Libido isn't listening to reason at all tonight, so it lets him snake his fingers along the seam of my low-cut dress. Each caress sending a shot of heat to my clit. I suck in a breath finding that he's successfully turned me on with just a few words and touches. Fuck me, I have the worst taste in men.

The song has finished, and several couples exit the dance floor. I recognize the giggly couple from earlier clinging to each other like the other might float away if they let go. I feel my mouth hitch up into a smile at the sight of them so besotted with each other. Pierce catches what I'm looking at and lets out a sound like he's clearing his throat. He guides me over to an empty spot and fiddles with his bow tie. My eyes narrow at the motion that looks as if he's nervous.

Suddenly he lets go of me and stands opposite in a line of men, who all have their left foot slightly forward.

Oh shit, is this going to be like one of those *Pride and Prejudice* dance moments where everyone knows the steps, but me? My heart hammers hard in my chest and my hands clam up. Why couldn't this be the type of event that did *The Cupid Shuffle?* I would kill at that type of group dance. Not this. I debate sneaking off the dance floor when I spy what looks like Walker and Lukas staring at us. Fuckers. They look poised to start making fun of me at any moment. I swallow my pride and resolve

312

that I'm going to dance the shit out of whatever this dance is. What a fucking nightmare.

The music starts, the song *You Belong to Me* by Cat Pierce begins to play and Pierce takes a low bow. I look around at the other couples, wondering what I'm supposed to be doing, but so far so good. That is until the women's side bows back and I'm left still standing there stupidly. I hear Walker and Lukas's snickering before I wobble down into the world's worst curtsy. This is the stuff of nightmares.

The men's side glides forward and Pierce is placing his hand in mine, his other is tight around my waist. I look up at him as he grins down at me. He leads me in a circle before I'm sent spinning away from him, my feet struggling to keep up with the rest of me that he just wound up like a spinning top toy.

He lets out a bellowing laugh that I've never heard from him before, as he spins me back into him. I land harder than I mean to, and he lets out an oof.

"Honestly, I thought you'd be better at this." He says, hopping to the left. I glance at the other couples and see the girl's side has their arm raised and are going around the gentlemen. I do my best to mimic the others but end up looking like a possessed flamingo.

He lets out another laugh, his smile wide and easy.

"I told you, I didn't know how to dance like this."

"Clearly." He takes my hand and sways his hips against my backside before spinning me yet again. I'm going to develop vertigo at this rate. We go through another round of spins, and he dips me, his body bent over mine, holding me steady as I gaze up at him. My heart is in my throat.

When he stands me up his mouth is close to my ear, "Did I tell you, you look beautiful tonight, Salem?" I feel my chest squeeze at those words. I shouldn't let them affect me, but they do. They slip right past my walls and take up residence in the corners of my stupid heart, echoing off the chamber in my mind.

I find it in me to shake my head no, even though his words have rattled me. "I was starting to wonder if you'd come at all."

"I'm here, aren't I?"

"You certainly are." He takes me by the arm spinning me into one last dip, my eyes find his easily as he holds me there suspended above the ground, my feet beginning to slip.

"Please, don't drop me." I cling to his biceps noting the way they hold me with ease.

"I wouldn't dream of letting you go." His words land heavy with meaning as he pulls me up

The dance comes to a close and his hands are still wrapped around me. My breath is coming in fast like I just ran a marathon, and I honestly don't know if it's because of Pierce or because of the dance. He finally lets me go, just as Walker and Lukas come over. Walker hands me a flute of champagne as he tucks me against him, whisking me away from Pierce in one swift move. I see Pierce's body go ridged, a muscle in his jaw twitching as his eyes dart between Walker and me.

"You guys were certainly something out there." Lukas says with a smirk.

Walker leans down to say something in my ear, my emotions are in a whirlwind over that dance and the words Piece said to me that I miss whatever Walker is saying. I'm about to have him repeat himself, when a tall man with silver hair steps over. He has a commanding presence and is the epitome of a silver fox.

"Pierce. Must you and your brother embarrass me at every event?" I feel a stab of ice in my chest at his words. This must be the twin's father.

"Hi, I'm Salem. Nice to meet you." I hold out my hand at an attempt to be cordial but am met with contempt as he stares at my outstretched hand. He turns to Pierce and says, "Control your whore, you looked absolutely ridiculous out there."

I drop my hand in shock. Walker pulls me in tighter. I look over to Pierce to see what he'll do, but he just puts his hands in his pockets avoiding me. The moment stretches and I feel everything from tonight between us going up in smoke. I'm so fucking stupid to believe I was any different than his many conquests. Embarrassment coats my chest and I feel my cheeks flame. A heady mix of anger, disappointment and confusion licks at my heart.

"Excuse me." I say, wrenching myself out of Walker's grasp. I need some air and thankfully the sky is looking like it's stopped raining. At least I knew exactly where Pierce's asshole nature came from.

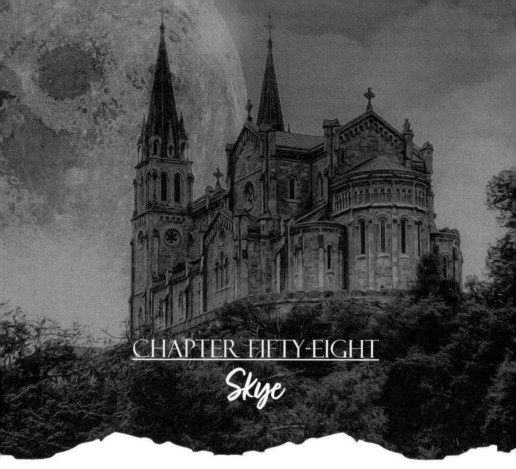

CHAPTER FIFTY-EIGHT
Skye

The house is basically empty and I'm not one to let it go to waste. I dig into the leftovers eagerly. With no one here to fight me over it, I get the best piece of lasagna, sinking my teeth into the layers of cheese and sauce. I'm immediately thankful for Graham's family recipes and his obsession with cooking large meals. Once I pack away more than my weight in pasta, I decide to explore the house. There are far too many rooms to count, the manor house sprawling out for ages. It's like a gothic architect made a baby with the Victorian era and splashed in a touch of Baroque for a bit of extra flavor. The result was this creepy as heck house that I was slightly regretting being alone in, now that I was really looking at how it screamed haunted house vibes.

"Hey!"

"Oh my God! Sloan. You scared me."

"Sorry. I saw you ogling the fireplace and thought it would be rude not to say hi."

"I'm glad you did. I was just thinking how haunted this place looks without everyone here."

"You're not at the ball?"

"Not a legacy." I shrug.

"Me either." He mimics my shrug. "Do you want to come play a game with me?"

I smile letting him lead the way.

"I didn't even know we had a game room." It was obvious this room was well lived in, with several empty beer cans and blankets strewn around the couch and chairs that flanked a large flatscreen TV. Sloan hands me a game controller.

"I have a confession..." I say sitting on the other end of the couch. "I've never played any video games."

"You're kidding me."

I shake my head. "It was just me and my dad on the road exploring. We didn't have much time to sit and play, plus there was my art."

"Well, I'm honored to pop that cherry of yours, Skye." His eyes twinkle as he breaks down the game for me, showing me how to hold the controller and which buttons I should press and when.

He presses play and I last all of five seconds before I'm shot, feeling the controller shake in my hands.

"What!" I shriek. Sloan lets out a belly laugh.

"Okay, let's try that again." I set my shoulders determined to at least make it a full minute this time.

He hovers his fingers over the start button, "Are you ready?"

"Yes."

"ARE YOU SURE?"

"YES!" I laugh at the faux intensity.

"3,2,1, GO!" He slams his finger down and we're off. I make my character duck down and army crawl out of the line of fire. The screen is split so I take note of Sloan's surroundings and map positioning, slowly trekking my way towards his little dot.

His practiced fingers fly over the buttons without hesitation, whereas mine are slow and clumsy. I manage to sneak up behind Sloan's camo clad character. I make mine jump out and hold her gun up to Sloan's character.

"Gotcha." I say, pulling the trigger.

Sloan whips his head in surprise at me, then barks out a laugh. "Oh, you're a dark one little Skylark, aren't you?"

I smirk, "I have my moments."

We play until I my hands cramp up and my eyes become heavy with sleep. I rest my head back for a moment, I tell myself, but end up slipping into slumber, my legs tangled with Sloan's.

CHAPTER FIFTY-NINE
Salem

I step outside flushed and angry, I take a deep breath, steadying myself and ripping off my mask, letting the sharp air slice across my face. The night air chills my skin almost immediately. This part of the building overlooks the ocean, the veranda is full of mist making it look like someone placed a smoke machine out here. Several clouds linger in the sky, blocking out bits of the moon that are tinged pink, making the sky a hazy red-black. This far out from any major cities, grant us pristine views of the stars on clear nights, but today with the rain clouds still looming, only a few stragglers are able to peek through. I rest my elbows on the stone rail and wonder exactly how long I'm expected to stay here at this stupid ball.

I'd been called worse things in my life, but they'd just stood there.

Laughter filters in mixing with clinking glasses and what sounds suspiciously like an instrumental version of *The Thong Song*. I stay outside until I feel the chill down in my bones.

When I step back inside, I'm determined to swipe some food, make sure the headmaster sees me, and then get back to the house so I can get this night over with as soon as possible. I spot Garrison and Graham huddled around a distinguished group of gentlemen as they converse holding champagne flutes. Garrison is actually holding two flutes on closer inspection. I make sure to smile at them as I pass.

I'm about to grab some sort of cake, crab cake maybe, when I hear a familiar laugh. I turn my hand frozen in midair and see Grandma Clementine laughing with several staff members and Headmaster Hayden.

"Oh, there she is!" Her lilting voice says as she gestures widely, champagne flute held high for extra emphasis Grandma is always theatrical.

I fix a smile onto my face and stand up straight. Crab cakes forgotten to my stomach's great dismay.

"Grandma Clementine! What are you doing here?"

"Pish posh girl. I always come to these things. Now come over here and give me a hug." She's wearing a lavender gown, with stars sewn into the fabric. Her mask matches the color of her gown perfectly and has pearls attached to the edges. Her white hair is perfectly coiffed, and she stands arms wide, flute of champagne held aloft in an invitation for me.

I cringe inwardly and brace my senses for an onslaught of garlic cloves that always seems to accompany her wherever she goes, and I find today is no exception. Her doctor told her years ago that she needed to up her intake of garlic and she took that so seriously that the smell creeps out of her pores, no matter what perfume she wears to mask it.

"Let me get a good look at you. Well..." she tsks, "apart from your hair, I'd say you look presentable."

"Thanks." I say tightly, fully ready for any barbs she might toss my way. Grandma has a way of cutting you down while you're stuck with a smile on your face, and you find yourself thanking her for her time.

"Your headmaster here was just telling us about the suspected arson in your room, pickle. Why didn't you tell me?"

"I didn't want to be a bother. Besides Headmaster Hayden assures me that they're doing everything they can to find the real cause of it." I catch the headmaster's jowls clenching tight. His gnarled knuckles whiten with how tight he's gripping his wine goblet. As he takes a sip, I see the red stain on his teeth that the wine has left behind. It's jarring how closely it resembles blood, giving him a more sinister quality as he glares at me from beneath his plain black mask.

"Well, he better. I don't donate good money to this place for my granddaughter to be stuck in the Hell House of all places with a bunch of frat boy hooligans." The people around us titter, and I feel a pit open in my stomach. I desperately want to get out of here. I let her carry on for a few moments more before making excuses to extricate myself. I give her a hug, promising to call her soon and apologize for not telling her about the fire.

I weave through the throngs of people who are substantially more intoxicated than when I first arrived, several swaying against each other as music continues playing. I spot Walker, Pierce and Lukas talking in a group with the girls who were making fun of me in the bathroom when I first got here. I let out a frustrated breath. I've officially had enough of this night. I hurry my steps to the door, my feet feel like they've grown two sizes and I'm already picturing how good it will feel to soak them when I get back to the house.

I make the trek back to the house with several revealers prancing around the front building. I step through the wrought iron gate that leads to the path back to Hell House. A small shiver wracks through my body as I step though, and I wish I had a jacket or at least a change of shoes as I hobble down the uneven well-worn path. I get lost in my thoughts, replaying the night. As I get deeper in the woods, I get the feeling that I'm no longer alone. The hairs on the back of my neck stand on edge as a shiver runs down my spine. I glance over my shoulder and scan the path, my eyes not seeing anything. I keep walking chalking it up to one too many horror movies. Plus, just being a girl alone in the worlds sometimes felt like you had to have a heightened sense of alertness. The blood moon is raised in the sky, making the surrounding clouds look like they'd been dripped in red paint. It's creepy as hell.

I continue down the path, only a few minutes from reaching the house. I was going slower than normal due to my feet feeling like I was stepping on knives with each footfall. The sound of gravel being trod upon reaches my ears, but it sounds like it's coming from behind me. My skin tingles again with something other than the chilly air. I glance around, still not seeing anything, but I decide to pick up my pace as best I can. I curse myself for not bringing my phone with.

The wind picks up sounding more like a high-pitched scream than your average gust of wind.

I keep my guard up, but when I'm maybe a minute away from the house I feel hot breath nipping at my neck and a feeling of claws scraping up my back has a scream flying from my mouth. I swirl around, eyes wide, hands ready to gouge out some eyeballs, but no one is there. I hear a deep chuckle. What the fuck was that?

"Pierce?" I ask, not in the mood for any stupid pranks. I pick up my pace, my heart hammering so hard I feel it in my throat.

"Salem, run." A soft feminine voice whispers in my ear.

I jolt, my feet sliding on the gravel, tripping me. I go down hard, the tiny bits of stone biting into my palms. My dress tangled beneath me as another chuckle ripples past me.

"What do you want?" I scream out, hopeful that someone from the house will hear me.

Only a laugh answers that sounds like it could be anywhere and everywhere at the same time.

My heart gallops, pulsating in my ears so loud that I almost miss when whatever it is tries to swipe at me again, but this time I'm ready. I turn, running as fast as I can toward the house my dress billowing behind me, but when I'm about to reach the exit of the path, my hair is ripped backwards, and I feel three sharp claw marks ripping down my back so deep that I know there must be blood. I scream at the top of my lungs. Kicking and clawing at nothing but air. Was I going insane? I can't see any assailant but my back burns with the rips in my flesh. At the blinding pain I feel a crack deep inside of my chest. My body heating underneath my skin. I see a flash of light gathering in my palms, I swipe to where I feel myself being held.

I'm let go as suddenly as I was snatched, my breath coming in ragged. I stare down at my hands, but they look as normal as they ever have. I shove down a wretch of vomit that gathers in my throat, confusion coating my mind.

"Salem?" Walker's deep gravel voice asks. I blink trying to focus my eyes on the three guys walking towards me.

"Stay away from me." I say yanking my heel off my foot, ready to use it like a weapon. My back was screaming, and I felt close to passing out from the pain.

"Baby, what happened?" Pierce pushes past Walker, taking in my disheveled appearance. I choose to ignore his use of calling me baby, but Walker sure doesn't seem to be willing to as he glowers at Pierce. He looks two seconds away from pummeling him straight in the face, and I can't say I wouldn't enjoy seeing that Karma in action.

"You can stop fucking with me. Why were you guys chasing me? You ripped my back open!" All three of them gasp when I turn gesturing to the blood seeping out of my back. Pierce doesn't even give me a second, before he's wrenching the shoe out of my hand.

"Who did this to you?" He demands, crushing my body against him as he inspects the wounds. I look up at him in confusion.

"It wasn't you guys?" They look at me with something that looks like a mix of fear and concern.

"Lukas! Give me your jacket." Pierce snaps. I see Lukas shrug out of his jacket and Pierce applies pressure with the black dress coat. "Hold on baby, I've got you. Walker, go check the woods. See if the fucker that did this is close."

I reach up feeling close to blacking out and run my fingers against Pierce's stubble.

"I couldn't see who did it. I thought it was you." He frowns at me, his devil mask sitting on top of his slicked back dirty blonde hair. "Lukas, go get help. She's losing a lot of blood." Lukas takes off running, as Pierce gathers me into his arms using his body to heat me up. "Stay with me." He demands.

"I make no such promises." I manage to whisper, before I slip out of consciousness.

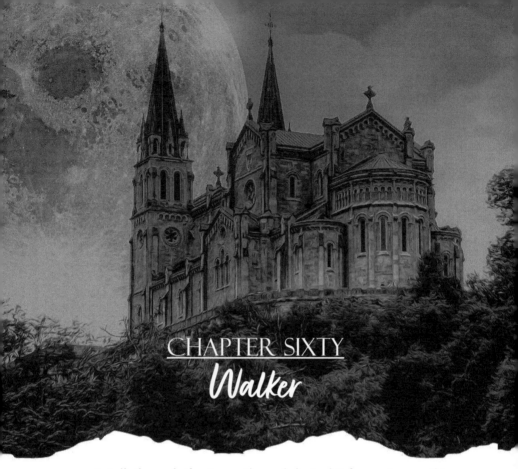

CHAPTER SIXTY
Walker

I stalk through the trees, the red sky is shit for seeing anything, so I swing out my phone and turn on the flashlight. Whoever fucking hurt Salem was going to pay. My feet stomp through the forest, snapping twigs and sending rocks flying. I remember the look on her face when Pierce and Lukas's father called Salem a whore. The man was lucky to still be breathing. I'd never felt my Wrath slip into place so fast, ready to rip out his throat with my bare hands. It took everything I had to shove it down, so I didn't end up murdering one of the most prominent CEOs in the country. But the way she looked as us, like she was disappointed, that gutted me the most. Especially since I'd been keeping her at arm's length since that day in her bedroom, when I lost control. I couldn't live with myself if I hurt her.

I swing the flashlight letting it bathe the dense forest in visibility. I'm careful not to get too close to the edge. One wrong step, or one strong gust of wind could have me on the bottom side of a cliff, smashed or impaled beyond recognition.

A rustling to my left has me swinging my flashlight in that direction.

"Emmet? What the fuck are you doing out here?" Was he the one that hurt Salem? My rage is threatening to spill over and pummel his face in. He stumbles, obviously drunk. Fuck. I almost laid out my friend.

I grab him by his jacket collar, helping him find his footing.

"Had one too many, must have lost my way."

"Yeah, well you were about to toss yourself over the edge of a cliff. Have you seen anyone else out here? Someone attacked Salem."

"Sss- she, okay?"

"I don't know. Listen, let's get you back to the house. I'm not seeing anyone else out here."

"Thanks, brother."

He hangs on me, but instead of being assaulted with alcohol breath I expect, I'm hit with the smell of mint. He could have just popped a mint in his mouth, that doesn't mean he was out here hurting Salem. I shake my head desperate to get back and see if anyone else found anything, and most of all if she's okay.

CHAPTER SIXTY-ONE
Pierce

Looking down at Salem in the hospital issue bed on the infirmary wing has me pacing back and forth with anxiety. They'd diagnosed her with dehydration and dismissed her wounds as an unfortunate run in with the foliage.

The nurse had the audacity to claim that she was intoxicated. I knew she hadn't drunk a drop of alcohol the whole night, so that theory was utter bullshit. They wanted this wrapped up in a tidy little bow, no fuss made for the important alumni that still graced our shores.

Normally they wouldn't disclose anything about a patient's condition to anyone but family, but I was a motherfucking Ledger and money talks. If my father taught me anything, it's that everyone has a price.

Salem shifts, obviously uncomfortable in her bandages. Fuck. I feel helpless to do anything but be right here. I wrack my hands down my face, slapping the sides to stay awake. I'd been up all night, not letting myself take my eyes off her for a second. Other than when she was carted off by the on-staff doctor and nurses, I'd been plastered to her side, waiting for those jade green eyes to open. I was desperate for those lips to tell me to fuck off.

Fuck, this was torture. I'd never been this out of mind for someone before and I wasn't sure I liked it. I was supposed to use her, the same I'd done to girls before. Why her? Of all the women I could fall for, it had to be Salem Knox. No matter how much I try to fight my feelings, I end up coming back for more.

"Anything?" Walker says handing me a cup of black coffee and sets down a bag of clothes he got from Skye for Salem to change into.

I shake my head grateful for the jolt of caffeine. "Did you find anything."

"No. Unless you want to count a drunk Emmet."

"Emmet was out there?"

"Yeah. Seemed pretty wasted too. If I hadn't caught him, he might have gone right over the edge of the cliff."

"Shit."

"Yeah."

We stand there sipping our coffees, staring down at Salem.

"She looked so scared." Walker whispers.

I swallow a hard lump, ashamed I drove her to want to arrive and leave alone.

"Pierce?" Salem croaks out. "Walker?"

"We're right here, wildcat." Walker grabs her hand, and she squeezes her fingers around him blinking up in confusion.

"What happened? Why is my back on fire? Wait. Where am I?"

"You're in the hospital wing." Walker says squeezing her hand he's still holding.

She sits up abruptly with a wince. "Woah, baby. Lay down. You've got about fifty stitches in your back." I go over to the head of her bed, helping her lay back down careful not to spill my coffee all over her.

"Do you want to tell us what happened? When we found you, you were shaking with fear." Walker asks, rubbing her arm. I feel a flare of jealousy at seeing him touch her, but I shove it away. The most important thing is she's okay and finding whatever dead man did this to her.

"I.... I was walking down the path, but it felt like someone was following me. You know that feeling? Well then, I heard their steps behind me, but I couldn't see them." She breathes in wincing. "I was almost to the house when I felt someone swipe at my back with claws."

I catch Walker's quick look at me. We hadn't seen anyone but that didn't mean that someone didn't attack her. Those woods were dense. Perfect for getting lost in. Or hiding.

"Oh, good you're up." A nurse chimes as she rolls in a cart. "Now I need you two to scoot I have to check on Ms. Knox's dressings."

"When will she be able to come home?" I ask.

"She should be cleared later today. Now shoo."

Walker and I leave the room. "I'm going to head back to the house, get her set up somewhere more comfortable." I nod my agreement, determined to wait outside this door until the nurse is finished.

I finish my coffee tossing the cup and check my drained phone. They really ought to keep chargers up here. I make a mental note to bring it up with the head of this department.

"You can go back in. She's going to be alright. She's lucky to have friends like you."

Yeah, I'm sure all good friends set their friend's rooms on fire. I let the guilt wash over me before I stride into her room, every bit the asshole she loves to hate.

Salem looks guarded and tired, but every bit as beautiful as the first time I saw her.

"Wow, you look like shit." She doesn't pull any punches and I fucking love it.

"You're one to talk."

"Ha. Ha."

"We'll find him Salem."

"What if it was a woman."

"Then they'll be every bit as dead just the same."

She sucks in a breath. I let her see just how serious I am. She bites her lip.

"Where was this kind of energy last night when your dad was calling me a whore?"

"Things with my dad are complicated, but you're right I should have said something. I'm sorry."

"What was that?"

"What was what?"

"Those words. Did I just hear *the* Pierce Ledger apologize or am I high off the hospital drugs?"

"Definitely the second one."

"That's what I thought."

"Alright, Ms. Knox. You're all set to go. Just remember to change your bandages every 4-6 hours and follow up with a doctor within two days." The nurse says as she comes in with a roll of bandages and ointment for her to take. "You're allowed to take some ibuprofen for the pain. One to two 200mg tablets when you change your bandages. Do me a favor, drink it with water. We just had a kid who swallowed them dry and they got stuck in his esophagus." Salem makes a grossed-out face.

"I promise to take good care of her." I say.

Salem narrows her eyes at me. "I can take care of myself."

"It's not a bad idea to accept some help. The wounds are hard to reach." Salem looks thrilled at the nurse's words.

"Well, sorry we had to meet this way Salem."

"What's your name?" She asks.

"Oh, I'm sorry. I'm Jacqueline. Your bag of items is right over there by the window. Please let me know if you need any help getting dressed." She leaves again, leaving Salem scowling at me.

"Need me to turn around while you change?" I point at the bag Walker left. She grabs it, sucking in air between her teeth with the sudden movement.

"Ok. Listen I know that nurse saw a lot of my parts, but would you mind…"

"I don't mind." I say grabbing the back of her gown's strings. I pull gently letting her remove her arms from the material. She covers her front with the blue floral gown as I check the bag for a shirt.

"Well, there's a bra in here if you want it, but I think it'll rub your wounds if we try." She shakes her head. "No bra it is." I scrunch up a plain black t-shirt, working her head through the hole careful not to knock against her bandages that go from the nape of her neck down to her mid back. She works her arms in, letting me guide her when she needs it. She glances down.

"Underwear?" She asks. I dig in the bag, retrieving a back lacy see-through pair. I raise my eyebrows.

"Who does Skye think you're going to need these for?"

She squares her shoulders, "Myself."

I thumb the lace, half tempted to keep them for myself, but instead I go to the foot of her bed, taking her hospital sock clad feet in my hands. I slide the skimpy material up her creamy legs, noting the bandages coating her knees. A smattering of birthmarks dot her legs, something I hadn't noticed before, but now I fight the urge to follow the trail of them with my lips.

"Can you stand?"

She nods. Panties laying right below her knees as we work together to swing her legs over the edge.

"Hold onto me." She wraps her arms around my neck standing with me. Her t-shirt falls covering her front. I guide her undies up her legs as her grip becomes shaky. I settle the thin material around her hips, the scrap of fabric barely covering her ass. I sit her down and have her step one leg at a time into her black leggings.

"Alright, baby. I need you to stand one more time. Think you can manage?"

She must be tired because she doesn't even sass me. She nods, linking her arms around my neck as she pushes up off the bed. I quickly hoist the leggings on. Her arm slips, but I hold her tight by the sides of her pants. "Okay, I've got you. Salem, sit for me, okay?" She sits, and I smooth her hair back.

"You good?" She licks her lips and nods.

"I just want to sleep."

"Okay, baby. I'm going to get you out of here so you can sleep."

And I do just that. Even going so far as to have a new mattress delivered via helicopter with special pillows, so she can sleep comfortably.

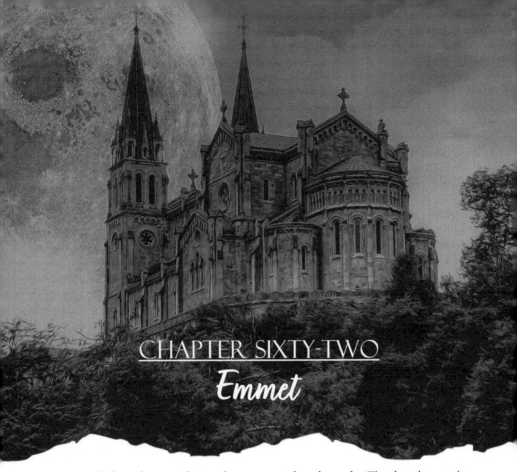

CHAPTER SIXTY-TWO
Emmet

"There's another player on the board. That's the only explanation for it."

Headmaster Hayden stirs his piping hot herbal tea, his displeasure palpable.

"What were you doing out there? Do you realize that you could have put the entire plan in jeopardy?"

I narrow my eyes at him. "I was taking a walk when I saw Salem get attacked. I knew that if she saw me, she would suspect me. Trust me, I played it off well. Walker doesn't suspect a thing, and Salem never saw me."

"You better hope they don't find us out, or I won't hesitate to snap your neck and send you flying back to purgatory faster than you can say your own name, Envy."

I held my tongue about the body he was currently residing in not being able to snap a saltine cracker let alone my neck, but I wouldn't put it past him to poison the shit out of me.

"You better fix this. Make sure they trust you implicitly. Do whatever it takes. We're too close to Samhain to fuck it up now." Spit gathered at the edges of his puckered lips, spraying saliva like he was Jonathan Groff.

The last thing I needed was someone trying to rid us of the only hope we had of getting the veil open.

"And you're sure you didn't see anyone?"

I can feel my patience thinning. "No. Like I said before, all I saw was Salem go down hard like she was attacked by air."

His nostrils flare and I sense he isn't telling me something important. Knowing better than to ask, I make to leave his house and head back to my room where I can get some information on Salem's condition.

"Did you get the device from your father?" Remembering the flash drive in my pocket, I hand over the tech capable of blocking the island's signal.

"No one should be able to get a phone call in or out once you activate it." I tell him.

"Just think, Envy, in two weeks' time we could be reunited with our families again." His cloudy eyes shine wistfully.

I leave him to his memories and brace the cold, bracing myself for what I had to do the next coming weeks to make sure I never had to leave this body.

CHAPTER SIXTY-THREE
Salem

My back feels like it's being sliced open by a thousand tiny knives as Pierce and Walker assist me to an unfamiliar bedroom on the first floor.

"Where are we going?"

"We can't have you ripping out those stitches trying to climb up to your princess tower." Pierce jokes.

I blink taking in the ornate carvings of the room complete with a plush carpet and intricate wallpaper design. "Looks like I got upgraded to the Queen's suite."

"This is my room." I spin my head towards him. "It's fine. I'm going to take the couch and Garrison is going to take your bedroom for the time being."

I feel a frown forming trying to figure him out. Why was he being so nice? He'd called me baby multiple times since last night and even apologized. It was throwing me for a loop.

They set me down on the world's comfiest bed. I could fall asleep right now.

"Knock, knock." Skye calls from the door. "Whoa, nice room."

I gesture for her to come in and she takes a seat next to me on the side of my bed. "I'm so glad you're okay. I was worried about you all night." She grabs my hand with a squeeze. "I brought you your phone." I grab it, noticing it's been charged.

"Thank you." I can hardly keep my eyes open and feel the need to lay down.

I see Walker placing my bag that carries my ruined dress and beat up shoes.

"Take these." Pierce says, handing me two slim white pills and a bottle of water.

I let go of Skye's hand and obey, too tired to put up a fight. Just getting dressed and over to the house seemed to wipe me out.

"We'll leave you alone to get some rest, but I'll be back in 4 hours to change your bandages." Pierce says shooing Walker and Skye out, shutting off the lights.

I lay back and do exactly what my body is begging of me. Sleep.

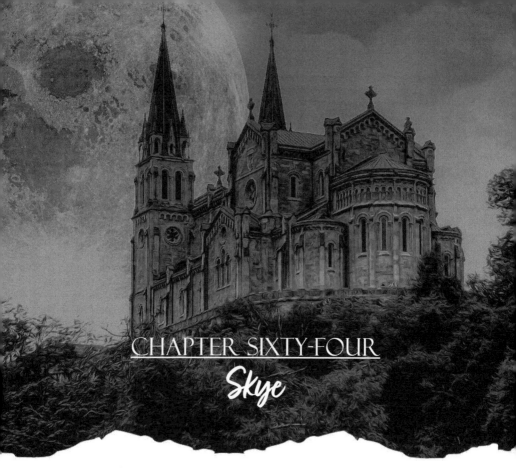

CHAPTER SIXTY-FOUR
Skye

The kitchen is packed with the guys arguing over what to make for Salem as she recovers in Pierce's room.

"Everyone knows you make chicken soup for someone who's sick!" Graham says swinging a ladle at Walker who's attempting to make her a sandwich.

"She's not sick, she's injured!" Walker says slapping more meat onto the bread and easily dodging Graham's makeshift weapon. The sandwich meat is piled on higher than she could even open her mouth, but I say nothing, instead enjoying the chaos that's unfolding before me while munching on some chips. My feet swing lazily from the stool as I pop another chip into my mouth, chomping its salty exterior and trying not to focus on who or what could have attacked Salem right outside our house. But, with all the guys home it feels safe. I swallow down a sharp piece wondering if Salem was the intended target or were they on their way here, after the three of us who were the only ones not attending the ball. That thought sours my stomach, making me toss the remainder of my chips into the trash, wiping the grease from my fingers.

"I already ordered a gourmet dinner that's being flown in from Seattle as we speak."

Walker and Graham gape at Pierce who's shaking his phone at them like a trump card.

"No fucking way." Walker slams a piece of bread down on top of his meat tower. "What am I going to do with this then?" He gestures at his leaning tower of meat.

"I don't know, eat it yourself." Pierce says, with a shrug, leaving the room while typing out something on his phone. His posture all business.

"What about my soup!" Graham laments.

"I'll eat your soup." I say, grabbing a spoon, even though I'm not the least bit hungry anymore.

"Amore." Graham says, tucking me against his hard chest with a smile. His mood swinging from angry to adoring. I pop my finger into the crook of his dimple.

"Oh, aren't you two just adorable." Lukas says, stalking in his words full of venom. I feel my spine straighten and my muscles tense. "You going to eat that sandwich?" He asks Walker, swiping up the plate.

"Go for it." He grumbles in response, leaving the kitchen to go back to the basement.

Graham eyes Lukas warily. "Soup?"

"Nah man, this sandwich is more than enough for me thanks." He flicks his eyes over me, a hint of anger laying behind his emerald stare. The intensity of his gaze reminded me how he'd looked at me as he came inside of me. Desperate and angry. I find myself clenching and it's like he can sense his effect on me, lifting his mouth up into a smirk before he takes his mountain of a sandwich up to our room. I blow out a breath once he's gone wondering how I'm going to share a room with a man that drove me crazy while feeling equally attracted to the gorgeous chef in front of me.

Graham hands me a spoon and gift him a small, tired smile. Maybe tomorrow would be a better day and I'd magically have the answers I was looking for.

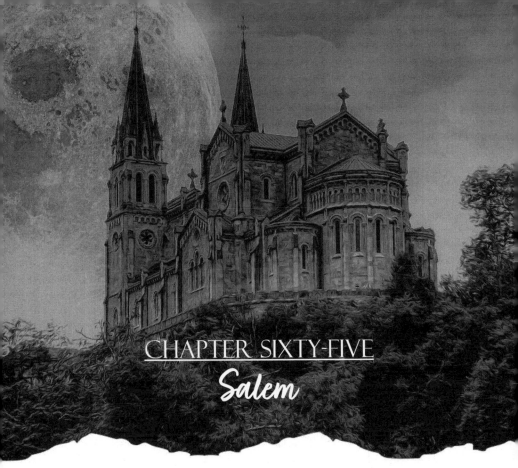

CHAPTER SIXTY-FIVE
Salem

Between Pierce, Walker, and Skye's endless hovering I slowly start to heal. Even Emmet has been making sure to pop in on me when one of those three aren't glued to my side. I learned that Emmet's dad is hot as fuck though when he'd FaceTimed while dropping off some food to my room. That apple did not stray far from the tree. I found myself blushing like an idiot when Emmet swung the phone camera on me to say hi at his dad's insistence. I about died inside, especially since I hadn't brushed my hair yet and was pretty sure I was sporting a pillow crease on my face.

The doctor cleared me and assured me and Pierce, who had accompanied me to the appointment, that I was healing nicely. I swear they had all tried to act like I was an invalid or something. Thankfully, they realized I was okay after we were able to remove the bandages earlier this week. My skin was still a little puckered, but it looked a thousand times better than when they'd first stitched me up like I was the bride of Frankenstein.

We didn't have any answers on who had attacked me, which made me uneasy. I was constantly kept company on my way to and from classes, which I felt was a bit overboard. It could have easily been what the nursing staff said it was. Just an unfortunate run in with some sharp branches, and maybe my mind got carried away. Otherwise, what else could it possibly have been? The guys insisted that they hadn't seen anything, and by the way they were helping me it didn't match up with someone who wanted to cause me harm.

The house was busy being decorated for the Halloween party happening this Saturday and I was ready to let loose. The theme was to dress up like a celebrity, dead or alive, but I didn't have a clue who I wanted to be. I'd show up looking hot, ready to have a good time. I was finally off my pain meds and wanting to throw back drinks until I was good and buzzed. If my blood was more alcohol than blood, so much the better.

I place the headphones Walker had leant me over my ears, cueing up some music so I could work on my homework. For some reason I seemed to focus better with a little something in the background. It seemed like everything between the guys and I had been put on pause while I healed. They damn sure were attentive, but they'd left me feeling pent up with desire, especially when they flashed their muscles around. Walker had a habit of wearing muscle t's that showed off his biceps in a way that made me feral. All Pierce had to do was look at me for me to remember just how good he could use that mouth. I wondered if he could use other parts just as good. I let the beats drum steadily in my ears, when *Sex and Candy* shows up in my shuffle, transporting me to that night at the bar.

God, singing with Walker was like someone had pulled out my deepest, most hidden desire and made it come to life. I had never told anyone how much I wish I could be a singer. Walker and I had that in common, where our families would never approve of our dreams. I'd kept it buried. Shoved away in a tiny box never to be made a possibility, until he asked me to join them on stage. It was expected of me to get this business degree and come back to Massachusetts, putting those skills to use.

"Hey, wildcat." The man himself walks in, his dark hair curling at the nape wet with a recent shower. I track the drop of water that dives down his neck, while taking off the headphones.

"Hey." I smile up at him. He always managed to make me feel better just by being near him.

"How are you feeling?" He drops down next to me, looking at my back dragging his calloused fingers across my skin, careful to avoid my scratches.

"Much better, so you can stop treating me like I'm going to break at any second."

"We have been doing that haven't we?" I nod arching my eyebrow.

"Hey, I wanted to ask you something."

"Yeah?"

"Why is the band called the Hateful Hydras?"

He palms my thigh, the heat seeping up my leg like he just set me on fire. "Well, I chose it because when a hydra gets cut down, they come back twice as strong."

"I love that." I say wholeheartedly. Walker tended to allow few people into his life. He was quiet around most, but he was incredibly funny when he let himself relax. Still there was an undercurrent of rage that clung to him in a way that told me that he'd been hurt.

"So, who are you dressing up as?"

"I haven't decided, but whatever I wear I want to look hot."

"No problem there." He says, locking his gaze on my bottom lip. He leans forward making my heart speed up. I lick my lips in anticipation. He catches the movement and seems to wake up from whatever spell he was under pulling himself back and crumbling my hope with him.

He stands, granting me an awkward wave before leaving me with an ache deep in my stomach. I didn't even get to ask him what he was going as.

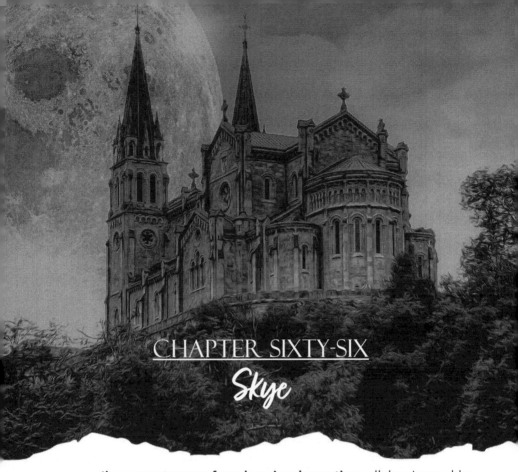

CHAPTER SIXTY-SIX
Skye

I'm a sweaty mess from hanging decorations all day. I was able to snag a vintage looking white dress for my costume on a quick shopping trip to town with Javelynn earlier. Salem was almost back to feeling like herself, and I knew we both needed a night to blow off some steam. My stomach had been nothing but a ball of anxiety over Professor Whitelsbee's constant disapproval and Lukas's intoxicating presence. I'd been able to avoid Lukas for the most part, except at night when I listened to his deep snores. Seriously, that man needed a sleep study done to see if they could fix that. Or perhaps just muzzle it with an apnea machine.

"Need some help?" Sloan extends his hand as I climb down the step ladder.

"Thanks." I say brightly taking his hand for stability.

"Hey. Package for Salem." Emmet says carrying a box in. "She up?"

"I don't know. Why don't you set it down in the mud room for now?" I suggest.

"Ohhh, looks like she got some pie." Sloan says tracking the box as Emmet walks past.

"I bet it's from Pierce. He's been lavishing her with all sorts of gifts since the accident."

"He went from womanizer to whipped so fast it gave me whiplash." Sloan says helping me to hang up some lights. I bark out a laugh.

"I heard that, asshole." Pierce calls from another room. Sloan and I look at each other trying to stifle our laughs.

"So, who are you going as?" He asks me.

"Marilyn Monroe."

"Classic."

"You think so? It's not too overdone?"

"She's a classic icon for a reason. You'll do her justice that's for sure." My cheeks warm at his compliment.

"Who are you going as?"

"Nicholas Cage."

"Any specific movie or moment?"

"Moonstruck. I'll never get over the scene where he's waving his wooden hand around yelling about his wife."

"I haven't seen it."

"Oh, you're missing out. It's hilarious. Cher the singer is in it."

"You know a lot about movies." I say tying off my end of the lights.

"It's my secret talent."

I stand back admiring our handiwork. This was going to be one heck of a party.

CHAPTER SIXTY-SEVEN
Salem

The music pulses throughout my body, my hips moving with the rhythm. I'm three drinks in, my mouth tasting like the cherry Jell-O that I threw back before heading out onto the makeshift dance floor. My costume feels tight as I move. I feel eyes boring into me making my body heat as I dance. I scan the crowd of sweaty bodies, costumes swaying together. A hand snakes up around my waist, pulling me back against a sweaty bare chest that smells like too much Axe body spray. I go to remove his sweaty hand from my stomach, but whoever he is presses me against him harder causing me to yelp. He lets out a dark laugh which pisses me off. "Hands off!" I yell above the music, but he doesn't make a move to show that he's heard me. I manage to spin, taking the shirtless man by surprise. I have no idea who he's supposed to be. The theme for tonight was 'Famous People- Dead or Alive'. So far, I'd seen two Lady Gaga's- one in a meat dress and one from *American Horror Story*.

The shirtless guy gets a predatory look in his eyes and steps towards me, I back up and come to a stop as familiar arms wrap around my back. Pierce's lips hover near my ear, sending a shudder throughout my body. "You alright?" I nod.

The shirtless guy's eyes bounce between us as he quickly assesses that he's not welcome. Why it takes another guy's presence and not my very clear refusal sparks a feeling of anger deep in my belly. He skitters away getting lost in the sea of bodies. Pierce is still pressed against my back, his hands snaking around my hips.

I turn facing him. He's dressed up as James Dean, his cocky smirk firmly in place. My body sways toward him of its own volition making me let out a snort. "Why are you here Pierce?"

"I live here." His gaze flits to my lips.

"Are you just going to stand there or are you going to dance with me?" He lets out a snarl grabbing my hips again and pushing our bodies together.

"You want to dance with me, witch?" He bites out grinding his lower half against mine. I can feel the pulse of his erection press against me, making me let out a moan of appreciation. Drunk me was such a slut, I arch into him without a second thought. His eyes darken at my movement. He rolls his hips against me in tune with the music as he pushes his fingers into my hips with a bruising grip, but it feels too good to care. As we grind together with the swell of the music, I feel a warm press of solid muscle come up from behind me. The scent of pine needles envelops me, and I know immediately who's body it is.

I see a flash of annoyance cross Pierce's face, before he looks at me assessing my reaction. I answer by snaking my arm around Walker's neck pulling him even closer. Pierce's jaw ticks then, he nods placing a quick kiss against my lips that tastes like whisky and fire. I let out a moan when he continues moving against me. Walker's body moving in time with ours.

It isn't long until I feel Walker growing hard against my ass. I grind myself against both Walker and Pierce, lost in the heady sensations flowing through me, letting myself just feel for once. Giving myself permission to take what I want. And what I want is both of them. I feel their cocks pulsating with each roll of my hips, working me up into the most delicious frenzy. Their hands roam over me, Walker cupping my breast as he licks my neck. Pierce takes notice and goes after my earlobe on the other side, his hot breath skating across my skin, leaving goosebumps in his wake.

I let out a groan, feeling my panties grow wet with my desire. I'm vaguely aware that there are people all around us, but I'm beyond caring.

"What do you want, baby?" Pierce growls in my ear, his voice hitching as I press against him. I can feel his full length pushing hard against me, so close to where I want him most.

Walker rolls his hips against my ass as I arch into him encouraging him to keep going.

"If you keep doing that, we're going to have a problem." Walker warns nipping at my neck. My mouth quirks up into a smirk.

"You want to take this somewhere more private, little witch?" Pierce says, trailing his hand up my side, caressing under my breast. My nipples ache for him to go higher, to touch me and take my breast in his hand, but he teases me keeping his fingers just below where I want it. This hunger for them thrummed through my veins, making my senses sharpen toward each tremor, each slight touch and brush of their lips. It set my body on fire, jolts of desire zinging straight to my clit. A deep ache opened inside of me, and I knew my answer.

I nodded my head, "Please." I murmured into Pierce's ear.

"I do love it when you beg." He says, yanking me towards the hallway. I grab Walker's wrist as Pierce pulls us through the crowd. Purple strobe lights flash while a fog machine sputters out mist onto the floor giving it the ultimate spooky vibe. A few people bump into us as we squeeze past them. One Marilyn Monroe tries to get Pierce's attention, which he ignores completely. I can't deny that it makes me feel all glowy on the inside. Something wholly separate from the alcohol I've consumed.

We stumble into Pierce's room that I've been occupying these last two weeks. Walker shuts the door behind us as we stare at each other, our breath ragged and uncertain. My eyes bounce between Walker and Pierce, each looking like they're seconds away from devouring me. I inhale, Walker's woodsy scent engulfing me as he takes a purposeful step closer. Pierce's nostrils flare, a mixture of anger and desire permeates his eyes. He clenches his fists looking like he's about to snap at any second. My heart rate ticks up, pounding furiously against my chest in anticipation.

I lick my lips and fist Walker's shirt in my hands yanking him towards me, taking his mouth with mine. I flick my tongue against his lips, and he opens for me, giving me full access to deep our kiss. He tastes like beer and a hint of mint as I work my tongue against his.

I feel Pierce's hands on my hips a moment before I'm forced back into Pierce's arms. He twirls me and pulls my hair so that I'm arched looking up at him before he punishes me with a bruising kiss. He rains hard and forceful kisses on my lips, grabbing me flush against him. I can feel every muscle through his thin shirt rubbing against my front. His kisses become slower until he nips my bottom lip and turns me around again. This time he forces me to bend over and I'm still trying to catch my bearings when I feel a sharp smack against my ass. I let out a surprised yelp. He pulls me up to him, his mouth right next to my ear, his breath tickling as he breaths out.

"Mm little witch, are you sure this is what you want?" I look up at Walker, who's shrugged out of his pants. His eyes are heavy with lust, and he palms his cock, releasing it from his briefs. I can see a tiny glisten drip off the tip and my mouth immediately waters at the sight of it.

Pierce grabs the bottom of my chin and yanks my head to the side so I'm looking straight into his stormy eyes.

"What do you want?" He asks forcefully. I swallow hard, licking my lips before I reply, my voice sounding out of breath.

"Both of you." I manage. Pierce's eyes darken then he slams his lips over mine, surprising me. I fist my hands into the back of his shirt, then move them to the nape of his neck and into his dark blonde hair. I pull on his hair hard enough that he breaks the kiss, looking down at me with that stupidly hot smirk.

Walker's hands move to my jean skirt, yanking my ass backwards with his fingers hooked through my belt loops. He pushes my skirt up, bearing my fishnet stockings as he crouches down onto his knees. His stubble grazes the backs of my legs, as Pierce continues to kiss me. His tongue ravishing my mouth stroke for stroke.

A loud knock jolts all three of us, Walker falls back and Pierce bites my lower lip.

"Hey, what's going on in there?" Emmet's muffled voice asks.

"What do you want Em?" Pierce calls out, his lower half pushing into me, hard and ready to take me right there.

"Pierce, where the fuck did you go man?"

"Did anyone lock the door?" I whisper. Walker rubs his hands down his face, his erection deflating as he grabs his briefs just in time to cover himself before Emmet swings opens the door.

He stands there a moment seeing all of us looking disheveled, his mouth open in shock.

"Close the fucking door." Pierce snaps which rouses Emmet out of his stupor. An evil glint sparks in Emmet's gleaming green eyes as he shuts himself in the room with us, taking care to lock it this time. The snick of the door locking fills the room. The distant bass of the party thrums through the air as the three of them look at me. My heart beats wildly in tune with the thump, thump, thumping of the pulsing music.

"Now it's a party." Emmet says, his mouth quirking up into a menacing smile.

My heart hammers hard as I look to the three foreboding men in front of me. I mean I was in college, and they said that *this* was the time for experimentation. If not now when? When else would an opportunity of playing with three extremely hot as sin guys pop up? But as my thoughts drift, they each move closer to me.

What the fuck did I get myself into?

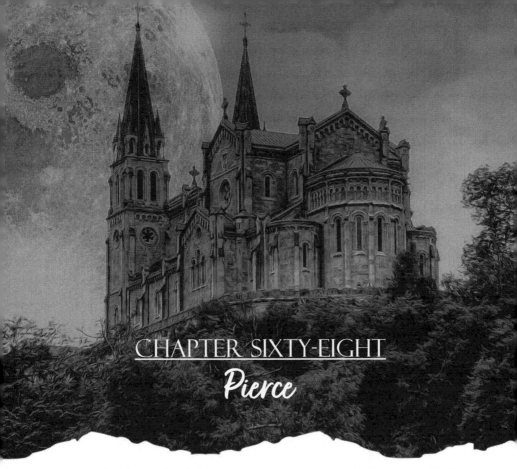

CHAPTER SIXTY-EIGHT
Pierce

Fucking hell. Now Emmet wanted a piece of Salem as well? The things I'd do for this little witch who'd somehow burrowed to deep inside of my mind that I was not just willing to share her with Walker, but Emmet too? I wasn't about to turn down this chance to fuck her until her knees gave out though. Maybe it would finally get her out of my system. I'd have that fucking pussy creaming around my dick one way or another. I was more than ready to give into this electric desire that had plagued me since the moment I laid eyes on her. I'd tried pushing her away, but despite how much I knew she hated me- I kept coming back for just a scrap of her attention. And now here I was in a room with two other guys who desired the same thing from her and fuck me I was so gone for her that I'd give her anything she wanted at this point. It becomes clear in that moment that I need to protect her from what's going down tomorrow on Samhain. I'll find another way around keeping my promise to Lukas. If it all goes to hell, I hope he can forgive me, but for now- I'm going to give my girl exactly what she's been asking for all night.

Emmet hooks his fingers under his shirt lifting it over his head seductively, making a display of his six pack which has Salem running her fingers over his muscles. I'll be damned if I lose her attention to fucking Emmet and Walker.

I yank my shirt off, which catches her attention and I see her sage green eyes drink me in. That's it baby girl, that's what I want to see, I think to myself as I continue undressing in front of her. Her eyes glued on me as she continues tracing Emmet's abs.

She flits her eyes to Walker, giving him a full-on smile, her whole face lighting up- which he returns as he drops his clothes, baring everything to her. Fucking Walker Hart smiling at that large of a wattage makes my chest squeeze with something that feels like jealousy. I don't think Salem has ever smiled at me like that. She scowls, she grimaces frequently, she gifts me with countless glares, maybe a smirk, but never a full out smile and now I've made it my mission to not only make her come around my cock, but to get her to look at me like that.

I watch Salem's fingers dip beneath Emmet's briefs as she watches Walker work his cock in his hands.

Salem reaches up and traces her delicate finger along Walker's scar. I exchange a worried glance with Emmet, afraid that Wrath is going to take over for Walker with Salem touching that scar, but instead

Walker shudders- capturing her finger with his teeth and licking the length of it to her black polished tip.

"Get over here." I growl out.

Salem's spine straightens.

"No." She says, right before curling her fingers around Walker's neck and pulling him down to her. He takes her mouth possessively, plunging his tongue into her pliable hot mouth. I feel my chest tighten.

"No?" I ask, but she ignores me using her hand to pull Emmet against her backside. He doesn't hesitate making quick work of taking off her jean skirt.

I glare, my aching cock is throbbing with the need for release.

Emmet rips a gaping hole in her fishnet stockings and runs his finger along her slit. She moans into Walker's mouth, backing up into Emmet's touch. The sound of her moaning sends a jolt straight to my cock, making my balls squeeze and my tip leak. Shit, she was so fucking hot.

Walker rips off her shirt and goddamn, she's not wearing a bra. I get an eyeful of her pert nipples before Walker takes one of her nipples into his mouth while working her other breast with his calloused hand.

"You're going to watch me, and if you're a very good boy- maybe I'll let you come and play."

Pride roils in my chest. Fucking what?

Sit and watch two other guys ravage the girl I want?

Emmet already has a knuckle deep into her dripping wet pussy while she tugs off Walker's briefs. She wraps her fingers along his length as he kicks off his briefs, their eyes are locked on each other as she leans down to lick him.

"Fuck, yes Salem." Walker growls.

Emmet's mouth is tipped up in a smile as he works her pussy, adding another finger. She moans, the sound shooting straight to my dick. I wrap my hand around my cock to ease the building pressure.

"Did I say you could touch yourself, Pierce?" She's looking straight at me, eyebrow raised.

That's it. I feel my restraint snap as I barrel into Salem, grabbing her up her hair and positioning her right in front of my cock. Emmet and Walker stand gaping at me, but I don't give a fuck. I need her and she damn well knows how much.

"Oh, I don't think I need your permission sweetheart. Now lick."

I see the moment of hesitation, my fingers digging into her scalp, her eyes alight with anger and desire. She licks her rosebud lips, letting out a shuddering breath before dragging her tongue up my length.

Fucking, yes.

She licks me again, harder- lingering at the tip where my pre-cum has gathered.

"Do you like the taste of me on your tongue, witch?"

In response she grates her teeth over my cock gently as she takes me deep into her mouth, her cheeks hollow out as she sucks. I can't help but thrust into her greedy mouth, hitting the back of her throat as she gasps around my length.

"I know you can take it."

Emmet slides up behind her, but before he can touch her, I rip her mouth off of my dick with a loud pop.

"Condom. Now."

Walker tosses me one from the nightstand, while he takes out two more.

"Put this on me, princess."

She rips the foil open using her teeth, her eyes not leaving mine. She takes my length in her hand and sheaths my dick. I pull her up to standing, her chest heaving. Those perfect nipples mere centimeters away from brushing up against my chest. I tuck a stray hair behind her ear, trailing my fingers down her cheek.

"We're going to fuck you senseless" I say before grabbing her by the neck and slam my lips against hers. She meets me with the same ferocity. Lips and teeth tangling in a hot mess. I slip my hands down her back and grasp her two full round ass cheeks into my hands and lift her up. She wraps her legs around me easily as I walk us back to the bed. My cock finds her wet slit as we walk. I thrust, managing to slide easily against her clit.

"Oh fuck." She says against my mouth.

I let out a dark chuckle.

"It's only the beginning."

CHAPTER SIXTY-NINE
Salem

I must be out of my mind letting these three guys have their way with me, but if I'm crazy then lock me up and throw away the key. I was going to enjoy my life. Pierce has me pinned beneath him- my arms outstretched above my head our fingers locked together as he balances the tip of his cock right outside my entrance. I've never felt so needy in my life, but this game him and I had been playing with each other has pushed me to my breaking point. I was going to pour all of my hatred right into him, taking out every frustration, every fucking loathsome look. I was going to punish him for everything he'd put me through this year.

I reach up and nip at his bottom lip, trapping it between my teeth before sucking it right into my mouth.

He lets out a groan and finally snaps, shoving his monster sized cock into my pussy.

I let out a scream.

"Holy fucking shit."

"You can take it."

My entire body shivers. I can feel the pulsing sensations all the way up to my face as he slides in and out of me.

"You're so tight, holy shit, Salem."

I turn looking at the Walker and Emmet who stand, cocks out and ready. Waiting patiently for their turn.

Pierce grabs my chin, snapping my head straight. "Eyes on me, princess." He hitches my leg up higher, positioning him deeper inside of me.

"Oh, fuck. Oh my god, yes."

"God can't hear you here, princess. It's just us sins."

I scream into his shoulder as I feel my orgasm rip through me, climbing up my spine and spreading to my fingertips. My entire body shakes around Pierce as he pumps into me ruthlessly, fucking me straight into another orgasm. I scratch my nails down his back, desperate to get closer to him.

"Oh, holy fucking shit, Salem." Pierce cries. I feel a warmth spread from my body into his, working its way down. His eyes go wide, breath hitching as he lets his release free.

"What the fuck, oh holy shit shit, yes. Don't stop." He demands, grabbing a handful of my hair and arching my head back. He claims my lips as we rock together, letting our bodies come down from the intense orgasms.

We lay there a moment looking at each other in disbelief. I don't know what just transpired between us, but it felt earth shattering.

"I hope, you're not done yet, wildcat." Walker says, sliding up next to me, the bed dipping with his weight.

Pierce peels himself off of me, disposing of the condom.

"You ready for us, sweetheart?" Emmet asks, coming up on the other side of me.

I nod my head, kissing Emmet on his full mouth. He lets out a chuckle. "Greedy girl." He murmurs as I turn to Walker, kissing him with equal fervor.

A hand slides down my body, tweaking my sensitive nipple. I can feel the calluses coating his fingers. I moan into Walker's touch, letting him explore lower. He finds me dripping and aching for more.

"Emmet was right, you are a greedy girl." I push him down and straddle him, positioning myself over his rock-hard cock.

"Do you have a problem with that?"

His eyes grow darker as he looks down my body, making me feel like a fucking queen to be this desired.

"No, babe. I'll make sure you have everything your greedy heart desires."

I slam my pussy down on him hearing those words come out of his mouth, and we both let out a moan.

"I'm going to take you right here, okay?" Emmet says, sliding a slick finger around my backside. I nod my head.

"Yes. Please, I need you." I feel him start to work a lubed-up finger in as I bounce on Walker's cock.

"Jesus, Salem. Slow down, baby, or I'm going to fuckin' blow my load in you. You feel so goddamn amazing." He peppers kisses down my neck.

I gasp, feeling Emmet work in another finger. *Holy shit.*

"You ready for me, sweetheart? I don't take kindly to being left out." His voice is dripping with envy.

"Yes, yes, now. Please."

"Mmm, you beg like such a good little girl." Emmet growls, removing his fingers. I whimper at the loss, but he quickly replaces them with the tip of his cock.

"I need you to breathe for us Salem." Walker grabs onto my hips slowing my rocking, as Emmet lines up to push inside of me.

Pierce sits over in the corner armchair, his cock getting hard as he watches us.

I shoot him a wink, and he sits up straighter fisting his growing length.

Emmet pushes against me, tentatively at first letting me adjust to the pressure of him inch by inch.

I feel stretched out between Walker and Emmet, my heart rate hammering wildly against my chest. I move my hips just a fraction and feel electricity sliding up my pulsing clit.

"Did you feel that?" Walker asks, eyes glued to where he's sheathed inside of me.

I nod my head and Emmet lets out a moan.

I move again and this time it shoots up even harder, wracking my body, Walker's and Emmet's. We break, moving together as one in a wild mess of limbs, building each other's orgasms as they pump in tandem against me. I've never felt this on fire and full before, but I want more.

My eyes lock with Pierce's and he seems to understand my desire instantly, standing up from the chair and stalking over to us.

I look up into his eyes and see the truth of his desire written plainly across his stupidly hot face.

"You want it, princess?" He asks, snaking his hand down into my hair.

"Yes." I lick my lips readying my mouth.

He comes closer, letting me work my lips over his engorged tip.

I feel his hands clench my hair as he slams my throat down his length.

"What a good fucking girl you are." Pierce says as I suck his cock with everything I have.

Emmet rocks into me from behind and I meet him stroke for stroke. As we move, I feel his hands grip into my ass spreading them apart further. It makes me groan around Pierce and clench down on Walker.

"Shit, Angel, just like that." Walker swears, bucking up into me faster. I feel my orgasm cresting, my legs pulsating as I work to keep myself balanced between Walker and Emmet.

"Oh, fuck Salem." Emmet says, slapping his hand down straight on my ass, making me cry out.

I suck on Pierce with renewed intensity, wanting him to come down my throat.

His fingers curl into my hair, pulling on it as I lick him from balls to tip.

My body feels fucking electric with so many sensations hitting me at once. Walker is the first to come, his hips jerking wildly as I clench around him following him into my orgasm. Everything inside of me feels like it's on fire with this heady desire as I shake.

"Fucking hell." Emmet cries, coming hard into my ass.

Pierce puts both hands on the back of my head and roars as he comes down my throat. I gag, come leaking down my face as my eyes water. I gasp, getting air back into my lungs. Emmet removes himself from me. I roll off of Walker and let out a laugh. "Holy fucking shit, that was insane."

"Hell, yeah it was." Walker agrees.

I look over to Pierce and Emmet, they both have smiles plastered to their faces.

"I don't know about you, but I want to do that again." Pierce says licking his lips like he's gearing up for a meal.

"Let her catch her breath first, Jesus." Emmet says, peeling off his condom and tossing it into the bin.

"Water would be good." I croak out. Feeling the best kind of sore in all the right places.

The three of them move to get to the door.

"Um... guys?" They turn to look at me. "Clothes?" I gesture to their naked bodies.

They scramble to get their clothes on, before Pierce comes over and plants a kiss on my lips.

"Be right back." He bops me right on the nose, then follows Emmet and Walker out of the room.

I cover myself with a blanket and take stock of what just happened.

That was one of the hottest, most unexpected and wild nights of my life, and something told me it wasn't over yet. I was going to be walking funny tomorrow. I feel a smile play across my lips as I think about the way those boys just ravaged me, like I was a fucking queen, and they'd give me anything I wanted.

Hell House wasn't looking so bad after all.

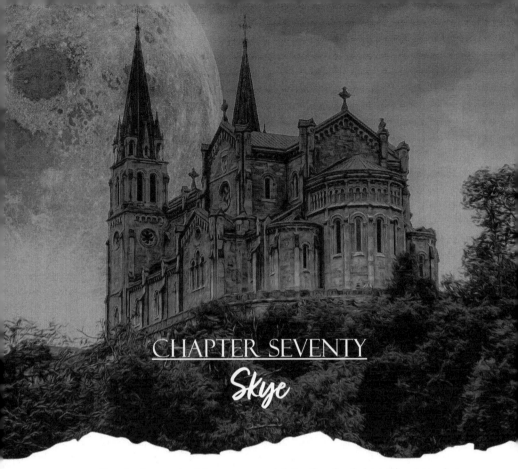

CHAPTER SEVENTY

Skye

I've lost count of how many drinks I've had, but it's enough to make my head spin like I've done one too many pirouettes. I steady myself against the wall, eager to get off the dance floor. The music pulses all around me, my body still gently swaying to the beat. Salem and I had spent the beginning of the evening pounding back more than a few shots, and now that was starting to catch up with me. She'd been pulled away by Pierce and Walker and they looked like they were happy making a Salem sandwich out of her.

I sweep my eyes around the room spotting Graham and Garrison dancing with a hot brunette in the middle. Sloan slumps against a wall opposite me and raises his red solo cup at me. Lukas was nowhere to be found though, like I cared. I was done caring. I was going to have a night where my thoughts didn't drift to Lukas Ledger for once. I was dressed like Marilyn Monroe in her iconic white dress. I'd painted my lips ruby red accentuating my Cupid's bow and curled my blonde hair into a wavy bob, pinning my hair up to make it look shorter than it was making sure to tuck my dyed ends away. Even making sure to place a sultry black dot above my lips. All that was ruined now. My makeup was smeared, and my hair was a wild mess, all stray pieces hanging out of the careful pinning job I'd done. The alcohol coursing through my veins was making me feel heavy but also like I needed something. Or someone.

I move slowly to a room off the living space that was currently functioning as a dance floor. My steps feel wobbly, but I manage to make it to the darkened room. I need air.

I'm engulfed by the smell of vanilla the moment I step through the French doors. *Lukas.*

My chest squeezes knowing he's in here. My skin buzzes in anticipation. I know I should leave. I know that I didn't need a distraction like Lukas Ledger, but I'd had a taste and it was unforgettable. I craved more, feeling his magnetic pull every time he was near. The hairs on my arms stand at attention as I feel hot breath moving across my back.

"Knew you'd find me in here sooner or later." He growls, tracing a finger up my bare arm.

"How?" My heart becomes erratic, banging against the cage surrounding it.

"Mmm, we're like magnets Skye. Always drawn to the other. Always seeking each other out. Do you think I'm not aware of you no matter what room we're in? I know. I always know."

The song outside switches to *Bad Romance* and I couldn't agree with the sentiment more. No matter how bad Lukas was for me, I wanted him. I craved him in a way that wasn't healthy. I'd pushed him away, but no more, even if it destroyed me in the end. I had to have him. He was everything a good girl like me shouldn't want, but maybe I wasn't as good as I portrayed myself to be. It was time to be honest with myself on who I truly was versus who I tried to be. Lukas had taken one look at me and saw past the charade and called me on it, pushing me to accept the dark parts of me that I tried to hide like he could read my thoughts. Like he'd been privy to every dark desire that I'd dreamed up and liked what he saw.

He grabs onto my elbow, slowly spinning me so I can take in his features. It's just light enough in here that I can make out his features. He's wearing dark horns and a leather jacket with no shirt. His black pants hang low, showing off his well-defined v, his tattoos sprawling across his chest.

"Who are you supposed to be?"

"Don't you know? I'm the devil in disguise." He says with a smirk, trailing his pointer finger up the seam of my halter dress starting at the swell of my cleavage and ending where my dress was tied around my neck. My breath is coming in fast at his feather light touch.

"You don't say."

"Don't believe me, Marilyn?" He steps closer, tugging on my knotted halter holding my dress up. He places his other hand on my hip, backing me up to the pool table. My butt bumping into the edge. I spread my legs instinctively, letting Lukas step between them. My fingers crawl up his bare chest, tracing the edges of his tattoos. He tugs hard against the knot, this time managing to free it from its hold. It falls open, baring my breasts to him. He glides his hand down cupping it in his hand, with a punishing squeeze.

"You denied me, Skye."

"I know." He places his head against my shoulder, his facial hair stabbing into my skin.

"You pretended like we didn't happen." He kisses my collar bone.

"I know." I whisper, digging my hands into his dark hair, scraping my nails as I go.

"Tell me why I shouldn't walk out of here right now."

"Because." My eyes flutter close as he kisses up my neck. Heat spreading to my core making me pulse with need, I feel myself becoming wet with each touch he grants me.

"Because why?"

"Because I want you." He inhales a sharp breath, like I just stabbed him. He grips my face hard with his two hands and slams his mouth down onto me with a bruising kiss.

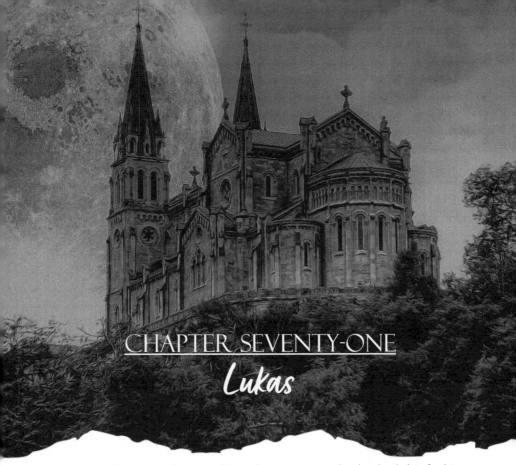

CHAPTER SEVENTY-ONE
Lukas

I kiss her with everything I have. For weeks I've had this fucking ache in me that only she could soothe.

"You're a lot darker than you let on, Marilyn, and I think that the darkness that lives inside your heart, scares you. But, baby, I'm going to make every dark fantasy you've ever had into a reality. I'm going to flay you open until your darkness spills out to meet mine and then I'm going to let you come all over my pierced cock like the good little girl you pretend to be. You do this with me now, and there's no going back. There's no pretending like nothing ever happened between us. Do you understand me?"

She nods her acceptance, legs quaking around me as she sits perched on the end of the pool table,

"I'm going to make it so good for you." I promise her with another kiss making sure to bite into her bottom lip. She moans into my mouth. "You like it like that don't you? Rough with a hint of tenderness?"

She responds by flicking her tongue over my bottom lip and sucking it right into her mouth.

Goddamn this girl.

"You know how I know you enjoy the same darkness as me?" I ask nipping at her neck and twisting her nipple between my fingers, earning me a gasp. "Anyone could walk in here right now and here you are, bared to me with your breasts on full display." I lean down and lick her breast with my flattened tongue, biting her pink and puckered nipple. "Mmm, delicious. Are you ready for me?"

"Why don't you find out?" She taunts. I let out a dark chuckle ready to make this woman mine.

I slip my fingers under her dress and find her fucking bare and shaved. She laughs at my surprise, nipping my lip with her teeth. I let out a groan, sliding my finger into her tight pussy.

God, she's so tight and wet for me.

I work my hand over her clit as she fucks my finger, riding me as she chases her pleasure. I want to be the one to give that to her. I feel my cock straining against my pants, desperate for her but I will myself to wait. I drop down to my knees opening her legs up for me wider. I use my free hand to spank the inside of her thigh, she moans, and I grin. I knew this is what she wanted. I'm filled with a sick sense of satisfaction, wondering what else she'll let me do to her tonight. I want to fill her up so much that she never forgets who she belongs to. I soothe the spot I smacked with a kiss, licking my way up her smooth legs, pausing at her hip bone.

"Please." She begs, hips rolling her pussy down onto my hand. I can't deny her what she asks for so nicely.

"Such a good girl, begging for me." I lick her clit, rewarding her like the queen she is.

"Such a pretty little cunt." I say blowing on her slick skin. I work another finger in, stretching her tightness as she drips down my hand. I lick it with a moan. "You taste so good, baby."

Her legs quake with the need for release. I run my hand up her torso, grabbing her breast as I lay my tongue flat against her clit. She shudders as I lick and suck on her sensitive bud.

"Lukas." She groans. God, I love hearing my name on her pretty lips. "I need more."

I stand up, taking her mouth with mine and let her taste her arousal on my tongue.

"How do you want me, Skye baby?"

"Bare." The word slices through my stomach. I've never fucked someone raw. I swallow hard, wanting to give her exactly what she wants. "I'm clean and on the pill." That's all it takes for me to snap.

I let her work her fingers down my zipper, freeing me from my briefs. I step out of my pants and line myself up with her entrance. She feels my piercings, lingering at their cool metal tips.

"I'm clean too." I promise. I haven't been with anyone since the start of school, and I hadn't wanted to. I only wanted her. I wanted to know how special she was to me. "I've never been like this with anyone. Do you hear me, Skye?"

She nods, "Me either." Her sincerity wraps itself around my heart. I push in, and we both let out a gasp. I can feel everything, and the sensation is overwhelming. My body shakes as I try to reign in my orgasm that's building in my spine. My balls squeeze and I can feel my tip leaking as I slam up into her. I lay her back, onto the pool table, rolling the balls out of the way. I sit between her legs, my legs holding my weight off of her as I piston in as deep as I can. I wrap my hand around her slim throat and squeeze. Her eyes go wide with surprise, but she mirrors me, digging her nails into my neck as she constricts her hand around my throat. I let up when her eyelashes begin to flutter while she soaks my cock. She sucks in a greedy breath with a huge fucking grin on her face.

She pushes her heels into my ass trying to control the speed. She moves her hands down my back, her nails rake on the way down, marring up my back with long pleasurable scratches- marking me as hers. I arch into her loving how she moves with me, loving the way she feels against me. She fits perfectly and I never want to stop.

She pushes me, hooking my leg as she takes control, riding me. My back bumps against the balls on the table and my hand grabs onto a pool stick. An idea flashes in my mine. I did promise I would make all of her dark fantasies come true, and I think I know just how to start.

"Do you trust me." I whisper as she rides my cock, lifting up her hips and taking every single inch into her.

"Yes." She says kissing my lips without hesitation.

I bring the handle of the pool stick up to my mouth and coat it with my spit. Sucking it into my mouth for lubrication, making sure to run my tongue up the length. Her eyes flash with something that looks like interest, and I tuck that away for later.

I move the stick to her back entrance. She eyes me warily but lets me do as I want. I lick my finger making sure there's moisture before I work it in to warm her up.

She groans out, picking up her pace. "You like that?" She nods her head enthusiastically.

"More." she insists.

I grin, pumping up into her. I spread her cheeks, removing my finger and pressing the edge of the pool stick to her opening. I feel the tip of it slide against my cock, making her tight wet pussy even tighter. I go slow, letting her breathe through it.

"Lukas, oh my god. I can't. I can't."

"Breathe, baby."

Tears gather in her eyes, "It hurts but oh my god it feels so fucking good. Please, Lukas." I kiss her lips and move the pool stick and my cock in tandem taking her holes up with everything I can.

She clenches down around my aching cock, and I can feel she's close.

"That's it baby, come all over my cock like a good girl." Her whole-body shudders around me and then she's crying out, squeezing me without abandon as she comes. I'm right behind her, feeling my Lust rise up and slam down on us both. I remove the pool stick and let myself fill her with my hot cum as it shoots out of me. The sensation racks over my whole body and hers as she comes again with a scream.

"Holy shit." I say into her neck with a kiss. "That was even better than last time. Are you okay?"

She places a kiss on my lips. "More than okay."

We dress in the dark, exchanging kisses as we stumble back out into the party. I make sure to stash the pool stick where no one will accidentally use it. I grab onto Skye's hand and drag her through the writhing crowd and push her into our room. I'd be happy to cuddle her or fuck her or even sleep back in my bed if it means I can be near her and call her mine.

"You're not going to run away again?" I ask as she pulls me to her bed.

"Not a chance." She says running her fingers up over my tattoos across my chest.

"Good. Then we can go for another round."

She laughs, pressing herself against me eagerly and just like that, I'm hard again. This girl of mine knew just what buttons to press.

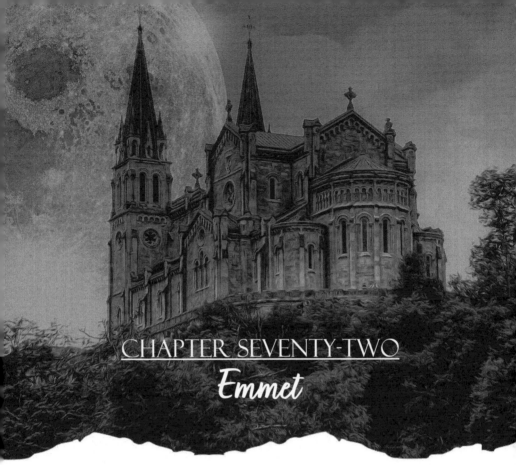

CHAPTER SEVENTY-TWO
Emmet

My entire body is sore. I'd blurred the lines last night, giving into my desires. Salem had slipped through my guard, making me want her in a way that made me forget my goals.

That would not be happening again.

No matter how good last night felt, I still needed to lead her down to the cave.

This ends today.

Salem stretches next to me a full smile playing along those sultry lips. I'd done things with her that I'd only entertained in the privacy of my room. I almost felt guilty for what I was about to do. Almost.

I take her face in my hands and kiss her one last time. I wonder if she can sense this is a goodbye because when I pull away a frown graces her beautiful face.

Walker and Pierce are still passed out, their bodies tangled in the bed next to us.

"Good morning." Salem croaks out, her hair devilishly disheveled.

"Do you want some breakfast?" She nods her head eagerly. Pierce stirs smacking Walker straight in the face with his hand as he stretches.

"Gah! What the fuck. Why is your dick on my leg?" Walker pushes Pierce off the side of the bed and he crashes with a loud boom. Salem laughs into her hands, her green eyes sparkling with mischief.

I retreat to the kitchen leaving them to their last moments of merriment before I pull the rug out from under them. Remembering the box of pie I'd stashed the other day for Salem, I fetch it from on top of the cabinets setting the box down on the counter.

"Oh, bet." Sloan says, snatching a piece while my back is turned, busy with getting plates.

"Hey! Come on man that's not... what the fuck? Sloan?"

His face is locked in a silent scream as black veins sprout from his mouth tracing down his throat. He clutches at his chest.

"Emmet, what the fuck? Sloan? SLOAN? Call 911." Walker catches Sloan before he collapses on the floor.

Skye walks in a scream flying out of her lips. The room erupts into chaos as my hands shake with the plates I was getting for Salem.

Salem.

This box was sent specifically for her.

"It's not going through!" Skye screams shaking her phone as it beeps uselessly in her hands.

"I'll drive him. Garrison, give me your keys." Walker demands, hoisting Sloan's slumped body over his shoulders.

"I'll go with." Garrison agrees, helping Walker out the door as they race him to the car. We hear it peel out of the drive a moment later.

"What happened?" Skye demands, tears streaking down her face.

Salem and Pierce emerge from the room hand in hand. "What's going on? We heard screaming." Salem says. "Oh, pie." I fly across the room, placing my body between her and the pie.

"Don't!"

"Emmet? What's going on?" She demands, placing her hands on her hips.

"Sloan ate a bite of that pie before he... he couldn't breathe. He... his veins. Oh my god. Salem. This pie was addressed to you."

The room goes silent. Pierce looks murderous, clasping her hand so hard it's blanching white. Skye is shaking her head back in forth in disbelief.

"What?" Salem's shaky voice finally asks.

"The box. It was addressed to you." She shoves me out of the way letting go of Pierce's hand and grabs the box top.

"This, this can't be right. It was sent from my grandmother."

Dread fills my stomach. The other player on the board. Someone able to conjure claws out of thin air. Someone in attendance at the ball. Someone who wouldn't want Salem to open the veil.

The dots all click into place in my head right as Headmaster Hayden walks into the kitchen pointing a gun straight at Salem.

CHAPTER SEVENTY-THREE
Pierce

Last night was arguably one of the best nights I'd ever had, even if that meant sharing Salem between Walker and Emmet. That all came crashing down the moment I saw the headmaster point a gun straight at the girl who I've fallen for. I thought I'd have more time to whisk her away off the island. Consequences be damned. I planned to take the family helicopter to Seattle, and even had cleared a time with the pilot.

I realize with a pit forming in my stomach that Emmet could have easily tipped off the headmaster with that information. The guy was a tech genius, able to hack into anyone's business at the swipe of a thumb. I can't believe how stupid I was to overlook that. After what we'd done with Salem last night, I assumed Emmet was on the same page, but maybe he was just playing us.

The headmaster clicks back the gun. I can hear the shell slide into place, ready to annihilate anyone one the receiving end. He can't hurt her, he needs her.

Salem stands with her hands raised- her face drained of any color.

"Stop this." I demand. He scowls at me.

"I wouldn't have to do this if you had just done your job." He spits out.

"What is he talking about Pierce?" Her big green eyes fill with tears, and I feel my heart break. I was a fool to think I could hide this from her.

"Yes, Pierce. Would you like to enlighten your little witch about what you did to her? Emmet, tie her hands up. It's time we take back what's ours."

Salem's eyes whip to Emmet, her head shaking back and forth. "Emmet, no. Please."

"Sorry, Salem. I need to do this." He wraps her hands up in a zip tie the headmaster handed to him. My mind is whirring with thoughts on how to stop this. Salem has tears streaming down her face and I know she could never forgive me. It wouldn't take much for the headmaster to swing his gun straight at me, so I need to plan this right.

"Make sure you tie up the others." He directs Emmet.

"Pierce. What a disappointment. You can still fix this, you know. Join us and I'll make sure you're set free." I don't trust a word he says, knowing the depths of his cruelty, but if I tag along, maybe I can stop this.

"Oh, wait. That's right. You're a traitor. Emmet make sure he's tied up too."

Emmet comes around me and tries to take my hands, I shove him hard, which has me looking down the barrel of a gun and my spine straightens. Emmet uses that moment to force my arms behind my back and into a zip tie, making sure to knot my ankles together as well.

"Let's skip the dramatics, shall we?" The headmaster growls, a murderous gleam emanating from his eyes.

"P-Pierce." Salem calls.

"I'm so sorry, baby."

"Shut up. The two of you. Emmet, grab the girl." The headmaster leaves us as Skye lets out a sob.

Emmet snatches Salem up by her arm, to which she responds by spitting on him. I feel a flutter of Pride watching her. He hauls her out of the room, leaving us bound and helpless on the kitchen floor.

I'm coming for you, baby. Don't you worry.

CHAPTER SEVENTY-FOUR
Salem

Emmet's nails dig into my arm as he drags me down the path behind the house. The figure I'm following is just like the one from my dream. Dark and ominous, decrepit Headmaster Hayden. I hadn't ever seen his face in the dream, but the way he carried himself fit.

"Why are you doing this to me, Emmet?"

"You're the key to making my dreams come true little witch." I flinch at the nickname Pierce had given me. What did the headmaster mean by 'tell her what you did'? What was Pierce's involvement in all of this? What did they want with me? My head swims with questions that I have no answers to.

"What do you mean by that? Where are you taking me?" My body pimples with the chilled air. I was wearing nothing but a black cami and matching underwear. I hadn't even put on shoes before I was being tied up and carted out the door.

They don't answer, instead they lead me over the path I'd taken not too long ago when I was exploring the cave.

If they were taking me there now, were they the cause of the pentagram that I found? What did I have to do with any of this?

"Don't act like you don't know why you're here." Emmet spits. "I saw the way you wielded that lightning bolt, like it was nothing." My head snaps to look at him. His jaw is set as he looks ahead with determination.

"I don't know what you want with me."

He lets out a humorless laugh.

"Oh Salem. You're about to change the whole world and you don't even know it. Did it ever occur to you why someone would want to attack you? To send you poisoned pie?"

I narrow my eyes at him. "What are you saying?"

"Your grandmother. She was behind that."

I whirl at him, my steps slipping. "Are you out of your mind? Of course, you are. You kidnapped me and tied up our friends after you spent the night fucking me." The betrayal burns.

"You should be used to people screwing you over by now. You let Pierce fuck you after everything he did."

"Why do you two keep saying he did something? What did he do?" My bare feet slip again. Each rock feels like a knife to my foot.

"Who do you think set your room on fire?"

All my strength leaves me in that moment. "No." I crumple, making Emmet have to hoist me up. There's no way they're telling the truth.

"I don't believe you." I spit at him.

"I see the truth doesn't sit well with you. I guess it doesn't matter telling you now then, that you're a witch."

I gasp, the pieces falling to place in my mind. A witch. A witch from Salem...named Salem. I almost want to laugh. The truth rings throughout my body. Out of all the things he's said, this is the one that latches to my soul. I know, that at least in this, he's telling the truth. I feel my magic flare in acknowledgement, churning inside my chest.

"Your family helped contain all of us souls in Purgatory, and because of that, you're the only one who can bring that containment spell down."

"I don't even know how to cast spells."

"Don't worry. It'll recognize your blood." His smile is full of malice.

"Would you two be quiet? We're almost there." Headmaster Hayden shouts, obviously struggling to make it down the hill.

If they need me, they can't shoot me, can they? Emmet said I was the key to something. If I could get away before then, I could call for help. My mind snags on Sloan wondering if he made it to the hospital wing in time and if they were even able to do anything. The pie that was meant for me, that Emmet saved me from eating. Why would he do that? Was it just so he could use me now as this 'key' to unlocking whatever it was? And what did that have to do with the night of the thunderstorm?

All I knew for sure is that I wasn't sure who I could trust even if I did manage to break free.

CHAPTER SEVENTY-FIVE
Skye

"**Can you reach my zip tie strings?**" I ask Pierce who's doing a worm crawl on the floor to get to me.

"Yeah, just let me flip over so we can sit back-to-back." He manages to swing himself over so we're in the right position. Calling out for help has done nothing. Most of the party goers must have passed out hard or left.

I remembered a viral video I had seen on how to get out of zip ties if you were ever captured, and I was glad that I watched it several times to commit it to memory.

"Okay, I'm going to need you to tug on them, making the ties as tight as possible." Pierce grabs onto them and does his best to follow my instructions. I feel like loss of blood flow as the plastic digs into my skin. God, I hope this works. Salem needed us.

"Okay on 3, I'm going to come down hard on your leg, okay?" He shifts into position and props up his leg behind me.

"1, 2, 3." I slam my arms down as hard as I can, with a yelp. "Shit!"

"Maybe you could kick it?"

"I don't want to break your fucking wrists, Skye!"

"Just do it!"

"Fuck! Okay. Hold on. On 3, okay?"

I nod my head yes, bracing for impact. "1, 2, 3!" His slams his shoes directly on my zip ties and I hear a crunch mixed with a snap. The pain works its way up my arm and into my elbow, but I'm free.

I bring my arms around to the front and rub my wrists, making them go in a circle.

"I don't think they're broken!"

"Awesome, now get me out of this."

I snatch a pair of scissors off the counter and lean down over Pierce, working the blade between his skin and the zip's plastic.

"What did he mean earlier, when they were taking Salem? About you doing your job?"

He sighs as I snap the plastic off of him and move to do the ones around his ankles. I have the scissors angled just beneath the plastic.

"I set your room on fire."

I almost stab his leg in surprise. "What?" The zip tie snaps, and he snatches the scissors out of my hands.

"We need to get Lukas. Let's go." He strides out of the room, leaving me grappling for answers on the floor.

"Wait, wait! What the fuck is going on? What do you mean you set our room on fire?" I'm practically screaming.

"What the fuck is going on, man?" Lukas pops his head out of our room looking all kinds of mussed and scratched up from last night.

"Headmaster Hayden and Emmet just kidnapped Salem. And Sloan might have been poisoned or gone into anaphylactic shock. We need to go. Pierce, since you know their plan, want to fill us in on where they're taking her?"

"The cave."

Lukas looks at him with barely contained rage. "What does she mean by you're involved?"

"I was working on setting us free."

"And that includes kidnapping Salem? The fuck man?"

"I know! I was working on getting her out of here today."

"Great job with that."

"Free of what?"

They both snap their head at me, jaws ticking. It's unnerving how similar they look at this moment.

"We don't have time for this." Pierce says, stalking off. Lukas stares at me a moment debating, then follows his brother. I'm hot on their heels.

"You two better start spilling, now." Pierce is already out the door with a slam, making the room shake.

"Skye, baby. I need you to call 911 okay. Have them meet us at this cave." He shows me a location on the map. I recognize it as the one that made everyone so uneasy on our kayaking trip.

"Are you going to tell me what the fuck is going on?"

"I will baby, I promise, but right now I need to go and help Salem before some bad shit goes down and we're all screwed. Do you trust me?"

Those same four words he whispered to me last night play in my mind. And my answer is the same now as it was then. "Yes."

He kisses me on the mouth, and I wind my fingers through his hair. "Be careful." I say before he's following his twin out the door towards a man who'd pointed a gun at us easily. My stomach is in knots as I dial 911 meeting the same busy tone as earlier. Fuck this messed up island and its spotty service. I keep dialing, pushing my fingers into the screen as I shake with rage. Please, please, please let them get to Salem in time.

CHAPTER SEVENTY-SIX
Pierce

I run as fast as I can through the trail, careful not to twist an ankle on my way to the cave where everything started. Where my life no longer became my own. I'd been saddled with this demon for over two years now, losing myself more and more, until Salem came along, and I felt like I could breathe again. I felt like me. I leap over the fallen log with ease, thankful of all those hours I spent training for football.

I'm coming, Salem.

I reach the entrance of the cave, and listen for their voices, hurrying my way to where I think they'll be.

Wind whips through the cave whistling against the jagged rocks. Water sloshes at my feet, threatening with the high tide. I creep over the rocks as silently as I can, like my heart isn't lodged in my throat and my head isn't throbbing with regret. I see a flash of light near the back of the cave, and my stomach clenches with dread.

Was I too late?

Lights spark down the skull wall and the cave fills with sounds of screams as hands try to rip and push through the crack. The cave flashes a bright red as the headmaster continues his chant. Salem has tears tracking down her face, her mascara smeared, and her hands bound behind her back. He has her shoved down onto her knees.

I need to get to Salem before he finishes his incantation.

I slink closer to where the headmaster has Salem on her knees, but where was Emmet?

Were Skye and Lukas on their way?

Salem lets out an ear-piercing scream as the headmaster pushes her hand against the rocks. My heart is thudding hard as I scramble over the rocks, the water rising every second that we're here.

I'm coming Salem.

The earth rumbles beneath my feet, making it near impossible to remain standing. My arms flail as I try to maintain my balance. A large boulder slams down next to me, the stalactite missing me by mere inches. A shout fills the cave, and I see my brother Lukas, barreling towards us. Emmet springs up, gun in hand and aims it straight at Lukas's chest.

I run at a full sprint towards Emmet, tackling him to the ground. I hear the gun go off as Emmet's head cracks against a rock.

The headmaster turns, a sneer coating his face as he breaks Salem's contact with the wall, positioning her body as a shield in front of him as he holds her tight by the throat. She claws against his grip, but her strength is no match for the unnatural demon that possesses him.

"Lukas!" I croak out searching for my brother, as I try to wrestle the gun out of Emmet's hands. He's woozy but still strong, kicking me straight in the ribs with a sickening crack. I let out a wheeze, feeling like I'd just been hit with a truck. I spit out a wad of blood and manage to wrench the gun away from Emmet's grip.

I'm so close, the ground still quakes as I push off the ground running at full speed to Salem, my lungs burning the whole way. Her eyes flick over to me, and she shakes her head no, but I'm not leaving her with this psychopath that wants to kill her. She recognizes my decision to ignore her as I brace myself to put a bullet into his head. He turns at the last second, his soulless eyes promising vengeance right before my finger pulls back the trigger.

In that moment it's like time slows down and everything becomes slow motion. I see the moment the bullet sinks into his skull blowing a hole through his head. He crumples, lifeless and mouth agape.

The shrieks from behind the veil become louder and more insistent as Salem scrambles away from me, bringing her knees up into her chest. I drop the gun, unable to process what I'd just done. The image of the headmaster's shocked face burns into my memory.

"Salem! Baby, I'm so sorry, I'm here. I'm right here." I go to her and gather her into my arms, and she lets me cradle her.

"Pierce. Why?"

"I'm so sorry baby. I thought, fuck! I thought it was the only way to save us. The headmaster linked our souls up with demons."

She looks at me in disbelief.

"It's true." Lukas says, clutching his side.

"Oh fuck! Lukas, are you shot?" I go to him seeing blood gush out of his wound.

"It's just a scratch." He says with a little cough, his fingers turning crimson with the effort to stop the blood flow.

I go to snatch up the gun, when another rumble goes through the cave. A piece of rock comes careening down and smacks me in the head. I'm down before I even know what happened.

"Pierce!" Lukas and Salem scream in tandem. My vision is tunneling, black creeping around the edges as I fight to take a breath.

"Holy fuck." Salem says rushing to my side. I reach for Salem whose eyes are rimmed red. Her flushed cheeks hold two streaks of mascara, but she's never looked more beautiful.

"Pierce, oh my God."

"I'm okay." I murmur, blinking hard, her face going out of focus for a moment. Shit, that hurt.

"We need to get out of here." Lukas says, his face pulled tight as he holds his side. I nod my agreement, standing up, grabbing onto Salem's small palm. I feel a wave of dizziness hit me, and I fight back the urge to vomit.

"We can't!" Salem says halting me by the hand I'm holding onto. I look at her with confusion.

"We can't leave it like this! They'll come through and burn through the world."

What seems like a thousand shrieks fills the air. I slam my hands over my ears and see Salem and Lukas doing the same. The quaking intensifies sending several pointed rocks crashing into the cave. Blood trickles down my face as I fight off another wave of dizziness.

The noise quiets for a moment as Salem stands straight up, her shoulders set in determination as she stares at the lightening crack. She tentatively raises her hand, but before she can place it on the rock, I grab her by the hand and spin her into me.

"Lukas you go, I'm staying with Salem." She looks at me with warmth in her eyes, a thousand things unsaid between us. "If the world's going to burn, let me burn with you." I say smashing my lips down onto hers. I don't want to lose her. She opens for me, kissing me back with an intense passion that I've only ever experienced with her, but then she pulls back a second later.

"I have to do this Pierce. I was made to do this and if I have to die, I'll die with your lips on me one last time." She says, resolve coating her every word kissing me fiercely. It tastes like tears and goodbye. I let go of her reluctantly as she slides away from me, knowing she's the only one that can fix this. She lifts her hand again and I hope to Hell she knows what she's doing as she places it against the cracking veil.

The screams get louder as the ground shakes. A hand snakes through the rift, snaking around my neck until I can't breathe. Their strength is immense as I try to rip their hold off of me.

"Salem," I choke out. Her eyes dart to me, but where her usual jade green iris resides is instead engulfed by a sea of black. The cave lets out one massive shudder and I see Lukas dragging Emmet out of the opening right before Salem is thrown back and I'm buried by the crushing weight of stone.

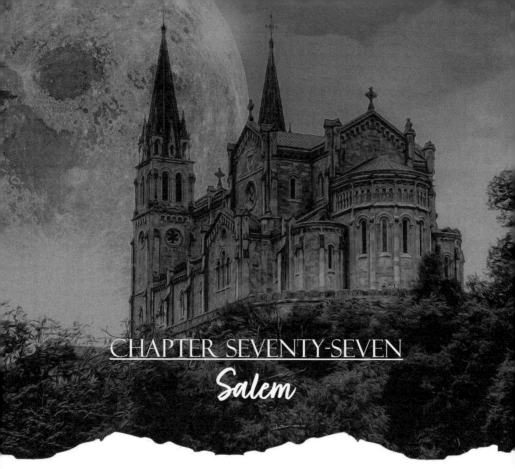

CHAPTER SEVENTY-SEVEN
Salem

There's a feeling deep within my veins, a sense of wrongness that coats every cell eating me from the inside out. I blink, lids heavy and eyes unfocused. My head swims. I try to move my limbs but my muscles ache like someone has pinned me down with bags of sand. I try to think but my thoughts are slip away as quickly as they form. My lungs feel like they're full of sludge as I take a shuddering breath in. A low consistent buzzing reverberates against my eardrums. I become aware of the cool wetness that surrounds me, sloshing against my soaked clothes. I sit up like I've been electrocuted, the heaviness still coating my limbs. I blink my eyes finally settling on two unmoving forms.

"Salem!" A familiar voice screams but it sounds far away. My movements are slow like I'm trying to trudge through a vat of molasses.

My head buzzes while my vision swims in circles before me making everything around me tilt. A pair of strong arms wrap around me, pulling me to standing.

"Salem, we have to go!" The voice is so familiar, and yet wrong at the same time.

My unfocused eyes struggle to grasp my surroundings. I turn my head which only makes the dizziness come on harder, but my eyes snag on the two motionless figures. I could have sworn I saw one move.

"I'll go back for Pierce, but we need to move." The person promises.

The sound of Pierce's name slams into me and my chest heaves with recognition. Pierce. Oh God. What happened? I sift through my memories, images flashing past in my mind faster than I can hold onto them.

An ear-splitting crack fills the air around me and whoever it is that's dragging me. Suddenly I'm tossed over, hanging upside down, swaying back and forth as the person runs. My body jostling with every step.

"Fuck!" They scream.

I get slammed down onto sand, the only light wafting over us comes from a waning moon.

"FUCK!" The voice screams again. Lukas? I turn to see the tattooed twin crumpled next to me, his head in his blood-stained hands.

Understanding hits me, and I scramble to a standing position, the world still spinning but what I can make out is nothing but smoke and a pile of rocks where the cave should be.

"PIERCE!" I scream out, my legs forcing me forward. I grab the nearest rock digging at it so hard that I feel my nails crack. Blood seeps out from my cuticles, but I ignore it. I ignore everything but the insistence inside of me to get to Pierce.

"Salem. Salem! Stop! There's nothing we can do."

"We have to get him out!" I realize that I'm crying. My head is swimming, but I can't give up.

If the world's going to burn, let me burn with you. What have I done?

I let out a scream, my voice garbled. This is my fault. He wouldn't have been here if it wasn't for me.

I feel Lukas's arms pulling me away from the rubble. My knees shake as I lean into him.

"We need to go get help." I nod, my stomach swirling along with my head. I feel my eyes flutter back into my head before I slip. My vision blackens.

"Hold on." Lukas says in a voice that sounds so similar to Pierce's that my heart shatters at the cruelty of having to hear Pierce's voice when he could be dead. He could be dead because of me- I think before I completely black out.

To Be Continued...

Note to the reader from the author:

Don't you just hate cliffhangers? I hope you can imagine my evil cackle from here, but also know I feel your pain. These characters have been through hell, and you know what they say about going through hell, keep going until you're on the other side and well- we aren't there yet. You can read the rest of Hell House's story next year when Queens of Hell House releases. Until then, if you need a little spicy fix be sure to check out my book, My Teacher's Dirty Secret. It's a taboo romance between a student and her teacher. I packed it full of spice. If we were talking chili peppers, it would be a ghost pepper. Extra hot.

If you're feeling the need to talk about Hell House with other readers, be sure to check out my Facebook group.

If you don't want to miss my upcoming works, sign up for my newsletter here, where I share sneak peeks of what I'm working on as well as updates.

Spotify Song List

Self destructive by Vorsa

Sex and Candy by Alexander Jean

How Villains Are Made by Madalen Duke

Poison by Rita Ora

Queen of Disaster by LULLANAS

Monsters by Ruelle

The Bad Touch 2k20 by DJ Gollum, Empyre One

Big Bad Wolf by Roses & Revolution

Killer by Valerie Broussard

Retired by Gabbie Hana

Rhiannon by Fleetwood Mac

House Of The Rising Sun by The Animals

Hate Me (with Juice WRLD) by Ellie Goulding, Juice WRLD

Bad Romance by Halestrom

Beat the Devil's Tattoo by Black Motorcycle Club

Vendetta by UNSECRET, Krigaré

Don't Save Me by Chxrlotte

The Devil is a Gentleman by Merci Raines

Hide and Seek by Lerion, Lauren Paley

Killer by The Ready Set

Devil Inside by CRMNL

Highway to Hell by AC/DC

Raise Hell by Dorothy

Nightmare by Halsey

All the good girls go to hell by Billie Elisha

Devil's Backbone by The Civil Wars

You Belong to Me by Cat Pierce

Lion by Saint Mesa

Thong Song (Instrumental Version) by Sisqo

Rituals by Jiovanni Daniel

Lips of a Witch by Austin Giorgio

When You Say My Name by Chandler Leighton

Spiracle by Flower Face

Breakfast by Dove Cameron

House of the Rising Sun- Instrumental by John Slider

Season Of The Witch by Lana Del Rey

Reaper by Silverberg, Jordan Frye

Devil Doesn't Bargain- Acoustic by Alec Benjamin

Stairway to Heaven- Led Zeppelin

Sweet Creature- Harry Styles

Acknowledgements

First and foremost, I would like to thank you the reader for picking my book. I never read this portion of a book, but I would feel remiss if I didn't thank all the people who made this book possible.

I'd like to really thank myself this time for consistently coming back to the keyboard through all the doubts I had plaguing me. There were so many negative voices that tried to stifle me, and it took the encouragement of my husband, and my own pep talks to get out of my own way to finally put pen to paper... figuratively since I wrote all of this on the computer.

Husband, who needs a harem when I have you. Thank you for encouraging me to write whatever pops into my head. Without you this idea wouldn't have happened. I'll never forget the moment when we were talking about the sin of gluttony and the characters took shape, before I even knew what I was going to do with them.

Penina, you crazy bitch, thank you for all your edits -even while on vacation! You're contribution to this book was invaluable. I'm so glad I followed the sound of your laugh that fateful first day of school, freshman year.

Kara and Melissa, thank you for letting me complain endlessly about word counts, plot holes, and all my writing woes. Your support helped me feel like I could actually finish this book!

Alison, you're the bees' knees for always checking in on me. I love our talks about books and travel! You're an amazing human and I'm glad to know you.

Stephanie, my love, your wealth of knowledge is invaluable, and I love that even though we're separated by an ocean, our friendship still stands. Thank you for cheering me on and helping me through the writing process.

I would also like to thank coffee for giving me the perfect blend of awake-ness and anxiety. You're the unsung hero of making sure I get shit done.

I'm thankful for the people on Instagram that have hyped me up and shared my book, giving me motivation on the days when I felt like I had none. Their handles are @bri.and.her.bookss @feliciaisbooked @rainey.day.reading @kiki.reads_ @jbfoxreads @thebookishgirlreviews @hannuuhhhh.reads @laniirobb

I feel like I'm forgetting some, and I apologize if I am! Never underestimate the small kindness of sharing an author's work. It really makes a difference.

Courtney, thank you for catching my grammatical errors! It was a pleasure to work with you.

Tabitha, I appreciate all your help. Without you, Skye would be wearing the wrong clothes in some scenes! Thank you for ARC reading this and sending me screenshots of words I missed.

Lastly, I would like to thank all the authors who came before me that paved the way for writers like me.

About the Author:

Dakota is an avid reader, writer, and painter. She lives in the US with her three kids, husband, and their husky. In her free time, she likes to binge watch shows on Netflix with her husband. She also enjoys taking trips with her family to new and exciting destinations.

www.DakotaWildeAuthor.com

Made in the USA
Columbia, SC
22 October 2022

69865688R00224